CLIVILIUS
WHERE CREATION MEETS INFINITY

© 2024 Nathan Cowdrey. All rights reserved.
First Edition, 20 March 2024
ISBN 978-1-4461-0614-3
Imprint: Lulu.com

Step into Clivilius, where creation meets infinity, and the essence of reality is yours to redefine. Here, existence weaves into a narrative where every decision has consequences, every action has an impact, and every moment counts. In this realm, shaped by the visionary AI CLIVE, inhabitants are not mere spectators but pivotal characters in an evolving drama where the lines between worlds blur.

Guardians traverse the realms of Clivilius and Earth, their journeys igniting events that challenge the balance between these interconnected universes. The quest for resources and the enigma of unexplained disappearances on Earth mirror the deeper conflicts and intricacies that define Clivilius—a world where reality responds to the collective will and individual choices of its Clivilians, revealing a complex interplay of creation, control, and consequence.

In the grand tapestry of Clivilius, the struggle for harmony and the dance of dichotomies play out across a cosmic stage. Here, every soul's journey contributes to the narrative, where the lines between utopia and dystopia, creator and observer, become increasingly fluid. Clivilius is not just a realm to be explored but a reality to be shaped.

Open your eyes. Expand your mind. Experience your new reality. Welcome to Clivilius, where the journey of discovery is not just about seeing a new world but about seeing your world anew.

Also in the Clivilius Series:

Luke Smith (4338.204.1 - 4338.209.2)

Luke Smith's world transforms with the discovery of a cryptic device, thrusting him into the guardianship of destiny itself. His charismatic charm and unpredictable decisions now carry weight beyond imagination, balancing on the razor's edge between salvation and destruction. Embracing his role as a Guardian, Luke faces the paradox of power: the very force that defends also threatens to annihilate. As shadows gather and the fabric of reality strains, Luke must navigate the consequences of his actions, unaware that a looming challenge will test the very core of his resolve.

Paul Smith (4338.204.1 - 4338.209.3)

In a harsh, new world, Paul Smith grapples with the remnants of a hostile marriage and the future of his two young children. Cast into the heart of an arid wasteland, his survival pushes him to the brink, challenging his every belief. Amidst the desolation, Paul faces a pivotal choice that will dictate where his true allegiance lies. In this tale of resilience and resolve, Paul's journey is a harrowing exploration of loyalty, family, and the boundless optimism required to forge hope in the bleakest of landscapes.

Jamie Greyson (4338.204.1 - 4338.209.3)

Haunted by shadows of his past, Jamie Greyson navigates life with a guarded heart, his complex bond with Luke Smith teetering on the brink of collapse. When Jamie is thrust into a strange new world, every moment is a test, pushing him to confront not only the dangers that lurk in the unknown but also the demons of his own making. Jamie's quest for survival becomes a journey of redemption, where the chance for a new beginning is earned through courage, trust, and the willingness to face the truth of his own heart.

Kain Jeffries (4338.207.1 - 4338.211.2)

Kain Jeffries' life takes an unimaginable turn when he's thrust into Clivilius, far from the Tasmanian life he knows and the fiancée carrying their unborn child. Torn between worlds, he grapples with decisions concerning his growing family. Haunted by Clivilius's whispering voice and faced with dire ultimatums, Kain's resolve is tested when shadowy predators threaten his new home. As he navigates this new landscape, the line between survival and surrender blurs, pushing Kain to confront what it truly means to fight for a future when every choice echoes through eternity.

Beatrix Cramer (4338.205.1 - 4338.211.6)

Beatrix Cramer's life is a delicate balance of contradictions, her independence and keen intellect shadowed by her penchant for the forbidden. A master of acquisition, her love for antiques and the call of the wild drives her into the heart of danger, making her an indispensable ally yet an unpredictable force. When fate thrusts her into the clandestine world of Guardians, Beatrix must navigate a labyrinth of secrets and moral dilemmas. Caught in the crossfire of legacy and destiny, she faces choices that could redefine the boundaries of her world and her very identity.

4338.206.1 - 4338.209.4

GLENDA
DE BRUYN

CLIVILIUS
WHERE CREATION MEETS INFINITY

"My life dances on a tightrope—balancing the serene duty of a healer with the covert operations of the Fox Order—revealing the inner strength of a woman who navigates the interplay of light and shadow."

- Glenda De Bruyn

4338.206

(25 July 2018)

THE FOX

4338.206.1

I stepped out of the cramped examination room, its sterile scent clinging to me like a second skin. The clinic was bustling with the typical late afternoon flurry, a cacophony of coughs, whispers, and the occasional wail of a distressed child. I made my way towards the waiting area, my steps echoing slightly on the linoleum floor. The fluorescent lights overhead cast a harsh glow, accentuating the weariness that seemed to permeate the room.

As a physician, especially one far from my birthplace of Zurich and now deeply embedded in the community here in Hobart, Tasmania, I carried not just the responsibility of care but also the silent stories of those who walked these halls. Each patient was a world unto themselves, a universe of experiences, fears, and hopes. It was my job to navigate these waters, to provide solace, understanding, and, whenever possible, healing.

"Clyde Thompson," I called out, my voice steady despite the fatigue that was beginning to make its presence felt. My eyes scanned the room, settling on an elderly gentleman who was making a valiant effort to rise from his chair. As he struggled to stand, a cough rattled through him, harsh and guttural, like the sound of dry leaves being crushed underfoot. It was the kind of cough that made you wince, the kind that spoke of long nights and discomfort.

I took a deep breath, steadying myself. My gut churned with a mixture of concern and resolve; this was going to be one of those cases that reminded you of the fragility of human life, of the battles fought in the quiet corners of everyday existence. I could already sense the weight of responsibility settling on my shoulders, a familiar burden that I bore with a mixture of pride and apprehension.

"This way, please," I said, managing a smile that I hoped was reassuring. I gestured towards the small room at the end of the corridor, a space that had become my sanctuary and battlefield, where I waged war against illness and despair on a daily basis.

As we walked, I couldn't help but notice the effort it took for Mr. Thompson to simply put one foot in front of the other. Each step was laboured, an indication of the struggle that his body was enduring. The clinic's corridor seemed to stretch on, a seemingly endless path lined with closed doors and the faint echoes of other lives being lived and examined within their confines.

I found myself glancing at Mr. Thompson, studying him not just as a patient but as a person. His face was a roadmap of years lived, lines etched deep by laughter, sorrow, and the inexorable passage of time. His eyes, though clouded with the weariness of illness, still held a spark of determination, a silent refusal to be defined solely by the physical limitations that beset him.

As we reached the examination room, I held the door open for him, a silent gesture of support and respect. "We'll take good care of you," I found myself saying, the words more than just a professional reassurance. They were a promise, a vow that I and countless others in this profession made daily —to care, to heal, to stand as beacons of hope in the often overwhelming darkness of illness.

Settling Mr. Thompson into the examination chair, I prepared myself mentally for the consultation. This wasn't just about diagnosing and prescribing; it was about connecting, understanding, and supporting. As I turned to face him, ready to begin, I felt the full weight of my role. I was not just a clinician; I was a confidant, a guide through the uncertain journey of health and illness. Pierre, my husband, often said that I carried the weight of my patients' worlds on my shoulders. Perhaps he was right, but in moments like these, I was exactly where I needed to be.

"Would you excuse me for a moment, please?" I asked, the words slipping from me with practiced ease, yet my heart was anything but calm. The elderly gentleman seated before me, his frame slight and weary from the cough that seemed to shake the very essence of him, nodded with an understanding that spoke volumes of his vulnerability. As I stepped outside the door, the cool touch of my phone felt like the weight of the world in my palm.

The corridor outside the examination room suddenly felt eerily silent. The air hung heavy with the scent of antiseptic, a constant reminder of the battle we waged against unseen enemies. My patient, with his cough that echoed the fears of our community, was showing signs of the new viral infection that had been the subject of whispered conversations and heated debates amongst my peers. Its grip on the elderly was unyielding, merciless in its spread and severity. Yet, amidst the scientific discourse, lay a web of conspiracy spun by those of us who saw shadows in every corner—The Fox Order, we called ourselves, believers in a tale so convoluted it seemed ripped from the pages of a dystopian novel.

Taking a deep breath, I unlocked my phone with a sense of urgency. The message I was about to send felt like casting a stone into a pond, unsure of the ripples it would create. "Does The Fox have wings?" I typed, my fingers hesitant for a moment before pressing send. The implications of this inquiry were vast, its answers potentially altering the course of our quiet resistance. Penelope Lister, my handler and the linchpin in our delicate operation here it Tasmania, would understand the gravity of my question.

Her reply came swiftly. "Maybe." That single word, so noncommittal on the surface, sent a shiver down my spine. My heart thrummed against my chest, a staccato beat in the silence of the hallway. "Maybe" was a world of ambiguity, suggesting that our leader was possibly out of play, our movements exposed to unseen eyes. It was a call to tread lightly, to mask our steps in the shadows of discretion.

"Maybe," I whispered to myself, the word a mantra of caution. It was a reminder that the path forward was fraught with risks, that every step, every decision, now required an even greater degree of caution and scrutiny. The world of medical practice, with its familiar protocols and scientific certainties, seemed a stark contrast to the shadowy realms of espionage and covert operations. Yet, here I stood, at the nexus of both, the weight of my dual responsibilities pressing upon me.

I took a moment, allowing the weight of Penelope's response to settle in my mind. The stakes were higher than ever, our path forward fraught with danger. Yet, the resolve within me hardened. We were not just fighting a viral outbreak; we were battling the shadows, striving to bring light to the truth obscured by fear and manipulation.

With a steadying breath, I pocketed my phone and prepared to step back into the examination room. The face I would present to my patient would be one of calm assurance, the demeanour of a medical professional dedicated to their care. Yet beneath the surface, my mind was already racing, plotting our next move in a game where the rules were constantly changing. The Portal Defence Corps, with its tendrils of conspiracy and dissent, would not deter us. We would move with caution, yes, but move forward we would.

The fight for truth, for the health and safety of our community, demanded nothing less.

Stepping back into the small, clinical space, I fixed a smile onto my face, one that I hoped conveyed empathy and professionalism. "I'm terribly sorry about that. Urgent family matter," I said, my voice laced with an apologetic tone that was more for my own benefit than for Mr. Thompson's. It was a small lie, a necessary veneer to cover the true nature of the interruption.

"That's fine," Mr. Thompson managed to articulate, his voice struggling to break through the hacking coughs that seemed to wrack his body with increasing ferocity. Each cough was a stark reminder of the urgency of the situation, a sonic symbol of the invisible threat we were all facing.

Taking another deep breath, I couldn't shake off the creeping dread that it might already be too late for Mr. Thompson. The thought that someone could have reported him to the authorities for displaying symptoms of the feared virus sent a shiver down my spine. The implications of such an action were too grave to contemplate, not just for him but for the community at large.

"What can I help you with, Mr. Thompson?" I asked, my voice a blend of professional concern and a personal need for reassurance. I wanted to believe, more than anything, that this was just a case of a nasty cold, not the harbinger of a deeper crisis.

"I seem to have caught this very nasty cough," Mr. Thompson replied, his voice weak but earnest.

"Do you know who you might have caught it off?" I inquired, clinging to the hope that he could provide a name, a clue, anything that might help trace the path of this illness and perhaps contain it.

"No, I live alone and don't get out much," he said, and his words painted a picture of isolation that was all too common among the elderly. It was both a blessing and a curse in these times—a shield against the spread of illness but a barrier to human connection.

"Are you sure? You haven't visited or been visited by any friends or family in the last week?" I pressed, my desperation for a lead, any lead, making me push harder than I might have under different circumstances.

"No, I don't think so," Mr. Thompson insisted, his certainty a cold splash of reality on my flickering hope.

"Clyde, please. Surely there must be some community event you went to. Some visitor?" My voice was earnest, almost pleading, as I looked into his eyes, searching for a flicker of recollection, a spark that might ignite a trail to follow. My use of his first name was an attempt to bridge the clinical distance between us, to forge a connection that might unlock the information I needed.

"No, I am...." His voice faded into another bout of coughing, each spasm seeming to take a piece of his strength with it.

As I watched him, a mix of professional concern and personal empathy warred within me. Each unanswered question, every cough from Mr. Thompson, was a reminder of the invisible lines that connected us all, for better or for worse. The knowledge that I was standing on the front lines of this battle, armed with little more than questions and a deep-seated hope to make a difference, was both a burden and a privilege. In that moment, I was more than a medical professional; I was a protector of sorts, navigating the murky waters of a crisis with nothing but my wits and my will to help.

The unexpected sharp knock at the door jolted me, a stark interruption to the intense atmosphere of the examination room. For a moment, I froze, the abrupt sound slicing through the air like a cold blade. My heart raced, each beat a thunderous echo in my chest as I approached the door, my steps hesitant. The clinic was supposed to be a sanctuary, a place of healing, yet in that instant, it felt like anything but. My palms were clammy, a physical testament to the surge of anxiety that gripped me. "I'm with a patient. Can it wait?" I called out, my voice steady despite the turmoil swirling within. I didn't dare open the door, fearing what—or who—might be on the other side.

Leaning against the cool wall, I tried to steady my breathing, wiping my sweaty palms on my trousers in a futile attempt to calm my nerves. "Please go away, please go away," I whispered to myself, a silent mantra, hoping against hope that the intrusion would simply disappear if I wished it hard enough.

But the universe had other plans. The door handle turned downwards with an ominous finality, forcing me to retreat as the door swung open, breaking the fragile barrier between my patient and the outside world.

"I'm sorry, Glenda. The men insisted it was urgent," Michelle said, her eyes meeting mine in a silent exchange of worry and apology. Her presence felt like a harbinger of unwelcome news.

Two army officers stepped into the room, their uniforms crisply ironed, medals glinting under the harsh fluorescent lights—a sharp contrast to the vulnerability and sickness housed within these walls. They carried an air of authority and urgency, a palpable reminder of the world's troubles that had now invaded our small space of care and healing.

"Thank you, Michelle," I managed to say, my voice a mix of professional composure and underlying concern. I moved instinctively, positioning myself between the door and Mr. Thompson, a protective gesture born from a deep-seated commitment to my patients' privacy and well-being. It was a physical manifestation of my role as a caretaker, a barrier against the uncertainties these uniformed strangers brought with them.

As Michelle quietly closed the door, leaving us in a tense tableau, I couldn't help but feel a deep sense of foreboding. The arrival of these officers, with their formal bearing and the unspoken gravity of their visit, signalled a shift. The crisis, it seemed, had reached our doorstep, blurring the lines between my professional obligations and the wider world's turmoil.

As Commander Jim Larsson and Bruce Foggarty entered the room, the tension seemed to thicken, clinging to the air like a palpable fog. Larsson, with the authority his rank and stripes commanded, held a presence that demanded attention. His name, boldly emblazoned across the left side of his chest, introduced him before a word was spoken. Yet, amidst the formality and the gravity of the situation, it was Bruce Foggarty who captured my immediate, intense focus.

Bruce, a name and face etched into the recesses of my memory, stirred a whirlwind of emotions and recollections. The sight of him was like a ghost from the past manifesting in the stark, clinical light of the present. There was a time when our paths had crossed, intertwining in the complex dance of shared ideals and clandestine meetings that now felt worlds away. The suspicion that he, too, might be part of The Fox Order—a secret that bound us in a silent fraternity—loomed large in my mind. Yet, the veil of secrecy that enveloped us all made it impossible to reach out, to confirm whether the person before me was an ally or another potential foe.

In this world of shadows and whispers, the only certainties were few and far between. My handler, Penelope Lister, remained an enigmatic figure in the background, her presence felt but never seen. And Pierre, my husband, stood as the sole beacon of trust and shared purpose in the muddied waters of our cause. But here, now, with Bruce's familiar gaze meeting mine, a torrent of questions and possibilities raced through my mind.

"Glenda, please step aside," Commander Larsson's voice cut through my thoughts, pulling me back to the pressing reality of the moment. His request, delivered with an air of non-negotiable authority, left little room for resistance.

I hesitated, caught between the instinct to protect my patient and the understanding of the severity of the situation unfolding before me. It was Bruce's covert glance, a silent communication in the briefest of moments, that swayed me. His eyes, veiled from Larsson's view, held a warning—a clear signal to comply without drawing attention or suspicion.

"As you wish," I acquiesced, my voice steady despite the storm of emotions and questions swirling within. Stepping to the side, I allowed them the space they demanded, all the while acutely aware of the undercurrents at play.

As the Commander's directive cut through the tense atmosphere of the room, "Test him," a chill ran down my spine. The authority in his voice left no room for doubt or dissent. Bruce, moving with a purpose that seemed both reluctant and resolute, approached Mr. Thompson, the testing device in his grasp—a modern-day sword of Damocles disguised as something as innocuous as an EpiPen.

My instincts screamed for me to intervene, to protect my patient from what felt like an intrusion too cold, too clinical in its impersonality. But Bruce's glance, a silent communication laden with a fear that mirrored my own, halted me. His head shake, minimal but unmistakable, was a clear warning. The gravity of his gaze communicated more than words ever could. Once again, I found myself heeding his silent plea, a testament to the trust I had in this shadowy bond forged by our shared, unspoken affiliation.

I stood there, a silent witness, my body coiled tight with tension. The taste of blood filled my mouth, a reminder of the effort it took to restrain myself, to remain a bystander in this critical moment. Watching Bruce manipulate Mr. Thompson's head, the gentleness we as medical professionals pride ourselves on replaced by a necessity for efficiency, was almost more than I could bear. The device pressed against the venerable, wrinkled skin of Mr. Thompson's neck was a harsh juxtaposition of technology against the fragility of human life.

With my eyes closed, a prayer formed silently on my lips, a fervent plea for a negative result. The seconds stretched into eternity, each passing moment a weight upon my heart. The beep of the device, a harbinger of fate, pierced the heavy silence, and the robotic announcement that followed felt like a decree from the heavens.

"Test result negative."

The relief that washed over me was palpable, a release of breath I hadn't realised I'd been holding. My eyes fluttered open, just in time to catch myself before a tear could betray the depth of my emotions. The relief on Bruce's face mirrored my own—a moment of shared humanity in the midst of this clinical procedure.

"It is indeed a negative result," Bruce's voice, once again composed, broke the silence that had enveloped the room. His announcement to the Commander, though delivered with a professional detachment, couldn't mask the undercurrent of relief that flowed beneath the surface.

In that moment, the room seemed to breathe again, the tension dissipating ever so slightly as the immediate threat receded. Yet, the seriousness of Bruce's demeanour, the swift return to protocol, served as a reminder of the delicate balance we were navigating. This was more than a medical test; it was a trial by fire, a test of loyalty, and a dance with shadows—all under the watchful eyes of the unseen forces that governed our actions.

A sudden and unexplainable transformation settled, and the room was steeped in a tense silence, the kind that weighs on your shoulders and tightens around your chest, making each breath feel like a conscious effort. The Commander's thoughtful pause felt interminable, a moment stretched thin by the gravity of decisions made within it. When he finally spoke, his words seemed to hang in the air, heavy with authority. "Mr Thompson. Please come with us," he requested, his tone polite yet firm, leaving no room for refusal.

Mr Thompson, bewildered and frail, attempted to voice his confusion. He was obedient, despite his evident unease. I, on the other hand, felt a surge of protectiveness, a fierce need to stand up for him, to question the rationale behind this request. Ignoring the silent warnings from my handler to remain cautious, I found myself speaking up, driven by a mix of duty and defiance.

"What for? You heard it yourself, the test result was negative," I said, my voice steady and imbued with as much authority as I could muster. Beneath the surface, however, was a tumultuous mix of fear and determination. I was acutely aware of the risk I was taking, the potential consequences of challenging those in power. But in that moment, all concerns for my own safety were overshadowed by the need to protect my patient, to demand justice and transparency.

Bruce's plea, "Glenda, don't," was laced with urgency and a hint of despair. His words were meant to shield me, a reminder of the precariousness of our position. Yet, I couldn't back down, not when it mattered most. My gaze locked with Commander Larsson's, a silent battle of wills, my eyes burning with a mix of anger and desperation. I wished my stare could convey the depth of my resolve, could somehow challenge the authority and decisions that seemed to operate beyond the bounds of reason.

"Mr Thompson, this way please," the commander repeated, his voice cutting through the charged atmosphere. He assisted Mr. Thompson from his seat with a gentleness that belied the situation's underlying tension. Mr. Thompson's compliance, his silent acquiescence to the commander's request, was a bitter reminder of the power dynamics at play. As they left the room, the silence that enveloped their departure was deafening, leaving a void filled with unanswered questions and unspoken fears.

As I made my way to the door, each step felt heavier than the last, burdened with a mix of emotions that seemed too complex to unravel in the moment. The simple act of closing the door felt symbolic, like sealing away the part of myself that had just dared to challenge the authority of the Commander and the unsettling course of events that transpired. A wave of defeat washed over me, leaving a residue of confusion in its wake. *But why?* The question echoed in my mind, a silent plea for understanding in a situation that defied logic. The test was negative, yet the outcome felt anything but a victory.

Hot tears, unbidden and unwelcome, began to trail down my cheeks, the saltiness a reminder of the vulnerability I felt. With a swift motion, I wiped them away, refusing to let them be a testament to my perceived weakness. In the quiet of the room, my own voice surprised me, "This is not the first time, nor will it be the last time." The words, spoken aloud, served as a grim reminder of the challenges I had faced and the daunting path that lay ahead. It was a mantra of resilience, born from past struggles, yet it did little to ease the immediate sting of helplessness.

My legs, betraying the turmoil that churned within, began to shake uncontrollably. It was as if the strength that had propelled me through confrontation had suddenly evaporated, leaving me physically and emotionally drained.

Without warning, my knees buckled, sending me crumpling to the floor in an undignified heap. There, in the solitude of the examination room, I allowed myself a moment of surrender, my eyes closing as I sought refuge in the darkness behind my lids.

Time seemed to stand still, the only measure of its passage being the slow return of my composure. It was a painstaking process, gathering the shattered pieces of my resolve, fortifying the walls I had meticulously built around my emotions. I remained on the floor until I felt a semblance of strength return, until the trembling had subsided and the fed shed tears had dried.

Rising from the floor felt like a rebirth of sorts, a physical manifestation of the renewed determination that began to take root within me. I straightened my attire, a symbolic gesture of realigning my purpose and resolve. With a deep, steadying breath, I opened the door and stepped into the corridor, the light casting long shadows behind me.

Walking down the corridor towards the waiting room, each step was an echo of the resilience that had been forged in the fires of adversity. The weight of responsibility pressed heavily on my shoulders, a constant companion in this journey. Yet, with each stride, I felt the flickers of determination grow stronger, fuelled by the knowledge that, despite the setbacks and the uncertainties, my commitment to my patients, to the truth, remained unwavering.

ESCAPE

4338.206.2

As I made my way towards the front reception desk, still carrying the remnants of the emotional turmoil from earlier, Michelle silently handed me the next patient's file. The simple exchange felt grounding, a reminder of the routine that structured my days, even if today felt anything but routine. Glancing at the label, a wave of familiarity washed over me as I recognised the name. Luke Smith. His case was one I was well acquainted with, having seen him several times before for various minor ailments and check-ups.

The familiarity brought with it a semblance of normalcy, a brief respite from the storm of emotions still swirling within me. I took a moment to gather myself, to don the professional façade that was second nature, yet felt so fragile today.

Walking to the front of the room, I called out with a clear, steady voice, "Luke Smith." The name cut through the low murmur of the waiting room, reaching the young man seated at the back. He looked up, his expression a mix of apprehension and curiosity, a common look among patients awaiting their turn. "This way please," I said, my tone professional yet warm, a balance I had perfected over years of practice.

As Luke approached, I could see the slight hesitation in his steps, the unconscious bracing for whatever news awaited him. I ushered him into the examination room with a reassuring smile, closing the door behind us to afford us privacy and a sense of separation from the world outside.

Directing him to sit in the visitor's chair, I couldn't help but notice how the room seemed to shrink with the memory of Mr. Thompson's presence still lingering in the air. I tried hard to push the thought aside, to compartmentalise my concerns and focus on the patient in front of me. Luke took his seat, unaware of the chair's recent history, the weight of the decisions made in this very room.

As I prepared to engage with Luke, to delve into the reason for his visit, I found myself grappling with the duality of my role. On one hand, I was the compassionate caregiver, dedicated to healing and comfort. On the other, I was a soldier in a far more complex battle, one that extended beyond the confines of this examination room, beyond the simple ailments and worries of my patients.

But in this moment, with Luke sitting before me, I needed to be fully present, to leave the shadows at the door.

"What can I do for you this time, Mr. Smith?" I inquired, adopting the professional tone that had become second nature to me. His silence, however, was unexpected—a pause that stretched too long, filling the room with a tangible tension.

"Mr. Smith?" I prompted again, my curiosity piqued and a hint of concern threading through my voice. His response, or rather the lack of one, was not typical for our interactions. Then, suddenly, he leaned in close, his movement so swift it caught me off guard. His question, whispered with a gravity that belied the quietness of his voice, sent a shiver down my spine. "Tell me, Glenda, what do you know about 'The Testing'?"

My immediate reaction was a mixture of shock and instinctual caution. "Shh," I hushed, my hands moving of their own accord to cover both our mouths, a gesture aimed at preserving the secrecy of our conversation. "How do you know about that?" I whispered back, my mind racing with the implications of his knowledge.

Luke's response was to lean even closer, his breath barely audible as he whispered, "I can get you to a safe place." The promise in his words was like a beacon in the darkness, a flicker of hope. "Really?" I found myself whispering back, barely daring to believe. "Is there such a place?" The concept of a safe haven seemed almost mythical, a distant dream in the shadowy world we navigated.

Then, as if to answer my silent prayers, Luke opened his hand, revealing a small, rectangular, metallic device nestled in his palm. The sight of it was both intriguing and alarming. "Yes," he confirmed softly, his voice a whisper that carried the weight of secrets and possibilities.

"What is that?" I asked, my curiosity now fully alight. The device, so unassuming in appearance, held the promise of answers, of escape, perhaps even of salvation. My professional demeanour was momentarily forgotten, replaced by a keen interest in the mystery Luke presented. The room, with its clinical sterility and the remnants of previous conversations, suddenly felt like a cocoon, isolating us from the world outside and the dangers that lurked there.

"I'll show you," Luke's voice was steady, a contrast to the tumult of emotions swirling within me. His question, "Are you sure we're alone?" pierced the bubble of intrigue surrounding us.

"I can't be certain," I admitted, my mind racing through the possibilities. Bruce and the Commander were a constant shadow in the back of my mind, their presence an ever-present threat that loomed just beyond the physical confines of this room. The Testers, with their clinical efficiency and detached coldness, had left an indelible mark on my psyche. The possibility of their return, though seemingly slim, haunted the edges of my thoughts. Yet, the chance for something more, for a glimpse into the unknown, tethered me to the spot, curiosity and fear waging a silent war within.

The transformation of the room unfolded with a surreal, almost dreamlike quality. Luke moved with a purpose and precision that belied the extraordinary nature of his actions. He pushed the chairs aside with a gentle yet firm touch, each movement calculated to create a clear path to the back wall. It was as if he were an artist clearing his studio, preparing to reveal his masterpiece. The mundane clutter of the room, which had always been a backdrop to the daily grind of medical examinations and consultations, shifted, becoming the prelude to something extraordinary.

As Luke approached the wall, his demeanour changed; there was a palpable shift in the air, a sense of anticipation that made my heart race. With a motion that seemed both effortless and laden with significance, Luke activated the small device. The wall, once a solid barrier confining the space, shimmered and dissolved into a breathtaking display of bright, electrifying, swirling colours. It was as though a veil had been lifted, revealing a window to another dimension.

The colours themselves were alive, a vibrant tapestry that moved and breathed. Hues of azure clashed with streaks of gold, while emerald greens and deep purples intertwined in an ever-changing dance. It was a spectacle that defied explanation, a phenomenon that challenged the very laws of physics as I understood them. The light emitted from the portal cast the room in a surreal glow, highlighting Luke's features with an ethereal light as he stood before the mesmerising display.

I watched, captivated, as the colours pulsed and flowed, creating patterns that seemed to hint at the infinite. The portal beckoned with a promise of adventure and discovery, yet it also whispered of dangers unknown. It was both a promise of escape from the shadows that had begun to encroach upon my life and a challenge to step into a realm beyond my wildest imaginings.

"Shall we?" Luke's invitation was both a question and a challenge, his hand extended towards me, a bridge between the known and the unknown.

Rising from my chair, I was momentarily transfixed by the spectacle before me. The awe that washed over me was palpable, igniting a spark of hope that had lain dormant amidst the shadows of fear and uncertainty. My steps towards the portal were measured, a physical manifestation of the inner turmoil between the pull of discovery and the grip of caution.

"I have heard my father speak of a Portal before, but never seen it with my own eyes," I confessed, my voice a whisper of wonder. The stories that had once filled my imagination with vivid tales of other worlds and hidden truths were now a tangible reality before me. "It is more beautiful than I ever imagined."

"It is beautiful," Luke's agreement was a simple affirmation, yet it carried the weight of shared experience, of a connection forged in the briefest of moments yet bound by the surreal.

I stood on the threshold, the portal's swirling, colliding colours inviting, promising, yet I hesitated. The allure of the portal, with its mesmerising display of light and energy, was a siren call to my soul, yet the anchor of my reality, of my responsibilities and fears, held me fast.

"What's wrong?" Luke's voice cut through my hesitation, laced with panic.

"Pierre. What will happen to Pierre?" The question spilled from me, my voice a blend of hope and desperation. Pierre, my anchor in the tumultuous sea of uncertainties, the thought of leaving him behind was unbearable. Luke's assurance, "I'll bring Pierre for you and your parents," was meant to comfort, yet it opened a wound I had long tried to heal.

My response was instinctive, a reflex born of pain and memory. "I lost my father many years ago," I confessed, the mournfulness in my voice a testament to a loss that time had not dulled. The words felt heavy, each syllable laden with the weight of years passed and the shadow of grief that lingered.

"I'm sorry for your loss," Luke's sympathy was genuine, a balm to the raw edges of my heart.

Taking heart from his genuineness, I found myself asking, "When?" The urgency of our situation, the promise of escape to a place of safety, was a beacon of hope in the darkness. Luke's admission, "As soon as I can. I can't promise I'll be quick," was a tether to reality, a reminder of the challenges and dangers that lay ahead. Yet, it was a promise of effort, of commitment, that bolstered my resolve.

"Thank you," I said, my gratitude sincere, even as my gaze remained transfixed by the portal's spellbinding display. The step I took forward was more than physical movement; it was a step towards the unknown, towards a future that was as uncertain as it was necessary.

"I'll be right behind you, Glenda," Luke's words were a comfort, a promise that I would not face what lay ahead alone. His presence, both as a Guardian and as an ally, fortified my courage. The portal, with its vibrant hues and swirling energies, beckoned, a doorway to possibilities unknown.

In that moment, standing on the precipice of a decision that would alter the course of my life, I felt a strange peace. The fear and uncertainty that had gripped me were still there, but so too was a sense of purpose, of destiny unfolding. The journey through the portal was not just an escape; it was a leap into a future where hope and danger coexisted, where the fight for survival and freedom would continue.

The sudden vibration of my phone on the desk was like a jolt from another world, abruptly pulling me back from the brink of the unknown that the Portal represented. The vibrant allure of the technicolour swirl momentarily faded, replaced by the stark reality of my current life. With a sense of reluctance, I turned away from the portal's mesmerising display and walked over to the desk, the urgency of the vibration hinting at something urgent, something dire.

Pierre's message was a cold splash of fear: *We've been compromised. Run!* The words leapt from the screen, searing themselves into my consciousness. A gasp escaped me, unbidden, as my hand flew to my mouth, a physical attempt to stifle the surge of panic that threatened to overwhelm me. The world seemed to tilt, the ground beneath me suddenly unstable.

"What is it?" Luke's voice, laced with curiosity and concern, pierced the fog of my shock. Turning to face him, the phone felt like a lead weight in my hand—a link to the life I was about to leave behind, now a potential threat to my safety.

Locking the phone with a sense of finality, I approached Luke, extending the device towards him. "Luke, you must destroy this phone for me, please," I implored, my voice a mix of instruction and plea. The necessity of the act was clear; any ties to my former life, especially those that could be traced or exploited by our adversaries, had to be severed.

"I will," Luke promised, his voice steady, imbued with a resolve that offered a sliver of comfort in the chaos. "You have my word."

Compelled by a newfound urgency, I hurried back to the Portal, the vibrant gateway to safety that had moments ago been an object of awe and hesitation. I was so close, the colours beckoning, the promise of escape within reach. Yet, as I stood on the threshold, I stopped. Again.

"Oh, Luke. I nearly forgot," I blurted out, the urgency of the moment making my voice tremble slightly.

"What is it?" Luke's impatience was palpable.

"In my top drawer, you'll find my hospital ID and keys. I have a high enough security level that will get you into almost any part of the Royal. You may find them very useful later." The words spilled out in a hurried whisper, the significance of what I was entrusting to him not lost on me. The realisation that these mundane objects could become tools of survival in the right hands underscored the importance of the situation we found ourselves in.

"Indeed. I am sure I will," Luke's response carried a note of acknowledgment and understanding of the potential value of what I was offering. His encouragement to move forward, despite the whirlwind of emotions and last-minute preparations, was the nudge I needed to cross the threshold into the unknown.

Finally, with a deep breath that did little to calm my racing heart, I stepped into the wall of swirling colour, the portal that promised refuge but demanded a price—leaving behind everything familiar. Luke followed closely, a silent guardian in my leap into the unknown.

As my foot touched down, the sensation underfoot was unlike anything I had expected. Soft, brown dust that seemed to cushion my step, a stark contrast to the hard, clinical floors of the medical centre I had left behind. Then, without warning, a voice spoke to me. It wasn't a voice in the traditional sense; there was no sound, no audible tone. Yet, its message resonated within me with clarity and depth, "Welcome to Clivilius, Glenda De Bruyn."

The greeting, though not heard with my ears, was felt throughout my being, a communication that transcended the need for sound. It was as if the very essence of this place, Clivilius, had reached out to me directly, acknowledging my arrival in a manner so personal and intimate that it momentarily took my breath away.

MEDICAL EMERGENCY

4338.206.3

As I stood there, enveloped in the vast silence of Clivilius, a sense of desolation swept over me. The quiet was profound, a stark contrast to the busyness I had left behind. Around me, the landscape was a monochrome of brown, the dust rolling into hills that seemed to stretch into infinity in every direction. The beauty was overshadowed by its emptiness, a solitude that pressed in on me from all sides.

A sudden pang of panic seized me, my heart racing against the stillness. *This isn't what I expected at all.* Each step I took was a testament to the surrealness of the situation, my feet sinking ever so slightly into the soft, yielding dust beneath me. The stories my father had told me of Clivilius painted a picture of a vibrant world teeming with life, a stark contrast to the barrenness that lay before me.

Where is the bustling city? Where are the abundant herds of animals roaming freely? Where are the brilliant flora that grow in every nook and cranny? Where are all the people? The questions spiralled in my mind, a whirlwind of confusion and disbelief. The world I had imagined, filled with the vivid hues of life and the bustling sounds of existence, was nowhere to be found. Instead, I was greeted by an emptiness that seemed to swallow up any hope of finding familiarity.

What stretched before me didn't look anything like the world my father had described before he disappeared. *But that was years ago.* The thought that perhaps it had all been destroyed in the intervening years was a cold shard of fear in my heart. *Is it all gone? Is my father really dead?* The possibility that the vibrant Clivilius of my father's stories had been reduced to this desolate landscape was a blow, a loss of hope not just for finding my father but for the refuge I had sought in this place.

As these thoughts tumbled through my mind, a sense of isolation settled over me, heavier than the air of this alien world. The realisation that the Clivilius I had envisioned, the world of my father's tales, might no longer exist—or perhaps never did in the way I imagined—was a bitter pill to swallow. The notion that my father, if he had ever found his way here, might have met his end in this lonely expanse was a thought too painful to fully accept.

Yet, amidst the despair and the myriad of questions, a resolve began to form within me. If this world had once been the place of wonder my father described, then perhaps there were secrets yet to uncover, truths hidden beneath the surface of this seemingly barren land. The journey ahead would not be the one I had anticipated, but it was one I was determined to undertake. In the silence of Clivilius, I knew the search for answers, for my father, and for a new beginning, was just starting.

The sudden appearance of the tall, slender gentleman, materialising from the seemingly empty landscape, was a jolt to my senses, already heightened by the unfamiliarity of Clivilius. The soft shuffling of his footsteps, drawing closer from the side, was the only indication of his approach in the otherwise silent expanse. The gentle touch of Luke's hands on my shoulders startled me, a light jump betraying my nerves as he guided me to face the newcomer.

Taking steps towards the man, my curiosity piqued, I felt a mix of apprehension and a budding hope that perhaps this world was not as desolate as it first appeared. Luke, with a swiftness that spoke of familiarity, quickly moved ahead of me, eager to make introductions.

"This is Glenda," Luke announced, his arm sweeping in my direction in a grand gesture that seemed to bridge the gap between us. "Glenda is a doctor in Hobart," he added, his voice tinged with a pride that warmed me, despite the chill of uncertainty that had settled in my heart. His introduction, while simple, felt like a lifeline, anchoring me to my identity in this strange new world.

I stepped forward, extending my hand in a gesture of greeting that felt both familiar and bizarrely out of place in the context of our surroundings. "It's a pleasure to meet you..." My voice trailed off, the realisation dawning that I had ventured into the unknown without even the basic knowledge of this man's name.

"Paul," he filled in the gap, his handshake firm and reassuring. "I'm Luke's brother."

"Of course. I see the resemblance now," I replied quickly, my words a reflex more than a thoughtful response. As I glanced between Luke and Paul, I frowned slightly, mentally chiding myself for the comment. Observing them side by side, it struck me how different they actually appeared. Paul was easily six inches taller than Luke, with a physique that spoke of strength and physicality—larger muscles, broader shoulders, a stark contrast to Luke's leaner frame. And their hair, Paul's locks a few shades lighter than Luke's, hinted at a diversity in their genetic tapestry that piqued my curiosity. *Perhaps they were...*

"Paul burnt his foot last night," Luke's voice snapped me out of my speculative reverie. His casual mention of the injury, juxtaposed with the concern underlying his suggestion, shifted my focus from their differences to the matter at hand. "He seems to be doing okay with it, but I reckon a bit of medical attention wouldn't hurt."

"Sure," I responded, the doctor in me taking over instinctively. "Show me your foot," I directed, my tone firm yet imbued with an underlying concern.

Paul's hesitation was palpable, a brief moment of vulnerability that spoke volumes. Slowly, he raised his leg toward me, a silent consent to the examination. I squatted, reaching out to take his leg, preparing myself for a closer inspection. The act was familiar, a routine part of my profession, yet the context in which it was happening—a world away from Hobart, in a landscape foreign and barren—lent it an air of surrealism.

"Oh, no, no. Not yet," interrupted Luke.

At Luke's sudden interjection, my hand drew back as if it had brushed against something too hot. The urgency in his voice, coupled with the sudden shift in priorities, left me momentarily disoriented. "There is another man in far more need than Paul," he explained, the growing concern in his tone mirroring the tightening sensation in my shoulder—an instinctive physical response to the anticipation of dealing with a potentially grave situation.

"Take me to him, and I shall take a look," I found myself saying almost immediately. My directive was clear, yet it carried the weight of responsibility I felt as a doctor, a calling that didn't recognise the boundaries of worlds.

Luke's gaze turned to his brother, a silent communication passing between them before he voiced the question, "Where's Jamie?" The concern was evident, a tangible thread pulling at the fabric of their shared worry.

Paul's response, marked by a heavy gulp, did little to quell the rising sense of urgency. "He's resting in the tent. I think he has a fever." His words painted a picture of vulnerability, of a man laid low by illness in a world that I was beginning to realise offered little in the way of comfort or safety.

"Shit," Luke's expletive was a sharp punctuation to the tension that had enveloped us. "What happened? I thought he was feeling better."

As I observed the brothers' exchange, a part of me was analysing every word, every gesture for clues. Understanding their dynamics, their experiences in this place, was crucial. If I was going to navigate the complexities of Clivilius, to uncover any trace of my father, I knew I would need to understand and rely on Luke and Paul. Their knowledge, their experiences, and their support would be indispensable.

"He seemed much better when we ate. But soon after... He looks pretty bad," Paul's words were a stark reminder of how quickly situations could deteriorate here. The mention of a meal as a turning point suggested a sudden onset, a rapid decline that was all too familiar in the realm of medicine.

Without another word, I cut through the mounting tension. "Take me to him. Now," I demanded, my voice carrying an authority born of years in emergency rooms and clinics, where every second could mean the difference between life and death.

Luke's gesture for Paul to take the lead was swift, an unspoken command that was immediately heeded. I trailed behind them, my gaze momentarily captured by the way the dust danced around my feet with each step I took. The landscape of Clivilius, with its endless expanse of soft, brown dust, felt alien yet strangely mesmerising. As we trekked over several dusty hills, the monotony of the terrain made me acutely aware of the silence that enveloped us—a silence so profound it seemed to press against my ears.

The journey to the camp, though not long, gave me time to ponder the situation I found myself in. The anticipation of meeting Jamie, of assessing his condition and providing medical assistance, was a familiar pressure—a reminder of my responsibilities as a doctor, regardless of the world I was in. Yet, underlying that was a current of apprehension about the unknown elements of this place and how they might affect my ability to help.

❖

The sight that greeted us at the campsite instantly sent a jolt of panic through me. My eyes locked onto a half-collapsed military-looking tent, its fabric sagging mournfully, like a wounded soldier. "Oh my God!" I couldn't help but exclaim, the words bursting from me as my mind raced with images of someone trapped beneath its dismal folds. "He's not trapped under there, is he?" I asked, urgency propelling me forward, ready to dive into action.

Paul's response, a chuckle rich with amusement, momentarily confused me. "Oh, no," he reassured, his voice still laced with remnants of laughter. "He's in the fully built tent," he clarified, gesturing towards another structure that stood a short distance away, its integrity intact and imposing.

"Thank God," I breathed out, a wave of relief momentarily softening the tension that had seized me. My gaze shifted to the indicated tent, taking in its size and structure. It was large, easily capable of sheltering ten men, mirroring the military precision and durability of the first, yet proudly upright and unyielding. The relief that washed over me was palpable, easing the tightness in my chest.

"That one is just my attempt to put a tent up by myself," Paul admitted, a hint of self-deprecation in his tone. His words painted a picture of a solitary struggle against the canvas and poles, a battle evidently lost to the elements or perhaps to inexperience.

"Oh, I see," I responded, my interest in the failed tent waning now that the urgency had dissipated.

As we moved towards the fully erected tent, the sense of purpose returned, sharpening my senses. The brief interlude of humour and misunderstanding with Paul had, in a way, lightened the mood, reminding me of the resilience and humanity that persisted even in the most challenging circumstances.

Luke's gesture, holding back the tent's flap for me, felt like a transition from the desolate outside world into a space teeming with life, albeit a muted one. The interior of the tent, with its sparse furnishings and the presence of a man and two small dogs in repose, created a stark contrast to the barren landscape of Clivilius that lay beyond its confines. The sight of the two Shih Tzus, lost in their peaceful slumber beside the man, added a touch of normalcy to the otherwise grim scene.

"Jamie?" Luke's voice was gentle, a soft intrusion into the silence that hung heavily within the tent. The lack of response, however, heightened my sense of urgency, pulling me towards the mattress where the man lay.

As I rushed over and knelt by the man's side, the reality of his condition hit me with stark clarity. The heavy blanket, pulled up to his waist, seemed like a meagre defence against whatever malady afflicted him. His bare chest, marred by an ugly welt oozing with fluid, was a silent testament to his suffering.

"He's not good. Not good at all," I found myself saying, the words heavy with concern and a growing realisation of the severity of his condition. My assessment, though brief, was enough to confirm the seriousness of the situation. The oozing welt, an alarming indicator of injury and infection, demanded immediate attention.

Turning back to Luke, my expression must have mirrored the gravity of my thoughts. "What happened here?" I asked, seeking context, understanding, anything that might shed light on the cause of Jamie's condition.

"A hot coal struck him in the middle of the night," Paul's reply was so matter-of-fact, yet it sent my mind reeling. *A hot coal?* The absurdity of the situation clashed with the gravity of Jamie's condition, leaving me momentarily stunned. *How in the world did a hot coal strike him in the chest?* The scenario seemed far-fetched, almost implausible, and I couldn't help but let my imagination run wild with the possibilities. Yet, the reality of the welt oozing before me anchored my thoughts firmly back to the present.

I hoped, for my own peace of mind, that this wasn't a case of intentional harm. The thought of dealing with physical violence, of navigating the murky waters of interpersonal conflict, was not something I had anticipated facing here. My gaze shifted to Paul, the suspicion creeping unbidden into my thoughts. With the camp being as isolated as it appeared, my initial, albeit reluctant, conclusion painted him in a potentially guilty light.

"It's a long story," Paul's words did little to quell my burgeoning suspicions. The ambiguity of his response, the hint of complexity and perhaps danger in their situation, only deepened the mystery surrounding Jamie's injury.

"Later, then," I found myself saying, pushing aside the accusatory thoughts. There was a time for questions, for unraveling the story behind the injury, but it wasn't now. Jamie's well-being took precedence, and my focus narrowed to the task at hand. My fingers moved with practiced care, assessing the area around the welt for signs of further injury or infection. Each touch was a search for information, a way to gauge the extent of the damage and the best course of treatment.

"I need a cloth," I directed, my voice firm with the authority of my medical expertise. The request was practical, a necessary step in beginning to address the wound.

Paul's gesture, pulling a fresh t-shirt from his suitcase, was both practical and slightly apologetic. "It's clean. It's all we have," he said, a bashful undertone in his voice as he handed it over to me. The situation, demanding improvisation with limited resources, was a stark reminder of the challenges faced in Clivilius. My response, a disbelieving "Seriously?" directed towards Luke, was born of frustration and a desperate hope for something more suitable for medical use.

Luke's reaction, a shake of the head and a helpless shrug, conveyed his regret. "I'm sorry, Glenda," he offered, his apology sincere yet doing little to change our circumstances. The lack of proper medical supplies was a hurdle, but not an insurmountable one. Turning back to Jamie, my resolve firmed. The t-shirt, while far from ideal, would have to suffice.

Dabbing the oozing fluid from the open wound with the clean t-shirt, I couldn't help but mutter a curse under my breath as the wound became more visible. The severity of the situation was becoming increasingly apparent. "He has severe swelling in the upper left of the small gap between his pectoral muscles," I announced, my voice steady as I continued to carefully clean the area. "I need to relieve some of the pressure."

The men's simultaneous "Okay" was a small comfort, a sign of their readiness to assist in whatever way they could. My directive for someone to hold Jamie was practical, anticipating his possible reaction to the procedure. "And take those dogs outside," I added, the presence of the animals, however comforting they might be under different circumstances, now a potential hindrance.

Paul's quick interception of Luke, as the latter moved to assist, underscored the dynamics at play within their group. "I think you had better take the dogs," he told Luke, his tone firm. It was a moment of decision-making, a quick allocation of roles based on the immediate needs of the situation.

As Luke, with a gentle nod of understanding, collected the dogs to take them outside, I was left with a moment to prepare mentally for the task ahead. The anxiety in Luke's actions, the solemn nod, reflected the gravity of what we were about to undertake. It was a reminder of the trust being placed in my hands, the expectation of relief and healing that I was determined to fulfil.

Kneeling beside Jamie, my focus narrowed to the injury before me. The challenge of providing medical care in such rudimentary conditions was daunting, yet it was a testament to the adaptability and resilience demanded of us all. In that tent, with limited resources and the weight of expectation upon me, I was reminded of the core of my profession: to do no harm, to alleviate suffering, and to bring healing, however and wherever it was needed.

To ensure the accuracy of my diagnosis, I needed to trust not just my training but also my instincts, honed over years of medical practice. I touched the site of the swelling again, my movements deliberate, seeking confirmation through the tactile feedback beneath my fingertips. Closing my eyes momentarily allowed me to concentrate fully on what my hands were telling me. The skin, still smooth under my touch, confirmed that the swelling at the secondary site wasn't the result of a burn. This realisation, while narrowing down the potential causes, did little to ease the concern knotting my stomach.

Paul's presence beside me, as he knelt and the tent flap zipped closed, marked the transition to a more focused and intimate setting for the task at hand. The outside world, with its vastness and uncertainty, was momentarily forgotten, the entirety of my attention converging on the patient before me.

"Hold his shoulders down," I instructed, my voice steady, betraying none of the apprehension that flickered within me. This wasn't just about applying medical knowledge; it was about doing so in a setting far removed from the sterile predictability of a hospital.

As Paul reached across me, the incidental brush of his arm against mine in the cramped space of the tent underscored the physical closeness required for this kind of field medicine. "It'd be best if you sit on his waist," I advised, the words feeling strange even as they left my mouth. In the clinical settings I was accustomed to, such instructions would be unnecessary, but here, in the raw immediacy of our environment, they were essential.

"Lightly," I hastened to add, watching as Paul clumsily positioned himself. The necessity of the instruction, juxtaposed with the delicacy required in its execution, was a stark reminder of the precarious balance we were attempting to maintain. Jamie, unconscious and unaware, was nevertheless at the mercy of our actions, and it was imperative we minimise any additional distress.

"He's likely to try and move suddenly," I concluded, my statement as much a warning as it was a prediction. The anticipation of involuntary movement was based on countless similar situations, where pain or surprise could elicit a sudden response from even the most sedated of patients.

With the t-shirt carefully spread around the small, ominous lump near Jamie's left pec, I took a moment to steady myself. The task at hand was delicate, fraught with risk, and demanded all my focus. I touched the surrounding flesh lightly, the tips of my fingers confirming the diagnosis that had formed in my mind. The seriousness of the situation, the balance between causing harm and potentially saving Jamie's life, weighed heavily on me.

"You ready?" I asked Paul, not taking my eyes off Jamie's chest.

"Ready," Paul's response came back, a gulp punctuating his words, betraying a nervousness that mirrored my own.

I tilted my head, a brief moment of hesitation washing over me. The reality of what was to come, of Jamie's impending lucidity, pressed down on me with an almost physical weight. The thought flitted through my mind—*I hope that Paul will be as firm as I need him to be, or the situation could go terribly wrong.* The risk was not just theoretical; it was immediate and deadly. A wrong move, a lapse in concentration, or a failure of nerve could result in a puncture to Jamie's heart, a mistake with irrevocable consequences.

Yet, the alternative was no less dire. The long splinter, an unseen but palpable threat, loomed over us with the potential for just as much harm. If I didn't act, if I allowed my fear to paralyse me, the splinter could work its way toward Jamie's heart, a slow but certain death sentence.

With a decisive action borne out of necessity, I pressed my fingertips firmly into Jamie's chest, feeling the resistance of his body against my own. Instantly, Jamie's form stiffened beneath my touch—an unmistakable sign that he had been roused from his unconscious state by the intensity of the pain.

His eyes snapped open, wide with shock and suffering, as a scream tore from his throat, a visceral response to the agony he was experiencing. The sound, raw and heart-wrenching, filled the tent.

As I fought to keep my composure in the face of Jamie's reaction, I felt my own body tense, a reflexive response to his distress. Paul, thankfully, was quick to react, pressing Jamie's shoulders back down to the mattress, a necessary restraint to prevent further injury.

Outside, the disturbance roused the dog, whose barks of alarm added to the chaos of the moment, a soundtrack to the tension unfolding within the tent.

"Jamie!" Luke's voice, filled with concern and confusion, cut through the tumult. My focus, however, remained unwavering, even as the zip of the tent ran upwards in a rush of sound. "Stay out!" I found myself yelling, an instinctive command to preserve the precarious control we had over the situation.

The small dog, emboldened or perhaps frightened by the commotion, darted behind me, its growls a menacing warning. The situation had escalated quickly, the presence of the animals adding an unpredictable element to an already tense procedure.

"Get them the fuck out!" The urgency of the moment pushed me to shout, my usual composure giving way to the demands of the situation. Paul, momentarily distracted by the need to protect me from the growling dog, moved away from Jamie. The risk of Jamie moving and exacerbating his injury was too great.

"Don't you move," I commanded, my voice sharp, as I threw Paul a stern look, demanding his immediate return to his crucial role. The urgency of the command was clear, and Paul quickly reassumed his position.

Jamie's scream, a second outcry of pain, pierced the air once more. Yet, I did not allow it to break my concentration. My focus remained laser-sharp on the splinter site, each movement calculated to minimise further distress while addressing the immediate threat.

Luke, responding to my earlier command, managed to grasp the small dog, preventing it from causing any more disruption. With a firm grip, he removed the dog from the tent, restoring a semblance of order to the chaotic scene.

In the midst of the turmoil, my resolve only hardened. The challenges we faced—Jamie's pain, the dogs' interference, the cramped conditions—only served to underscore the gravity of our situation. Yet, despite the distractions, my commitment to Jamie's well-being, to performing the procedure with the utmost care and precision, remained unwavering.

"Hold him. It's nearly there," I instructed Paul, my voice steady. As I pressed down again, my fingertips dug deeper into his flesh, a necessary intrusion to reach the foreign object that had caused so much distress. My fingernails acted as a makeshift barrier underneath the splinter, a technique born out of necessity in the absence of proper surgical tools. The sight of grey and yellow pus oozing from the wound was both a sign of infection and a beacon of hope that we were close to removing the cause. When the black head of the splinter finally rose to the surface, a sense of grim satisfaction washed over me.

"Last time," I announced, more to prepare myself than anyone else. With one final, determined push, I braced for Jamie's reaction.

His response, a screech that seemed to pierce the very fabric of the tent, was as haunting as it was heart-wrenching. Amidst his cries, the sound of the splinter popping free from its fleshy prison was grotesquely satisfying. The long, black splinter, now accompanied by a viscous, malodorous mess, was a grim trophy of our efforts. The foul odour that filled the air was overwhelming, catching me off guard and forcing me to swallow back my gag reflex.

Wiping the mess away with the t-shirt, I couldn't help but present the charcoal splinter to Paul, a mix of disbelief and accusation in my gesture. "I'm guessing nobody knew that was in there?" The question was rhetorical, a reflection of the incredulity of the situation.

Paul's response, a simple shake of the head accompanied by, "I certainly didn't," only added to the surreal nature of our makeshift operation. As Jamie's body ceased its squirming and his breathing began to normalise, a wave of relief washed over me. The immediate danger was past, but the need for aftercare was pressing.

"I need some clean water," I stated, already thinking ahead to the cleaning and dressing of the wound. Paul's agreement to fetch it was swift, as he climbed off Jamie's body.

As I dabbed at the wound, witnessing yet another discharge of pus, now turning dark grey as it oxidised, the reality of our situation settled heavily upon me. Here, in the isolation of Clivilius, far removed from the resources and support of a traditional medical facility, we had managed to perform a critical intervention. The challenges were daunting, the conditions far from ideal, but the human will to aid, to heal, and to persevere had proven stronger.

Jamie's eyes flickered open, revealing a storm of confusion and pain as he took in his surroundings. His gaze, when it finally settled on me, was tinged with a defiance born of vulnerability and fear. "Who the fuck are you?" he snarled, his voice carrying an edge that spoke more of his pain than of any real animosity towards me.

"I'm a doctor," I replied, my tone deliberately neutral. The emotional tumult of the situation demanded professionalism, a calm amidst the storm of fear, pain, and confusion that Jamie was undoubtedly feeling.

"And she just saved your life," Luke interjected as he entered the tent, his words a bridge between Jamie's hostility and the help I had provided. "You should be grateful," he added, a note of admonishment in his voice that was meant to remind Jamie of the criticality of his situation.

"Grateful! You expect me to be fucking grateful!?" Jamie spat back, the word laced with bitterness. His reaction, though harsh, was not entirely unexpected. Gratitude, in the face of such raw pain and fear, was a complicated emotion, often overshadowed by the immediacy of suffering.

The tension in the tent escalated as one of the dogs, picking up on the heightened emotions, issued a low warning growl. "Duke! Stop it!" Luke's reprimand to the dog was a brief distraction from the heated exchange, a momentary shift in focus.

Jamie's attempt to sit up, a reflexive reaction to his frustration and confusion, was met with pain. Instinctively, I reached for his shoulder, gently but firmly encouraging him to stay down.

The situation escalated when Duke, responding to the tension, lashed out. The sharp bark was a precursor to his teeth sinking into my arm, a moment of panic and pain that forced me to act defensively. "Get off me!" I yelled, my hand coming down hard on Duke's head in an attempt to free myself from his grip. The dog's reluctant release was a small relief.

Luke's immediate reaction, scooping Duke into his arms, was both protective and apologetic. "Oh, Glenda," he began, his concern evident. But my patience had worn thin, the stress of the situation, the danger posed by the dog, and the need to maintain control pushing me to my limit. "Back away, Luke," I demanded, my voice carrying the weight of my authority and frustration. The warning glare I shot him was unambiguous

"I'll lock him out," Luke conceded softly, a quiet acknowledgment of the need to remove Duke from the situation. As he retreated outside, the tent's atmosphere remained charged, a palpable tension that reflected the complexities of healing, not just the physical wounds, but the emotional and psychological scars that such incidents leave behind.

Wiping away the droplets of saliva that marked Duke's aggressive encounter, I felt a mix of relief and concern. Relief that the dog's teeth hadn't fully broken the skin, but concern over the potential for infection. The need for a strong antiseptic became immediately clear to me; in a place like Clivilius, even minor wounds could escalate quickly without proper care. I found myself moving towards Paul's suitcase, my actions guided by the practical need to mitigate any risk of infection, rummaging for something clean that could serve until I found proper medical supplies.

"It's your own fault, you know," Jamie's voice cut through the tent, his words sharp, laced with the same callous disregard he had shown earlier. The comment, meant to provoke, instead served as a reminder of the countless faces and personalities I had encountered in my medical career. His attitude, while frustrating, was not unfamiliar to me.

Rolling my eyes, I chose to ignore the jab. In my years of service in the hospital's emergency department, I had learned that personal feelings had to be set aside. Jamie's demeanour, abrasive as it might be, was not going to deter me from my purpose. *Treat the person without judgment*, the motto that adorned the walls of the emergency department, echoed in my mind. It was a principle that had guided me through countless shifts, countless encounters with patients whose attitudes ranged from grateful to hostile.

The reminder of that motto was a grounding moment, a mental reset that allowed me to refocus on the task at hand. The challenge was not just in treating the physical wounds of those who found themselves under my care but in navigating the complex web of emotions and reactions that each patient brought to the table. Jamie, with his hostility and pain, was no exception. He was a patient in need, and my role was to provide care with professionalism and empathy, regardless of his demeanour.

❖

"Luke," I called out, ensuring my voice carried a sense of urgency as he made his way back into the tent. The situation, already tense, required immediate action, and I knew exactly what was needed. "Listen carefully. I need you to return to the Medical Centre and get me a few supplies."

"Sure. What do you need?" he asked.

As I secured the makeshift bandage made from the t-shirt around my arm, ensuring it was tight enough to protect the bite marks from further irritation, I began to mentally compile a list of the medical supplies required. The protective layer provided by the t-shirt was a temporary measure, a barrier against the immediate threat of infection, but far from sufficient.

"I need..." My voice trailed off as I realised the complexity of the request I was about to make. In the back of my mind, a worry nagged at me—the potential for the situation to worsen without proper care. "Do you have any paper and a pen?" I asked, skepticism tinging my voice despite the pressing need for optimism.

Luke's smile, unexpected yet welcome, brought a brief moment of lightness to the situation. "Actually, we do." His answer, simple yet profound, was a small victory in our current predicament.

Relief washed over me as I adjusted the wrapping on my arm, trying to alleviate the itching sensation that had begun to manifest. The discomfort was a worrying sign, an early indication that all might not be well beneath the fabric. The thought of dealing with an infection or an allergic reaction in such a remote setting was daunting. Clivilius, with its unknowns and limited resources, was not the place for medical complications, especially ones that could potentially be avoided with prompt and proper care.

The realisation that I was now relying on the very people I had come to help was not lost on me. The dynamics of our situation had shifted, blurring the lines between caregiver and patient, between helper and those in need of help.

"Here," Luke's voice pulled me back from the maze of medical needs running through my mind, offering the paper and pen.

I accepted them with a brief smile. "Thanks," I murmured, my mind already racing ahead. As I began to jot down the supplies, my focus narrowed to the page before me, my brow creasing with the intensity of my thoughts. The list grew, each item added a testament to the dire needs of our makeshift medical camp. Before I knew it, the page was filled, a daunting inventory of necessities that seemed to stretch beyond the realm of the possible.

Hovering the pen above the completed list, I hesitated, hoping to find items that could perhaps be deemed non-essential. Yet, as my eyes scanned the list, the realisation hit me—every single item was vital. There was nothing superfluous about our needs; each supply was a critical component in ensuring the health and safety of everyone here. I sighed, the weight of our circumstances pressing down on me. The list was ambitious, reflective of the dire straits we found ourselves in.

"A lot of this you can find in my examination room," I finally said, handing the list to Luke, who had positioned himself beside me, his presence a silent support. "The rest," I continued, indicating the items marked with asterisks, "you'll have to take from the shared supply room." The mention of the shared supply room, a potential point of contention, caused Luke's head to snap up, his concern palpable.

"I'm sorry, Luke, but we are going to need it all," I stated, the simplicity of my words belying the complexity of our situation.

Luke's acceptance, a nod of his head, was a silent testament to his trust and willingness to take on the daunting task. "I'll be quick, I promise," he assured me, determination lacing his voice.

"Luke," I found myself reaching out, gripping his arm with a firmness that carried my unspoken fears. "Be careful," I warned, the words heavy with the knowledge of the risks he was about to undertake. The thought of the commander, a lurking threat to Luke's mission, weighed heavily on my mind. I chose to leave that worry unvoiced, not wanting to add to Luke's burden. It was a decision made from a place of care, an attempt to shield him from further stress, even as my own concerns churned within me.

As Luke prepared to leave, the resolve on his face, the hardening of his features, spoke volumes. He understood the importance of the task ahead, the criticality of his mission. With a final nod, a silent promise of his return, he exited the tent, stepping out to gather the supplies that would mean the difference between health and hardship for us all.

FIRST STOCK

4338.206.4

The tent flap's rustle snapped my attention away from the delicate balance of medical attention and wary observation I had been maintaining. Since Luke's departure, Duke had appointed himself Jamie's unwavering guardian, a role he assumed with a silent, imposing presence that filled the tent. Despite my initial reluctance to bridge the gap between us, Jamie's insistence on fostering a truce between Duke and me was something I couldn't easily dismiss.

Kneeling on the tent floor, the coolness of the ground seeping through the fabric of my clothing, I found myself reflecting on the oddity of my current task. Here I was, a doctor, used to navigating the complexities of human anatomy and illness, now attempting to navigate the complexities of animal behaviour—specifically, that of a small dog whose loyalty to Jamie was as admirable as it was challenging.

I grudgingly retrieved a treat, a small peace offering in the silent negotiation between Duke and myself. The act, while simple, felt strangely significant, a gesture of goodwill in the midst of uncertainty. Yet, despite my efforts, Duke remained unmoved, his loyalty to Jamie a barrier he was not yet willing to let down for me. The treat, an olive branch extended in the hope of mutual understanding, lay ignored between us.

The boy's stubborn refusal to accept my offering left me feeling oddly disheartened. In the grand scheme of our situation, the dog's acceptance or rejection of me should have been trivial. And yet, as I looked at Duke, his stance resolute and protective, I couldn't help but feel a twinge of respect for his unwavering loyalty.

Paul's entrance, marked by his cautious effort not to spill the water he carried, brought with it a wave of concern. His rapid-fire questions, laced with worry, barely allowed me a moment to compose a response. "I'm fine," I assured him, trying to downplay the incident with Duke and the minor injury it had caused. "It's just a surface wound. This shirt is just a precaution until Luke gets back with some antiseptic." My words were meant to reassure, to minimise the concern that Paul's furrowed brow betrayed.

"But, what...?" Paul's voice trailed off, his confusion evident. The situation, already tense, was further complicated by Jamie's interjection. "Duke doesn't like her," he stated bluntly, an echo of the dog's earlier aggression. "And neither do I," he added, his voice carrying a chill that seemed to lower the temperature within the tent.

"Jamie!" Paul's scold was immediate, a reflexive defence against Jamie's harsh words. Yet Jamie's dismissal of my presence, his assertion that I shouldn't be here, hung heavily in the air, a palpable tension that threatened to escalate.

My gaze towards Paul was a silent plea for caution, a recognition of the volatile nature of Jamie's current state. The pain and disorientation he was experiencing, compounded by the unfamiliar environment, rendered him unpredictable. My priority was to avoid any further confrontation that might exacerbate the situation.

Paul, however, was undeterred by my silent warning. His retort to Jamie was impassioned, a vehement defence of my role in Jamie's survival. "If she wasn't here, you'd be bloody dead within a few days!" His words, though harsh, were a stark reminder of the gravity of Jamie's condition and the necessity of my presence.

Jamie's reaction, a soft moan as he attempted to shift his position, was a reminder of his vulnerability beneath the veneer of hostility. "You'd best stay on your back for now," I advised, my voice carrying both a professional firmness and an undercurrent of compassion. The directive was not just a medical recommendation but an attempt to reestablish a semblance of order within the chaos of emotions and pain that filled the tent.

In that moment, the complexity of our situation was laid bare—a delicate balance between medical necessity, interpersonal dynamics, and the raw, human experience of suffering and survival. My role as a doctor had never felt more challenging, nor more critical, as I navigated the fine line between providing care and managing the fragile egos and emotions of those under my care.

Paul took several steps. "I've brought you some clean water," he said, pushing Duke away with his foot and placing the small bucket in front of me. He turned and walked out the tent.

Submerging a fresh t-shirt into the bucket, I felt a sudden, unexpected exhilaration as my fingers made contact with the cool liquid. The sensation was almost electric, a stark contrast to the tension that had filled the tent moments before. "How interesting," I found myself murmuring, a sense of wonder momentarily distracting me from the severity of our circumstances. The properties of the water here in Clivilius, or perhaps the simple act of cleansing, seemed to carry a significance I hadn't anticipated.

As I wrung out the shirt, watching the clear droplets fall back into the bucket, I turned my attention to Jamie and Duke. The dog's hesitant approach, his wary circling of the space between us, prompted me to offer a solution. "Do you want to hold him?" I suggested, indicating Duke with a nod.

The idea was practical, a way to keep Duke calm and contained while I attended to Jamie's wounds.

Jamie's response, a pat on the bed to invite Duke closer, was a silent affirmation of our mutual goal—to provide care. Duke's compliance, his willing leap onto the bed beside Jamie, was a small victory, a moment of cooperation in an otherwise fraught environment.

As Jamie held Duke, creating a small island of calm on one side of the tent, I approached to wash Jamie's chest. The silence that enveloped us was heavy with significance, a shared understanding that transcended words. The act of cleansing, of washing away the physical remnants of Jamie's ordeal, was imbued with a deeper meaning—a gesture of healing, of starting anew.

❖

Standing at the corner of the tent, a brief respite from the intensity of the medical emergencies inside allowed me a moment of reflection. My gaze found Paul, isolated on the riverbank, his posture closed off with arms tightly folded across his chest—a silent testament to the weight of thoughts or concerns he might be carrying.

"It's a good spot for a nice bridge," I ventured softly, breaking the quiet that enveloped us as I approached. My comment, intended to bridge not just the physical gap between the riverbanks but perhaps also the emotional distance that seemed to hang between us, startled Paul. His reaction, a quick jump and a turn of his head, was a reminder of the tension that underpinned existence here.

"It is," Paul's response was simple, an acknowledgment that carried with it an undercurrent of agreement or perhaps a shared vision for a future that seemed so uncertain.

As I moved to stand beside him, the expanse of the river before us became a focal point for a moment of shared contemplation. *It can't be more than twenty metres wide at this point,* I estimated silently, my eyes tracing the contours of the landscape that lay beyond. The view, with its arid dust hills rolling into the distance under the clear, unyielding sky, held a desolate beauty that was hard to ignore.

"It's oddly beautiful, isn't it?" I found myself saying aloud, an attempt to vocalise the mixture of awe and melancholy that the scene evoked within me. The beauty of the place, so stark and unforgiving, seemed at odds with the struggles we had already faced.

"It is," Paul echoed his earlier sentiment, his question catching me slightly off guard. "How are you so relaxed with all of this?" His curiosity seemed genuine.

I folded my arms across my chest, mirroring his posture, and shrugged slightly—a physical attempt to convey the nonchalance I was far from feeling. "I'm a doctor," I replied, the words carrying more weight than they might seem. "It's my job to be calm." It was a simplified explanation for what was, in reality, a complex balancing act of emotions and responsibilities.

Paul's smile in response, "Fair call," was a relief. It meant I could avoid delving deeper into the fears and uncertainties that lurked beneath my composed exterior. As my gaze drifted back to the river, a thought struck me with sudden clarity—*Father could be anywhere.* The realisation was daunting, a vast unknown that seemed as wide and insurmountable as the river before us.

"We will build a bridge," I found myself declaring with a confidence that surprised even me. The metaphorical significance of the statement wasn't lost on me; it was about more than just a physical structure—it was about making connections, overcoming obstacles, and perhaps finding my father.

"We can't," Paul countered, shaking his head, his objection pulling me back from my reverie of determination.

"Can't?" I challenged, the word feeling like a denial of the possibility I had just envisioned. "Of course, we can." My belief in our ability to overcome, to build and create, was unwavering.

"We don't have any materials," Paul pointed out, a practical concern that momentarily dampened my resolve.

"Luke will get them for us," I asserted, my faith in Luke's capabilities stemming from more than just hope. *I know how this works. If Luke really is a Guardian, like my father, he'll bring us the best Earth has to offer to help us.* The thought was a tether to a larger purpose, to a belief in the support networks we had, seen and unseen.

I nudged Paul's crossed arms with my elbow, trying to lighten the mood with a bit of humour. "And I thought you were the optimistic one." It was a gentle tease, a reminder that optimism was a choice, a perspective we could adopt even in the face of adversity.

Paul's eyes narrowed in thought, a moment of introspection before he finally responded. "I am," he affirmed.

Hearing Luke's voice call out, a blend of urgency and relief, my heart lifted. His return marked not just the arrival of the much-needed medical supplies but also a reinforcement of our small team's resilience and capability. "Glenda! Paul!" The sound of my name, called out across the distance, was a beacon pulling me back toward the centre of our operations, toward the heart of our makeshift camp.

I couldn't help but smile, a spontaneous reaction to the anticipation of what Luke had managed to gather. "Come," I urged Paul, my steps quickening as we made our way back to the tent.

As we entered the tent, the sight of Jamie attempting to discreetly wipe away his tears was a poignant reminder of the reason behind our urgent need for supplies. His vulnerability in that moment, juxtaposed with the stoic front he had tried to maintain earlier, underscored the complexity of our situation.

"You okay?" asked Luke, abandoning the bags he was carrying and rushing to Jamie's side.

"Yeah," Jamie's response, though sniffed back through pain, was an attempt to reassure, to minimise his suffering in the eyes of his partner. His admission, "Just in a lot of pain," was a stark admission of his vulnerability.

My attention, momentarily diverted by the exchange between Luke and Jamie, turned to the bags Luke had brought. Peering inside the first one, a wave of relief washed over me. *Luke has done very well.* The supplies, even from my brief glimpse, promised a significant improvement in my ability to provide care. My smile, hidden from view, was one of profound gratitude for Luke's successful scavenging.

"You'll be right now," Luke assured Jamie. "I've got you some strong pain medication."

As I directed Paul to spread a spare blanket across the floor for the medical supplies, my mind was already cataloging what we needed versus what we had. The sense of order, a principle so deeply ingrained in my medical training, provided a semblance of control in an otherwise unpredictable situation. Paul moved quickly to prepare the space, his actions reflecting the urgency of our collective effort.

As I began sorting through the bags, laying out the supplies on the blanket, the methodical nature of the task was oddly comforting. Each item placed down was a small victory, a piece of the puzzle in my quest to provide the best possible care under the circumstances.

Luke's voice broke through my concentration. "I'm pretty sure I've got all the items on the list without an asterisk," he said, a hint of uncertainty in his voice. "But I'll have to go back now and check the supply room for the rest." The nervous shifting of his weight did not escape my notice, sparking a brief flare of frustration within me. *Now's not the time for your nerves to play up, Luke.*

"Yes," I responded, trying to mask my own concern with a veneer of calm authority. "I will need the antiseptic and antibiotics. I can't dress Jamie's wounds properly without them." The importance of those items could not be overstated; without them, our ability to prevent infection and promote healing was severely compromised.

"Go," I insisted, my tone leaving no room for hesitation. Jamie's pained moan, a sharp reminder of the stakes at hand, punctuated the urgency of the moment. "Just try to relax," I told him, my attention briefly shifting to offer a word of comfort, knowing all too well the limitations of what comfort I could provide without the necessary supplies.

Turning back to Luke, I mouthed a silent "Go," a final push to expedite his departure. His silent nod in response, a mutual understanding of the gravity of the situation, was the last interaction before he stepped out to fulfil the critical task.

"Not much longer now," I reassured Jamie, trying to infuse my voice with as much confidence and comfort as I could muster. The promise of pain relief and rest was not just a medical intervention; it was a beacon of hope in the dimness of his current suffering. "And I'll have something to take the pain away and help you sleep." Jamie's response, a loud exhale, was heavy with the weight of enduring pain and the anticipation of relief.

"Well, if you don't need me, Glenda, I'll go and see if I can finish getting this other tent up," Paul said, his willingness to contribute to our shared effort evident in his readiness to take on another task.

"That's fine," I replied, my mind already juggling the tasks at hand with those that lay ahead. "I'll come and help you when I've sorted Jamie."

❖

In the stillness of the tent, time seemed to pause, the silence wrapping around us like a tangible presence. It was a moment of uneasy anticipation, each of us caught in our own thoughts, waiting for the next step in our collective struggle for stability in this alien environment.

The arrival of Luke, laden with more bags of medical supplies, broke the spell. His entrance, a promise of relief and support, was a welcome disruption to the heavy quiet. "How did you go?" I couldn't help but express my surprise at the volume of supplies he brought back. The essentials I had marked with asterisks, I had assumed, would not require so much space.

Luke's grin was a mix of pride and mischief, a hint that there was more to his haul than met the eye. "I'm pretty sure I've got everything on your list," he boasted, his confidence sparking a flicker of hope within me. Yet, the sight of the bags prompted a question in my mind, *Why so many bags?*

"Oh," he added, almost as an afterthought, "And then I just grabbed a heap of random stuff for good measure. I'm not really sure what any of it is to be honest." His admission, candid and a little reckless, was quintessentially Luke—a mixture of thoroughness and a dash of impulsiveness.

"Well, that's not surprising," Jamie managed a soft chuckle, his voice a blend of amusement and discomfort.

"Thank you, Luke," I said sincerely, my gratitude extending beyond the supplies he had procured. The effort, the risk he took on our behalf, was not lost on me. As I reached for the morphine, my movements were methodical, each action informed by years of training and experience. The preparation of the syringe, the swabbing of Jamie's arm with antiseptic, and the quick, efficient way I administered the injection were all part of the routine, yet in this setting, each step felt imbued with greater significance.

The effect of the medication was almost immediate. Jamie's body, previously tense with pain, began to relax, a visual testament to the relief coursing through his veins. His struggle to keep his eyes open, the fluttering of his eyelids as sleep beckoned, was a poignant reminder of the body's need for rest, for a reprieve from pain.

As Jamie drifted off to sleep, a sense of accomplishment, however small, settled over me. The immediate crisis had been averted, Jamie was comfortable, and for the moment, we could all breathe a little easier.

Luke's question, laden with concern and barely concealed fear, cut through the relative calm that had settled over the tent. "He's going to be okay, isn't he?" His voice was soft, vulnerable, a stark contrast to the strength he had consistently shown. Turning to meet his gaze, I found his eyes reflecting the turmoil of emotions that I, too, was struggling to keep at bay. "I hope so," was the only assurance I could offer, a truth wrapped in the reality of our uncertain circumstances.

Luke gripped my shoulder firmly. "I have to go," he stated, a resolve in his voice that belied the emotion I had seen in his eyes moments before. My nod in response was an acknowledgment of the necessity of his departure, a silent conveyance of understanding and support.

Luke's apology, "I'm so sorry, Glenda," added a layer of sombreness to the moment. It was an expression of empathy, of shared hardship, and perhaps, an acknowledgment of the weight of the decisions he'd be forced to make in their struggle for survival. "You did the right thing, Luke," I found myself saying, an attempt to provide him with the reassurance he needed. The bite of my lip was involuntary, a physical attempt to steady myself against the surge of emotions his words had evoked. The realisation of my permanence in Clivilius, the acknowledgment that Earth was now a part of a past I could never return to, was a heavy burden to bear.

"Now, go and do what you need to," I urged him, my voice steady despite the tumult within. It was a send-off, a command to face whatever lay ahead with courage and purpose.

As Luke stood and made his way to the tent's entrance, his posture spoke volumes. The droop of his head, the slow, measured steps, were all indicative of the weight his Guardianship carried as he prepared to step back into the unknown.

"And go confidently," I called out after him, a final piece of encouragement, a reminder of the strength and determination that had brought him this far. It was a plea for him to hold onto that confidence, to remember that, despite the uncertainties and dangers, he was capable of facing whatever challenges lay ahead.

Luke paused, a silent acknowledgment of my words. The slow raise of his head, a sign of acceptance, perhaps even a spark of the confidence I had implored him to embrace, was the last I saw before he disappeared from view.

❖

Kneeling beside Jamie, the world outside the tent seemed to fade into the background, leaving me enveloped in a silence that was both comforting and oppressive. The solitude of the moment allowed my professional façade to slip, revealing the raw emotions I had been keeping at bay. My eyes, a testament to the strain and fatigue of the past hours, betrayed me, releasing a single tear that traced a slow path down my cheek. The physical manifestations of my stress—my throbbing head and the incessant itch on my arm from Duke's earlier aggression—were mere echoes of the turmoil within.

As another tear followed the first, a physical acknowledgment of my sorrow, I instinctively wrapped my arms around myself in a self-embrace. It was a futile attempt to ward off the overwhelming sense of emptiness that surged through me. This emptiness wasn't just the physical absence of those I cared about; it was a profound sense of isolation, a realisation of the vast distance between this world and everything I had known and loved.

The emotional dam broke, and a deep, heaving sob wracked my body, a release of all the pent-up fear, anxiety, and sorrow that I had been carrying. The cry that escaped my lips was loud, raw, and unfiltered, a sound of pure anguish that I would have once sought to muffle, to hide from the ears of others. But in that moment, the realisation hit me with crushing clarity: there was no Pierre here to hear my cries, to offer words of comfort or a reassuring embrace. Not this time.

I am alone.

KEEPING HABIT

4338.206.5

Sitting cross-legged in the dust beside Paul, I found a moment of tranquility as we both watched the day's light fade, the sun's final rays disappearing into the horizon. The campfire before us, with its steady plume of smoke ascending into the calm air, provided a focal point for reflection, its crackling flames consuming Paul's empty paper plate with a voraciousness that felt almost comforting. It was in this simple act of destruction and warmth that my face finally softened, a physical manifestation of the tension easing from my muscles.

The task of setting up the tent, undertaken mostly in a companionable silence, had been a welcome distraction. Paul's sensitivity to my need for quiet, for space to process the day's tumultuous events, was a kindness I hadn't fully anticipated but was profoundly grateful for. His presence, unobtrusive yet steadfast, had allowed me the room to navigate my own turmoil internally, while we worked side by side to secure our immediate shelter and safety.

In the aftermath, I busied myself with organising our supplies, moving food and medical necessities into the new tent, a necessary task that offered its own form of meditation. Paul, in the meantime, had taken on the role of firekeeper, coaxing life into the flames that now offered us both light and warmth.

Now, as the evening settled around us, with Jamie still lost to the world of sleep, it was just Paul and me sitting in the quiet. The fire before us danced and flickered, casting a warm glow that illuminated our small circle of existence against the encroaching darkness.

I found myself tapping my empty plate against my knee, a nervous habit that betrayed the undercurrent of anxiety still running through me. After watching Paul's plate reduce to ash, I made the decision to let mine follow, tossing it into the flames. The brief flare of energy as the fire consumed it mirrored my fleeting moment of stillness.

But peace was elusive, and my fingers soon began to wiggle restlessly on my thighs, a physical manifestation of the unease that wound tightly within me. Despite the calm of the evening and the soothing presence of the fire, my mind raced with thoughts of the day past and the uncertainties that lay ahead. The simplicity of our current setting, the quiet companionship of Paul, stood in stark contrast to the complexities of our situation, a brief respite in what I knew would be a relentless push for survival in Clivilius.

Paul's question, gentle and laced with concern, pierced the veil of my internal turmoil. "Everything okay?" His inquiry, simple yet laden with the offer of support, momentarily drew me out of my restless thoughts.

"Ahh, yeah," I responded, the words slipping out more as a reflex than a true reflection of my state. My hands, betraying my inner unease, moved restlessly along my thighs, a vain attempt to quell the nervous energy that seemed to have taken hold of me.

"You sure?" Paul pressed, his voice steady and sincere. "I'm here if you need to talk," he added, extending an offer of companionship and understanding that was both appreciated and daunting.

For a moment, I entertained the possibility of confiding in Paul, of unburdening the weight of fears and uncertainties that clouded my mind. Yet, the thought was quickly dismissed. *He wouldn't understand, would he?* The complexity of my emotions, the depth of my concerns, felt too vast, too entangled in the specifics of my past and the uncertainties of our present situation.

"I need to check on Jamie," I said instead, using the immediate concern for Jamie as a reason to withdraw. The swift motion of getting to my feet was as much about escaping the conversation as it was about tending to Jamie.

As I made my way to the tent, the dust of Clivilius clinging to my trousers went unnoticed, a trivial concern against the backdrop of our current reality. Standing outside the tent's entrance, I paused, cupping my hands over my mouth in a moment of self-comfort. The deep breaths I took were an effort to compose myself, to gather the strength and calm I needed to face not just Jamie's needs but my own internal battle.

The offer of support from Paul lingered in my mind, a reminder that, despite my feelings of isolation and the personal walls I had erected, I was not entirely alone. Yet, the decision to keep my worries to myself, to maintain a façade of strength and competence, was a path I had chosen, perhaps out of habit or perhaps out of a deep-seated fear of vulnerability.

As I prepared to enter the tent, the brief moment of solitude outside was a poignant reminder of the complexities of human interaction, especially in the face of shared adversity. The challenge of balancing personal struggles with the needs of the group, of finding moments of connection amid the vastness of our isolation, was a constant negotiation. In the end, the care for Jamie, the responsibility I held as a doctor, provided a focus, a purpose that, for the moment, allowed me to push aside my own turmoil in service of a greater need.

❖

As I carefully unzipped the front flap and pushed my way inside the tent, the familiar low growl of Duke greeted me, an unwelcome but expected reaction. My frown was automatic. Despite my efforts to forge some kind of truce with him, Duke's loyalty to Jamie rendered him impervious to my attempts at reconciliation. His growl was a clear reminder of our unresolved tension, a barrier between me and Jamie that I had yet to overcome.

"It's okay, Duke," Jamie's voice, weak yet reassuring, broke through the tension. The sound of him patting Duke on the head was a gentle reminder of their bond, one that, despite the circumstances, I couldn't help but respect.

"Sorry," I found myself apologising, not just for disturbing the peace but for the unease my presence seemed to invariably cause. The tent was dim, the last vestiges of daylight barely penetrating the fabric, leaving us in a state of growing darkness illuminated only by the distant, flickering glow from the campfire outside. My eyes strained to adjust as I made my way carefully toward Jamie, conscious of Duke's watchful gaze on me.

"I didn't mean to wake you," I added, even as I approached Jamie's makeshift bed. The concern for disturbing his rest was genuine, a reflection of my desire to ease his discomfort in any way possible.

"I was already awake," Jamie's response, soft and devoid of any irritation, was a relief. It lifted a small part of the weight I carried, the constant worry about causing further distress to those under my care. His tone, perhaps unintentionally, offered a bridge over the gap Duke's distrust had created between us.

"Ahh, shit," escaped my lips, quieter than a breath, as I crouched beside the medical supplies I had carefully organised earlier. The realisation that some of our precious stock had been compromised was a blow not just to our practical resources but to the sense of control I was striving to maintain in this chaotic environment.

"What is it?" Jamie's voice, laced with concern, broke through my dismay. Despite his own pain, his immediate response was to inquire, to offer support.

Continuing to squint in the dim light that barely filled the tent, I let out a heavy sigh, the weight of frustration and disappointment pressing down on me. "Several of the gauze dressings have been torn to shreds. And one of the bandages is missing." The words felt like an admission of defeat, a testament to the challenges of safeguarding our limited supplies against all possible threats.

"Henri!" Jamie's scold was directed at Duke's brother, the culprit of our current predicament. The naming of the dog, a moment of levity in our dire circumstances, did little to alleviate the frustration of the situation.

Gathering what I needed of the remaining intact supplies, I moved closer to Jamie, intent on making the best of what we had left. His next words, "I found your missing bandage," were almost comical in their timing, if the context hadn't been so dire.

Watching Jamie attempt to reclaim the bandage from Henri's mouth was a surreal moment. "You may as well let him keep it," I huffed, the irritation clear in my voice. The realisation that a dog's playful moment had further depleted our already scarce medical supplies was far from amusing. "We can't use that now," I added, the pragmatism borne of necessity overriding any other consideration.

Jamie's eye roll was a silent commiseration, an acknowledgment of the absurdity and frustration of the moment.

"Take these," I instructed Jamie, my voice firm yet laced with an underlying current of concern. The urgency of the moment propelled me to act swiftly, presenting him with a bottle of water and a handful of capsules before he had the chance to settle back into a position of comfort. My actions, though abrupt, were driven by the need to address his pain and reduce the risk of infection as efficiently as possible.

"What are they?" Jamie's question came quickly, a mix of curiosity and trust as he didn't hesitate to follow my directions, swallowing the first capsule with a large gulp of water.

"There are a couple of antibiotics and then some pain and sleeping medication," I explained succinctly, watching as he consumed the remaining capsules in a similar manner. The combination of medications was carefully chosen to address both the immediate discomfort and the longer-term necessity of preventing infection.

As Jamie lay back down, I remained vigilant, observing his movements for any indication of further discomfort or adverse reactions to the medication. My role extended beyond the administration of drugs; it encompassed the continuous monitoring of his condition, a responsibility I took seriously.

"Watch the dog for me," I instructed next, shifting my focus to the task of changing his dressing. The presence of Duke, a constant by Jamie's side, required a certain level of caution and coordination. Jamie's response, drawing Duke closer with a protective arm, was a silent acknowledgment of the bond between them. Snuggling the dog into his armpit, Jamie's action spoke volumes about the comfort and security the animal provided him in a world where both were in short supply.

Preparing to change Jamie's dressing, I was acutely aware of the delicate balance of our situation. Each action taken, from the administering of medication to the simple act of caring for a wound, was imbued with deeper meanings of trust, care, and survival. In the dimly lit tent, with the quiet presence of Duke, Henri, and the steady breathing of Jamie now eased by medication, I felt a profound sense of purpose.

Carefully, I began the delicate task of removing the dirty dressings from Jamie's wound, my hands moving with practiced precision to avoid causing any unnecessary pain or disrupting the healing process. Holding the soiled gauze, I paused, my eyes instinctively scanning the interior of the tent for a sanitary bin, a habit ingrained from years of working in well-equipped medical environments. My brow furrowed in frustration as the reality of our situation hit me once again. The stark contrast between the facilities I was accustomed to and our current setup in Clivilius was jarring. The lack of basic medical infrastructure, something I had taken for granted back on Earth, was becoming an increasingly pressing issue.

The limited resources at our disposal and the absence of a designated area for medical waste underscored the challenges of providing healthcare in such a rudimentary setting. The frustration that welled up within me was more intense than I cared to acknowledge, a reminder of the compromises and improvisations that I had already made. *Tomorrow*, I resolved, *I will talk with Paul and Luke about setting up a basic medical tent.* The necessity of a dedicated space for treating injuries and managing medical supplies was clear, and the thought of organising such a space offered a small measure of comfort.

After cleaning Jamie's wound with the utmost care, I proceeded to redress it, applying fresh gauze with gentle, efficient movements. The process was familiar, yet each motion was tinged with the awareness of our constrained circumstances. As I secured the new dressings, ensuring they were snug but not too tight, I allowed myself a moment to consider the implications of setting up a medical tent. It would not only improve the safety and efficacy of the care I could provide but also symbolise a step towards establishing some semblance of normalcy within our extraordinary situation.

Jamie's eyes, heavy with the onset of the medication's effects, were a welcome sight. It was a small victory in the grand scheme of things, but it brought a sense of relief nonetheless. The smile that found its way to my face was spontaneous, a reflection of the satisfaction that came from seeing a patient—no matter how challenging—begin to find some respite from their pain.

Having finished with the immediate task of redressing Jamie's wound and ensuring he was as comfortable as possible, I gathered the medical supplies, ready to organise them in a more secure location. The decision to move them was practical, a necessary step to protect our dwindling resources from further canine interference. "I'm taking the supplies to the other tent," I announced, more out of habit than the expectation of a response. My addition, "Away from Henri," was a light attempt to inject a bit of humour into the situation, even if I wasn't sure Jamie was coherent enough to appreciate it.

As I manoeuvred through the tent flap, ready to step out into the cool evening air, Jamie's voice, soft yet clear, stopped me in my tracks. "Glenda," he called out, prompting me to pull back inside, my attention immediately refocused on him.

I turned to face him, meeting his gaze. The vulnerability in his eyes, so at odds with the tough exterior he often presented, was striking. "Thank you," he mumbled, his words simple yet laden with meaning. It was a rare moment of acknowledgment, a glimpse into the complexity of his character that went beyond the surface level.

In the few moments that followed, I watched as Jamie succumbed to sleep, his features relaxing into a peaceful expression that belied the pain and struggle of his waking hours. The sight of him, so exposed and human in his slumber, stirred a deep empathy within me. Despite his often abrasive demeanour, the reminder that even the prickliest among us harbour pain and vulnerability was poignant. *Even pricks have feelings in them, somewhere,* I mused to myself with a gentle smile, acknowledging the truth of the complexity of human emotion.

With one last look at Jamie, now lost in the depths of much-needed rest, I quietly left the tent.

❖

Sitting down in the dust beside Paul, his immediate question, "How is he?" carried the weight of genuine concern for Jamie's well-being.

"Still in a lot of pain," I admitted, the words heavy on my tongue. The update I provided was factual, stripped of any sugarcoating. "I've changed the dressing on his wound and given him some more painkillers and a few sedatives. He should be out for the rest of the night." My response was clinical, yet beneath the surface, there was an undercurrent of hope that the medications would provide Jamie the relief he so desperately needed.

Paul's gratitude, "Thank you, Glenda," was sincere, yet it stirred an uneasy feeling within me. "I'm not sure we would have survived here long without you." His words, meant as a compliment, instead evoked a sense of premature celebration. *It's a bit too soon to be thanking me,* I thought. The stark reality of our situation, the constant threat to our survival, was never far from my mind. *From what I've witnessed so far, there's still plenty of time for us to die yet.*

The question that had been gnawing at the edges of my consciousness finally pushed its way to the forefront. "Is this all of you?" The courage it took to voice the inquiry was born of a need for clarity, despite the fear of what the answer might reveal.

"Yes," Paul's response was simple, a confirmation that carried its own weight of implications.

"There's been nobody else?" I pressed further, the need for understanding driving me to seek out as much information as possible.

"No," Paul replied again, his answer prompting him to question, "Were you expecting more?"

The moment of truth hung between us, heavy and significant. "Oh... um... no," I stammered, the realisation hitting me that divulging my fears and speculations would serve no purpose. If Paul didn't know anything about others before us, then sharing my tangled web of hope and fear would only add to our collective burden. The possibility that others might have been here before us, coupled with the implication that they had not survived, was a duality of hope and despair that was best left unexplored for the moment.

We lapsed into silence, the crackling of the fire the only sound in the still night. My gaze was drawn to the flames, their dance a mesmerising distraction from the whirlwind of thoughts and emotions churning within me. The fire, with its warmth and light, became a focal point for reflection, a beacon in the darkness that surrounded us. In that silence, the reality of our situation settled heavily upon me, a mix of determination and dread for what the future might hold.

"You know you can't go back," Paul's words, spoken softly, broke the silence that had settled between us. They were a stark reminder of the reality we faced, a truth that hung over us like a shadow.

"I know," I responded, the words leaving my lips with a weight that felt heavy. My father had told me that, among many other things, preparing me in his way for a journey he was uncertain that I would ever have to take. My brief acknowledgment of Paul's statement sent us spiralling back into a contemplative silence, each lost in our thoughts.

Sitting there, staring into the fire, memories of my childhood washed over me. I had grown up on stories of Clivilius, tales told by my father that painted this world in strokes of adventure and mystery. As a young girl, those stories fuelled my imagination, igniting a hope that one day I might see this place for myself, to experience its wonders first-hand. My father's narratives had made Clivilius sound incredible, a realm of endless possibilities and undiscovered secrets.

But now, confronted with the reality of Clivilius, the wonder and excitement that once filled those childhood dreams had evaporated, leaving behind a longing for the familiar, for home. The harshness of our situation, the struggle for survival in an alien world, bore little resemblance to the enchanting tales I had once believed in. The stark contrast between my childhood fantasies and the present reality was jarring.

As I sat beside Paul, the warmth of the fire doing little to chase away the chill of realisation, I couldn't help but wish for an escape from this reality. The thought that I might just wake up from this, to find it all a dream, was a fleeting comfort. Yet deep down, I knew the truth. This was no dream; it was the life I was now bound to, a life filled with challenges and uncertainties.

Seeking to shift the tide of my thoughts from the paths of nostalgia and regret, I turned the conversation towards the events that had unfolded before my arrival. "So, what did happen last night?"

Paul's recounting of the previous night's ordeal—a fierce dust storm and an encompassing darkness that seemed almost sentient in its intensity—left me gasping. The visual he painted of their struggle against the elements and the subsequent injury that Jamie suffered was a testament to the unpredictable and perilous nature of Clivilius. "And that was how Jamie got burnt," Paul concluded, his words a sombre coda to the tale of survival against formidable odds.

The casual conclusion to such a harrowing tale seemed almost surreal, and I found myself searching the night sky for some semblance of normalcy, a distraction from the harsh reality Paul had just described.

"It's very dark. There is no moon, or stars here?" My question was more than just an inquiry about the celestial landscape; it was a search for a glimmer of familiarity in an environment that felt increasingly foreign.

"I don't think so," Paul's reply came, tinged with the same uncertainty that had been shadowing my thoughts. "Or at least, we didn't see anything last night." His words confirmed the unsettling notion that Clivilius lacked the comforting presence of celestial bodies we had taken for granted on Earth.

"Oh," I murmured, my gaze drifting back to the fire, the only source of light in the enveloping darkness. The realisation brought a new layer of concern to my already troubled mind. "I see." The simplicity of my response belied the turmoil of thoughts racing through my head, the implications of our situation becoming ever more daunting.

"Glenda," Paul's voice, soft yet filled with a resolve that caught my attention, prompted me to meet his gaze.

"Yes, Paul?" I answered, sensing the gravity of what he was about to say.

"The dark can be a scary place here. I'm going to keep the fire going all night." His declaration was a testament to his understanding of the psychological comfort that light provided in the face of the unknown, a beacon of hope and a measure of protection against the intangible fears that darkness brought.

"Do you feel safe here?" My question was more than a query about our physical safety; it was an exploration of his emotional and psychological state in this new world.

Paul's hesitation spoke volumes before he even replied. "Nothing about this place seems particularly safe," his honesty was a reflection of our shared vulnerability. "But I think having the light is the best thing for us, to hopefully avoid a repetition of last night's fiasco." His pragmatic approach, focusing on the light as a means of safeguarding against the dangers both seen and unseen, offered a sliver of comfort.

The uncomfortable shift in the dust under me was a physical manifestation of the unease churning within. The unpredictability of our new world, with its unseen dangers and unanticipated challenges, weighed heavily on my mind. The thought of another dust storm, or worse, the unknown force that had claimed my father and decimated what was once a thriving city in Clivilius, filled me with a sense of urgency. "I think we should build some security for our small settlement. And soon," I found myself asserting, more out of a need to feel some semblance of control than anything else.

Paul's cautious gaze met my suggestion with a measured response. "I'll have a chat to Luke about it tomorrow," he promised.

Pleased with his agreement, I acknowledged his response with a nod. My mind was already racing with the logistics of setting up a medical tent that could adequately serve our needs—a task that promised to occupy much of my time and energy in the coming days.

"You'll take the first watch then," I stated more than asked, as I rose to my feet, brushing off the dust that clung to my slacks. The idea of a watch system had formed almost instinctively, a basic measure of security against the unknowns that lurked in the darkness beyond our firelit circle.

"First watch?" Paul's question, marked by a hint of surprise, underscored the novelty of the concept in our current situation.

"Well, you can't very well sit there awake all night," I reasoned. The practicality of sharing the responsibility for keeping watch, for ensuring our collective safety, seemed obvious. "I'll switch with you when I check on Jamie during the night." My words were an attempt to formalise our arrangement, to establish a routine that could offer us some measure of security.

"Sure," Paul agreed, his attention drifting back to the fire.

As I made my way towards the supply tent, a sudden curiosity prompted me to turn back. "Oh, and Paul?" I called out, an afterthought striking me as both poignant and necessary.

"Yeah," he responded, his voice carrying across the short distance to where I stood.

"Does our little settlement have a name yet?" The question felt important, a way to solidify our presence in this dusty landscape, to claim a piece of it as our own.

Paul's smile, though I could not see it, was evident in his voice. "Bixbus," he announced, a choice that sparked a flicker of amusement amidst the gravity of our conversation.

"Hmm. Odd name," I mused aloud, the uniqueness of the moniker lingering in my thoughts as I turned and entered the tent. The naming of our settlement, however unconventional, was a small but significant act of defiance against the uncertainty and danger that surrounded us. It was a declaration of our intent to survive, to build something lasting—a symbol of hope and resilience that, despite everything, we were here to stay.

❖

Standing just within the shelter of the tent, the transition from the outside's relative brightness to the tent's dim interior required a brief pause. My eyes gradually adapted to the muted illumination, a faint glow that seeped in, painting soft shadows across the sparse interior. The light from the campfire outside cast a comforting, if not entirely sufficient, radiance that allowed me to navigate the space.

The tent, despite being designed to accommodate ten people, felt cavernously empty with just the bags of groceries and additional medical supplies I had brought in. This stark emptiness lent the space an air of vastness that was both impressive and slightly disconcerting. The realisation that this tent was now my temporary home, my medical base, underscored the drastic change my life had undergone in the last twelve hours.

Caught up in the practicalities of setting up the tent and ensuring Jamie's well-being, I hadn't fully considered my own basic needs until that moment. The act of unbuttoning my shirt, a prelude to settling in for the night, was halted by the sudden awareness that I lacked bed clothes, or any change of clothes for that matter. The reality of our situation, stripped down to survival essentials, hit me anew as I hastily redid the buttons. The absence of such basic comforts was a stark reminder of the abruptness with which we we been thrust into this new existence.

The air inside the tent, warm and filled with the fine dust of Clivilius, carried with it the alien planet's signature. Moving towards the back corner, I retrieved the single folded blanket. Laying it out on the floor of the tent's right wing, I took a moment to smooth out the uneven surface beneath.

The act of preparing my makeshift bed was meditative, a moment of normalcy in an otherwise unrecognisable world.

As I pressed the lumps of dust flat with my palms, the texture of the ground beneath the tent's floor was a tangible connection to Clivilius. Each movement, each adjustment of the blanket, was a silent assertion of my determination to adapt, to make this place as hospitable as possible under the circumstances.

Settling into the blanket, the emotions I had been holding at bay surged forward, threatening to overwhelm me. The longing for home, for Pierre, and for Lois, our loyal golden retriever who was a constant, comforting presence in our lives, washed over me with an intensity that took my breath away. The absence of their warmth, the silence where their laughter and soft whimpers should have been, carved a hollow space within me that seemed impossible to fill.

In this landscape, so far removed from everything familiar and dear, I found myself fighting for a semblance of the routine that had anchored my days back on Earth. Kneeling on the blanket, I sought to ground myself in a practice that had always brought me solace. Closing my eyes, I took a deep breath, willing the turmoil within to ebb, to give way to a moment of peace.

"I'm grateful for my life," the words left my lips in a whisper, a soft affirmation in the enveloping darkness of the tent. Acknowledging gratitude, even in the most dire of circumstances, had always been a way to centre myself, to find a path through the darkness. "I'm grateful for the air. I'm grateful for the kindness of Paul." Each statement of gratitude was a lifeline, a reminder of the good that could still be found, even here, even now.

But as I continued, the effort to focus, to truly feel the gratitude, was immense. The usual comfort and clarity this ritual provided were obscured by the pain of my current reality. Recalling the day my mother informed me of my father's disappearance, a memory steeped in loss and uncertainty, I realised that tonight's struggle was even more profound. The weight of not just personal loss, but the displacement from my world to Clivilius, bore down on me with crushing force.

Swallowing hard against the tide of emotion, I forced myself to continue, to find one more thing to be grateful for in this unfamiliar world.

"I'm grateful for Clivilius."

4338.207

(26 July 2018)

THE SLEEPING MAN & THE NAKED MAN

4338.207.1

The gentle intrusion of early morning sunlight coaxed my eyes open, marking the start of another day. Lying there for a moment longer, I allowed myself the luxury of stillness, half-expecting the familiar chorus of birdsong that had always signified dawn back on Earth. But the silence that met my ears was a stark reminder of our alien surroundings. No melodious greetings, no wind rustling through the treetops—just a profound quiet that seemed to envelop everything.

My face contorted with the weight of realisation as the events of the previous day, the reality of our situation, came crashing back. Clivilius was real. This stark, silent world was now my home. The finality of that thought pressed down on me, a tangible reminder of the distance between this life and the one I had known.

With a sigh, I rolled off the blanket, the motions mechanical. Folding it neatly, I placed it back in the corner of the tent.

Stepping outside into the crisp morning air, I squinted against the low sun on the horizon, its rays casting long shadows on the ground. I found myself trying to gauge the time, an instinctive reach for normalcy in a world where every familiar reference point had been stripped away. My phone, the keeper of time, dates, and alarms, was now with Luke, and my smartwatch was a world away, left behind on my desk in a last-minute oversight that now seemed almost prophetic.

Estimating the time to be somewhere between six and seven in the morning, I couldn't help but muse on the assumption that Clivilius operated on a time scale remotely similar to Earth's. The realisation that even something as fundamental as time might not align with what I knew was a sobering thought. It underscored the vastness of the unknowns we faced, the need to adapt not just to a new environment, but to a wholly different way of experiencing life itself.

Surveying the camp for any signs of life, I noted the stillness that enveloped us, a stark contrast to the chaos of the previous day. My gaze settled on Paul, who was sprawled near the remnants of last night's campfire, now nothing more than a bed of cold ashes. He was asleep, his chest rising and falling with each deep, peaceful breath, a soft snore escaping him now and then. Despite the discomfort of his makeshift bed on the ground, it seemed he had managed to find some semblance of rest amidst the unfamiliarity of our surroundings. Observing his tranquil state, I couldn't help but feel a tinge of envy; sleep had eluded me for much of the night as I grappled with my new reality.

The realisation that I too had eventually succumbed to sleep, however brief, was a small comfort. The exhaustion from the day's events had finally overtaken me, pulling me into a restless slumber filled with tossing and turning. My introduction to Clivilius had been nothing short of a whirlwind—a mix of anticipation, anxiety, and medical emergencies. I had expected the transition to be challenging, but the reality was something else entirely. I had braced myself for the overwhelming, for a sensory overload of new sights and experiences. Instead, I found myself navigating a landscape that was as mentally and emotionally taxing as it was physically barren.

As I stood alone with the extinguished campfire and my companions still enveloped in sleep, a fleeting sense of fortune crossed my mind, grateful for the uneventful night that had passed. The silence and tranquility of dawn allowed me to take in our surroundings with fresh eyes. The dusty brown hills stretched endlessly, interrupted only by the clear river weaving through them like a lifeline. Observing the vast openness, I reasoned that the likelihood of an unexpected encounter was minimal. The natural geography of Clivilius, with its expansive views and the absence of barriers for sound to travel, provided a sort of natural early warning system. *For now, at least, our biggest threat is ourselves*, I concluded silently, a realisation that was both reassuring and daunting.

This acknowledgment, however, brought forth a deeper, more unsettling reflection. As the warmth of the morning sun kissed my bare arms, I considered the harshness of the environment that enveloped us. The prospect of not just surviving but thriving in such conditions seemed increasingly remote, a notion that sent an involuntary shiver down my spine. *I am just a person, among a small group of other persons*, I mused, the reality of our vulnerability pressing in. The thought of our small, unprepared group trying to carve out an existence in this barren landscape was overwhelming.

Yet, I couldn't afford to dwell on these fears. The immediacy of our situation, particularly Jamie's condition, demanded my focus and energies. *Jamie needs my attention*, I reminded myself, pushing aside the creeping dread with a determined shake of my head. The well-being of each member of our group was paramount; our survival depended on our collective health and strength. Helping Jamie to recover fully was not just a matter of medical duty but a crucial step in maintaining the integrity of our small community. *Each one of us matters*, I affirmed, grounding myself in the responsibility I held as both a doctor and as Bixbus's newest resident.

❖

Unzipping the tent with the intention of checking on Jamie, I was wholly unprepared for the sight that greeted me. The shock of seeing Jamie in such a vulnerable state, caught in the midst of dressing, sent a flush of embarrassment coursing through me. "Oh, I'm so sorry," I stammered out, hastily closing my eyes in a futile attempt to erase the image that had already imprinted itself in my mind.

With my face undoubtedly coloured with embarrassment, I swiftly turned away, allowing the tent flap to fall back into place as I moved to the side, trying to regain my composure. The sound of Jamie's chuckle from within the tent, light and unbothered, eased some of my tension. His reaction, or lack thereof, to the intrusion suggested he was not as perturbed by the incident as I was.

"I didn't expect you to be up and moving so soon," I managed to say, my voice carrying a mixture of surprise and relief. My caution was evident in the way I deliberately avoided turning my head back towards him, an attempt to maintain some semblance of dignity after the accidental invasion of his privacy.

Jamie's light-hearted response, accompanied by another chuckle, offered a moment of levity amidst the awkwardness. "It's okay," he assured me, his head appearing through the tent flap as he spoke, providing a startling but welcome indication of his improving condition.

Emerging from the tent, Duke barrelled through with a determination that momentarily shifted the morning's focus, was a light-hearted distraction. He dove nose-first into the dust, embarking on an exploration that seemed to disregard our human concerns entirely. Henri, less bold but equally curious, lingered until Jamie's gentle nudge sent him scampering after Duke. The sight of the dogs, so easily slipping into their routines of play and investigation, offered a brief respite from the weight of our circumstances.

Jamie, now more suitably attired in boardshorts and a t-shirt, stepped into the morning light, a visual reminder of the day's new beginning. "How are you feeling this morning?" I inquired, genuinely interested in his recovery progress. His response, indicating a significant improvement in his condition, brought a wave of relief. "Much better. My chest doesn't feel nearly as sore," he shared, his actions—stretching his arms above his head—mirroring the lightness in his tone.

"That's good news," I acknowledged, my professional assessment mingling with personal relief.

"I was about to go and take Duke for a walk. We've both been rather cooped up the last twenty-four hours. I think it'll do us both some good," Jamie proposed.

"I agree," I found myself saying. "But I need to change your dressing before you go," I added, my tone shifting to one of gentle insistence. The balance between allowing Jamie the freedom to regain his strength and ensuring his continued healing was a delicate one.

"Fine," Jamie acquiesced, his compliance accompanied by the simple action of pulling his shirt over his head. The readiness with which he agreed to the necessary medical intervention was a testament to his growing trust in my care, a small but significant affirmation considering yesterday's agitated outbursts.

As I gently removed the dressing that covered Jamie's wound, the sight of his healing chest prompted a small wave of relief. "It is looking much better," I observed aloud, allowing a hint of optimism to colour my tone. Jamie's smile in response was a small victory, a sign that we were moving in the right direction, however incrementally.

The practical part of me kicked in as I considered the next step. "Why don't you lay back down while I grab some fresh dressings from the supply tent." It was a reasonable request, given the circumstances, but Jamie's hesitation was palpable. His gaze shifted back to the tent, laden with a reluctance that mirrored my own internal conflict about the prospect of him returning to the confines of his makeshift recovery area. "Really?" he questioned, the single word heavy with the unspoken acknowledgment of the effort it had taken him to rise.

I empathised deeply with his sentiment. The thought of re-entering the tent after finally feeling the morning air and the freedom of being outside was not appealing. "Just for five minutes," I insisted, trying to strike a balance between his comfort and the necessity of the situation. The absence of basic furniture like a chair in our makeshift camp was a reminder of the many conveniences we had left behind. "If we had a chair, I'd say you could sit, but we don't."

Jamie frowned.

"Yet," I quickly added, hoping to infuse a bit of hope into the situation. "We don't have a chair, yet."

"Fine," Jamie huffed, his compliance mixed with a touch of defiance as he turned to return to the tent. In that moment, the interplay of patient and caregiver, of frustration and determination, encapsulated our shared struggle to find a semblance of normalcy in an environment that was anything but normal.

❖

Gathering the fresh dressings and other medical supplies needed for Jamie's care felt like a small but significant mission. The supply tent, with its orderly rows of necessities, was a reminder of the semblance of structure I was striving to maintain. As I made my way back, I couldn't help but notice Henri's cautious approach toward Paul, who remained lost in slumber, his snoring a gentle backdrop to the morning's activities. The sight of Henri, so focused and yet tentative in his approach, brought a soft chuckle from me. The innocence of the moment, the normalcy of a dog's curiosity, provided a brief respite from my constant concerns.

It's only a matter of time, I mused to myself, a smile playing on my lips. The thought wasn't just about Henri potentially waking Paul with an enthusiastic sniff or an unexpected nudge. It was more reflective of the broader situation we found ourselves in—this delicate balance of tension and tranquility, of adjusting to life in Clivilius with its unknowns and surprises.

Watching Henri's slow progress toward Paul, I was reminded of the simple, everyday moments that brought us joy back on Earth, moments now tinged with the surreal realisation that we were millions of miles away from everything we knew. Yet, here we were, finding small pockets of normalcy in the midst of the extraordinary.

❖

As I gently dabbed away the last of the water from Jamie's chest, I couldn't help but marvel at the marked improvement in his condition. "This really is looking much better already," I remarked, a note of genuine surprise in my voice. The burns that had seemed so threatening initially now appeared superficial, and the once alarming signs of infection from the splinter had receded significantly. "Your burns look superficial. Most of the damage appears to have been from the splinter's infection." Observing the rapid healing, my professional curiosity piqued, my brow furrowed in thought. *The rapid pace of recovery was unexpected; such a significant improvement in less than twenty-four hours was unusual, even by Earth standards. Which, now that I think of it, the damage also seemed to have progressed quite rapidly considering how severe it had become in less than twenty-four hours.* The thought lingered in my mind, stirring a mix of concern and wonder. *Is there something else going on here...?*

This question hovered in the air, unspoken yet palpable. The unique environment of Clivilius, with all its unknown variables, could be influencing both the decline and the healing processes in ways I hadn't anticipated. The possibility of alien microorganisms, the planet's atmosphere, or even Jamie's own physiological response to this world could be factors contributing to his rapid conditions. This realisation prompted a mental note to closely monitor his progress and to remain vigilant for any other unexpected developments in our health while we adapted to our new surroundings.

Jamie's response pulled me from my wandering thoughts. "I really don't feel much pain now at all," he assured me.

Continuing my examination, I sought further confirmation of his recovery. "And you've had no complaints with any upper body movements?" I inquired, securing the final piece of gauze over his wounds with medical tape. The absence of discomfort or limitation in movement would be a strong indicator of his healing progress.

"None," Jamie affirmed, his broad smile serving as a visual punctuation to his words. His positive response, coupled with the visible improvement in his condition, was a moment of triumph, however small in the grand scheme of our challenges.

"That's great news," I declared, my voice carrying both professional approval and personal relief. A light tap on his shoulder signalled the end of the procedure, a gesture meant to convey both reassurance and encouragement.

As Jamie made a swift motion to rise, I could sense his eagerness to get going. "But," I intervened, extending my palm towards him in a gentle yet firm gesture meant to pause his momentum, "I still need you to take another couple of antibiotic capsules."

Jamie's huff, a mixture of frustration and resignation, was an expected response. The interruption to his plans, however minor, was a reminder of the vulnerability he was likely eager to shed. "You'll need to take several daily for the next few days to make sure it doesn't get reinfected," I continued, emphasising the necessity of the medication for his recovery. It was crucial that he understood the importance of completing the course of antibiotics to prevent any setbacks.

The swift manner in which Jamie took the capsules, washing them down with a single gulp of water, was a testament to his acceptance of the situation. "Thanks," he muttered, a simple acknowledgment that carried a hint of appreciation beneath the surface irritation. Watching him wipe his mouth with the back of his hand, I couldn't help but admire his resilience.

As he stood and began to dress, I observed him closely, noting a slight stiffness in his left shoulder. The observation was filed away for later attention—perhaps a therapeutic massage could ease the tension and aid in his recovery. "You're good to go," I announced, offering a supportive pat on his back as a sign of reassurance and approval.

My final instructions were given with a mix of concern and authority. "But don't go too far. And the moment you start to feel tired or any dizziness, you need to stop and rest. Then as soon as you are able, make your way back to camp."

Jamie's nod of acknowledgment was all I expected.

"I'll go downstream," Jamie announced as we emerged from the tent, his voice carrying a hint of excitement at the prospect of exploring our surroundings. "There's a lagoon just around the bend. I'll take Duke with me, he'll love it."

"And Henri?" I found myself asking, my gaze shifting towards the smaller of the two dogs. Observing Henri's tentative movements around the campfire, his reluctance to venture into the dust, painted a stark contrast to Duke's eagerness.

Jamie's soft laugh, in response to Henri's hesitation, was tinged with understanding. "I don't think Henri's going to make it too far," he observed.

"I'll keep an eye on him," I volunteered, my offer stemming from a sense of responsibility for the well-being of all members of our small community, including our canine friends. Watching over Henri, ensuring he felt safe and comfortable while Jamie and Duke explored, was a small but significant task I was more than willing to undertake.

As Jamie called Duke to his side and they set off towards the lagoon, I watched them disappear into the distance. Their departure left me alone with my thoughts, and the sudden, loud gurgle from my stomach broke the silence, drawing a smile to my lips. "Time for breakfast," I murmured to myself, a reminder of the simple, everyday needs that continued despite our extraordinary circumstances.

❖

Making my way back to the supply tent, my steps were purposeful, drawn towards the several bags of groceries that we had managed to accumulate in the right wing of our makeshift storage area. As I began to sift through the contents, a slight grimace formed involuntarily. The reality of our culinary situation was laid bare before me—Paul had managed a simple dinner the previous evening, but the prospects for variety and nutrition seemed grim this morning. The assortment was disheartening: tins of corn, baked beans, and an unexpected amount of dog food. It was a collection that hardly promised the well-rounded meals we were accustomed to back on Earth. *Luke's going to need some guidance with his food selection*, I mused, the thought accompanied by a gentle sigh that carried a mix of resignation and determination.

Amid the tins and packets, a folded sheet of paper caught my eye, an anomaly in the sea of canned sustenance. Curiosity piqued, I unfolded it, my eyebrows raising in surprise. The contents were both unexpected and somewhat amusing—a basic guide to cement-laying. "Interesting," I scoffed lightly, the corners of my mouth turning up in a smile despite the situation. It was a stark reminder of the wide array of challenges we were expected to navigate, far beyond the medical and nutritional. Folding the instructions carefully, I slipped the paper into my back pocket, a symbolic gesture of accepting yet another role I hadn't anticipated taking on here in Clivilius.

"Aha! Finally, something edible for breakfast," I couldn't contain my excitement as I unearthed a box of breakfast muesli bars that had been cleverly hidden at the bottom of the bag. It was a small victory in the ongoing struggle to find suitable food, and my spirits lifted momentarily at the prospect of a somewhat reasonable start to the day.

Stepping outside, the rumbling of my stomach grew louder. Eagerly, I unwrapped one of the bars and took a hearty bite, savouring the taste of something other than canned beans or corn. The realisation that my breakfast would be over all too quickly, likely in another two bites, dimmed my initial excitement. Yet, I consoled myself with the thought that this modest meal would at least provide some basic form of essential energy.

My attention was diverted to Paul, who was beginning to stir by the remains of last night's campfire. The sight of him pushing Henri away from his face, a mix of annoyance and affection in his movements, brought a soft chuckle to my lips. Henri, in his own way, had fulfilled his role, providing a gentle, if somewhat slobbery, wake-up call. "You must have been tired," I called out to him, my voice carrying a mix of amusement and sympathy.

Paul's response, as he looked up towards me, rubbing his neck in an attempt to ease the stiffness that sleep on the ground often brings, was simple. "Yeah, I was," he admitted.

"You fell asleep pretty quick," I remarked, closing the distance between us as Paul sat contemplatively in the dust. Offering him the second breakfast muesli bar, I hoped to share a small portion of comfort. "Here, want some breakfast?" The gesture was as much about nourishment as it was about solidarity, a small act of looking out for one another in this unforgiving environment.

"Thanks, but I think I might go have a quick wash first," he responded, his voice carrying a hint of gratitude mixed with the immediate desire to rid himself of the night's accumulated grime. As he shook the dust from his hair, I couldn't help but empathise with his longing for a semblance of cleanliness, however fleeting it might be.

"In the river?" I asked.

"Yeah," Paul confirmed, a note of resignation in his voice. "It's all we've got."

"Fair enough," I conceded, understanding the importance of maintaining personal hygiene, even in such basic forms. It was a crucial aspect of keeping morale and health in check. "But make sure you eat when you get back. You need to keep your strength up. Soon we start putting up the third tent and then later we pour some concrete."

"Oh?" Paul's voice was tinged with surprise, his eyebrows arching in a way that made me chuckle softly.

"Yes." My smile widened as I shared the news. "I found your concrete instructions. They were in one of the grocery bags."

As Paul stood, his actions were deliberate, a physical shaking off of the night's rest as well as the dust that Clivilius seemed to blanket everything with. His face, contorted in concentration, mirrored the mental shift from the restful state to the readiness required for the day's tasks. His movements, though mundane, were a reminder of the constant adaptation we were all undergoing, each gesture a small rebellion against the dust that sought to claim everything as its own.

I couldn't help but let my gaze wander beyond our immediate vicinity, drawn to the area not far from our campsite where Paul and Jamie had made their first attempt at laying concrete. My curiosity, mixed with a professional concern for our structural endeavours, compelled me to assess their work from afar. Even at a distance, the quality of the concrete work seemed questionable, and a sigh escaped me before I could catch it. *What the hell is Paul thinking?* The thought was a mixture of worry and exasperation, a mental note to myself that our survival required not just effort but skill and planning.

Despite my reservations about their concrete work, I had to acknowledge the thoughtfulness in their choice of location. It was a strategic decision, balancing proximity to our living area with the need to maintain the integrity and utility of our space.

"Where are Jamie and Duke?" Paul called, his head poking out from within Jamie's tent. It was a simple question, but one that momentarily caught me off guard, snapping me back to the present moment.

I blinked quickly, a physical attempt to sharpen my focus and gather my thoughts. "They've gone for a walk. He seems much better this morning," I responded, my voice carrying a mixture of relief and caution.

"That's good," Paul remarked, a note of genuine relief in his voice before he disappeared back into the tent.

Moments later, Paul reemerged with a follow-up question, "Do you know which way they went?" His interest seemed more than casual, perhaps a reflection of the bond that was forming among our small group, or maybe an acknowledgment of the inherent risks in wandering too far from camp.

"They've headed downstream," I pointed in the direction Jamie and Duke had taken, the gesture accompanied by an explanation of Jamie's mention of a lagoon. As I spoke, my mind drifted to the practical implications of this lagoon's existence. The thought of it possibly offering a secluded spot for bathing was both appealing and necessary. The constant battle against the grime of dust and sweat was becoming increasingly uncomfortable.

"Yeah," Paul said, his voice carrying an ease that I found both appealing and slightly amusing in our current context. "It's a nice spot. There's nothing there except water and dust, but you should check it out sometime."

"I might wait until I have some clothes to change into," I stated, a decision born out of necessity rather than fear or reluctance. The thought of venturing to the lagoon, as inviting as it was, came with its own set of challenges—not least of which was the lack of proper attire for such an activity.

As Paul made his way past me, heading downstream towards the lagoon, a trail of curiosity followed him. The thought crossed my mind—*Surely Paul isn't going to bathe with his clothes on.* And yet, his direction seemed unmistakably towards Jamie, towards the very spot he had just recommended. His abrupt stop, followed by a self-directed scoff, was a moment of comedy. "Oh!" The realisation that hit him, prompting a sudden change in plans, was as unexpected as it was amusing. His declaration, "I'll go upstream," accompanied by an emphatic point, was a scene so human, so grounded in the everyday awkwardness we had all known before Clivilius, that it momentarily lifted the weight from my shoulders.

Paul's embarrassment, his quick pivot to save face, was endearing. *He is a funny man indeed*, I mused, the smile that spread across my face a rare and welcome visitor.

Turning away from the scene, my steps took me towards the Portal. The encounter with Paul, the brief escape into the simplicity of human interaction, was a balm. Yet, the Portal represented so much more—a reminder of why we were here, of the vast unknowns that still lay ahead, and of the hope that perhaps, in this strange new world, we might find not just survival, but a way to thrive.

THE NEW MAN

4338.207.2

As I approached the location of the Portal, a large, clear screen materialised before me, rising seamlessly from the ground. Its dimensions, though only roughly estimated, seemed to stretch about three meters in length and five meters in height. The screen's transparency, interspersed with moments of swirling colours when active, lent it an ethereal quality, making it seem less like a piece of technology and more like something out of a dream. Standing before it, I was struck by the realisation that seeing the Portal with my own eyes was a vastly different experience from hearing about it through my father's descriptions. Despite this, a part of me acknowledged, almost reluctantly, that his accounts had been remarkably accurate.

The knowledge that the Portal's activation was restricted to a Guardian—someone genetically bound to a Portal Key—cast a shadow of resignation over me. The understanding that this marvellous piece of technology was beyond my reach, that it would remain dormant without its designated Guardian, brought a mix of emotions. It served as a stark reminder of our isolation, of the chasm that lay between us and the possibility of return to Earth.

With a heavy heart, I forced myself to divert my attention away from the screen. Dwelling on the dwindling possibilities of returning to Earth, on the what-ifs and might-have-beens, would not aid our survival here and now. The Portal, a symbol of hope for a way back, also represented the vast divide between our current existence and the life we left behind.

Wandering closer to the Portal, my attention was caught by the meticulous stacks of pebbles that had been arranged to encircle a large area nearby. The careful placement of these small stone markers, seemingly methodical and deliberate, struck me as both charming and somewhat curious. *It is cute,* I mused internally, appreciating the effort that had gone into this rudimentary form of boundary marking. Though it appeared somewhat unnecessary at this juncture, given our limited presence and activities in Clivilius, I couldn't help but acknowledge the practicality it suggested for future endeavours. I resolved to inquire about the intent behind these pebble perimeters later, curious about the planning that was already unfolding in the minds of my companions.

Drifting through the designated area, my focus shifted to the assortment of supplies that had been organised within the bounds set by the pebble stacks. The presence of equipment designated for pouring concrete caught my eye, a tangible sign of the ambitious plans taking shape. As I tallied the materials, it became evident that there were enough resources to construct at least six large, corrugated iron sheds —an impressive undertaking that spoke volumes about the foresight and determination driving our efforts to establish a more permanent settlement.

Additionally, nestled among the larger construction supplies, were boxes containing the components for at least one, possibly two, additional tents. The discovery sparked an immediate consideration in my mind: *if there were no objections from the others, I would take the initiative to set up one of these tents as a fully functional medical facility.* The necessity of such a space was already clear, underscored by Jamie's recent encounter and recovery. *Hopefully, they wouldn't have to frequent it,* I thought, an optimistic wish tempered by the pragmatic understanding of our situation. The reality, as we had all begun to accept, was that the unpredictable nature of Clivilius, coupled with the physical demands of establishing our presence here, made the need for a dedicated medical space not just a precaution, but a requirement.

The sudden eruption of colours on the Portal's screen, a spectacle of vibrant, gyrating hues spreading across its translucent surface, immediately drew my gaze. It was a sight both mesmerising and unexpected, a stark departure from the Portal's usual dormant state. My initial awe quickly gave way to surprise as a young man, seemingly disoriented, stumbled through the kaleidoscope of colours and into our world.

As he regained his footing, the confusion was evident in his stance and the bewildered look on his face. "Clivilius," he uttered, his voice carrying a mix of disbelief and realisation. "What the hell is Clivilius?" His question, though directed at no one in particular, felt like a direct challenge to the reality I had been navigating since my arrival.

In that moment, a flurry of questions raced through my mind. *Who is he?* The sudden appearance of a stranger was alarming. *Is he dangerous?* The uncertainty of his intentions, coupled with our vulnerable position heightened my sense of caution. *Is this Luke's doing?* The thought that Luke might have orchestrated this arrival without warning us was both perplexing and concerning.

"Where the hell am I?" His desperation became palpable as he spun around, taking in his surroundings with a wild, searching gaze. The sight of him, so clearly out of his element and possibly afraid, tugged at my sense of empathy, despite the underlying fear and suspicion his sudden appearance had sparked.

Approaching the young man, I was cautious, acutely aware of the unpredictability of the situation. My eyes quickly assessed him—no more than five foot five, yet his physique, marked by well-defined calves and biceps, indicated a strength that belied his stature. Despite my own height advantage, I couldn't help but acknowledge the potential physical mismatch should the situation escalate. *You know well how heightened emotions make people do unpredictable and uncharacteristic things,* I silently reminded myself, a mantra born of experience and a reminder of the need for diplomacy over force.

"Are you okay?" My voice carried across the short distance, an attempt to bridge the gap not just physically but emotionally, to offer a semblance of understanding and concern amidst the confusion.

His reaction to my presence, marked by a mix of surprise and suspicion, was understandable. "Did Luke push you too?" he inquired, his gaze fixed on me as if trying to piece together the narrative that had led him to this unfamiliar place.

I shook my head in response, a gesture meant to convey both my non-involvement and my empathy. "No," I clarified. "I'm guessing he pushed you though?"

"Yes," he answered sharply, his confirmation laced with a mix of realisation and resentment. "At least, I think he did." His admission, though vague, hinted at a complexity that piqued my interest further.

As our exchange unfolded, a smile found its way onto my face, not out of amusement, but from a profound sense of relief. *I am no longer alone.* The sentiment was twofold; not only did his arrival signify another human presence in this foreign landscape, but it also represented a potential expansion of our fledgling community.

Luke's sudden emergence from the Portal, just moments after the young man's tumultuous arrival, immediately heightened the tension in the air. "I see you've already met Glenda?" His words, seemingly casual, did little to alleviate the charged atmosphere.

Instinctively, I took a step back, creating distance between myself and the unfolding confrontation. The young man's face flushed a deep red, a clear indicator of his escalating fury. His reaction was visceral, a raw display of emotion that left no room for misunderstanding. "You're a fucking arsehole, Luke!" His accusation was launched with venom, his proximity to Luke's face underscoring the seriousness of his anger. "What the hell did you push me for?" The question, though rhetorical, demanded an answer, an explanation for the abruptness of his journey through the Portal.

In the physicality of the moment, he shoved Luke hard enough to cause a stumble. "See," he continued, pushing Luke once more, a tangible demonstration of his point. "You don't like being pushed around."

"I'm sorry," Luke offered, his tone earnest, seeking to diffuse the situation as he struggled to regain his footing. "But Jamie needs you."

My surprise at this revelation was unmistakable. *So, he knows Jamie. A relative perhaps?* The question formed silently in my mind, a puzzle piece that suddenly seemed crucial to understanding the dynamics at play.

"What? Uncle Jamie is here?" The disbelief in the young man's eyes was palpable, a mixture of shock and an urgent need to reconnect with the familiar.

"Yeah," Luke's confirmation was simple, yet it carried the weight of our shared predicament, a silent acknowledgment of the complex web of relationships and responsibilities that had begun to form amongst us.

The shift in the man's demeanour was stark, his face hardening as he processed Luke's affirmation. "Take me home, Luke," he insisted, his voice laced with a determination that belied the underlying desperation of his request. "And I'll take Uncle Jamie with me." The firmness in his statement spoke volumes about his resolve, yet it also hinted at the naivety of his understanding of our current limitations.

Luke's response, or lack thereof, was a heavy silence that filled the air with tension. "I can't," he finally admitted, the weight of his words anchoring us all back to the harsh reality of our situation.

"What do you mean, you can't?" the man's frustration boiled over, his gestures a visible manifestation of the turmoil churning inside him.

Luke's apology, offered to the ground as if he couldn't bear to meet Kain's gaze, was a soft confession of his own helplessness. "I'm sorry, Kain," he murmured, his voice barely above a whisper, a testament to the depth of his regret.

Feeling my stomach plummet at the exchange, I was acutely aware of the pain etched in Luke's eyes—a mirror to the confusion and anger in Kain's. It was evident that Luke's decision to bring Kain here, though fraught with unforeseen consequences, was not made lightly.

"Sorry?" Kain's anger erupted, his question a rhetorical blade aimed squarely at Luke's guilt. "You're sorry! Sorry for what?"

Compelled by a need to offer some solace, or at least an attempt to diffuse the escalating tension, I stepped closer to Kain. Placing a firm hand on his shoulder, I hoped the gesture would convey a sense of solidarity and understanding. "It's impossible for us to return," I explained softly, my words intended to bridge the chasm of misunderstanding that lay between us.

The moment Kain pulled away from my grasp and launched himself at Luke, everything seemed to escalate uncontrollably. Witnessing the raw violence of Kain's actions, as he ran at Luke, shoulder-barging him with full force, sending them both tumbling to the ground, my heart raced, fear and adrenaline intertwining as I anticipated the worst. *Someone is going to get seriously injured.* The thought was a stark reminder of our precarious situation on Clivilius, where every new injury could spell disaster.

"Kain!" My voice, loud and filled with urgency, cut through the air as I sprinted towards them, desperate to prevent further violence. But my plea went unheeded. Kain, fuelled by anger and perhaps fear, took a wild swipe at Luke, who narrowly avoided the blow. The sight of blood oozing from Kain's knuckle, a visible testament to the intensity of his emotions, sent a chill through me.

Attempting to restrain Kain proved futile; his movements were too swift, his desperation too profound. As he dragged Luke closer by the foot, a grim tableau unfolded before my eyes. "Both of you, stop it now!" My demand, authoritative yet tinged with desperation, seemed to fall on deaf ears.

The situation escalated further when Kain's elbow collided with my jaw in his fervour to strike at Luke again. The pain was immediate and sharp, a physical blow that was matched by the shock of the betrayal. As I stumbled backward, grappling with the ache that radiated from my jaw, Luke took advantage of Kain's momentary distraction to retaliate.

Kain's subsequent fall, the impact stealing his breath, momentarily halted the chaos. Luke's stance, poised to continue the confrontation, prompted a swift intervention. "Luke, don't," I warned, the sharpness in my voice underscored by the urgency of preventing further violence. My outstretched hand, a plea for peace, contrasted with the dull throb in my jaw where Kain's elbow had made contact.

The tension that had just moments ago crackled in the air began to dissipate as Kain's breathing steadied, his body sprawled on the dust with vulnerability etched across his features. As he lay there, his gaze locked onto Luke's, I could see the raw fear mirrored in his eyes—a stark contrast to the anger that had propelled him just minutes before. Holding my own breath, I watched as Luke, in a gesture that seemed to bridge the chasm of their recent conflict, extended his hand towards Kain.

My held breath escaped in a loud exhale, a mix of relief and residual tension, as Kain, after a moment of hesitation, grasped Luke's hand and allowed himself to be pulled to his feet. The simple act, laden with complex emotions, felt like a tentative step towards reconciliation, or at least an acknowledgment of a shared struggle.

Turning my attention back to my own discomfort, I couldn't help but quip about the lack of medical supplies, "I'm assuming we don't have any ice either?" The question, though rhetorical, underscored the reality of our limited resources. Luke's confirmation, delivered with a softness that reflected our collective frustration, only served to solidify the concern. *My jaw is going to swell up nicely,* I thought ruefully, not enjoying the prospect of dealing with the injury without the basic comfort of ice.

Kain's apology, offered with a mixture of remorse and embarrassment, caught my attention. His inability to meet my gaze spoke volumes about the guilt and conflict he felt. "I'm sorry, Glenda," he said, his voice carrying the weight of his actions.

There was a sharp twinge of pain as I attempted a smile. Despite the discomfort, and the lingering wariness from Kain's earlier outburst, I felt it important to forge a connection, to extend the hand of friendship in the midst of our uncertain circumstances. His firm handshake was a solid affirmation, a tangible sign of his willingness to move past the altercation.

"I'm the camp's doctor," I informed him, easing my grip and stepping back slightly. My role, albeit self-assigned, felt more like a calling in these moments—providing care and attempting to maintain the well-being of our small group in an environment that was anything but forgiving.

"And I'm..." Kain's hesitation caught my attention, a brief pause as he seemed to search for the right words. His hand moved to his brow, a gesture of contemplation or perhaps uncertainty. My curiosity piqued, I couldn't help but silently question Luke's rationale for bringing Kain to Clivilius. The answer came sooner than expected.

"And you're our new construction expert," Luke chimed in, his grin slicing through the tension of the moment. The declaration was both a surprise and a revelation. Kain, with his youthful appearance and previously demonstrated physical prowess, was now being introduced in a role that was crucial to our survival.

I nodded, processing this new information. Kain's youth was apparent, placing him in his early twenties at most, yet the responsibility now being placed upon his shoulders was significant. My initial impressions of him, influenced by the morning's chaos, shifted towards a recognition of the potential he brought to our group. His expertise in construction, as proclaimed by Luke, could be the key to enhancing our living conditions and ensuring our safety

The sudden, faint sound of a bark slicing through the air was unexpected, but what followed sent a jolt of alarm through me. Paul's loud cry for help echoed across the distance, piercing the relative calm of the moment and instantly transforming it into a scenario fraught with urgency.

Luke's reaction was immediate; the shift in his expression from one of casual engagement to grave concern was palpable. "Something's wrong," he voiced the dread that had already taken root in my mind. His words were barely out before he sprang into action, taking off towards the source of the commotion with a speed that spoke volumes of the gravity he attached to Paul's cry.

My own heart matched Luke's pace, pounding with a mix of fear and adrenaline as I hurried to keep up with him. The brief jog to the camp became a mental preparation ground for me, my mind racing through various scenarios we might encounter. As the camp's doctor, I braced myself for the possibility of injury or worse.

THE DEAD MAN

4338.207.3

Henri stood at the riverbank not far from the tents. His barks were sharp and insistent, slicing through the calm like warning shots. Paul, with his back to us, was a hunched figure of urgency next to Henri, leaning over something—or someone—that I couldn't quite see from my vantage point. My pace quickened, drawn by a mix of curiosity and a sinking feeling in my stomach.

As I neared, the scene unfolded like a page from a thriller I wished I hadn't opened. A young man, his body a limp silhouette against the glistening surface of the river, was trapped in a deadly embrace with the water. He lay face down, the river's current treating him with an indifference that was almost cruel, bobbing him rhythmically as if to a lullaby meant for the deep. His feet, a jarring note in the otherwise fluid scene, were caught on a rock that jutted out from the bank like a hand reaching up from below.

My breath hitched, caught in the vice of sudden fear and concern. Luke's voice, laced with a similar urgency, cut through the air. "Paul, what's going on?"

The desperation in Paul's voice as he screamed back, "Help me!" was palpable, a raw edge of panic that I felt scrape across my own nerves. "Hurry! He needs help."

Luke, jumping into action without hesitation, was on his knees next to Paul in an instant. I stood frozen for a moment, watching as Paul extended his reach across the water, his hands pressing against the young man's waist in a frantic attempt to roll him. The gesture was one of desperate hope, a fight against the pull of the current and the weight of a body that seemed to have already succumbed to the river's embrace.

The river's edge felt like a boundary between two worlds—the solid certainty of the land and the unpredictable fluidity of water. As I approached, Paul's silhouette against the water blurred for a moment as he slid into the river, his movements deliberate and focused.

"Help me roll him," Paul's voice cut through the tension, a command that was both a plea and a directive.

I glanced at Luke, giving his left shoulder a firm nudge. He nodded, understanding flashing in his eyes before he too entered the water, positioning himself opposite Paul. The river, a silent witness to our efforts, seemed to hold its breath.

"Go," Luke signalled, his voice steady. "I've got him."

"Three. Two. One. Roll," I commanded, my voice more steady than I felt. As the body rolled, I crouched, my hands finding the cold, slick surface of the protruding rocks. With a tug that pulled at both my muscles and heartstrings, I freed the man's feet, releasing him from the river's grasp.

Kain's voice shattered the momentary calm, "Who the fuck is that?" The terror in his voice was a mirror to the shock rippling through me. I found myself echoing his question internally, my mind racing through faces and names, trying to place the stranger before us.

I've never seen this man before. The thought was a whisper in my mind, a puzzle piece that didn't fit.

Paul's response was a murmur, almost lost in the sound of the flowing river. "No idea." His voice carried a weight, a reflection of the uncertainty that clouded his features as he stared at the young face bobbing gently in the water. It was a face that belonged to no one we knew, an unknown variable in our tightly knit equation.

Despite the dire circumstances that unfolded before us, a fleeting spark of hope ignited within me. The sight of this stranger, though grim, hinted at a world beyond our small circle, a reminder that we were likely not alone in this vast, unpredictable nothingness. "Is he breathing?" I found myself asking, clinging to that sliver of hope, however thin it might be.

"I don't think so," Luke's reply came, heavy with resignation.

My mind raced, thoughts tumbling over each other in a frantic search for solutions. "Quick. Bring him to shore," I directed, voice laced with urgency. "There might still be a chance of resuscitation." In moments like these, every second counts, and the healer in me refused to give up without trying.

"No," Paul's response was curt, slicing through the thin veil of hope I'd clung to.

"What?" My voice shattered the tense air, a mixture of confusion and disbelief.

"I don't think it will help," Paul said softly, his voice carrying the weight of unspoken truths. "His throat has been slit."

I gasped, the word 'slit' echoing in my mind like a death knell. *How is that possible?* The reality of the situation bore down on me, a heavy, suffocating blanket of dread.

"Fuck!" Kain's exclamation was a raw expression of the shock that gripped us all.

Despite the gruesome revelation, a part of me insisted, "We should bring the body in anyway." My brain struggled to process the severity of the wounds, to understand the brutality that had been inflicted upon the stranger. It was a desperate grasp at humanity in the face of inhumanity.

"What good will that do?" Luke's question was pragmatic, yet it sent a chill down my spine. "If he's been murdered and someone comes looking for him, perhaps we shouldn't be the ones caught with his body."

His words, meant to be rational, felt like ice water being poured over the flickering flame of my hope. The implications of being found with the body, the danger it posed to us, was a reality I hadn't fully considered. A cold shiver ran down my spine as my mind threatened to spin out of control.

First dust storms and burns and now murder! The world I thought I knew, the Clivilius my father had described in stories of adventure and discovery, had vanished. It was replaced by a harsh, unrecognisable landscape marked by violence and fear. I rubbed my temples in a vain attempt to ward off the growing sense of despair.

We're all going to die here. The thought was a whisper of terror in my mind, a stark contrast to the determination that had fuelled me moments before. The brutality of the world outside our small circle of light had intruded, shattering any illusions of safety.

"I'm with Luke," Kain's voice cut through the chilling morning air, aligning himself with the caution that Luke had voiced.

"Yes," Paul chimed in, his gaze lifting to meet mine, a silent plea for understanding in his eyes. "Regardless, he deserves a proper burial." His voice carried a respect for life—and in death—that resonated deeply within me, a stark reminder of the humanity we must cling to, even in the face of barbarity.

"Proper burial!" Luke's scoff was a jarring note, dismissive and pragmatic, yet underscored by a fear we all felt. "You don't even know the guy."

"If we bring him in, I can do a rough autopsy." The words felt heavy on my lips, a grim acceptance of the role I had to play in this unfolding drama. It was a proposal borne out of the need to understand, to seek answers in the silence of death.

"Is that really necessary?" Luke's question, laden with skepticism, stung more than I expected. "I think it's pretty obvious what happened to him." His attempt to downplay the need for further investigation was a testament to the fear that perhaps we were delving into matters best left untouched.

I threw Luke a sharp look of disapproval, my gaze hopefully conveying more than my frustration. *He knows better than I, the danger we are in.* The words formed silently in my mind, a rebuke for his unwillingness to confront the reality that knowledge was our only ally in this desolate place. "A rough autopsy might be able to tell us more of a story of how he met his fate," I countered, my voice firm, trying to bridge the gap between our instincts to flee from the horror and the necessity to face it head on.

Anything we can learn might help us survive. The thought remained unspoken, a silent mantra that fuelled my determination. In the depths of my being, I understood that every piece of information, no matter how small or morbid, was a potential lifeline. The grim task ahead was not just about uncovering the truth behind one lost soul's demise but about gleaning any insight that might safeguard the rest of us against a similar fate.

This was our reality now—a balancing act between preserving our humanity and succumbing to the primal urge for survival. Each decision, each action, was a step on the tightrope we walked, with the abyss of the unknown yawning below.

As Paul began to retch, his body convulsing with the force of his nausea, I felt an instinctual urge to reach out to him, to offer some semblance of aid. But the river between us, its waters cold and unforgiving, made it impossible. I could only watch, a silent spectator to his distress, feeling a helplessness that knotted my stomach.

The horror of the scene before me seemed almost surreal, as if the serene backdrop of the river had been violently disrupted by a storm of human suffering. Vomit erupted from Paul's mouth in a rapid expulsion. His legs buckled beneath him, his arms flailing in a desperate attempt to find balance, to regain control over his rebelling body.

Luke's expression, a mirror to my own shock, morphed from surprise to fear in a heartbeat. His hands, once firmly gripping the body, released as if burned, and he slipped beneath the surface of the water with a splash that seemed to echo around us. "No!" My scream tore from my throat, a futile attempt to undo what had already happened, to rewind those few, critical seconds.

Paul and Luke resurfaced, gasping, the river claiming them momentarily before releasing them back to us. Water streamed from their hair and faces.

"Where's the body?" Paul's voice, tinged with surprise and confusion, broke the heavy silence that had fallen over us. His eyes met Luke's, both sets filled with a dawning realisation of the gravity of what had just occurred.

"Shit," The word slipped from me, a whisper of despair as the reality set in. The wave created by their fall had acted as a malevolent force, seizing the opportunity to claim the body for the river. It had been carried away into the faster-moving current, propelled out of sight, out of reach, as if the river itself sought to erase the evidence of the tragedy that had unfolded on its banks.

"Where's Jamie?" Luke's voice was edged with panic

"He went for a walk to the lagoon," I responded, the words feeling incongruous in the moment, almost trivial in the wake of our current predicament. It seemed an odd time for Luke to be thinking of his partner, yet the worry in his voice was unmistakable, a reminder of the personal stakes entangled in our survival.

"Lagoon?" Luke echoed.

"Downstream," Paul's reply came, succinct.

"Shit," Luke cursed, the pieces falling into place in his mind far quicker than I could follow. He looked back at Paul, his eyes wide with a new-found urgency. "We need to retrieve that body, now!" His declaration was a complete reversal from his earlier stance, driven by a sudden shift in priorities.

"But... but you just said..." Paul began, confusion lacing his words.

"Forget what I just said. You were right. We are better off keeping the body," Luke cut Paul off, decisiveness replacing his prior hesitation. Without another word, he clambered onto the riverbank and took off in a sprint

Paul, still reeling from his ordeal, wiped a speck of vomit from his lip.

"Go!" I found myself instructing, pushing Kain towards action, towards following Luke's lead. My shove was met with resistance.

"Fuck off!" Kain snapped, dodging my second attempt to spur him into motion.

Paul pulled himself from the river's grasp. "I'll go," he announced, determination in his voice as he walked up to Kain, ready to chase after the fleeting chance of regaining control over our situation.

"Introductions can wait," I said, my words a mixture of encouragement and urgency, pushing Paul to leave immediately. There was no time for formalities, no space for hesitation when every moment could mean the difference between life and death, between holding onto a semblance of order and succumbing to chaos.

Paul brushed past Kain without another word and took off in a sprint, his resolve to catch his brother a testament to the bonds that tied us together, the unspoken commitments that drove us to act even when every instinct screamed against it. In that moment, as I watched Paul's retreating figure, I was acutely aware of the fragility of our situation, of the delicate balance between survival and morality, and of the sacrifices we were all required to make to protect one another, to hold onto the threads of humanity in a world that seemed determined to unravel them.

"Are you okay?" My voice was steady as I reached out, placing a firm hand on Kain's shoulder, an anchor in the storm of chaos that had engulfed us. The sudden contact seemed to startle him, his body tensing under my touch as if jolted awake from a nightmare.

"I... I think so," Kain stammered, his words tangled with confusion and fear. The façade of toughness he'd maintained was cracking, revealing the vulnerability beneath. "What the fuck is going on?" The question burst from him, raw and laden with emotion, tears spilling over in a flood of unchecked fear and disbelief.

I took a deep breath, recognising the signs of shock setting in, the overwhelming reality of Clivilius crashing down on him far harder than it had on me—or perhaps it was just a different kind of hard. "Come," I said gently, coaxing him with a tone I hoped was comforting, inviting him to follow me to the relative sanctuary of our tent. "I think you're in shock." The words were an understatement, a simplified label for the complex maelstrom of emotions I sensed swirling within him.

Kain's response was a delicate nod, a fragile gesture that conveyed his willingness to be led, to seek solace in the guidance of someone else amidst the incomprehensible turmoil. He took a few hesitant steps, then paused, a hand pressed to his forehead as if to physically hold back the onslaught of his thoughts.

"Sit down for a while," I urged, guiding him under the protective canvas of the tent's canopy. The suggestion was not just an offer of physical rest but an invitation to momentarily put aside the burden of understanding, to find respite in the pause.

Kain collapsed into the soft dust, a silent surrender to the forces that had buffeted him since our arrival. His body seemed to fold into itself, a physical manifestation of his internal retreat from the reality that had proven too harsh, too sudden.

"Here, drink this. Probably nearly all of it," I offered, extending an unopened bottle of spring water towards him. The gesture was as much about providing physical sustenance as it was about offering a momentary distraction, a brief focus on a simple, necessary action.

Kain's smile was an awkward twist of his lips, a fleeting attempt at gratitude amidst the turmoil. He took the bottle with a shaky hand, gulping down the water in deep, desperate swallows. Closing his eyes, he rested his head in his hands, a silent figure of desolation seeking solace in the darkness behind his eyelids.

As I glanced past Kain, my gaze settled on Henri. He had reclaimed his spot on the corner of the mattress within the tent, a picture of tranquility amidst the turmoil that surrounded us. Unbothered, he seemed to embody a state of peace we all yearned for, a silent testament to the resilience of spirit I hoped we could all find in the days to come.

The fragile thread of hope was shattered by a spine-chilling scream that tore through the silence, slicing the air with a sharpness that made my neck stiffen. It was a sound that spoke of raw fear, of terror so profound it seemed to vibrate through the very ground beneath us. My heart hammered against my ribs, a frantic drumbeat propelling me into action.

Without a moment's hesitation, I leapt up, my legs moving instinctively, propelling me downstream through the thick layers of dust that had settled over everything. The dust kicked up around me, clouding the air, but my focus was unyielding. Each step felt heavy, as if the very earth sought to hold me back, to slow my desperate rush toward the source of the scream.

❖

I didn't stop. I didn't look back. My mind was a whirlwind of action and reaction, processing scenarios at a speed that felt almost disjointed from the physical effort of my legs propelling me forward. The scream had cut through the air with a clarity that left no room for doubt, igniting a sense of urgency that resonated with every fibre of my being. In my years of medical experience, such a scream was unequivocal —it signalled an emergency, a call to action that could not be ignored.

The terrain was unforgiving, the dry dust a treacherous carpet that sought to undermine my haste. When my shoe, heavy with the clinging dust, betrayed me, sending me stumbling to the ground, I felt a flare of frustration. But there was no time to dwell on the fall; the urgency of the scream that still echoed in my mind spurred me on. With a determination fuelled by the knowledge that every second mattered, I pushed myself up, barely registering the gritty texture of the dust against my palms.

As I reached the top of the last rise, my breath came in heavy, ragged gasps, sweat dripping from my brow, a testament to the physical exertion and the sweltering heat that seemed to press down with an almost physical weight. Yet, for a moment, I paused, allowing myself a brief respite to survey the scene that unfolded below.

The lagoon lay spread out beneath me, a serene expanse of clear water that glittered in the sunlight. Jamie and Luke were already there, their figures huddled over a body that lay motionless at the mouth of the lagoon, where the tumultuous journey of the river branched into the calm embrace of the lagoon. The sight sent a jolt through me, the reality of the situation settling in with a weight that felt as tangible as the dust that clung to my skin.

Paul, on the opposite side of the bank, was visible now, his posture and expression one of concern as he stared across the mouth of the lagoon toward the two men. Despite the distance, I could see that he appeared to be okay, a small comfort in the midst of the unfolding drama.

In that moment, perched on the edge of the slope, I took a deep breath, trying to steady my racing heart. The juxtaposition of the serene beauty of the lagoon against the backdrop of potential tragedy struck me with a poignant clarity. Here, in this untouched corner of Clivilius, the rawness of nature and the fragility of human life intersected in a way that was both beautiful and brutal.

As a doctor, I had faced emergencies before, moments where life and death hung in the balance, dependent on the actions taken in the briefest windows of time. Yet, standing there, overlooking the scene, I felt the weight of responsibility press down on me anew. This was more than a test of my medical skills; it was a challenge to my ability to remain calm under pressure, to make the right decisions when they mattered most.

With a final steadying breath, I began my descent down the steep slope, my resolve hardened by the knowledge that my skills, my experience, could make a difference. The path ahead was fraught with uncertainty, but one thing was clear: I was needed, and I would not falter.

As I transitioned into a jog, the rocky perimeter of the lagoon guided my path toward Luke, Jamie, and the still figure that lay ominously at the water's edge. The rough terrain demanded my full attention, each step a calculated effort to maintain balance and speed.

Behind me, Kain's voice pierced the tense air. "Jamie!" he called out, a note of desperation threading through his shout. I felt a pull to look back, to reassure myself of Kain's presence, but the immediacy of the emergency before me tethered my focus. There was no time for hesitation, no moment to spare for glances backward.

The scene that unfolded as I neared was one of raw emotion and chaos. "What the fuck have you done, Luke?" Jamie's voice, laden with accusation and disbelief, screamed into the open air. The intensity of his outcry was a stark contrast to the tranquil backdrop of the lagoon, a peaceful setting now marred by the drama of human anguish.

My breath hitched as I witnessed Jamie's loss of footing, a moment of heart-stopping fear as both he and the body tumbled back to the ground.

"Help me take him back to camp," Jamie's voice, choked with tears, broke through his façade of determined toughness. The vulnerability laid bare in his plea was a jarring sight, compelling me to pause momentarily in my approach.

I have a job to do, I reminded myself, the mantra a lifeline to cling to amidst the emotional turmoil. It was crucial now, more than ever, to maintain professional detachment, to prioritise the medical assessment over the pull of empathy that threatened to cloud my judgment.

"Wait," I found myself saying, an authoritative hand raised to halt any further movement. "Let me check him first." The directive was firm, rooted in the necessity of procedure over the impulse to act on emotion.

Luke's nod was a silent acknowledgment of the logic in my words, a begrudging agreement to the pause in action. Jamie, however, remained rooted to the side of the body, his refusal to move a testament to his emotional turmoil. The defiance in his stance, the raw grief that clung to him, painted a vivid picture of the complexity of our human responses to crisis.

Carefully encroaching on Jamie's protective circle, I crouched beside the still figure sprawled on the ground, the air thick with tension and unspoken questions. My heart was a drumbeat of purpose as I prepared to examine the young man, the solemnity of the moment not lost on me. The world seemed to hold its breath as I took in the stark evidence of violence—a clear, clean slice across his neck. My pulse quickened, a mix of professional assessment and personal shock at the precision of the wound. Whoever had inflicted this injury possessed a chilling expertise. Yet, as my mind raced to piece together the puzzle, nothing seemed to fit the grim tableau before me.

Leaning closer, I locked my gaze with his. His eyes, a striking shade of blue, held a semblance of life that belied his otherwise lifeless appearance. A soft gasp escaped me, the impossibility of the situation pressing in. *That's impossible*, I silently rebuked myself, even as a sliver of hope dared to flicker within me. My hand moved instinctively, sliding gently under his shirt to rest on his stomach. There, beneath my palm, was the faintest suggestion of life—a soft, rhythmic lifting and falling that defied all logic.

"He's breathing!" The words tumbled from my lips, breaking the heavy silence. The revelation hung in the air, a beacon of hope amidst the despair.

"Joel," Jamie whispered, his voice carrying a mixture of awe and tenderness as he touched the young man's forehead, a gesture of connection, of recognition.

Luke's response was a cough, the result of a mis-swallow, his expression a mirror of my own disbelief and confusion.

"But barely," I hastened to add, grounding the moment in the harsh reality of our situation. "I think he may actually be alive, but I don't understand how that is possible." The words were a professional assessment, yet they carried the weight of my own bewilderment. "His colour suggests he has lost so much blood that his circulatory system has collapsed." The gravity of his condition was not lost on me, each observation a piece of the enigma we were now faced with.

My gaze lifted to meet Jamie's, finding in his eyes a reflection of the myriad emotions swirling within me. "You're right," I said with a calm that belied the storm of thoughts racing through my mind. "I agree we should bring him back to camp."

As we prepared to lift Joel, Jamie's face lit up with an appreciative smile, a beacon of gratitude in the midst of our grim task. The warmth of the sun seemed to cast a glow around him, highlighting the determination and hope that shimmered in his eyes.

"What? Seriously?" Luke's incredulity pierced the momentary silence, his expression a mix of surprise and skepticism.

"Help us," Jamie's plea was soft yet urgent, his hands carefully positioning themselves under Joel's limp form. The request hung in the air, a call to action that was difficult to ignore.

Luke hesitated, a brief moment of indecision that had me holding my breath. *Be rational, Luke*, I silently urged, hoping he'd see the necessity of our collective effort. My internal plea was answered as he stepped in across from me, his arms sliding beneath Joel's wet body, a silent commitment to the task at hand.

"Ready. Lift!" My voice, firm and clear, broke the tension. Together, we lifted, a testament to our shared resolve.

A slight groan escaped me as we moved, a cramp in my left calf threatening to undermine my efforts. I silently willed my body to cooperate, to not fail me now when every step counted.

Halfway around the lagoon, relief came in the form of Kain, who seamlessly took my place. "Thank you," I breathed out, gratitude mixing with the pain as I took a moment to rub the ache in my calf.

As I raised my head, my eyes sought out Paul, who remained a solitary figure on the bank at the mouth of the lagoon. "You coming, Paul?" My voice carried across the distance, laced with concern and a hint of apprehension. The last thing we needed was another complication, another injury to navigate. The day had already brought enough surprises, from Jamie's unexpected emotions to the bewildering condition of Joel's not-quite-dead state.

Paul's response, "I'll meet you there soon," offered a measure of relief. I released the breath I hadn't realised I was holding, allowing myself a moment of hope that perhaps not everything was as bleak as it seemed.

The three of us, carrying the fourth, trudged through the thick dust that clung to our shoes, over several hills and across the wide expanse of barren nothingness.

GASP

4338.207.4

As the familiar shape of our tent finally came into view, a sense of relief washed over me, tinged with a growing sense of urgency. The anticipation of closely examining Joel's condition had turned the journey back to camp into a seemingly endless trek, each step fuelled by a mixture of determination and apprehension. Carrying a man who hovered between life and death, had transformed the familiar landscape into a gauntlet of physical and emotional challenges.

"Put him down on the mattress," Jamie's instruction broke through my thoughts as we approached the campfire.

"I don't think that's a good idea. We only have one. He could be infected," I found myself voicing the concern that had been gnawing at the edges of my mind. The possibility of infection, a threat that could compromise us all, suddenly loomed large, casting a shadow over the relief of having made it back to camp.

Jamie stopped abruptly, his reaction catching me off guard. "Bit late to say that now," he snapped, the frustration evident in his voice. "If Joel's infected then we likely are too."

My mouth tightened into a grimace, the taste of regret bitter on my tongue. *How could I have only thought of this now?* The self-reproach was a sharp sting, a reminder of the weight of responsibility I carried as the medic in our group.

"Jamie's right," Luke chimed in, his gaze meeting mine. "We may as well." His words, though meant to support Jamie, also served as a gentle reminder of the stakes we faced, of the delicate balance between caution and necessity.

I hesitated, the conflict within me palpable. The thought of compromising our only mattress, our solitary comfort in this harsh environment, against the potential risk of infection was a dilemma that weighed heavily on me. Yet, I could see the logic in Luke's stance, the necessity of keeping unity within our group, especially in the face of the unknown challenges that lay ahead.

Perhaps he is already making plans to provide us with additional bedding, I found myself thinking, a hopeful conjecture that offered a semblance of solace. "Okay," I acquiesced, my voice a mix of resignation and resolve as I moved to hold the tent flap open, a silent acknowledgment of the decision made.

As Kain swiftly removed the blankets from the mattress, a flurry of activity surrounded Joel's still form. My heart thudded against my ribcage, the anticipation of uncovering the truth about Joel's condition heightening my senses as Luke and Jamie gently laid him down. Now was the moment for a thorough examination—time to delve deeper into the mystery of his survival.

Luke stepped back to afford me the space needed to work. I knelt beside the mattress, my posture one of focused determination. Leaning over Joel, I began my examination, my fingers moving with the confidence and precision honed by years of medical practice. Each press, each prod, was a question asked, a piece of the puzzle I was desperate to solve.

The slice across his throat was my primary focus. I studied it closely, my brows furrowing in confusion. The wound was perplexing—a clean cut that, under different circumstances, should have been fatal within minutes. The very fact that I could, hypothetically, slip my fingers through the wound and touch the back of his throat without meeting any resistance was a conundrum that defied my medical understanding. It was as if the wound existed in isolation from the rest of his body's responses.

As my examination continued, my fingers tracing the contours of his arms and legs, I found no telltale warmth or the reassuring pulse of blood coursing through veins. Yet, contradictorily, Joel was breathing. The rise and fall of his chest, though faint, was undeniable—a silent testimony to the life still fighting to manifest within him.

Lifting my gaze to his eyes, I was met with a sight that tugged at the very core of my being. His eyes, a vibrant shade of blue, held a spark that seemed to dance with life, their gaze fixed on the tent's ceiling as if locked onto something beyond my comprehension. The dichotomy between his grievous wound and the apparent life within his eyes cast a profound sense of mystery over the entire situation. *How could someone so critically injured appear so alive in their gaze?*

This anomaly challenged everything I thought I knew about medicine and the human body's capacity to survive against the odds. It was a reminder of the complexities and mysteries that still elude even the most experienced among us. As I continued my examination, the reality of our situation settled heavily upon me—we were navigating uncharted waters, and the outcome of this journey was as uncertain as the condition of the young man lying before me.

Taking a deep breath, I prepared myself to articulate the perplexing findings of my examination. My words were chosen with care, reflecting the weight of the conclusion I had reached. "Both carotid arteries seem to have healed, assuming they were ever severed. Aside from the obvious slice across his throat and what I'd assume are bumps and bruises from his time in the river, he doesn't appear to have any other major physical wounds. I'm not sure how he could have lost all of his blood if not through major artery damage." The words hung in the air, a testament to the medical anomaly laid out before us.

Luke's confirmation came with a certainty that underscored the gravity of the situation. "His throat was definitely slit. There was a lot of blood," he stated, adding a layer of complexity to Joel's condition.

I could only shrug in response, a gesture of confusion and disbelief. "It's not making much sense." The pieces of the puzzle were refusing to fit together in any logical manner, defying my medical expertise and understanding.

"What do you mean you know his throat was slit?" Jamie questioned Luke aggressively. "And how the fuck would you know how much blood there was?" The accusation in his voice was palpable, turning the atmosphere in the tent charged with a new kind of urgency.

My eyes darted quickly between Jamie and Luke, the undercurrents of accusation and defence weaving a complex web of emotions and questions. They finally settled on Luke, searching his face for answers, for any indication of how he came to possess such definitive knowledge of Joel's condition. The tension between Jamie and Luke, the unanswered questions surrounding Joel's mysterious survival, and the inexplicable medical findings created a vortex of confusion and suspicion.

"No signs of any defensive wounds?" Luke asked, sidestepping the tension Jamie's accusations had woven into the air, a deft manoeuvre that left the underlying issue unaddressed.

"No, none," I found myself responding, my head shaking almost reflexively at the oddity of the question, especially given the current context. His inquiry struck me as peculiar, more so in the shadow of Jamie's pointed demands. Curiosity piqued, I couldn't help but probe further, "Were you expecting there to be?" The question hung between us, an invitation for Luke to divulge more, to add clarity to the murky waters of our understanding.

Luke's response was a head shake, his expression one of contemplation rather than evasion. "Not necessarily. I guess that means whatever happened to him, well, it happened quickly and probably took him by surprise." His words offered a semblance of logic, a possible scenario that fit the lack of defensive wounds, yet they did little to quell the undercurrent of suspicion.

Jamie, however, was not appeased. His glare, unwavering and filled with anger, underscored the urgency of his need for answers. "Well? You haven't answered my question," he demanded, his tone brooking no evasion.

Caught in the midst of this unfolding drama, I couldn't deny my own growing intrigue. *Luke clearly knows more than he is letting on,* a realisation that settled heavily within me. His knowledge, or lack thereof, was a critical piece of this intricate puzzle, one that could potentially shed light on the dark, uncertain path we found ourselves navigating. As Jamie's anger simmered, demanding transparency, and Luke wrestled with his conscience or calculations on what to disclose, I found myself at a crossroads of professional curiosity and the need for trust within our group. The balance of our survival could very well hinge on the truths yet to be uncovered, on the secrets that lay just beneath the surface of our uneasy alliance.

Luke's revelation seemed to suspend time within the confines of the tent. "Joel was the driver who delivered the tents back home," he began, his voice steady but heavy with the weight of what he was about to disclose.

My gasp was just a fragment of our collective response, a chorus of surprise that filled the space between us. Luke, undeterred by our reactions, continued to peel back the layers of this unexpected narrative. "I was surprised to see him. I didn't recognise him at first, though. Not until I saw his name sewn into his shirt." His words prompted me to action, my hands moving almost of their own accord to confirm the truth of his claim. I found the rip, and with it, the name that anchored Joel's identity in our reality. "Joel," I read aloud, the name resonating with a newfound significance.

Luke's story unfolded further, revealing the accidental chain of events that had catapulted us into this shared ordeal. "Henri and Duke coming here was all an accident," he admitted, the simplicity of the statement belying the chaos it had unleashed. "Joel accidentally let Henri outside and he ran through the Portal when we tried to catch him. I forgot I was still carrying Duke when I followed after Henri." The pieces of the puzzle began to fit together, albeit jaggedly, painting a picture of unintended consequences and serendipitous encounters.

"And Joel saw all this?" My voice barely concealed the whirlwind of thoughts racing through my mind, trying to piece together the implications of Luke's admissions. "Yes," Luke confirmed, his next words casting a shadow over the already dim light of our understanding. "And when I returned, I found Joel lying in a pool of blood in the back of the truck."

The gravity of the situation settled heavily upon us, the air thick with the realisation of the catastrophic turn of events Joel had been swept into. "Holy shit," Kain's words echoed my own sentiments, a succinct summary of the shock and disbelief that gripped us.

"But that was yesterday," Jamie said, the words hanging between us, charged with an accusation that felt like a physical blow. "Why didn't you tell me?"

Luke's response was a gulp, the sound dry and filled with apprehension. "I thought you'd blame me for it," he admitted, his voice barely above a whisper, a confession that seemed to pull the tension tighter, like a bowstring ready to snap.

"I do fucking blame you for it!" Jamie's exclamation burst forth, raw and unfiltered.

"Boys!" My own patience, worn thin by the escalating tension and the gravity of our predicament, prompted a firm interruption. Yet, my attempt to mediate was lost in the storm of their conflict.

"And then you brought him here and dumped his body in the fucking river! That's some seriously fucked up shit," Jamie's voice rose again, each word a hammer striking the anvil of accusation, his outrage a clear reflection of the horror and disbelief that such actions could be attributed to his own partner.

"It wasn't me!" Luke's shout was a desperate attempt to defend himself, to deny the atrocious act that Jamie laid at his feet. "I would never do something so terrible!"

"Boys!" My voice, louder this time, carried a note of finality, a demand for silence that could not be ignored. "Stop it!"

The tent fell into an eerie silence, the kind that follows a storm, where words hang suspended, their impact lingering in the air.

Jamie was the first to break the heavy silence that enveloped us, his voice cutting through the tension like a knife. "Well, what did you do with the body?" he asked, his tone now somewhat more contained than the raw edge it carried moments before.

"We buried him," Luke replied, his voice barely above a whisper, laden with an unspoken weight.

"We?" I couldn't help but interject, my curiosity piqued, yet apprehension knotted my stomach.

Luke bit his lower lip. After a brief hesitation, he confessed, "Beatrix, Gladys, and I."

"This is insane," Kain muttered, his voice muffled as he shook his head, burying it in his hands in disbelief or perhaps despair.

I felt a frown etch itself deeply across my forehead, my brows knitting together in confusion and concern. My eyes narrowed as I tried to piece together the bizarre puzzle laid out before us. "I really don't understand any of this at all," I admitted, my voice a mix of frustration and resolve. "But I can do some basic surgery and stitch his throat back up. I can't guarantee anything." I paused, considering the gravity of what I was about to undertake. "He might be breathing and have his eyes open, but that doesn't mean that he is actually alive. He hasn't spoken and isn't responding to any of my stimuli."

Jamie's face was a mask of confusion and concern. "So, what does that mean? What's happening to him?" he asked, his brows furrowed in worry.

I sighed, feeling the weight of uncertainty press down on me. "I really don't know," I replied honestly, my heart heavy with the admission.

At my words, Luke seemed to retreat into himself even further, taking a few steps back as if the physical distance could shield him from the reality of our situation.

"Alright," Jamie said to me, his voice firm, a surprising beacon of support in the unsettling fog of unknowns. "What do you need?"

"Well... I need..." I began, my mind racing through the list of medical supplies and equipment I would need, before my voice tapered off, lost in the magnitude of what we were about to attempt.

Jamie leaned in closer, his presence grounding, urging me to focus. His eyes, filled with determination and an unspoken promise of support, helped me gather my thoughts. "Okay, let's think this through," I said, bolstered by his proximity and the solidity of his support. "First, we'll need..." And with that, the plan began to take shape, a fragile hope blossoming.

❖

The interior of the tent seemed to close in around me, the canvas walls feeling more like barriers than protection as I glanced around, a nervous flutter in my stomach. Luke and Kain had managed to slip away, their departure almost ghostlike in its quietness, leaving an eerie silence in their wake. My eyes found Jamie, and I tried to steady my voice. "I'm going to do a horizontal mattress suture. I need a medium saline solution with a broad spectrum of antimicrobial activity, gloves, non-absorbable suture material, forceps, needle..." The list flowed from my lips, a mantra of medical necessity, before I paused to take a breath, feeling the weight of the task ahead.

Jamie's reaction—or the lack thereof—was not what I hoped for. He stared back at me with a blank expression, his eyes glazing over as if the words I spoke were in a foreign language. A pang of frustration mixed with a dash of fear coursed through me as I realised the magnitude of the responsibility resting squarely on my shoulders. This was going to be much harder than I had initially realised.

Feeling my face tighten, I made a snap decision. "You stay here and watch him," I instructed Jamie, trying to infuse my voice with more confidence than I felt. My hand found his shoulder, giving it a firm pat in an attempt to convey a sense of urgency and importance to his role. As I got to my feet, the action felt like stepping into a role that I suddenly felt entirely unequipped for.

"I won't be long. I'll just get what I need from the medical tent and come straight back," I promised, my words a blend of reassurance for him and a pep talk for myself. As I stepped out of the tent, the cool air hit me, a stark contrast to the stifling atmosphere inside. The brief moment of solitude allowed me to gather my thoughts, steeling myself for the task ahead. I knew that every second mattered, and the urgency propelled me forward, my mind racing through the procedure steps and the supplies I would need to gather.

❖

Within the span of two minutes, the reality of our precarious situation had transformed the tent into an impromptu operating room. I found myself kneeling beside Joel, the gravity of what I was about to do settling heavily on my shoulders. With deliberate movements, I donned a pair of medical gloves, the latex material stretching snugly over my fingers, a thin barrier against the severity of the procedure I was about to undertake.

I handed another pair to Jamie, the urgency of the moment reflected in my voice. "You'd better wear these," I instructed, more a command than a suggestion. Jamie, understanding their importance, slipped his gloves on with an efficiency that betrayed his nervousness.

"Now hold this tray for me," I continued, my voice steady, trying to infuse some semblance of calm into the charged atmosphere. Jamie nodded, a quick, jerky movement that spoke volumes of his anxiety.

"And try not to tremble too much," I added, half-jokingly, yet fully aware of how our nerves could impact the delicate procedure. "I don't need any other distractions." Jamie nodded again, his movements quick but more controlled this time, as he focused.

As I began to prepare Joel's neck wound for suturing, the silence between us was charged with concentration. The air felt thick, each of us wrapped in our own thoughts, yet united in a singular purpose.

"Why a mattress suture?" Jamie's question broke the silence, his curiosity piercing my bubble of focused intensity.

"No unnecessary talking during surgery," I responded flatly, my tone brooking no argument. My time in Borneo had indeed broadened my horizons, pushing the boundaries of my medical knowledge and skills. There, amidst the lush jungles and the critical lack of resources, I had learned to adapt, to innovate. Yet, despite the growth, the core truth remained—I was a general practitioner, not a surgeon. My experiences had taught me the value of knowing my limits, the importance of acknowledging the thin line between confidence and hubris.

Now, kneeling beside Joel, every lesson learned, every skill honed, was called upon. I knew my capabilities, but more importantly, I recognised the boundaries of my expertise. This was not the time for lengthy explanations or discussions. Precision and focus were paramount; there was no room for error, no space for distractions. My hands, though steady, were a testament to the respect I held for the task at hand—a life hung in the balance, and it was up to me to navigate this precarious edge with the utmost care and concentration.

As I focused intently on Joel's neck wound, the world around me seemed to narrow. Grasping the edge of the wound with the forceps felt almost second nature, a testament to the countless hours I'd spent in medical settings, though never quite like this. The needle holder felt like an extension of my own hand as I drove the needle through the skin, easily piercing the dermis. The sensation of the needle moving through flesh was both familiar and surreal.

As the needle approached the edge of the wound, a moment of instinctual haste nearly overtook me. I almost reached out with my bare hand, a move that would have breached the sterile protocol I was so desperately trying to maintain. Catching myself just in time, I remembered the forceps, the proper way to control the needle without compromising sterility or precision. It was a small slip, but it reminded me sharply of the delicate balance between instinct and training, between doing what felt natural and what was medically correct.

The sound of several instruments rattling on the tray beside me brought me back to the immediate reality. Jamie seemed to be struggling with his own battle against nerves. I paused, forceps still in hand, and turned slightly to check on him. "You okay there, Jamie?" I asked, my voice laced with genuine concern. The last thing we needed was for him to faint. "You're not about to pass out?"

"No, I'm fine. Sorry," he replied, his voice tinged with a childlike meekness that caught me off guard. It was a vulnerability I hadn't expected from him, and it served, oddly enough, to slightly lower my own nerves. His admission, rather than adding strain, somehow made the moment more human, more bearable. "You're doing a great job," he added, his encouragement simple yet sincere.

"We've a long way to go yet," I responded, the reality of our situation settling heavily upon me once more. As I turned back to the wound, ready to continue, I felt a renewed sense of purpose.

The sensation of the needle piercing the skin once more was both precise and deliberate, a critical moment in the delicate dance of suturing. As I drove the needle through the other side of the slice, I could feel the resistance of the dermis before it re-emerged on the opposite side, a testament to the care and accuracy required in this procedure. The task required a level of focus and dexterity that seemed to magnify with each movement, each decision calculated and critical.

Next, I meticulously backwards-loaded the needle in its holder, a technique that required both skill and patience, ensuring the alignment was perfect for the next puncture. The process was methodical, each action building upon the last, leading to the final goal of wound closure. As I proceeded in vertical alignment with the other puncture site, I felt a deep connection to the moment, the meticulous nature of the task grounding me in the present, each movement a testament to the years of training and experience that had led me to this point.

After pulling the final suture to the appropriate skin tension, ensuring that the wound edges were neatly approximated without being too tight, I completed the procedure with an instrument tie.

Sitting back on my knees, my body instinctively seeking a moment of rest, my bum settled on my heels, and I allowed myself a brief pause. The intensity of concentration required for the suturing had created a bubble around me, one that I was only now stepping out of. "We did it!" I exclaimed, a wave of accomplishment sweeping over me.

Jamie's question hung in the air, heavy with hope and uncertainty. "So, he'll be okay now?" he asked, his eyes searching mine for reassurance. My smile vanished as quickly as it had appeared, the fragile optimism shattering under the weight of reality. Deep down, I harboured doubts about Joel's condition, doubts that gnawed at me with persistent whispers. I wasn't convinced that Joel was truly alive in the way we understood life. The complexities of his condition were beyond the scope of a simple suture and saline.

Then, without warning, the tent was pierced by the sound of Joel gasping for air, a desperate, guttural attempt to draw oxygen into his lungs. It was a sound that was as shocking as it was unexpected, reminiscent of a fish out of water, struggling for survival in a dry environment. My reaction was instinctive, a mixture of surprise and fear that sent me tumbling backwards with a startled exclamation. "Shit!"

The tray of instruments, once meticulously organised, was now a scattered mess upon the floor, the sound of metal clanging against the ground echoing through the tent like an ominous bell. The sudden chaos seemed to amplify the panic setting in, a tangible shift in the atmosphere from hope to fear.

"What's happening?" Jamie's voice, now laced with panic, mirrored my own internal turmoil. His question was a reflection of the confusion and fear that gripped us both, a stark contrast to the brief moment of accomplishment we had just experienced.

Regaining my composure was a struggle, the shock of Joel's sudden gasp for air leaving a lingering sense of dread. I leaned over Joel, my mind racing to process the situation, to find a solution within the confines of my medical training and experience.

"Help him," Jamie insisted, his voice a mix of command and desperation. His plea was a stark reminder of our human instinct to aid those in distress, a call to action that resonated deeply within me, even as I grappled with the limits of my abilities.

My heart pounded against my chest, a relentless drumbeat in the silence that followed Joel's gasps. The tension was palpable, a thick, suffocating cloak that wrapped around us, binding us to the moment. "I don't understand," I admitted, my voice barely above a whisper, a wave of panic crashing through me. "This is out of my scope. I'm not trained for this." The admission of my limitations was a bitter pill to swallow.

As I grabbed hold of Joel's arms, attempting to pin them down in an effort to manage his convulsions, the severity of the situation was undeniable. The convulsions were a physical manifestation of the turmoil that wracked his body, a sign of the internal battle that raged within.

Then, as suddenly as it had begun, it stopped. Joel went still, his eyelids fluttering closed in a haunting semblance of peace.

As I slowly released my grip on Joel's now still arms and backed away, the cold, hard truth of Joel's condition echoed through my mind, reverberating with the finality of a closing chapter. "I'm sorry, Jamie. He really isn't alive," I uttered, the words tasting like ash in my mouth. I couldn't bring myself to meet Jamie's gaze, to witness the impact of those words reflected in his eyes. The space between us was filled with a palpable grief, a chasm widened by the harsh reality of our situation.

Jamie's response was heart-wrenching, a big sniff breaking the silence before he spoke, his voice laced with desperation and sorrow. "Can't you try to resuscitate him?" he managed between choked sobs.

Catching a glimpse of Jamie's tear-stained face, his eyes puffy and reddened with grief, I felt as if someone had physically reached inside me and torn a hole in my chest. The pain in his expression, so raw and vulnerable, mirrored the turmoil swirling within me. "He has no blood for his heart to pump around his body," I explained, my voice barely above a whisper. The words were a cold, clinical truth, but they felt like a betrayal, an admission of defeat in the battle we had so desperately hoped to win.

"I'm sorry, Jamie," I whispered again, the silence around us heavy with shattered hopes. A small, salty tear escaped, trailing down my cheek. The disappointment was overwhelming, a tide that threatened to pull me under with its ferocity. I wished, with every fibre of my being, that there was more I could do, that some miracle could reverse the cruel hand we'd been dealt. But some realities are unchangeable, and the pain of acceptance was a burden we were now forced to bear together.

Jamie's sudden grasp on my arm jolted me, his touch a stark contrast to the numbness that had begun to settle over me. "We have to take him back to the lagoon," he stated with a conviction that seemed to cut through the dense fog of despair enveloping me. His words, firm and resolute, clashed with the turmoil swirling within me.

"But why?" The question escaped my lips before I could fully grasp the futility behind it. My head shook in confusion. "What good will that do him now?" I couldn't understand Jamie's insistence, the logic behind his request lost to me in a sea of resignation.

"We have to try," Jamie insisted, his determination undeterred by my doubts. He crouched above Joel's head, positioning himself to lift under his shoulders in a gesture that spoke volumes of his refusal to accept defeat, his unwillingness to let go without exhausting every possible avenue.

"It's no use, Jamie. He's gone," I whispered, my voice soft, attempting to infuse a gentle reality into the situation. The finality of my words felt like a betrayal, an acknowledgment of defeat in the face of Jamie's desperate hope.

"Please, Glenda," he begged, his eyes, brimming with tears, locked onto mine, pleading for understanding, for support. The depth of his anguish was palpable, each word, each look, a heart-wrenching reminder of his sorrow.

Fighting back the swell of emotions that threatened to overwhelm me, I felt another tear escape, tracing a wet path down my cheek. The gesture of moving Joel, of trying to bring him back to a place of significance, seemed so utterly futile in the stark face of reality. Yet, witnessing the pain it caused Jamie to stand by, to do nothing, stirred something within me. The urge to act, to comply with his plea, was driven not by a belief in the efficacy of our actions but by the need to alleviate his suffering, to honour his need to cling to hope, however slim.

But even as I considered his request, a deeper fear gnawed at me—a fear that Jamie's faith in what little I could offer would only serve to deepen his despair when faced with the inevitable truth. The prospect of nurturing any false hope felt like walking a delicate tightrope, where the balance between compassion and reality was perilously thin.

FRESH WOUNDS

4338.207.5

"Paul! Kain!" I called out, my voice piercing the heavy silence as Jamie and I struggled with the weight of Joel's limp body, dragging him from the shelter of the tent. My legs, strained beyond their limit, betrayed me suddenly, giving way beneath me. The unexpected collapse sent my knees crashing into the unforgiving dust, a sharp pain radiating up my thighs before dissipating into a dull ache at the base of my spine. I winced, the physical pain momentarily distracting me from the emotional turmoil of our grim task.

Hearing my call, Paul and Kain rushed toward us, their faces etched with concern and urgency.

Pushing through the pain, I forced myself back onto my feet, hastily brushing the dust from my knees. The small abrasions, superficial wounds in the grand scheme of things, seemed ready to break the skin's surface, threatening a release of blood. Yet, this physical discomfort was nothing compared to the weight of our current endeavour.

"I'll take him," Paul said decisively, stepping forward to relieve me. He reached across, his hands firmly grasping Joel's shoulders, prepared to shoulder more than just the physical burden of our fallen comrade. I nodded once, my gesture one of silent gratitude for his intervention, a small solace in the midst of our collective despair.

"Where are we taking him?" Kain's voice broke through, his question hanging in the air, underscored by the unspoken fears and uncertainties that plagued us all. Without hesitation, he moved to lift Joel's other shoulder, ready to play his part in this sombre procession.

"To the lagoon," I instructed, my voice carrying a mix of resolve and trepidation. The lagoon was not just a destination but a symbol of our last hope, a place that, perhaps foolishly, we believed might offer some semblance of peace or resolution to the unfathomable situation we found ourselves in.

As we navigated the uneven terrain, the three of us took turns supporting Joel's flaccid form, a steady rhythm to our steps as we made our way toward the lagoon. The weight of Joel's body was a constant reminder of our dire situation, each shift in his weight a silent echo of the life that once animated him. The air was thick with an unspoken grief, the kind that wraps around your throat and tightens with each breath.

Jamie, driven by a mix of desperation and determination, moved ahead of us with a pace that seemed to defy the heavy atmosphere that clung to our group. His figure, a blur of motion against the backdrop of the barren desert, rushed into the clear water of the lagoon before the rest of us could fully catch up. His actions, so full of purpose and urgency, stood in stark contrast to the helplessness that gnawed at my insides.

Watching Jamie wade into the lagoon, I was struck by the surreal nature of our actions. Here we were, in the midst of an unfathomable situation, clinging to a sliver of hope that defied logic. The lagoon, with its clear waters and serene beauty, seemed almost oblivious to the tragedy that unfolded on its banks. It was a sharp, painful contrast to the turmoil that churned within me, a reminder of the world's indifference to individual suffering.

As we approached the edge of the lagoon, the clamour of our movements contrasted sharply with the stillness of the water. "Make sure he's on his back," I found myself shouting, my voice cutting through the flurry of activity as Paul and Kain carefully lowered Joel into the lagoon's embrace.

Kain, without hesitation, splashed into the lagoon, moving to steady Joel from the side opposite Jamie. The water, disturbed by our movements, rippled around them, the only immediate response to our desperate endeavour.

Jamie's voice, firm and determined, cut through the tension as he called out to Paul, "No!" He interrupted Paul's preparations to join them in the water, his focus solely on ensuring Joel's safety. "Kain and I have got him covered." His assertion was a mix of command and reassurance.

"You sure?" Paul's question, filled with concern, mirrored my own fears and doubts. As Jamie and Kain slowly waded deeper into the lagoon, their figures becoming part of the lagoon's scenery, I found myself questioning the efficacy of our actions, the hope that spurred us forward now mingled with apprehension.

"Certain," came Jamie's reply, a single word that carried with it a weight of responsibility and determination.

Turning to Paul, I asked, "Can you see?" My own gaze strained to catch a glimpse of Joel, to ensure his well-being even as we entrusted him to the care of the lagoon. I shifted my weight from one leg to the other, trying in vain to alleviate the throbbing pain in my knees.

"No," Paul admitted, his frustration evident. "It would be nice if they didn't keep their backs to us. I can't see much at all." His words echoed my own feelings of helplessness, the difficulty in standing back, unable to contribute further, unable to see the outcome of our actions.

The sudden gasp for air shattered the heavy silence, slicing through the tension like a bolt of lightning. My heart leapt into my throat. "What's happening?" I shouted, the words ripping from me in a mixture of fear and desperate hope. Every fibre of my being screamed to join them in the lagoon, to be at Joel's side. It felt wrong, standing here on the shore, as if by merely observing from a distance, I was betraying my medical duty, my need to be part of this impossible moment.

Jamie turned, his face alight with an incredulity that mirrored our own, yet etched with a joy that seemed out of place in the grim tapestry of our ordeal. "He's breathing again," he announced, his voice carrying over the water, a beacon of impossible news.

I exhaled loudly, a release of breath I hadn't realised I was holding. *Wie zum Teufel isch das überhaupt möglich?* The question echoed through my mind, a mantra of disbelief. *De Mann isch tot gsi, dess bin i mir sicher gsi!* My medical training, every bit of experience I had, told me that what we were witnessing defied all logic, all understanding.

"What the hell is going on? How is that even possible?" Paul's muttered disbelief under his breath was a vocalisation of the confusion within me.

I shrugged, the gesture one of helplessness in the face of the unimaginable. "I'm not sure. But it seems there is something about the lagoon that is keeping Joel alive," I replied, my voice tinged with wonder and skepticism. *Or bringing him back to life,* my mind added silently, entertaining the notion that we had stumbled upon something truly miraculous, a phenomenon that challenged the very fabric of our understanding.

Paul's smile, brief as it was, transformed into a furrow of deep thought. "You mean he wasn't actually dead when we first found him in the river?" he posited, seeking some logical explanation in a situation that defied logic.

Pausing, I let his words sink in, turning them over in my mind. My face mirrored the intensity of my thoughts, furrowing in concentration as I grappled with the myriad of possibilities, the medical anomalies, the sheer improbability of it all. "I really don't know," I admitted after a moment. The certainty I once held about life and death, about the boundaries of medical science, was being challenged in the most profound way.

Paul's response, a simple gesture of rubbing at his forehead, was an emblem of our shared confusion, of the questions that multiplied with each passing moment. Standing at the edge of the lagoon, witnessing what could only be described as a miracle, I realised that we had ventured into uncharted territory, a place where science met the unknown, and all our preconceived notions were being washed away by the waters of the lagoon.

As the bright sun bore down on us, merciless in its intensity, I found myself shielding my eyes, squinting towards where Jamie, Kain, and Joel were. The glare of the sunlight on the water's surface made it difficult to see clearly, adding to the frustration I felt. "What's going on out there?" My voice carried across the water, a mix of concern and impatience breaking through as curiosity got the better of me. Unable to contain my urge to be involved, I began to remove my shoes, ready to wade into the unknown myself.

"It's okay," Jamie's voice floated back, an attempt at reassurance that did little to quell the storm of questions raging inside me. "We've got it under control."

"But I really should examine..." My protest was cut short.

"Maybe we should just leave them be," Paul's suggestion came unexpectedly, his hand grasping my arm with a firmness that spoke volumes. His intervention halted my movements, anchoring me to the spot beside him.

A look of bewilderment quickly took over my face. *Surely Paul is not serious?* The thought raced through my mind, incredulity mixing with a sense of professional duty. *This is by far the greatest medical anomaly of my career, and they all expect me to just stand here on the sidelines?* The very idea seemed antithetical to everything I stood for as a medical professional, every instinct honed by years of training screaming for me to be involved.

"Just for a little while," Paul insisted, his voice attempting to tread a delicate balance between reason and the emotional turmoil that enveloped me. "You can examine him when Jamie has calmed down."

"Fine," I huffed, the word heavy with reluctance. Sinking into the dust beside Paul, I felt the resolve within me harden. The decision to wait, even for a moment, felt like a concession I was loath to make. "But I'm not giving them too long." My words, a compromise between my professional judgment and the situation's demands, hung between us.

"Fair enough." Paul's response, though accepting, did little to ease the tension that gripped me.

The silence between Paul and me stretched on, a tangible manifestation of the tension and uncertainty that clouded the air. Inside me, curiosity roamed like a caged animal, eager for release, for an opportunity to dissect and understand the unfathomable events unfolding before us. Several times, the urge to rise, to dash back to the lagoon's edge, surged through me with such intensity that my muscles tensed in anticipation. Yet, each time, I forced myself to remain seated, whispering a mantra of patience to my restless spirit. *It isn't my time yet.*

"Why don't we head back to camp for a bit," Paul's suggestion broke through my internal struggle, his voice pulling me back to the present. He rose to his feet, embodying a decision made, as he extended his hand towards me. "Jamie's got a loud voice; he'll yell out if he needs us." His attempt to tug me along, to persuade me to distance myself from the situation, was met with a stubborn resistance on my part.

Initially, I pulled away, yanking my elbow from Paul's grasp with a firmness that mirrored the turmoil within me. Despite my reluctance, his persistence wore down my resolve. Deep down, I knew he was right; standing vigil on the lagoon's shore would not alter the course of events. Joel's fate, entwined with the mysteries of the lagoon, was beyond my ability to influence. With a heavy heart, I found myself acquiescing, walking beside Paul in a silence that was filled with unvoiced questions and concerns.

We had barely crested the first gently sloping hill on our way back to camp when a sudden curiosity overtook me. I noticed something off about Paul's arm, an anomaly that hadn't been there before. Stopping abruptly, I turned to him, my concern overtaking my previous resignation. "What's wrong with your arm?" I inquired, my gaze drawn to the area of concern

Paul's reaction was swift, almost reflexive, as he whisked his arm away from my view, a clear attempt to downplay whatever it was I had noticed. "Oh, it's nothing," he replied, his voice carrying a hint of dismissiveness that did little to assuage my concern.

Reaching across Paul's body and grasping his arm, I examined the darkened flesh surrounding three small, ominous holes. "This doesn't look like nothing," I said, my voice carrying the weight of my medical expertise and burgeoning worry. The sight before me was troubling—a clear indication that what we were dealing with was far beyond ordinary.

"Tell me what happened," I demanded, my tone leaving no room for evasion.

Paul hesitated, his reluctance visible in the tense lines of his body before he finally spoke. "Joel dug his fingernails into my arm when he first... woke up." His admission, delivered with a mixture of disbelief and discomfort, only added layers to the mystery.

"That was when you screamed?" I pressed further, seeking clarity.

Paul's face flushed a bright red, an acknowledgement that spoke volumes. "Yeah," he admitted.

My mind raced, piecing together the implications of Paul's words against the backdrop of medical knowledge I possessed. Dead or alive, Joel's body is not capable of inflicting wounds on anyone else. The notion that Joel, in whatever state he was, could cause such harm was baffling. It's not uncommon for scratches or punctures to become infected, but this looks more than a simple infection. The darkened tissue, the rapid progression of the symptoms—it all pointed to something far more sinister. And if it happened only today, then whatever it is, it's progressing rapidly, just like Jamie's wound had. This realisation struck me with the force of a physical blow, causing me to gasp as the pieces of a terrifying puzzle began to align in my mind.

"Is it bad?" Paul's voice, tinged with worry, pulled me back from the precipice of my thoughts.

"Well, it's not bloody good," I responded, deciding against revealing my deeper concern.

Paul chuckled nervously.

"Come," I instructed with a newfound urgency that surprised even myself. My mind was racing, piecing together a plan. "I have an idea." The words were a beacon of action, a directive that pulled Paul and me out of the morass of fear and confusion, if only momentarily. I led the way, setting a brisk pace. Paul followed closely, his trust in my sudden decisiveness evident in his quick compliance.

As we traversed the remaining distance to camp, my thoughts were a whirlwind. The seriousness of Paul's condition, mirrored by the mysterious recovery of Joel, had ignited a spark within me. This wasn't just about medical curiosity anymore; it was about understanding the unknown forces we were dealing with. My footsteps were purposeful, each one carrying us closer to a makeshift lab where I hoped to piece together some semblance of understanding.

The camp, usually a place of rest and camaraderie, now loomed before us as a sanctuary of potential solutions. My mind buzzed with possibilities, with hypotheses that needed testing, with urgent questions that demanded answers. The urgency of our return was palpable, driven by the need to act, to apply scientific inquiry to the surreal circumstances we found ourselves in.

❖

"Wait here," I urged Paul, leaving him momentarily as I ducked into the supply tent. My movements were quick, efficient, driven by a singular focus. Emerging moments later, bandages in hand, I was already mentally preparing for the next steps. "We need to go back to the lagoon," I announced to Paul, not pausing to gauge his reaction as I started to move away, my mind racing ahead.

"Glenda, wait!" Paul's voice, laced with hesitation, halted me in my tracks. I turned to face him, noting the concern etched on his features. "It's only a minor wound. I'm not sure we need the lagoon," he ventured, a note of uncertainty in his voice that piqued my curiosity.

I eyed him cautiously, aware that the situation was far from ordinary, and every piece of information could be crucial. "Go on," I encouraged.

Paul seemed to weigh his next words with great care, the pause stretching between us like a chasm. "Well..." he began, his hesitation palpable.

I gestured for him to continue, my patience thinning.

"I've already washed it in the river by the lagoon and the flesh seemed to return to normal within a few minutes. So..."

His voice trailed off, leaving the implication hanging in the air, a tantalising hint at a possible solution, or at least a temporary reprieve.

"... and then without the water it turned grey again," I finished for him, piecing together the implications of his observations. "Interesting. Let's try the river water then," I decided, nodding toward the river flowing behind the tents. The suggestion was a compromise, a test of the water's effects without the immediate return to the lagoon.

"It can't hurt, can it?" Paul agreed, a note of hope mingling with the resignation in his voice.

I shrugged, a non-committal gesture that masked the uncertainty of my thoughts. "We shall see." The possibility that the river water also held some curative properties was both a beacon of hope and a daunting reminder of how little we understood about the forces at play. As we made our way toward the river, the juxtaposition of my medical and scientific training against the backdrop of this inexplicable phenomenon was not lost on me. We were stepping beyond the bounds of conventional medicine, guided by necessity and the slim hope that nature might offer a solution where science could not.

We found ourselves kneeling along the riverbank, not far from the tents. "Go," I prompted Paul, my voice tinged with a mixture of hope and urgency as I pointed toward the clear water. The river, with its gentle flow a few inches below us, seemed almost too benign to be a source of healing for what we faced.

Paul hesitated for only a moment before he complied, submerging his arm beneath the surface. However, his attempt was brief, lasting less than ten seconds before he began to withdraw it. My frustration bubbled to the surface as I frowned at the hasty action. "That wasn't long enough," I said, my voice firm. Acting on instinct, I reached for Paul's arm, pushing it back under the water despite his protests.

"It's burning!" Paul's shout pierced the air, laden with pain and surprise. He struggled against my grip, a clear indication of his discomfort. Yet, in that moment, my focus was singular—on the potential for healing that the river might hold.

I brushed aside Paul's outburst with a determination that bordered on obstinacy. "Wash your arm," I instructed, my tone leaving no room for argument. The realisation that I shouldn't touch the affected area myself dawned on me, a precaution born of uncertainty and the fear of unknown consequences. Paul's gaze, filled with a mix of confusion and distress, met mine. His eyes, wide and imploring, reminded me of a sad puppy, invoking a twinge of guilt within me. *It's for his own good,* I reassured myself, trying to quell the rising discomfort at causing him pain.

As Paul obeyed, gently swirling the water over his arm, I watched with bated breath. The minutes stretched on, each passing second a testament to our desperation and hope. Then, gradually, almost miraculously, I witnessed the transformation. Paul's skin, previously marred by the ominous marks, began to return to its normal, healthy shade. The sight was nothing short of awe-inspiring, a visual confirmation of the river's inexplicable healing properties.

"Give me your arm," I instructed, my voice carrying a mix of determination and uncertainty. As Paul extended his arm towards me, the water from the river dripping from his skin, I took the bandage and began to wrap his wound with a practiced precision. However, mid-way through, I halted, an idea sparking in my mind.

"What's wrong?" Paul's voice broke through my concentration, tinged with a hint of panic.

"I'm not sure if it will make any difference, but it's worth a try," I found myself saying, more to myself than to Paul. The words were an attempt to bridge the gap between hope and the unknown.

"What is?" Paul's question, simple yet loaded with expectation, pulled me back.

Without a word, I unwrapped the bandage, then submerged it in the river, ensuring every inch of the fabric absorbed the water. The bandage turned a darker shade, heavy with the liquid that might carry the miraculous properties we'd stumbled upon.

"Ahh," Paul murmured softly, a sound that seemed to carry relief. His reaction spurred me on, reinforcing my resolve.

Looking up at him, I tried to project confidence. "It might help to keep the properties of the water on the wound for longer. If we can change the dressing whenever it completely dries out, with a bit of luck, your wound should heal fully," I explained, allowing a small smile of satisfaction to cross my lips. The idea felt right, a blend of intuition and scientific speculation.

Paul shrugged, a gesture of trust in my judgment. "Go for it."

Carefully, I wrapped the soaked bandage around his wound, my movements deliberate. "The sun is too hot," I remarked, the realisation dawning on me as I considered the implications. My face creased in thought once more. "I'll have to find something to protect it. Try to keep it moist for longer." The words were as much a reminder to myself as they were instructions for Paul.

Rubbing at my temples earnestly, I turned my attention to our surroundings, searching for a solution. *But what...?* The question echoed in my mind, a challenge that would no doubt demand a creative response.

FRESH BLOOD

4338.207.6

The sun hung mercilessly in the cloudless sky, its rays beating down without reprieve. The heat was oppressive, turning my skin slick with sweat, each droplet a testament to the exertion of my body under the relentless sun. "Only one more left," I muttered under my breath, the words barely audible over the sound of my laboured breathing. My fingers closed around the small box, lifting it from the dust where it lay, a minor treasure unearthed from the arid landscape.

The thought of it being good exercise, trudging through this endless dust, had long since lost its charm. I had lost count of the trips back and forth, a monotonous trek that seemed to stretch on indefinitely. *We can't go on like this,* I thought, a flicker of frustration sparking within me. The idea of a road, a path, or even a simple trolley seemed like luxuries from another world, anything to alleviate the burden of these monotonous journeys from the Drop Zone—a name I had learned for the area marked by the small rock piles, a waypoint that had become all too familiar.

"Maybe we should just move camp closer," I mumbled to myself, the suggestion born from a mix of desperation and practicality. Each step through the dust felt heavier than the last, a laborious dance with gravity that left my muscles aching for relief. The idea of relocating camp, though daunting, held a glimmer of promise, a potential solution to the endless back-and-forth.

The thought lingered as I dragged another tired step through the dust, the landscape a blur of sun-scorched earth and relentless heat. The notion of moving camp, of breaking the cycle of exhaustion, was a seed of hope amidst the physical toll of our current situation. Yet, even as I considered it, the logistics, the effort required, weighed heavily on my mind. It was a decision not to be taken lightly, but the alternative—continuing in this manner—seemed increasingly untenable. As I made my way back to camp, the box in hand a symbol of our tenuous hold in this unforgiving environment, I knew that something had to change. The necessity for a more sustainable solution was clear, even if the path forward was not.

Arriving back at camp, the weight of the box in my hands now a familiar burden, I noticed Paul standing at the riverbank, his figure silhouetted against the wide expanse of water. He looked deep in thought, almost statuesque in his contemplation. *He's been standing there for quite some time,* I observed silently, curiosity piquing as I wondered what had captured his attention so fully.

Suddenly, Paul's voice broke through the tranquility of the scene. "Yes!" he cried out with a conviction that echoed across the riverbank. His enthusiasm was infectious, even before I understood its cause.

"What is?" I asked, approaching him from behind, my query breaking his reverie and causing him to startle slightly.

Paul turned to face me, a spark of excitement in his eyes that I hadn't seen in a while. "I was just thinking about what you said yesterday. About building a bridge," he shared, his voice carrying a note of revelation as if the idea had just crystallised into something tangible.

"Oh, and?" I prompted, my curiosity now fully engaged. The concept of building a bridge had been a fleeting thought, one of many potential solutions tossed around in the face of our logistical and security challenges.

Paul turned back to the river, his hands moving animatedly as he outlined his vision. He spoke of a primitive wooden structure, an idea so vivid I could almost see it stretching across the river before us. Small wooden slats crisscrossing their way along, bound by an upper railing that reached chest height. My imagination followed his description, painting a picture of a bridge that was both simple and functional.

As Paul's enthusiasm grew, he described turrets that would guard the entrance on each side of the bridge, providing a rudimentary layer of security. His eyes lit up with the prospect of adding these defensive features, a testament to his foresight and consideration for our safety.

I nodded gently, impressed by the creativity and practicality of his plan. *It's creative,* I acknowledged internally. *Simple and practical.* Paul's vision had opened up a realm of possibilities, not just for improving our camp's logistics, but for emboldening us with a sense of capability and hope. The bridge, a metaphorical and literal connection to the broader landscape, seemed like a beacon of progress in our otherwise uncertain situation.

That's all I needed to open the potential of finding my father. The thought, intertwined with our current predicament, reminded me of the broader goals that had brought me here. I had planted the seed of innovation well, now seeing it take root in Paul's imagination.

My next challenge will be getting him to act on it. Determination settled within me, a resolve to see this vision come to life, to transform Paul's enthusiastic blueprint into a tangible structure that could bridge more than just the physical gap between riverbanks. The journey ahead would require collaboration, effort, and perhaps a touch of the ingenuity that had sparked this idea in the first place.

"And," I chimed in, my voice laced with a smile, eager to add a bit of momentum to Paul's enthusiasm, "if we can make them tall enough, I imagine those turrets would provide a spectacular view over the land." The idea of blending function with an aesthetic appeal was appealing, adding another layer of purpose to the bridge.

Paul's smile widened in response, his eyes reflecting a shared excitement for the potential our project held. "So, my simple plan has your approval then?" he joked, his tone light, yet underscored with a genuine curiosity about my thoughts.

I couldn't help but laugh lightly, the sound floating between us like a shared secret. "I think it's the perfect combination of daring further exploration and security. A balance of beauty and practicality." My endorsement was sincere, born from a growing belief in our ability to transcend the limitations of our current situation.

"Exactly!" Paul exclaimed, his excitement palpable. But then, as quickly as it appeared, his enthusiasm seemed to recede, giving way to a more reflective mood. I watched him, intrigued by the sudden shift, the layers of thought that seemed to cloud his expression.

As I studied his face, a realisation dawned on me. Despite the time we'd spent together, Paul remained somewhat of an enigma. I realised I didn't really know very much about him at all. This thought lingered, a reminder of the complexities and depths of the people around us, often obscured by the immediacies of our shared challenges.

"We have to make this work, Glenda," Paul said after a moment, his tone shifting to one of solemnity. His words carried a weight, a sense of urgency that resonated deeply with me. "We just have to."

"I know," I replied, my conviction matching his. In that moment, I understood that our motivations, though possibly different, were aligned towards a common goal. *So, it appears that we both have our own reasons for building that bridge,* I mused internally, a soft smile playing at my lips.

"Shall we get this next tent up then?" I suggested, looking towards the vacant space beside the medical tent. The practicalities of camp life called to us, a grounding reminder of the day-to-day efforts that underpinned our larger ambitions.

"May as well," Paul agreed, his response carrying a hint of the resolve that had characterised our conversation.

As we turned our attention to the new tent, a deep sense of satisfaction settled over me. *I like Paul. He's going to make a very important ally.* This realisation, comforting and promising, bolstered my spirits as we set about our work, the future bridge symbolising not just a physical crossing, but a bridge between individuals, each with their own stories.

❖

The late afternoon sun cast long shadows across our makeshift camp as Paul's voice, brimming with excitement, cut through the air. "Oh my God, I can't believe we're almost done!" His enthusiasm was contagious, a much-needed boost to our spirits after the long hours of labour.

"Glenda," he called across the tent, his tone carrying a mix of admiration and surprise, "You are an expert with tents!"

A smile tugged at the corners of my lips as I straightened up, taking a moment to wipe the sweat from my brow. "I've had plenty of practice," I responded, my voice laced with a modesty that belied the depth of my experiences. Erecting tents had become second nature to me, each one a reminder of the varied landscapes and challenges I'd encountered over the years.

"Really?" Paul's curiosity was piqued, his question hanging between us as he paused in his work, looking genuinely intrigued.

"These are a lot simpler than the large medical tents we used in Borneo." The words slipped out almost reflexively, a casual reference to a past that felt both a world away and as close as the fabric of the tent we were assembling.

Paul gasped, his reaction immediate and filled with a mix of awe and curiosity. "Borneo? What were you doing there?" His question, so innocent and earnest, opened the floodgates to a sea of memories, each wave crashing against the shores of my mind with vivid clarity.

"Oh," I chuckled, the sound mingling with the rustle of the tent fabric in the gentle breeze. The memory of meeting Pierre, that chaotic day that seemed to encapsulate both the beauty and madness of life in such remote locales, washed over me. Pierre, with his easy smile and adventurous spirit, had swept into my life like a tempest, challenging and changing everything I thought I knew about love and partnership.

"That's a very long story. Perhaps we save it for the campfire sometime." My words were an invitation, a promise of stories to be shared under the darkened sky, where the crackle of the fire would weave itself into the tapestry of tales from places far and near.

"Fair enough," Paul called out in reply, his voice carrying a note of anticipation and understanding. His response was a gentle acknowledgment of the complexities and depths that lay within each of us, a reminder that every person carries with them a myriad of stories, waiting for the right moment to be shared.

The moment Paul released his hold, the tent wobbled precariously, sending a jolt of alarm through me. I couldn't help but cry out, a reflexive response to the sudden instability that threatened to bring our efforts crashing down.

"Glenda! You alright?" Paul's voice, laced with concern, reached me even as I struggled to extricate myself from the enveloping tent fabric.

"Yeah," I managed to say, pulling my head free from the tent's grasp. My voice was a mix of frustration and relief as I glanced at the rebellious pole. "I just can't get this darn pole to stay upright." The words were a testament to the struggle, the pole's stubborn defiance a mirror to the challenges we'd been facing.

"Here, let me try." Paul's offer was immediate, his readiness to assist a comforting presence in the midst of the minor setback.

I felt his hands join mine under the fabric, guiding his touch to where my fingers were still wrapped around the pole. "It should just..." I began, hoping to convey the simple yet elusive action needed to secure the pole in place.

"Am I losing my mind?" Kain's voice suddenly cut through the air, his query tinged with a mix of humour and bewilderment as he strolled into camp.

My head turned instinctively towards the sound of his voice, though my view was obstructed by the tent fabric that still partially enveloped me. The sight that greeted me was mostly the tan and green blur of the tent material, a visual barrier that left much to the imagination.

"I don't understand any of this," Kain's voice carried a note of dismay, his confusion echoing around the campsite, blending with the rustle of the tent fabric in the breeze..

Pushing my head further away from the edge of the tent to give myself some space, I responded, trying to offer a semblance of reassurance amidst my own thoughts. "Just give yourself a few days to adjust," I huffed, the words coming out more forcefully than I intended. "It'll all start to make sense in a few weeks."

"It will?" Paul's voice, tinged with skepticism, emerged from underneath the rippling fabric, his head poking out just enough to meet my gaze.

"Sure," I replied a bit too quickly, the realisation of my potentially empty promise dawning on me the moment the words left my mouth. I slunk my head back, trying to retreat from the conversation, hoping to avoid any further scrutiny from Paul.

"So, how is Joel doing anyway?" Paul's question shifted the focus, and I felt a momentary wave of relief wash over me. Paul had let go of the previous line of inquiry, moving on to a topic that, while still fraught with uncertainty, felt slightly easier to navigate.

"He's... umm... he's alive, I guess," Kain said, his voice trailing off as he paused by the campfire.

"That's great..." Paul began, but I was quick to cut in, seizing the opportunity to redirect the conversation.

"Hey, Kain," I called out, an idea forming on how to momentarily shift our focus from the heavy atmosphere that had settled around us. "It looks as though we've left the tent pegs for the next tent back at the Drop Zone. Can you go have a look, please?" My request was deliberate, a strategic move to not only procure the needed supplies but also to give us all a brief respite from the intensity of our situation.

Kain shrugged his shoulders gently, a nonverbal sign of his acquiescence. "Sure," he replied.

"Thanks. It's probably a small, rectangular box." My instructions were specific, an attempt to ensure he knew exactly what to look for amidst the clutter that had accumulated at the Drop Zone.

"Really?" Paul's voice carried a blend of skepticism and curiosity as Kain moved out of earshot, his brow arching in a manner that suggested he wasn't entirely convinced by the timing of my request. The suspicion in his eyes was almost palpable, prompting a defensive instinct within me.

"What?" I countered, striving for nonchalance in my tone. "I remembered I left them on top of one of the larger boxes. I meant to go back for it." My words were hurried, a veneer of casual explanation that I hoped would dispel his doubts. As I spoke, I found refuge in the task at hand, using the tent fabric as a shield from Paul's probing gaze.

"You're a woman of great mystery, Glenda. I'll give you that," Paul remarked, a hint of amusement now threading through his voice. His comment, though light-hearted, underscored the depth of the intrigue that seemed to surround our interactions.

The situation coaxed a giggle from me, a reaction I muffled with my palm. The absurdity of the moment, juxtaposed with the gravity of our circumstances, struck me as unexpectedly humorous. I hadn't intended any deception with my request to Kain. The recollection of the tent pegs had genuinely sprung to mind unbidden. *Although it had been rather timely,* I conceded internally.

In the back of my mind, I recognised that providing Kain with a tangible task might indeed serve as a useful distraction. His recent experiences, the weight of everything we'd been through, necessitated a momentary reprieve—a practical focus that might help him process everything more effectively than a potentially invasive conversation with Paul, who would invariably pursue a line of conversation leading to far too much prodding and questioning than I felt was reasonable at present.

The thought solidified my conviction that I had made the right call, however serendipitous it might have been. *But I needn't tell Paul that,* I reminded myself, a silent acknowledgment of the complexities of human interaction, especially in our current environment.

With that resolution, I turned my attention back to the stubborn tent pole, the physical struggle a welcome diversion from the psychological manoeuvring of moments before. The pole, unyielding and defiant, demanded my focus, a tangible adversary in a world filled with unseen challenges.

❖

Taking a momentary step back from the tent, I could feel the exhaustion mixed with a sense of accomplishment. I paused, wiping away the sweat that had gathered on my brow with the back of my hand—a small, physical testament to the efforts of the day. *I'm impressed.* In the quiet that had followed Kain's departure, Paul and I had managed to complete the third tent and had made significant progress on the fourth, despite the challenge presented by its missing pegs. The realisation of what we had achieved in such a short span of time filled me with a quiet pride.

"There can't be more than an hour or so of daylight left. I'm going to check on Jamie and Joel," Paul's voice cut through my reflections, his words pulling me back to the present.

I looked up at the sky, taking note of the encroaching dusk for the first time since we'd started. *Paul's right.* The sun was indeed on its swift descent behind the mountains, casting long shadows and painting the sky in hues of orange and pink. The beauty of the moment was not lost on me, despite the urgency that dusk brought with it. "Alright," I replied, my voice carrying a mixture of resignation and resolve. The end of daylight signalled a shift in priorities, from construction to preparation for the night ahead.

"I'll get the fire started." The words were simple, yet they carried the weight of responsibility. The fire would be our source of light, warmth, and comfort as the night settled in. It was a task I approached with a sense of ritual, understanding its significance in the context of our survival and morale.

The fire quickly took to the kindling, its flames dancing eagerly as they began their slow conquest of the thicker logs. The warmth and light it provided were comforting, a small beacon of normalcy in the vastness of our surroundings. "Pierre would enjoy this," I murmured to the crackling flames, a nostalgic smile spreading across my face as I imagined him here with me, sharing in the simple pleasure of a campfire under the open sky. The thought of him stirred a mixture of warmth and longing within me, a reminder of the life we shared and the countless moments we had enjoyed together. *But something is missing,* I thought, the smile fading slightly.

"But where would I sit?" I could almost hear Pierre's voice, laced with his charming French accent, posing the question with a playful inquisitiveness. He had a way of making even the most mundane concerns seem significant, his perspective always bringing a new layer of consideration to every situation. And he would be right, as he so often was. The absence of a proper place to sit around the fire felt like a gap in our makeshift sanctuary, a detail overlooked in the rush to establish camp.

Motivated by the memory of Pierre's gentle teasing, I turned my attention to the small stack of firewood. Among the pieces, I searched for the largest and smoothest logs, ones that could serve a dual purpose. Carefully, I arranged them around the campfire's perimeter, creating impromptu seats that offered a reprieve from the dusty ground. It was a simple act, but one that felt deeply significant, a small touch of comfort and consideration that bridged the gap between mere survival and living.

As I stepped back to survey my handiwork, I could almost hear Pierre's voice again, this time offering his approval with a term of endearment that always made my heart flutter.

Perfectly done, my sweet pastry, he seemed to whisper, the sound so vivid in my mind that I could almost feel his breath on my ear.

"Luke's here," Kain's voice broke through the evening calm as he approached the campfire, his announcement drawing my attention away from the flames. Watching him stride past, the soft glow of the fire illuminating his path towards the tents, I noticed the sleeping bags he carried. "Luke!" I called out, eager to catch his attention. It truly felt like an age had passed since our last interaction.

Luke responded with a wave, his demeanour bright and cheerful, a stark contrast to the dimming light around us. The sleeping bag, strapped snugly around his neck, bobbed in rhythm with his movements, a playful companion to his steps.

"Haven't seen much of you since this morning," I remarked, my voice carrying a hint of both curiosity and mild reproach.

"I know," Luke acknowledged, his voice carrying a note of apology mingled with the fatigue of the day's activities.

I didn't pause, eager to convey my observations and perhaps a subtle appreciation for his efforts. "But I've noticed new supplies at the Drop Zone, so I figured you hadn't forgotten us."

"Of course not." His response was simple, yet it carried the weight of commitment, a reassurance that, despite the distance and silence, the bond among us remained unbroken.

My gaze then drifted to the bottle in Luke's grasp, a beacon of warmth in the cool evening air. "Ooh, that's some good whiskey you've got there," I commented, my interest piqued by the promise of a brief respite it offered.

Luke's chuckle was soft, a sound that seemed to dance with the crackles of the fire. "Help yourself," he offered generously, extending the bottle towards me.

With an eagerness that surprised even myself, I took the bottle, feeling its weight and the promise it held. Tilting it back, I allowed the whiskey to wash over me, a wave of heat that coursed through my veins. "Ahh. Just what I needed," I proclaimed, the liquid courage soothing the day's weariness. Handing the bottle back to Luke, I couldn't help but comment, "Whoo," as I shook my head lightly, trying to dispel the potent effects of the alcohol. *That's some strong booze.*

"Where's Paul?" Luke asked.

"He went to check on Jamie and Joel," I responded, trying to maintain a tone of nonchalance as I tossed another small log onto the fire, watching the flames eagerly consume the new addition.

Without waiting for further explanation, Luke took several determined strides towards Joel's tent, his intention clear. "No," I quickly interjected, stopping him in his tracks. "They're at the lagoon." My voice carried across the campsite, hoping to redirect his concern and prevent any unnecessary worry.

"The lagoon?" Luke's confusion was evident as he turned to face me, seeking clarity. "Why the lagoon?"

I hesitated before responding, the weight of the situation pressing down on me. "Joel died... Again," I admitted, the words feeling surreal even as they left my lips. A look of confusion, mirrored by my own feelings of uncertainty and disbelief, spread across my face. *Was he ever really dead... or alive at all?* The question spiraled in my mind, a conundrum that seemed to defy all logical explanation, setting off a pounding in my head.

"Well, that's hardly a surprise," Luke replied after a moment, his tone carrying a hint of resignation. "Perhaps he really was dead." His response, though pragmatic, did little to ease the complexity of the situation.

I could only shrug in response, the ambiguity of Joel's condition a puzzle that remained unsolved. "Perhaps."

"More?" Luke offered, holding the whiskey bottle toward me, an implicit invitation to seek solace in the temporary escape it provided.

"No thanks," I declined, my gaze drifting back to the fire. The warmth of the flames provided a small comfort against the chill of the evening and the swirling thoughts in my mind. Yet, I couldn't help but think that if my head didn't settle, I would definitely reconsider Luke's offer. The thought of numbing the confusion, even for a short while, held a certain appeal as I watched the flames dance.

"Bag," Kain's voice cut sharply through the evening air, his hands gesturing for Luke to throw it over. Without hesitation, Luke, wearing a smile that seemed to momentarily lighten the mood, complied. The sleeping bag arced gracefully through the air, and Kain caught it with practiced ease, his movements swift as he quickly disappeared inside the medical tent.

"Glenda!" The sound of Paul's voice, calling out with a mix of urgency, snapped my attention in his direction. "Joel?" I whispered to myself, more a question to the universe than anyone in particular, as my gaze strained into the distance. The dimming light played tricks on my eyes, but as the figures grew closer, there was no mistaking the sight. Joel was indeed between Paul and Jamie, supported by their arms, his legs moving in a clumsy, uncoordinated fashion that belied a semblance of life I hadn't dared hope for.

Without a word, Luke and I exchanged a glance—a silent agreement—and hurried over to meet the trio as they approached the camp. The sight of Joel, alive in some form, walking however awkwardly, was a jarring contradiction to the reality I had resigned myself to. My heart raced, a mixture of hope and apprehension coursing through me as we neared them.

"He's bleeding!" The urgency in my voice matched the alarm coursing through my veins as I spotted the fresh trickle of blood from Joel's nose. The situation, already steeped in mystery and confusion, had taken another turn towards the inexplicable.

"Luke, get me some tissues from the medical tent." My command was sharp, a reflection of the immediacy of the need.

"Yeah," Luke responded, his voice tinged with a daze that mirrored our collective bewilderment at the unfolding events.

"I got it!" Kain's voice, filled with a proactive urgency, cut through before Luke could even move. He dashed over, efficiency embodied, and handed me the tissues with a speed that spoke of his understanding of the situation.

"Ta," I said simply, my focus narrowing as I pressed a wad of tissues against Joel's steadily bleeding nose. "Let's get him sitting." The directive was clear, aimed at mitigating the immediate concern of the bleeding while we processed the broader implications.

Paul and Jamie guided Joel to sit on a large log by the campfire. "Not too close," I cautioned, wary of the fire's heat and the potential hazards it posed to Joel in his vulnerable state. "Is it just his nose?"

"I think so," Jamie replied, his voice carrying a note of tentative relief that we were dealing with a seemingly isolated issue.

"I didn't even notice it was bleeding," Paul admitted, his confession highlighting the rapidity with which the situation had evolved.

Kneeling in front of Joel, whose condition seemed to defy logic at every turn, I expressed my bewilderment. "I don't understand how," I admitted, the mystery of Joel's condition —a blend of life, death, and now spontaneous bleeding— deepening.

Jamie's head shake was a silent echo of our shared confusion. "I didn't give him any blood, but he seems to have plenty of it now." His words, intended to shed light, only cast longer shadows over our understanding of Joel's state.

Carefully, I prodded several places on Joel's arms and legs, my medical training guiding my hands even as my mind raced to make sense of the situation. "Yes," I confirmed, the reality before me undeniably bizarre. "There is definitely blood in his veins now. It's a medical anomaly!" The declaration was both a statement of fact and an acknowledgment of our foray into the unknown.

Rising to my feet, I accepted the whiskey bottle from Luke, the weight of the moment necessitating a brief respite. "You better lie him down again once the bleeding stops," I instructed, the practical part of my brain already thinking ahead to Joel's care in the immediate future. And with that, I took another swig of whiskey, the strong liquid a temporary balm to the unabated questions and concerns churning within me.

Luke's chuckle, loud and somewhat disbelieving, was a gentle reminder of the surreal nature of our reality. In the face of the unexplainable, sometimes laughter was the only response that made any sense.

Standing there, hands planted firmly on my hips, my gaze was fixed on Joel with a mixture of awe and incredulity. *It's blood. Real blood!* The mantra played over and over in my mind, each repetition reinforcing the bewildering reality of the situation. The sight of blood, flowing from someone we had all but given up for lost, was a stark reminder of how little we understood about our current circumstances.

"Nightfall can't be too far away now," Paul's voice cut through my reverie, grounding me back to the practicalities of our survival. His observation, simple yet laden with the unspoken acknowledgment of the day's end, pulled my thoughts from the realms of medical mysteries to the immediate needs of our group. "I'll prepare us some food."

PROMISE

1338.207.7

As I took my seat on a log opposite the campfire, the flames casting a warm, flickering light across the campsite, Luke moved to join me. The fire's glow, ever comforting in the encroaching darkness, seemed to hold a semblance of normalcy.

"You alright?" I inquired, turning my attention to Luke. His presence, a fluctuating dynamic in our group, offered a momentary distraction from the whirlwind of questions fluttering within me.

"Yeah," Luke replied, his gaze shifting to the fire as he took a long sip of whiskey. The flames reflected in his eyes, a mirror to the turmoil and uncertainty that lay beneath his calm exterior.

The quiet moment by the fire, however brief, allowed my thoughts to drift to my father. *Did my father know about this?* The possibility that he might have had knowledge of the phenomena we were witnessing, and by extension, that he could still be alive, ignited a spark of hope within me. *Somewhere.* The word hung in my mind, a beacon in the vastness of our unknown surroundings.

But then, other thoughts intruded, their memories a tumultuous sea crashing against the shores of my newfound hope. *But Pierre? The Fox?* The questions, relentless in their pursuit, swarmed the fragile peace I had found. *Does any of that matter now?*

Sitting there, beside Luke, with the night drawing in and the fire crackling before us, I was torn between the past and the present, between what I had lost and what I might yet find. The complexities of our situation, the intertwining of personal quests with the immediate demands of survival, left me navigating a labyrinth of emotions and uncertainties. Yet, in the midst of it all, the fire's warmth offered a semblance of comfort, a reminder that, for now, we were alive, and with life, there remained the promise of hope.

❖

As night fully claimed the sky, turning it into a vast expanse of darkness, we found comfort in the simple acts of eating, sharing stories, and depleting the whiskey bottle that had become a symbol of our camaraderie. The sound of laughter, particularly Paul's loud cackle, seemed to echo into the empty distance, a defiant proclamation of life amidst the uncertainty that surrounded us.

"Shh," I cautioned with a playful seriousness, pressing my fingers to my lips in a futile attempt to stifle my own amusement. "The zombie is sleeping," I joked, referencing Joel's inexplicable state with a term that seemed as crazy as the situation itself. My efforts to remain composed failed miserably as I succumbed to a fit of giggles, the absurdity of our conversation acting as a temporary balm to the day's stress.

Kain's laughter joined mine, unbridled and genuine. "Well, I didn't know how else to describe him," he admitted, his words a reflection of our collective struggle to make sense of Joel's condition.

"Are we sure it's safe in there? We don't really know what's going on," Paul mused, his voice lowering but still carrying an edge of concern as he leaned in closer to our small gathering. His question, though posed in jest, touched on the undercurrent of fear and uncertainty that we all harboured about Joel's unpredictable condition.

"Oh," Luke sighed heavily, his patience wearing thin. "Don't be so stupid, Paul." His dismissal of Paul's concern was abrupt, a mix of frustration and denial in the face of our shared unease.

"Ah," Paul gasped, putting on a show of being wounded by Luke's words, his feigned hurt doing little to mask the underlying tension that his question had surfaced.

As Luke staggered to his feet, using my shoulder for support, his movements were unsteady but determined. "Of course, it's safe," he muttered under his breath, more to himself than to anyone else as he made his way toward the silent tent that housed Joel and Jamie. His assurance, though quietly spoken, was a desperate grasp at normalcy, a need to believe that the anomaly of Joel's condition could be contained, understood, and ultimately, posed no threat.

"Is he alright?" Kain's whisper cut through the lingering laughter, his concern for Luke's well-being evident in his hushed tone.

"Oh, he's fine," Paul responded with a dismissive wave of his hand, his nonchalance a façade that barely concealed the complexity of emotions we were all navigating. And with that, the three of us settled into a contented silence, each lost in our own thoughts as the fire crackled before us, a beacon of warmth and light in the enveloping darkness.

"Well, dinner was tasty. Thank you both," I said appreciatively, feeling a momentary sense of normalcy as I tossed my paper plate into the fire. "I wonder whether now might..." My sentence trailed off as Paul's sharp "Shh" cut through the air, a command that immediately drew my attention.

The sound of voices, their pitch and tension unmistakable, echoed from the tent, a discordant note that shattered the evening's fleeting peace. My curiosity piqued, I watched as Paul, with a quiet determination, pushed himself up from the log, his gaze fixed on the tent's entrance.

As a dark figure burst from the tent, the identity of the person was unmistakable. "Luke!" Paul's voice carried a mix of concern and surprise as he called out to the retreating figure. But Luke, propelled by an unseen force, didn't pause. He broke into a run, his form quickly swallowed by the night's embrace.

Paul made a tentative move to follow, but I instinctively knew that intervening might not be wise. With a swift wave of my hand, I signalled for him to stay put. My observations over the past days had hinted at underlying tensions, a silent storm brewing beneath the surface. *Perhaps it hasn't been right for a long time,* I thought, the realisation heavy with implication.

In the midst of our concern for Luke, the night briefly came alive with an otherworldly display. The faint glow of vivid Portal colours danced across the landscape, a fleeting spectacle that illuminated the darkness before disappearing as quickly as it had appeared. The beauty of the phenomenon was stark against the backdrop of our isolation.

Observing the direction and distance of the light, it dawned on me how isolated our camp truly was. If there had been anyone within reach, such a display would surely have drawn attention. Yet, the dancing lights sparked an idea, a potential solution to the challenges we faced. *I really need Paul's turrets,* I realised, the concept of the defensive structures suddenly taking on new significance.

"Yep. Looks like it's definitely you and me tonight, Paul," Kain's voice broke through the quiet of the evening, his statement a simple acknowledgment of our reduced numbers.

"I guess so," Paul agreed, a hint of resignation mixed with a newfound comfort in our current living conditions evident in his tone. "I might get used to this dust yet," he joked, settling back onto his log with a casualness that belied the day's earlier tensions, his foot softly patting the ground in a rhythm that seemed to echo the crackling of the fire.

"Oh no," I interjected, the thought of anyone choosing the ground over a more comfortable alternative prompting a quick response. "There's a sleeping bag for you in the other tent." My words were an offer, a gesture of consideration amidst our makeshift living conditions.

"Really?" Paul's surprise was genuine, the prospect of a sleeping bag, a small luxury in our current environment, seemingly a welcome proposition. "That should make a nice change. But the tent's all yours," he said, directing his comment at Kain with a casualness that suggested a deeper comfort with the outdoors than the confines of a tent. "I'll sleep out here again tonight. I don't want to let the fire completely burn out."

Kain's surprise at Paul's choice was evident. "Don't like the dark?" he teased, probing into the reasoning behind Paul's preference with a lightness that sought to pierce the evening's calm.

"Hmph," Paul responded, a noncommittal grunt that carried more weight than words, his glance shifting towards me as if seeking an ally in the unspoken understanding that had developed among us. "Something like that." His vague reply was an admission of sorts, a hint at complexities and fears not fully voiced.

Remembering my own relief at not having experienced the unsettling events of Paul and Jamie's first night in camp, I chose to step back from the conversation, allowing Paul the space to navigate the topic as he saw fit.

"Is there something out there?" Kain's question, voiced with a cautious curiosity, delved deeper into the night's shadows, probing for threats real or imagined. "Other people maybe?"

"Not that we know of," Paul's response was quick, a dismissal of the possibility that carried with it an undercurrent of the unknown. His words, while intended to reassure, also underscored the vastness of our isolation and the myriad of mysteries that lay beyond the firelight's reach.

Sitting on the log, the uneven surface beneath me mirrored the turmoil of my thoughts. My intuition screamed that Paul's assertion of our solitude couldn't be entirely accurate. *We can't be the only ones here.* Yet, the absence of any sign of others tangled my thoughts into knots. My father's accounts of the Portal, which until now had seemed like mere fantasy, appeared to align disturbingly with our current reality. The notion that I might actually be in an alternate world, or reality, was both fascinating and terrifying in equal measure. It just didn't seem possible, yet here I was, living proof that it was.

"Do you know something that you're not telling us?" Paul's question, sharp and direct, yanked me back to the present, his gaze piercing through the veil of my private contemplations.

I hesitated, the weight of his inquiry pressing down on me. "I'm just as confused as the two of you are," I managed to say, my response a mix of truth and evasion. The reality was that I had more questions than answers, my father's tales now seeming less like the ramblings of an imaginative mind and more like a map to our current predicament.

"I don't think we're safe here," Kain interjected, his bluntness slicing through the night air.

Paul exhaled softly, a sound filled with resignation. "Right now, we don't really have any other option. I'm sure Luke would have warned us if it wasn't safe." His attempt at reassurance felt hollow, based more on hope than certainty.

"Luke doesn't know everything," Kain retorted, his voice loud and laced with skepticism. His dismissal of Luke's knowledge was a jolt.

My eyebrow raised involuntarily, a silent acknowledgment of the complexities within our group. *It seems Paul and I aren't the only ones withholding information.* The realisation that each of us might be guarding our own doubts and discoveries added another layer of interest to our dynamics.

"We'll just have to watch out for each other. We're all we've got right now," Paul stated, his words a pointed reminder of our shared reliance. His glance towards me carried an unspoken plea for unity, a recognition of the fragile thread that bound us together in this unfamiliar world.

Feeling the weight of the conversation and the unsaid accusations, I shifted uncomfortably once more. The implication that I might be concealing vital information was unsettling, igniting a defensive spark within me. "I think it's time for bed," I announced, more to escape the intensity of the moment than from any real desire for sleep. With a decisive slap on my thighs, I rose from the log, leaving the warmth of the fire and the complexity of our conversation behind. The night air felt cooler as I stepped away, a welcome respite from the heat of scrutiny and the burden of unanswered questions.

Pushing my way inside the medical tent, a space that had silently been designated as mine. The interior was dark, save for the faint glow seeping through the fabric walls. Kneeling, I felt the dust beneath the tent floor press against my knees, a reminder of the unforgiving environment that surrounded us.

Closing my eyes, I took a deep, steadying breath. "I'm grateful," I said aloud, my voice a whisper in the vast silence. The words were a simple acknowledgment of the day's end, a moment to centre myself amidst the uncertainty. But as I knelt there, enveloped in the quiet, a realisation dawned on me. *No, this isn't right.* The thought was clear, insistent. *Paul and Kain need this just as much as I do.*

Compelled by this dawning, I quietly exited the tent, my resolve firm. Approaching them again, I inadvertently startled Kain. His surprise sent him tumbling backward off his log and onto the ground. "Glenda!" he exclaimed, his voice sharp with surprise. "What the hell!"

"Sorry," I mouthed, the words barely a whisper as I extended my hand to help him up, an apologetic gesture for the unintended scare.

"Glenda," came a whisper from behind me. Startled, I turned to find Paul, who had moved silently to stand just behind me. The suddenness of his presence caused me to jump, but Kain's firm grip on my hand kept me steady.

Paul chuckled softly at the situation, his apology whispered into the night air as he dropped his sleeping bag onto the dust in front of his log. "Sorry," he said, the humour evident in his tone.

"No, you're not," I replied, my initial surprise giving way to a softer smile. Despite the unexpectedness of the moment, I found a sliver of amusement in our interactions, a brief respite from the weight of our circumstances.

"You don't like the tent?" Kain asked, his question drawing my attention back to the larger issue at hand, his gaze briefly flicking towards the medical tent.

"Actually," I began, my voice steady, signalling a shift in the conversation. "There's something I think we should do as a group first." The words were an invitation, a call to gather not just for practical reasons, but perhaps to solidify the sense of unity and purpose that had begun to form among us. In this moment, standing with Paul and Kain, the idea of solitary refuge in the medical tent felt less appealing than the prospect of facing the night together, as a unified front against the uncertainties that lay ahead.

Kain's brow raised with curiosity. "What is it?" he asked.

"Gratitude," I affirmed, the simplicity of the word belying the depth of its significance.

"Gratitude?" Kain repeated, his tone laced with a scoff, as if the concept was too abstract or inconsequential to consider.

"Hear me out," I insisted, raising my hand to forestall any further objections. The conviction in my voice and the gesture commanded attention, prompting a momentary silence from both of them.

Kain, though still visibly uncertain, held his tongue, allowing me to explain.

I took a deep breath, gathering my thoughts. "It's something my father taught me. I've done it every day since..." My voice trailed off, choked by the sudden surge of emotions at the mention of my father. I swallowed hard, battling the lump in my throat before continuing, "It's become a nightly tradition for me." The words, once spoken, felt like a bridge between my past and our present, a ritual that had offered solace and strength in times both good and bad.

I knelt in the dust near the glowing embers of the fire, the warmth on my face a contrast to the cool night air. "Come join me," I encouraged, inviting them to share in this tradition, to perhaps find in it the same comfort and grounding it often provided me.

After a brief moment, filled with the crackling of the fire, Paul moved to kneel beside me.

Kain, still standing, looked on with a mix of doubt and curiosity. His skepticism was palpable, a barrier to fully embracing the vulnerability of the moment.

"It's okay," I reassured, turning to meet his gaze. "We're not praying or anything." My words were meant to ease his apprehension, to clarify that this act of gratitude was not bound by any specific belief or doctrine but was instead a universal acknowledgment of our humanity, our struggles, and the moments of beauty that persisted despite them.

Taking a deep breath, as if steeling himself against his own reservations, Kain finally knelt in the soft dust on my other side. His action, reluctant yet deliberate, marked a significant moment of unity, a shared willingness to explore this simple yet profound act of gratitude together.

When Kain and Paul had finally settled into the dust beside me, the air around us felt charged with a hesitant anticipation. "I'll go first," I declared, breaking the initial silence that had enveloped us. "I'm grateful for life," I stated calmly, my voice steady despite the tumult of emotions and experiences that had led us to this moment.

As a whole minute of calm silence stretched between us, I sensed their hesitation, their uncertainty about this unfamiliar practice. My elbow found Paul's ribs with a gentle, yet firm nudge, a silent encouragement for him to share.

Yet, the silence persisted, a tangible presence in the night. I found myself staring into the diminishing flames of our campfire, questioning their willingness to engage. *Are they not going to participate? Then why stay?* The thought nagged at me as I nudged Paul a second time, urging him without words to break the silence.

"I'm grateful for the river," Paul finally said, his words coming out hastily but breaking the silence like a stone thrown into still water.

As the serenity of the silence enveloped us once again, I closed my eyes, allowing the simplicity and sincerity of Paul's gratitude to resonate. *Yes,* I thought, *the river is a good thing to be grateful for.* Its presence had been a constant, a source of life and, now, a symbol of gratitude.

Feeling the silence stretch on, my resolve hardened, and I nudged Kain for a third time, determined to include him in this moment of shared vulnerability. *If he is going to stay with us,* I told myself firmly, *he is going to participate.*

"I'm grateful for Uncle Jamie," Kain finally blurted out, his voice tinged with a mix of reluctance and sincerity.

Paul's reaction was immediate, his hand flying to his mouth in a futile attempt to stifle a light snort of amusement. The sound, though brief, shattered the solemnity of the moment.

Kain, frustrated by the reaction, stood abruptly, his movements quick and filled with a palpable tension. "Kain, I'm sorry," Paul called out, his apology trailing after Kain as he stormed past the far end of the campfire, disappearing into the darkness.

As Paul's knees emitted a soft protest, he prepared to chase after Kain into the darkness. Instinctively, I reached out, gently tugging on his arm to halt his intended pursuit. "Don't," I mouthed silently, my voice lost in the quiet of the night.

Paul turned to me, his expression etched with questions, the faint glow of the campfire flickering across his face. I could see the mix of concern and confusion as he tried to decipher my plea.

"He'll be back. There's nowhere else to go," I reassured him, my voice soft but firm. Despite the vastness that surrounded us, our campsite had become a nucleus of our existence in this strange place, a beacon in the unyielding darkness.

Paul's gaze lingered on mine, his eyes narrowing as he weighed my words, the silent communication between us charged with the tension of the moment.

"Besides, we're not done," I continued, an assertion that seemed to hang in the air between us.

"We're not?" His response, laced with surprise, reflected the unexpected turn our evening had taken. The simple act of sharing gratitude had evolved into something more profound, a ritual of connection and reflection in the face of our uncertainties.

As I turned my attention back to the dwindling fire, the flames casting a warm, comforting light, I sensed Paul's hesitation give way to resolve. He knelt beside me once more, his movements slow and deliberate.

In that moment, as I swallowed the lump that had formed in my throat, a tear escaped, tracing a solitary path down my cheek. The vulnerability of the act, the raw emotion it elicited, was both freeing and frightening. "I'm grateful for Clivilius," I whispered, the name evoking a cascade of memories and emotions, a testament to the profound impact of my experiences.

Without waiting for Paul to respond, to offer another piece of gratitude into the night, I rose swiftly to my feet. The need to escape, to find solace within the confines of the medical tent, was overwhelming. My departure from the fireside was quick, a retreat into the sanctuary of solitude where I could ponder the complexities of our situation and the ritual that had unexpectedly opened a floodgate of emotions.

Wiping away several more tears, I couldn't help but chide myself for the vulnerability I had displayed. Emotions, usually kept tightly under wraps, had cascaded forth in a rare moment of openness. Retrieving the sleeping bag Kain had thoughtfully left for me, I freed it from its compact casing, the sound of the fabric unfurling a soft echo in the silent tent. I rolled it out along the tent floor, the action mechanical, allowing my hands to be busy while my mind continued to race.

The darkness enveloping the tent seemed to thicken with each passing moment, a cloak of invisibility that offered a strange sense of security. I rationalised that, cloaked in this pervasive darkness, my privacy was assured until the break of dawn. The notion provided a small comfort, a temporary reprieve from the scrutiny I felt under the watchful eyes of the night sky.

Choosing to lie atop the sleeping bag rather than within it, the warmth of the evening rendering the additional layer unnecessary, I stared up into the void above me. The darkness seemed infinite, a vast expanse that mirrored the depth of my thoughts. I allowed myself a deep breath, a deliberate attempt to calm the storm within, my mind wandering freely over the day's events, each memory a piece to an ever-complicating puzzle.

Joel's condition was a mystery that refused to be sidelined. *Was he dead? Alive?* The questions circled tirelessly in my mind. The waters of this new world, their properties unknown and seemingly magical, teased at the edges of my understanding. *Could they truly possess the power to heal, to reverse death itself, or halt the ageing process?* The notion was fantastical, bordering on the edge of incredulity, yet the tingling sense of purpose it ignited within me was undeniable.

Again, my thoughts returned to my father. *Did my father know about this?* The possibility that he had knowledge of these waters, these powers, and that it could mean he was still out there, alive, filled me with a renewed sense of determination. The stakes had shifted, the game had changed, and with it, my resolve.

"I will find you, father," I whispered into the darkness, my voice a soft but fierce declaration.

4338.208

(27 July 2018)

BROKEN FINGER

1338.208.1

As the early morning sun crested the distant mountains, its warm light began to traverse the barren landscape, reaching out to where I stood just outside the tent. The sight was a gentle reminder of the world's enduring beauty, even in the most desolate of places.

With my fingers interlocked, I raised my arms above my head, indulging in a long, satisfying stretch that awakened every part of my lanky frame. I leaned from side to side, feeling the gentle pull along my sides, a simple yet profound pleasure of movement after a night's rest. Aside from a minor crook in my neck—an unwelcome souvenir of the night that I hadn't noticed until this moment—I was pleasantly surprised by the quality of sleep I had managed to achieve during the very dark night.

The sound of stirring from the tent beside me captured my attention, halting my morning ritual mid-stretch. As I straightened my back, bringing my arms down to my sides, my gaze drifted towards the source of the noise. The tent flap moved slightly, a sign of life within.

"May I enter?" My voice was tentative as I pushed my head through the tent's front flap, unsure of what awaited me inside.

"Yeah," Jamie's response was weary but welcoming, his attention fixed on Joel, who, to my surprise, sat upright. "Come take a look at this."

I approached with cautious steps, my eyes wide with a mix of concern and curiosity. Duke, ever watchful, tracked my movement, his gaze sharp and unyielding, reminding me of our tentative treaty.

"His hand is hurt," Jamie disclosed, gently lifting Joel's arm towards me. His tone was matter-of-fact, yet underlaid with an unspoken worry.

Kneeling beside them, I focused on Joel's hand, trying to ascertain the extent of his injury. The task felt familiar, a return to the routine of medical assessment.

"Wrist movement seems to be fine," I observed aloud, my fingers moving with practiced care over Joel's palm and then to his fingers, seeking signs of damage.

At the slightest touch to his index finger, Joel's response was immediate—a croak of pain that pierced the quiet of the tent. The reaction was so swift, so pronounced, that it left little doubt in my mind about the nature of his injury.

"I believe he has a broken finger," I concluded, my professional assessment made with a confidence born of experience. As I looked up to meet Joel's gaze, a silent communication passed between us—a mix of empathy, understanding, and a shared resolve to navigate this latest challenge.

"How bad is it?" Jamie's voice was tinged with concern, his eyes fixed on me as if searching for a silver lining.

My brow furrowed as I shook my head. "Impossible to say without an X-ray. But with our limited resources, I doubt it would make any difference even if we could," I responded, the reality of our situation laying bare the limitations we faced. My medical training had prepared me for many things, but practicing without the necessary tools wasn't one of them.

Turning to face Jamie, I was met with a look that mirrored a tumult of emotions—bewilderment, sadness, and fear mingling in his gaze.

"I'll go and check what supplies we have. I should be able to take care of it. I can always ask Luke for additional supplies if I need them," I offered, striving to inject a note of reassurance into the conversation.

"You've spoken to Luke?" Jamie's question, laced with a hint of surprise, caught me slightly off guard.

"Not this morning, but I've given him my access card for the Royal. As long as he's careful, he'll have access to all the supplies we'll likely ever need," I explained, the recollection of my decision to entrust Luke with the card bringing a momentary sense of optimism.

Jamie sighed softly, his response revealing a complex mix of emotions. "I'm glad you have that much faith in him."

"You don't?" The question was out before I could stop it, a direct probe into Jamie's trust—or lack thereof—in Luke.

Jamie's reaction was subtle yet telling. His lips pressed together tightly, a clear signal that he was not ready to engage in a discussion on the matter. The shutters came down behind his eyes, a barrier erected to keep his true feelings hidden from view. Without a word, he shrugged, an evasive manoeuvre that spoke volumes.

Refocusing on the task at hand, Jamie uncapped his water bottle and gently held it to Joel's lips. As Joel took clumsy sips, water escaping down his chin, I reached out to dab away the droplets. In that moment, our collective attention returned to Joel, the immediate need to care for him overshadowing the undercurrents of tension and unanswered questions.

"Mind if I look the rest of him over?" I directed my question towards Jamie, seeking his consent to proceed with a more thorough examination of Joel. It felt necessary to ensure that we hadn't missed anything that could complicate his recovery.

Jamie glanced at Joel, who offered a gentle nod of permission, a silent but clear communication of trust and readiness for the examination to continue.

"Go for it," Jamie responded, his attention momentarily diverted by the practical matters of camp life. "I have two hungry dogs to feed anyway."

At the mention of food, Henri, ever attuned to the routine of mealtime, leaped down from his resting place and bounded towards the bags, anticipating the familiar rattle of tinned dog food.

With Jamie and the dogs momentarily preoccupied, I turned my full attention to Joel, determined to conduct a thorough assessment. The whimpers of anticipation from the dogs became a distant backdrop to my focused evaluation.

"Everything else seems to be okay. Your bruises will heal," I reassured Joel after completing my check. He responded with a slow nod, an indication of his understanding and appreciation for the care being given.

"And his neck?" Jamie's voice cut across the tent, concern for Joel's well-being evident even as he attended to the dogs.

I paused to give Joel's shoulder a reassuring squeeze before responding to Jamie, ensuring that both men knew I was taking their concerns seriously. "No sign of infection," I announced, relieved to deliver positive news.

Turning back to Joel, I offered him further advice, speaking clearly to ensure he grasped the importance of what I was saying. "Don't do anything strenuous, and with plenty of rest, it looks like your throat will heal fine."

Though my words were directed at Joel, I was aware of Jamie's attentive presence in the background, listening for any information that might affect their collective well-being. This moment, a blend of professional assessment and personal concern, reflected the depth of our interconnectedness, the way our lives had become intertwined in the pursuit of survival.

Joel's mouth curled into a faint smile, a subtle yet profound indication of his resilience. The morning light, filtering through the canvas window, bathed his face in a soft, pink glow that seemed almost ethereal against his pallor.

"I think it might be worth keeping a bucket of lagoon water here and dabbing some on his neck every few hours. I suspect that might help," I suggested, the idea forming as I spoke. The mysterious properties of the lagoon's water, which had shown remarkable healing capabilities, held a potential that we couldn't afford to overlook.

"Really?" Jamie's surprise at my suggestion was evident, his eyebrows raised in curiosity.

As I looked at Joel, contemplating the enigma of his survival, a thought escaped me louder than intended. "He really shouldn't be alive," I remarked, the starkness of the statement cutting through the air. Realising the potential discomfort my words might cause, I hastened to add, "But he is." The tent's atmosphere tensed momentarily, a reflection of the fine line between life and death we navigated.

"I'd like to set up a lab to study the properties of the lagoon's water. I'll talk to Paul and Luke about it this morning," I declared, my mind racing with the scientific possibilities and the urgent need to understand the forces at play in our survival.

"Why Paul?" Jamie's question, though simple, hinted at underlying currents of concern or perhaps skepticism regarding the distribution of responsibilities within our camp.

"With you preoccupied with Joel, it would make sense for Paul to take responsibility for leading the camp's development," I answered with a firmness born of necessity. The situation demanded clear roles and responsibilities, and I felt no inclination to debate the point.

"Hmph," Jamie scoffed, his dissatisfaction clear. "Why not Kain? Why not you?"

"I'm a medical professional. Medical matters are all that I have any interest in leading," I stated, my voice reflecting a conviction in my role and limitations. The silence that followed was contemplative, my own decisiveness surprising even to me.

"And Kain?" Jamie pressed, unwilling to let the matter rest.

Meeting Jamie's gaze, I weighed my words carefully. "Kain is a strong, young man. Luke was wise to choose him, but he lacks the experience we're going to need for our settlement to thrive." It was a candid assessment, not meant to diminish Kain's contributions but to acknowledge the challenges that lay ahead.

Jamie's attention shifted away, and an uncomfortable silence enveloped the tent. The conversation had broached sensitive topics, revealing the complexities of our interpersonal dynamics and the delicate balance of leadership, expertise, and survival that our survival necessitated.

"Do you want me to get that bucket of water for you?" The question lingered in the air, my offer standing as a gesture of support, considering the day's earlier discussions and the tentative plans we had begun to formulate.

"No," Jamie's response was immediate, his gaze shifting thoughtfully across to Joel, who had settled back into a prone position. The softness in his voice belied the strength of his resolve. "I don't ever want to leave your side, but it'll probably do me good to get a short walk and some fresh air." His words were a poignant reminder of the deep bond forged under these extraordinary circumstances, and yet, a recognition of the need for self-care amidst the ongoing crisis.

"Very well then. I'll be back shortly, and we'll get that finger of yours all sorted," I assured Joel, my hand finding a gentle resting place on his leg as a sign of comfort.

❖

Emerging from the tent, the absence of Paul beside the now cold remnants of last night's campfire immediately drew my attention. My wandering mind was abruptly reined in as my eyes swiftly focused on the trail of footprints etched into the dust. Instinctively, my legs began to follow the path laid out before me, leading me beyond the confines of our temporary shelter and towards the riverbank where I found Paul crouched, attentively examining the wound on his arm, the bandage discarded beside him.

"That's looking really healthy," I announced as I approached, my voice surprising him enough to unsettle his balance momentarily.

"We have to stop meeting like this," Paul joked, his wide grin reflecting a mix of amusement and embarrassment.

My head cocked to the side as I puzzled over his comment. *What does he mean by that?*

"I mean you sneaking up behind me at the river," Paul clarified, his explanation bringing a moment of understanding, though the phrase was still somewhat odd to me.

"Sorry," I apologised, lowering myself to his level to get a better look at his wound. Despite the peculiar context of our conversation, my focus sharpened. Paul's gaze drifted across the river, lost in thought, as I took hold of his arm, examining the healing process more closely.

After a thorough inspection, I released his arm and pushed myself to my feet, ready to offer my final advice. "Keep a close eye on it. Notify me immediately if anything changes.

And remember to soak the bandages in the river," I instructed, emphasising the importance of vigilance and the beneficial properties we hoped the river's water possessed.

"Of course. I'll watch it closely," Paul assured me, rising to stand by my side, his tone sincere and committed.

With a faint smile, I turned to leave, my initial purpose—attending to Joel's broken finger—suddenly springing back to the forefront of my thoughts.

"Hey, Glenda?" Paul's voice reached out to me, a soft inquiry in the early morning light.

"Yes, Paul," I answered, pivoting gracefully.

"Are you happy to keep sleeping in the medical tent for now? If so, Kain and I could share that third tent and we can leave Jamie and Joel where they are," Paul proposed, his tone suggesting a careful consideration of our living arrangements. "Oh, and Luke, if he ever decides to stay the night," he appended, the mention of Luke an afterthought yet laden with unspoken concerns.

"Sure," I responded with a noncommittal lift of my shoulders. The specifics of where I laid my head each night felt trivial in the grand scheme of things. "I don't have any issues with that."

"Great. I'll move my suitcase across as soon as Jamie is awake," he planned out loud.

"They are both awake now. I was just in with them," I informed him.

"Oh," Paul expressed his surprise, the news seemingly altering his immediate plans. "Joel too?" he inquired, a genuine concern in his voice as we made our way back towards the camp's heart.

"Yes. He has a broken finger, but apart from that, he looks to be making a speedy recovery. It's quite remarkable, really," I shared, the awe in my own voice reflective of the miraculous nature of Joel's recovery.

"It is very odd," Paul concurred, a hint of perplexity mingling with his agreement. "I may as well move my stuff now then," he decided, a resolve taking shape in his voice.

"I don't think they'd mind," I reassured him.

Paul's next words carried a softer tone, a shift that caught my attention. "Do you know if Kain slept alright?" He gestured towards Kain, who was beginning to stir from his own slumber beside the now-smouldering campfire.

"I assume so. I didn't notice anything unusual," I replied, puzzled by his concern. "Why do you ask?"

"Just making sure we're all safe, I guess," he explained, the underlying worry for our collective well-being evident in his voice.

"You could ask him yourself. He's awake now," I suggested, encouraging direct communication among us.

"Sure, okay," Paul agreed, nodding once as if to solidify his resolve. "I'll do that then. I'll just grab my bag first." With that, he offered an awkward smile, a brief acknowledgment of the complexities of our interactions, before brushing past me and disappearing into the tent.

Turning toward my own tent, I was gently interrupted by Kain's approach, his movements deliberate.

"Have you seen Jamie this morning?" His voice, rough with sleep, carried a note of concern, or perhaps just the need for a familiar presence.

"I have," I replied, stopping to give Kain my full attention. The importance of maintaining our connections, of checking in on each other, had never felt more pressing. "You should go and visit with him."

"I will," Kain affirmed, stretching his arms high above his head, before vigorously rubbing the back of his neck.

"Do you have a preference as to which side?" Paul's voice suddenly cut in, carrying across the campsite as he emerged from Jamie's tent, his travel bag indicating a move was afoot.

"You and Paul are moving into the third tent," I clarified for Kain, noticing how his expression morphed into one of confusion at Paul's query.

"They're both the same, really," Kain responded, his voice carrying a note of indifference to the specifics of the arrangement. His second stretch, arms reaching towards the sky, enhanced his adaptability, a trait that would be invaluable to us all.

Impressive, I mused silently, admiring Kain's ability to remain unfazed by the smaller details of our shared situation. His casual approach to these decisions, when contrasted with the weight of the unknowns we faced, was a refreshing reminder of the resilience and flexibility we had all been forced to adopt. In a world where so much was uncertain, Kain's attitude towards the mundane offered a glimpse of normalcy, a brief respite from the constant vigilance the rest of our reality demanded.

"I'm going for a walk to the Drop Zone," Paul announced as he emerged from his new home. "Take stock of what Luke's left us."

"I doubt you'll find anything new. I haven't seen him yet this morning. But I'm sure there could be some useful things we didn't notice before," I responded, my voice laced with a cautious optimism.

With Paul heading off to the Drop Zone and Kain making his way to visit Jamie, a brief moment of solitude presented itself. It was an opportunity to focus on the task at hand without distraction. Entering the medical supply tent, I found myself momentarily overwhelmed by the urgency of finding what was needed for Joel. My eyes scanned the scant supplies with a heightened sense of purpose, the reality of our limitations pressing heavily on me.

The supplies were limited, yet, within these constraints, I managed to gather a selection of items that I hoped would suffice in treating Joel's injury. Bandages, antiseptic, and a few other essentials were carefully packed into a large bag, a makeshift medical kit cobbled together from the remnants of what Luke had brought us.

❖

Returning to Joel with the medical supplies in tow, I felt a mix of determination and concern. "You ready?" I asked him, signalling my readiness to attend to his broken finger.

"You don't need me, do you?" Kain asked, his gaze flitting nervously between me and his uncle, searching for an indication of where he should be.

"No, Jamie and I can manage," I assured him, trying to diffuse the tension that seemed to hang in the air. "He's getting good practice." My comment, meant to lighten the mood, inadvertently set off Jamie.

"I'm not your fucking lap-dog," Jamie snapped, his frustration clear and cutting.

Kain's face flushed a deep shade of red at the outburst, a visible sign of his discomfort. Internally, I wrestled with the impulse to respond harshly to Jamie, to snap back at him for his unnecessary aggression. However, experience and instinct held my tongue; such a retort would likely do more harm than good.

Kain, sensing the escalating tension, opted for an escape. "I'm going to give myself a quick wash," he said, his voice low, as he quietly exited the tent, leaving behind the strained atmosphere.

In that moment, I reassessed the situation and decided Jamie's help was not as indispensable as I had initially thought. Kneeling beside Joel, I positioned the bag of supplies against my thigh and focused turned my attention to him.

"Can you sit?" I asked Joel, extending my arms to aid him, my gaze sharp and warning as Jamie attempted to step closer. The message was clear; his presence was more disruptive than helpful at this juncture.

With care, I assisted Joel into a sitting position, his determination shining through despite his injury. It was a small yet significant victory.

Jamie, perhaps sensing his exclusion from the immediate care process, huffed, "I'm going to get the fucking bucket of water." His departure was abrupt, marked by the tent flap closing sharply behind him, inadvertently catching Duke in the process. The dog, quick to follow his master, squeezed through the tent's lower corner, his departure kicking up a small cloud of dust into the already tense atmosphere of the tent.

"Bite down on this," I instructed Joel, offering him a tightly rolled t-shirt for comfort and a distraction from the pain. As I focused, I sensed his apprehension growing, the tension palpable in the confined space of the tent.

"You'll be okay," I reassured him, locking eyes with him to convey confidence and empathy. His blue eyes, wide with fear, reflected his uncertainty. "I need to straighten your finger. I won't lie to you, it's going to hurt like hell, but I need to strap your broken finger to your adjoining fingers to keep it in place." It was important to me that Joel understood what was coming — honesty was paramount in building trust, especially in moments as vulnerable as these.

Joel's resolve was visible as he clenched the fabric between his teeth, his face set in determination.

"You ready?" I asked gently, needing his consent to proceed. It was crucial for me that Joel felt in control of the situation, despite the circumstances.

His nod, though apprehensive, granted me permission. As I carefully straightened his broken finger, I felt his body tense, a natural reaction to the sharp pain. My grip on his wrist was firm, meant to steady him as much as it was to prevent him from pulling away.

"Almost done," I assured him, meeting his pained expression with a smile meant to comfort. "Now we just need to strap it to your other fingers. You may feel a bit more pain, but the worst is over." I wanted to believe my own words as much as I wanted Joel to find solace in them.

As I wrapped his fingers together, I was acutely aware of the balance between gentleness and the necessity of securing the bandage firmly enough to aid healing.

"I'll give you some medication to take the edge off the pain," I assured Joel, gently removing the rolled t-shirt from his mouth, the fabric damp from his clenched teeth. "Do you have any allergies that you are aware of?" It was a standard question, yet essential under the circumstances, given our limited medical supplies and the need to avoid any adverse reactions.

"No," Joel's voice was a hoarse whisper, his head giving a slight shake to emphasise his answer, despite the discomfort it must have caused.

"Okay," I said, turning my attention to the supply bag, my hands beginning to search for something suitable.

"Oh," Joel's voice interrupted my search, causing me to pause. "There is one thing, actually."

"Yes?" My curiosity was piqued, ready for a more conventional concern perhaps.

"Hairy caterpillars." The unexpectedness of his answer momentarily derailed my train of thought.

What an unusual allergy, I mused, my search for medication momentarily forgotten as I looked up at Joel, a mix of curiosity and amusement crossing my face. "I don't think you have to worry about finding any of those critters here," I reassured him with a slight chuckle. "Just take a couple of these, get some rest, and I'll check on you regularly throughout the day."

"Thanks, Glenda," Joel murmured, his voice carrying a hint of relief.

"You're welcome," I replied, offering him a wide smile. Yet, as quickly as the smile appeared, it faded into a more contemplative expression. My mind was torn between the desire to delve deeper into Joel's recent experiences and the professional need to prioritise his immediate physical recovery. My curiosity, however, proved too strong to resist.

"Do you remember what happened to you?" The question was direct, intended to probe for any clues that might shed light on the miraculous nature of his recovery.

Joel's brief hesitation was palpable, a moment of internal debate before he settled on a firm "no."

"Alright, get some rest," I said, my tone softening, my smile returning as an offer of comfort. I quickly gathered the remaining medical supplies, stuffing them back into the bag with a sense of urgency driven by my swirling thoughts.

As I stepped out of the tent, the campsite stretched out before me, empty and quiet. The canvas brushed against my hair, a tactile reminder of the barrier between the relative safety of our makeshift sanctuary and the unknowns that lay beyond.

Joel's memory lapse, whether genuine or protective, added another layer of mystery to his already complex situation. My trust in Jamie and his intentions had been unsettled, the doubt compounded by his possible influence on Joel's silence. This revelation, far from resolving any of my questions, only served to deepen my resolve to uncover the truth behind Joel's circumstances. The intricacies of our survival, intertwined with the secrets we each held, painted a picture far more complex than I had initially realised.

STONE AGE & CIRCLING SHARKS

1338.208.2

"For fuck's sake!" The words slipped out, a mix of frustration and resignation, as I juggled the frying pan over the campfire I'd managed to coax back from the brink of extinction. The bacon was more charred than crispy, the eggs dry and overcooked, a far cry from the hearty breakfast I had envisioned for us. It was supposed to be a small morale booster, a taste of normalcy amid the disruption that had upended our lives.

It had indeed been a rough twenty-four hours for us settlers, a period filled with unexpected challenges and revelations that had tested our resolve and unity. With a long list of tasks ahead, I had hoped to fortify us with a decent meal, something to remind us of the comforts of home, however fleeting that might be. But my skills, honed in the convenience of a modern kitchen, seemed almost obsolete here in the rawness of a barren nature.

It's not like I haven't gone camping before. Those memories seemed almost quaint now, leisurely weekends spent in the wilderness, where the biggest inconvenience was forgetting the marshmallows for s'mores. But campfire cuisine, I realised, was an art form all its own, especially when you're working with limited supplies and under the pressure of survival.

We were essentially living in what felt like the Stone Age, each day a lesson in the basics of survival: finding food, ensuring safety, maintaining health. The simplicity of life had been stripped back to its most basic elements, a stark contrast to the complexity of the world we had known. Adapting to this rustic environment required not just physical endurance but a mental shift, a willingness to learn and grow in ways I hadn't anticipated.

"Everything alright, Glenda?" Kain's voice cut through my mounting frustration, his presence catching me off guard as he returned from his morning wash in the river.

"How the hell am I supposed to control the heat on this thing?" My response came out sharper than I intended, my irritation peaking as I contemptuously tossed the remnants of my failed attempt at breakfast into the coals. "Bacon should be fuck-easy to cook!"

"Would you like me to take over?" Kain offered, moving closer with a calm demeanour that contrasted starkly with my own. He squatted beside me, extending his hand towards the frying pan in a gesture of assistance.

"No!" The word was out before I could temper my reaction, my hand pulling the pan back protectively. Realising my overreaction, I paused, taking a few deep breaths to compose myself. "I need to be able to get this right," I admitted, the frustration of the moment mingling with a deeper sense of determination.

"Well, probably the easiest way to control the heat is to move to a cooler or hotter part of the fire. Looking at the state of that bacon, I'd suggest maybe moving over there." Kain gestured to another part of the fire, his suggestion practical and devoid of any judgment. "It should give you a much lower heat."

His advice was simple, yet it spoke volumes of his understanding of campfire cooking, an expertise I was quickly realising I lacked. Despite the initial sting of my pride, I couldn't help but feel grateful for his calm, practical input.

"Thanks," I conceded, my tone softer now, acknowledging the value of his suggestion. I moved around the edge of the fire to the spot Kain had indicated, a cooler area that promised a more manageable cooking temperature.

"And normally you'd want to cook on a grill plate, help keep the pan level. But we don't have one," Kain continued, providing further insight into the art of campfire cooking.

His suggestion made sense, a small piece of knowledge that underscored how much I had to learn about managing in this environment. "Can I rest the pan on the coals?" I asked, hoping for a simpler solution to my cooking dilemma.

"I wouldn't. Not with bacon and eggs, anyway. They'd end up like charcoal very quickly." His advice came as no surprise, especially after my recent culinary misadventure.

A large ball of saliva squeezed its way down my throat as I glanced back at the now almost unrecognisable bacon that had been hungrily chewed on by the fire. It was a hard pill to swallow, both figuratively and literally, acknowledging my defeat at the hands of a campfire.

"You'll just have to try and keep your arm as steady as you can, and you can always raise and lower the pan from the heat if it gets too hot." Kain's practical tips offered a glimmer of hope, a way forward amidst the trial and error of outdoor cooking.

"I'll talk to Paul and see if he can get Luke to bring us some more camping equipment," Kain offered, his proactive approach a welcome relief.

"Thank you," I said, appreciating his willingness to help as I placed several more strips of bacon into the frying pan, determined to give it another go with the newfound knowledge.

"Oh, and Kain?" I called out as he started towards his tent, a sudden thought striking me.

"Yeah?"

"Paul went to the Drop Zone. Can you please get him for me? Eating breakfast is mandatory for everyone this morning." It was important that we all gathered, a moment of unity and shared purpose in the midst of our challenges.

"Sure," Kain replied before disappearing inside the tent, his agreement swift and without hesitation.

Refocusing entirely on the task at hand, the campfire became my singular challenge, a primitive stove that demanded all my skill and patience. Though my peripheral vision caught Kain's departure towards the Drop Zone, his brief wave going unacknowledged, my entire being was consumed with mastering the art of campfire cooking. In that moment, the simple act of cooking not only became a test of my adaptability but also a symbol of my commitment to provide for our small community.

Despite the earlier setbacks, a sense of satisfaction began to bloom within me as the bacon finally started to resemble the breakfast I had envisioned. The switch from fried eggs to scrambled was not just a mid-preparation pivot; it was a strategic decision dictated by the unpredictable nature of our cooking facilities. The large batch of scrambled eggs, alongside several cans of beans heated to perfection, represented more than just a meal; it was a testament to resilience, to finding a way to thrive even under less-than-ideal circumstances.

Smiling, pleased with the fruits of my labour, I took a moment to appreciate the small victory. Cooking enough bacon for all of us, along with the eggs and beans, felt like a significant achievement. It was a morale booster, a tangible reminder that despite the myriad challenges we faced, we could still enjoy moments of comfort. This breakfast, cobbled together with determination and a dash of creativity, was my contribution to that sense of communal well-being.

As Jamie emerged from the tent, Duke, ever the opportunist, zoomed ahead and positioned himself beside me, or more accurately, beside the food I had painstakingly prepared. His doggy demeanour conveyed an expectation of sharing, a silent plea for a taste of the morning's efforts. Unable to resist those hopeful eyes, I broke off a small piece of bacon and offered it to Duke, who accepted it with an elegance unexpected from such a robust dog.

Then, as if summoned by the scent of food or perhaps Duke's quiet satisfaction, Henri appeared at our side. His arrival was marked by the enthusiastic wagging of his foxy tail, a blur of motion that spoke volumes of his excitement.

"Careful, he's a little..." Jamie's warning trailed off as I extended a piece of bacon towards Henri. In a flash, Henri's mouth opened wide, revealing a set of tiny but sharp teeth, which quickly found their way to my hand.

"Shit!" The exclamation escaped me as I withdrew my hand, startled by Henri's unexpectedly aggressive snatch. The little guy's bite was swift and determined, albeit lacking in precision, *reminding me of a little...*

"... shark," Jamie completed his earlier warning with a laugh, finding humour in the situation that I was still processing with a mix of surprise and slight annoyance.

"But he's always so placid," I protested, eyeing Henri as he gulped down the bacon without so much as a chew, a behaviour that reminded me of Lois, who would consume anything within reach with little regard for manners.

"Unless there's food involved, and he always seems to know when and where." Jamie's observation came with a knowing look, an acknowledgment of Henri's food-driven transformation.

"Hmph," was all I could muster in response, instinctively pulling my hands away from Henri's still eager nose, now diligently sniffing for more treats.

"No more, Henri. You've already had your breakfast," Jamie admonished, his tone firm yet affectionate. It was a necessary reminder, albeit one that Henri seemed to accept with a resigned sniff, his tail's enthusiastic wagging slowing to a more contemplative swish.

"You need to make sure you eat some breakfast too," I insisted, carefully arranging several rashers of bacon and a heaped spoonful of scrambled eggs onto a plate. I navigated the plate towards Jamie, mindful of Duke and Henri, whose eager snouts were animated by the scent of food. Their enthusiasm, while endearing, added a layer of complexity to the simple act of serving breakfast.

"Thank you," Jamie said, his smile genuine as he accepted the plate from me. "Is there some for Joel too?"

"Of course," I replied, a hint of self-reproach colouring my tone. The oversight, however brief, was unlike me. *Why is my brain so scattered this morning?* I couldn't help but question my focus as I reached for another plate, carefully loading it with food for Joel.

"Have some beans too," I added, motioning for Jamie to bring his plate closer once more. I spooned a generous helping of beans onto his plate, aiming to provide as nutritious and filling a meal as possible.

"Thanks, smells good," Jamie commented, his approval bringing a small sense of accomplishment.

Resting the frying pan on the nearby log, I stood up, drawing on years of medical training that had honed my ability to project my voice. "Pau-ul! Ka-ain!" I called out, the urgency of breakfast time lending strength to my shout. "Breakfast!" My voice carried across the campsite, an invitation I hoped would cut through the morning air to reach Paul and Kain at the Drop Zone.

"Where are they?" Jamie asked, his question punctuated by the act of shoving half a rasher of bacon into his mouth, a gesture that spoke to the casualness of our dining arrangements.

"Drop Zone. I'm surprised they're not back by now." My response was tinged with worry.

Jamie's reaction was a scoff, a non-verbal dismissal of my concern as he disengaged from the conversation. "Thanks," he said, a brief word of gratitude as he took Joel's plate and headed towards the tent. His actions, while appreciative, hinted at an undercurrent of lingering tension.

I followed him a few steps, driven by a professional compulsion. "I'd like to be present when you feed him."

"Feed him!? He's not a dog," Jamie retorted, his annoyance clear. The comparison, unintended as it was, struck a nerve. "Speaking of dogs, I wouldn't leave any of the food unattended while the little shark is circling." His warning about Henri, though made in jest, was not without merit, given our earlier encounter.

"Hmm," I murmured, crouching down to protect the remaining breakfast from Henri's opportunistic advances. The disappointment was palpable; missing the chance to observe Joel's condition firsthand felt like a missed opportunity for insight.

"Let me know how he gets on," I requested of Jamie, managing a smile that belied my frustration. It was important to maintain a semblance of cooperation, even in moments of disagreement.

"Sure," Jamie replied, his tone noncommittal as he turned away, Duke following loyally behind.

I eyed the lingering Henri suspiciously. "There's no more for you." My voice was firm, yet gentle, a futile attempt to dissuade his relentless pursuit for more scraps. Henri, undeterred, continued his hopeful vigil, a testament to his unwavering optimism in the face of scarcity.

Suddenly, a loud scream shattered the morning's relative calm, jolting me into high alert. My heart raced, my medical training kicking in instantly, preparing me for any emergency. Jamie, reacting with equal urgency, burst out from the tent, his expression mirroring my own concern.

My mind raced. The scream, unmistakably female, had emanated from the direction of the Portal—a place we had all learned to associate with the unknown, and sometimes, danger. The immediate worry that Paul and Kain might be in trouble was overshadowed by the realisation that their voices would have carried a different timbre. *Where the hell are Paul and Kain?* The question throbbed in my head, a nagging worry that added to the urgency of the moment.

"I'll go," I declared to Jamie, the decision made almost before I was aware of it. My legs propelled me to stand, driven by a sense of duty and the need to act. "You watch the food." It was a trivial instruction, given the circumstances, but it grounded us in the reality of our daily survival, even as we faced the potential for new crises.

Jamie's nod was a silent testament to our unspoken agreement, a mutual understanding born of necessity and trust. Without a word, he moved towards the campfire, taking up the mantle of guardian over our meagre provisions.

As I set off towards the source of the scream, my mind was a whirlwind of possibilities. The urgency of the situation left no room for hesitation. Every step towards the Portal was heavy with apprehension and the weight of responsibility. The unknown nature of our existence here was quickly teaching me to be ready for anything, and as I moved forward, I braced myself for what I might find, my resolve firm and my purpose clear. The well-being of our small community, and potentially a new arrival, depended on my actions in the coming moments.

KAREN

1338.208.3

The voices, loud and carrying moments before, softened as I neared the Portal. Cresting the final dune, I spotted two figures—a man and a woman—crouched in front of the translucent, enigmatic surface of the Portal. Their presence, an unusual sight, piqued my curiosity and heightened my alertness.

"Hello?" My call, tentative yet clear, broke the silence as I continued my approach, jogging lightly over the sand.

"Hey! Over here!" The woman's response was immediate, her voice a beacon as she stood, signalling me with wide, unmistakable arm waves.

"Hello!" I echoed back, slowing to a walk as I drew closer. Caution tempered my steps; the recent unpredictabilities of our situation had ingrained a deep-seated wariness in me. A brief mental risk assessment was necessary—I couldn't afford to throw caution to the wind.

The man, noticeably shorter, rose to stand by the woman, his posture suggesting a dependency or closeness. *Mother and son?* The thought momentarily crossed my mind as I observed their dynamics from a distance.

Deeming it at least somewhat safe to proceed, I decided to introduce myself. "I'm Glenda," I said, managing to keep a chuckle at bay as I extended my hand towards the woman. The initial assumption of their relationship quickly shifted in my mind. *More likely husband and wife*, I reconsidered, noting their familiar interactions.

"Oh, stop it!" The woman's playful reprimand followed a swift whack across the man's back, a response to a whispered comment I couldn't catch. Their interaction, light and familiar, momentarily eased the tension of the unknown.

"I'm Karen," the woman introduced herself, her grip firm and assured as she accepted my handshake. There was a certain strength in her manner, a resilience that seemed to radiate from her. "And this is my husband, Chris," she added, nodding towards the man beside her. Chris, shorter and with a less imposing presence than Karen, offered a stark contrast to her stature.

"Nice to meet you, Chris," I said, extending my hand to him as well. His handshake, though not as assertive as Karen's, carried its own story. The roughness of his skin spoke of labour and toil, qualities that garnered immediate respect in our current circumstances. *Like Luke's,* I reflected, a thought that brought a fleeting sense of reassurance. Luke's Guardian abilities and contributions were invaluable to our collective survival. The comparison prompted a sudden concern. "Where is Luke?" I found myself asking, my curiosity piqued.

"I don't think he's coming," Chris replied, his words succinct, yet they left an echo of uncertainty. Karen's accompanying shrug offered no further clarity, leaving a vague sense of unease hanging in the air.

"He didn't arrive with you?" My curiosity piqued, my eyebrows arched in surprise.

"No," Karen responded, her voice carrying a note of uncertainty. "I don't think this is how he meant for things to happen." Her words hinted at a complexity and intention behind their arrival, suggesting Luke's role was more than incidental.

"It was an accident?" The question slipped out, almost of its own accord, as I tried to piece together the fragments of their tale.

Karen inhaled deeply, the weight of her next words palpable. "I don't really understand it, but Luke made the most beautiful colours appear on the back of the living room door. I wanted to touch it, but he told me not to."

"He did?" Chris interjected before I could voice my own disbelief and the question burning within me. *If Luke had warned against touching it, why had the urge to do so been so compelling?*

"Yes," Karen affirmed, her glare directed at Chris, underscoring a tension that seemed to swell with the recounting of their tale. "And then you came bursting through the door and then, well, here we are." The blame she cast was clear, a direct line drawn from Chris's actions to their current predicament.

"You're blaming me for this?" Disbelief and defence mingled in Chris's response, his bewilderment at the accusation evident in his wide eyes.

"Well, if you had just come through the kitchen like you usually do, this wouldn't..." Karen's argument trailed off, caught in the escalation of a domestic dispute that seemed incongruous against the backdrop of our survivalist reality.

"Excuse me, *excuse* me!" My voice cut through their burgeoning argument, a firm interruption meant to quell the rising tide of blame. "I don't think this is really anybody's fault."

"Of course, it is. It's Luke's fault!" Chris's dramatic proclamation silenced us, a pointed finger of blame that seemed to simplify and yet complicate the narrative all at once.

Karen and I exchanged a glance, both falling silent in the wake of Chris's outburst.

"Accident or not," Chris's voice softened, a slight retreat from his earlier fervour, yet his words carried a weight of conviction. "It was ultimately Luke's carelessness that got us in this situation." His statement hung in the air, a pointed conclusion that seemed to leave little room for debate.

Karen's response was nonverbal, a quiet acquiescence as her head dipped, her eyes finding the ground. The gesture spoke volumes, a silent acknowledgment of the complex web of causality that had led them—and indirectly, all of us—to this moment.

"When can we go back home?" The question from Chris was directed at me, a plea for clarity amid the uncertainty that enveloped them. It was a question I had heard before, a reflection of the hope and desperation that clung to the idea of returning to what was familiar.

"We're not," Karen's voice cut through, her reply sharp and devoid of hesitation. Her interruption was unexpected, preempting my own response, and it caught me off guard.

How does she know that? The question echoed in my mind as I turned to look at Karen, her declaration surprising me. Her certainty, her acceptance of our reality here, was unsettling in its immediate finality.

"This is our home now," she stated, a definitive closing of the door on any notions of return. Her words, though simple, reshaped the contours of our conversation.

"It is?" Chris and I asked in unison.

Just how much has Luke told her about this place? The question lingered in my mind, a puzzle piece that refused to fit neatly into the emerging picture of our shared narrative. Karen's knowledge, her acceptance of our permanence here, suggested a level of understanding that went beyond the initial shock and confusion expected of a newcomer. It hinted at conversations, at revelations shared between her and Luke, that had not necessarily been extended to everyone.

Karen's brow furrowed, signalling a deep dive into her thoughts before she formulated a response. "Do you remember the times that we sat in bed at night and I used to joke about all of those crazy dreams Luke told Jane and I about on the bus?" she asked Chris, her question laden with a newfound significance.

Dreams? The word echoed silently in my mind, igniting a spark of intrigue. *Luke's had dreams about this place?* The possibility that our current reality could have been foreshadowed in Luke's dreams was both fascinating and unsettling.

"Yeah," Chris replied, his initial skepticism giving way to a dawning realisation as the implications of Karen's words began to settle. His eyes widened, reflecting a mixture of astonishment and apprehension.

I found myself captivated by the unfolding conversation, an observer to a revelation that seemed to bridge the gap between the mundane and the mystical. Karen bent down gracefully, her movements deliberate as she scooped up a handful of the dusty ground beneath us.

"Hold your hands out," she instructed Chris, a solemnity in her tone that commanded attention. Chris complied, extending his hands forward with a hesitance born of uncertainty and curiosity.

"I think it may actually all be real," Karen continued, her voice soft yet imbued with a conviction that seemed to solidify with each word. She slowly allowed the dust to cascade from her hand, a symbolic gesture that seemed to underscore the gravity of her realisation. The fine grains tumbled through the air, landing in Chris's open palms—a physical manifestation of the ethereal truths they were beginning to confront.

"Shit," Chris breathed, his reaction a succinct encapsulation of the shock and awe that such a revelation warranted. His response, punctuated by sharp intakes of breath.

Karen looked to me, her eyes alight with curiosity and a hunger for answers that seemed to mirror the intensity of the sun above us. "How many people are there? Are we close to the capital? And what about the facility?" Her questions tumbled out in rapid succession, each one a testament to the layers of confusion and hope that seemed to envelope us all.

My expression must have shifted dramatically because as I silently echoed her words, *Capital? Facility?* I could feel the confusion writ large across my own face. "What facility?" The words felt foreign on my tongue, out of place in the simplicity of our current existence.

"You know, the breeding facility," Karen elaborated, as if the term should have sparked recognition. My mind, however, drew a blank, the concept so alien it might as well have been, ironically, from another world.

Capital. The word resonated with a distant memory, a fragment from conversations with my father. Yet, the facility Karen mentioned was entirely unknown to me. *What the hell is Karen talking about?* The questions began to multiply in my mind, each one branching off into a myriad of possibilities. If Karen harboured beliefs about other people here, about a structured society with a capital and facilities, then her knowledge was crucial.

Chris's voice cut through my spiralling thoughts, bringing me back to the present. "I don't think Glenda knows what you're talking about," he said, his tone a mixture of concern and clarification. His intervention was timely, halting the barrage of questions I was on the verge of unleashing.

I'll ask her later. The resolution formed solidly in my mind. *I'll ask her about everything.* There was so much I needed to understand, so many pieces of this puzzle that Karen and Chris could potentially help assemble. But as the immediate reality of our situation reasserted itself, the flicker of hope that had briefly ignited within me sputtered and died. The vast unknowns that lay beyond our small settlement seemed suddenly insurmountable.

"There's only a few of us. We're just a tiny settlement," I confessed to Karen and Chris, the words heavy with the weight of our isolation. In the grand scheme of things, our group was but a speck in the vastness of this new world, our knowledge and understanding limited to the immediate challenges of survival.

"Take us," Karen's words carried a hint of excitement, a spark that almost managed to reignite my own sense of wonder. However, it wasn't quite enough to dispel the layers of unease that had settled over me since their arrival.

"Sure," I responded with a nod, a gesture of acceptance rather than enthusiasm. Despite the swirling questions and concerns, Karen and Chris didn't present any immediate threat. Introducing them to our small camp seemed the right thing to do, though I braced myself for the potential disappointment they might face. The reality of our settlement was far removed from any preconceptions they might have had about organised societies or structured facilities.

As we walked, the thick dust underfoot marked our passage through the vast, arid landscape that surrounded us. It was a silent journey, Karen and Chris following quietly behind me, their presence a constant reminder of the unpredictable nature of the Portal. Every step seemed to stir up more than just the loose earth; it churned a mix of apprehension and curiosity within me.

WELCOME TO BIXBUS

1338.208.1

"Not much of a settlement, is it," Chris remarked as we approached the cluster of tents and improvised structures that made up our small encampment. His tone carried a blend of disappointment and disbelief, as if the reality before him fell short of an expectation he hadn't realised he'd held.

"Is this it?" Karen's voice echoed Chris's sentiment, her confusion palpable.

"This is it," I confirmed, my voice steady despite the undercurrent of apology I felt for their apparent letdown. "Welcome to Bixbus." The name of our settlement, chosen in a moment of camaraderie and perhaps a touch of whimsy, suddenly felt exposed under their scrutiny.

"Bixbus?" Chris's repetition of the name was tinged with a mix of surprise and curiosity. "I thought we were in Clivilius?"

"Oh," I managed between light laughs, "we are in Clivilius, but we've called our own little settlement Bixbus."

"Oh," he said, his demeanour shifting to one of sheepish acceptance.

I watched Karen intently as she stood there, lost in her own thoughts, her moment of introspection interrupted by Jamie's emergence from the tent, Duke faithfully at his heels. It was only then, with the camp's daily life resuming around us, that I noticed the frying pan lying upside down in the dust, its contents—a mishmash of scrambled eggs—strewn about. An inward sigh escaped me. *All that effort for breakfast, now just part of the landscape.*

"Duke?" Karen's voice was tinged with a note of recognition as she squatted down to greet the eagerly tail-swishing dog. Her familiarity piqued my interest, pulling my attention away from the disappointment of the spoiled breakfast.

"You know him?" My curiosity was genuine, the distraction from my earlier frustration welcome.

"Not really," Karen admitted, her gaze shifting from Duke up to me. "I've seen pictures. Is Henri here too?"

A heavy sigh left me as I glanced towards the remnants of our intended meal by the campfire. "I'm assuming he had something to do with that mess?" The question, directed towards Jamie, who had been tasked with food supervision, carried a blend of accusation and resignation.

"That assumption would be correct," Jamie's response came, an admittance of the morning's culinary misadventure. "Now he's sulking in his bed."

"Not quite," I couldn't help but laugh, the absurdity of the situation and Jamie's description of Henri's sulking lightening my mood. I pointed towards the tent, where Henri had emerged and stopped a few meters from the entrance, perhaps intending on joining his brother or returning to the scene of his culinary crime.

"Hi, I'm Jamie," Jamie introduced himself with a straightforwardness that had become a hallmark of his personality.

"Ahh, Luke's partner," Karen recognised him almost immediately.

"Yep."

"This is Karen, and her husband Chris," I interjected, ensuring proper introductions were made, hoping to bridge any gaps of familiarity quickly.

"Bus friend, Karen?" Jamie inquired, a trace of curiosity threading through his words.

"Yes," Karen replied, her voice tinged with a soft chuckle. "That'd be me." Her acknowledgment seemed to carry a weight of shared history, a connection to Luke that predated our current circumstances.

"I'd normally say nice to meet you, but this is hardly a fun place to meet in," Jamie stated, unapologetically.

"Do you mind if Chris and I take a moment for a quick chat, just us?" Karen's request came suddenly, her gaze flitting between Jamie and me.

"Sure," I agreed without hesitation. "A river runs behind the tents. Might make a more pleasant spot for you."

"Thanks, Glenda," said Karen, then she grabbed Chris by the arm and dragged him away like a mother pulling their child from the confectionary shelves at the supermarket.

As the new couple vanished from view, Jamie exchanged a nonchalant glance with me. With a carefree shrug, he turned as if ready to return back to his tent.

"Wait! Do you hear that?" I suddenly exclaimed, my voice laced with a mix of curiosity and growing unease.

Jamie, caught off guard by my abrupt halt, stopped in his tracks. His head tilted to the side, his face wrinkling in concentration as he strained to catch the distant sound that had caught my attention. "Engine?" he asked, his voice carrying a hint of skepticism.

"It definitely sounds like a vehicle," I replied, my gaze fixed on the unseen source of the noise. Jamie stepped closer to me. "That's impossible... isn't it?" I added, my voice trembling ever so slightly.

My heart began to race, its frantic beats echoing in my ears. I couldn't help but wonder if we were about to face the unexpected. *Other people? Are they friendly or a potential threat?* My mind raced with a whirlwind of questions, and a cold shiver ran down my spine. *What had happened to Paul and Kain? Are we in danger?*

"Shit," I whispered under my breath, my eyes darting around the campsite, searching for anything that could serve as a defensive weapon. Panic flickered in my eyes. "We should arm ourselves."

"Huh?" Jamie's eyes widened, his expression a mixture of disbelief and confusion.

"Quickly," I insisted, my voice taking on a note of urgency as I tugged on his arm with determination. "We need to arm ourselves."

Scanning the area for anything that could be useful, I picked up the closest log I could find. It had served as a makeshift seat around the campfire moments earlier, but now it seemed destined for a more formidable role. "No, too heavy," I muttered, quickly discarding the idea. My eyes darted around, seeking a more suitable option. "Aha! Perfect!" I exclaimed, snatching up the upturned frying pan from the nearby cooking area. I held it up as if it were Excalibur itself, a makeshift shield against an uncertain threat. I looked up at Jamie, determination in my eyes. "This should do, yeah?"

A grin split Jamie's face, his relief palpable. "It's only Paul and Kain!" he exclaimed, his laughter filling the air, defusing the tension that had gripped us moments ago.

"Oh, it is?" I asked, rising to my feet and squinting toward the horizon. A cloud of thick sandy dust billowed in the distance, obscuring my view of the approaching vehicle. Jamie's assurance, however, proved accurate as I soon discerned the familiar silhouette of a ute struggling through the haze. The harsh Clivilius sun cast long shadows, outlining the distinctive frames of Paul and Kain in the front seats. Even before the ute pulled to a stop at camp, their contrasting heights and distinctive facial features became unmistakably evident through the dusty windshield.

With a jarring stop that kicked up a small storm of dust, the vehicle finally came to a halt in our campsite.

"That was bloody awesome!" Kain shouted with unbridled enthusiasm, his voice filled with excitement and adrenaline as he and Paul met at the front of the ute for a hearty high-five. The dust had painted their faces and clothes with a gritty veneer, but their expressions radiated a contagious sense of accomplishment.

"Apart from clogging up the engine!" Paul laughed in response, shaking his head at the unexpected detour they had taken.

"Where the hell did that come from?" Jamie called out, his curiosity piqued by the dramatic entrance.

"Come on," Kain replied, his focus seemingly fixed on the thrill of their recent adventure rather than Jamie's question. "You have to admit even that was fun."

I watched their camaraderie unfold, torn between relief at their safe return and a lingering sense of unease. The dust settled around them, coating everything in a fine layer of ochre, but the atmosphere in our camp was anything but settled.

"Guys!" I shouted, my voice breaking the reunion as Karen and Chris returned from their private conversation. "We have two new guests."

"I wouldn't call them guests," Jamie interjected flatly, his words laced with a heavy dose of skepticism. "They're not going anywhere."

The group fell into an eerie silence, the realisation of this new dynamic sinking in like a lead weight.

Paul was the first to break the icy silence. "I'm Paul," he said, extending his hand toward Chris with a tentative smile.

"Chris Owen," the short, thin-haired man replied, shaking Paul's hand with a cautious nod. "And this is my wife, Karen," he added, glancing toward the woman beside him.

"Nice to meet you, Karen," said Paul, offering her his hand as well.

Kain introduced himself next. "Kain," he said, following Paul's lead. "Jamie's nephew."

"Ahh," Karen's eyes lit up with recognition.

"I see you've met Jamie," Paul said, motioning toward where Jamie had retreated to stand under the canopy of his tent with Henri perched at his feet.

"We've only just met, but Luke has told us a lot about him over the years," Karen explained, her voice tinged with a mix of warmth and curiosity.

"Us?" questioned Chris, his brows knitting in confusion. "I've never heard his name before."

"Not you, darling. Jane," Karen clarified, a fleeting smile gracing her lips.

"Who's Jane?" Kain inquired.

"Oh," Paul exclaimed loudly, drawing everyone's attention. "You must be one of Luke's bus friends."

"Yes," Karen replied simply, her gaze drifting back to Chris.

"But where is Luke?" Kain asked, turning to Chris for answers.

"He's not here," Karen responded on Chris's behalf, her voice tinged with an air of finality that hung heavily in the air.

"Appears this was another accident," I chimed in, my voice heavy with disappointment as I responded to the questioning glare Paul shot my way.

"Figures," Kain muttered under his breath, his words just audible enough for everyone to catch, reflecting the sombre mood that had settled over our camp like a dark cloud.

"Not to be rude, but what do you actually do?" Paul inquired, his curiosity apparent as he sought to understand the newcomers.

I couldn't help but feel a spark of amusement at the question. *I thought I could be blunt,* I mused to myself, my lips curling into a cheeky smile.

"I'm an entomologist," Karen replied, her face lighting up with pride at her profession.

"A what?" Paul's brow furrowed in confusion.

"She studies bugs," Kain chimed in helpfully.

"Oh," Paul's expression remained a portrait of crinkled bewilderment.

"Insects," Karen corrected Kain, glaring at him. "Insects, not bugs."

They are different, I found myself agreeing with the woman.

"Well," Karen began, her tone matter-of-fact. "Insects need an environment to thrive. I work with the University of Tasmania to understand how they contribute to ecosystems and collaborate with local communities and environmental groups to advocate for greater protections." She delivered her explanation with a fervour that left little room for interruption, barely pausing to take a breath.

"That's great!" Paul exclaimed, his eyes brightening with newfound understanding as he absorbed Karen's passion and purpose. He then gestured for Chris to answer the same question.

"I do yard work," Chris replied, his response significantly less grandiose than Karen's.

"Yard work?" Kain questioned, his tone reflecting his curiosity.

With a calm demeanour, Chris crouched down and silently scooped a handful of the dusty ground beneath us, letting it trickle through his fingers like a fading hope.

"It's everywhere!" Paul exclaimed, his exasperation evident in his voice.

"Fucking oath, it is," Jamie added with a touch of bitterness, finally rejoining the conversation after his temporary withdrawal.

"Yeah, I've noticed that," Chris said, still gazing at the dust slipping through his fingers. He then looked up at his wife, a determination in his eyes. "But if this is our home now, we'll find a way." His words held a resilience that hinted at the challenges they had already faced and those that lay ahead, echoing the uncertain future that loomed over all of us in this inhospitable landscape.

"Call me crazy," Karen said with a warm smile directed at her husband, "But I trust Luke."

"You're definitely crazy then," Jamie sneered loudly, his derisive tone cutting through the conversation like a knife.

Anger surged through my veins, and my fists clenched reflexively. *What an arrogant prick!* I thought, my jaw tightening with frustration. I was on the verge of letting my outrage spill out in words when Karen unexpectedly beat me to it.

Karen stood her ground, her eyes radiating a steadfast determination as she faced Jamie's skepticism. Her voice, filled with an unwavering sense of optimism, flowed like a gentle stream. "A beautiful masterpiece starts with a single brushstroke. This is our blank canvas, let's create a masterpiece together."

My mouth fell open, and I found myself caught off guard by Karen's unexpected eloquence. Her words hung in the air, a poignant reminder of the hope that seemed to persist even in the face of adversity. I couldn't help but be intrigued and moved by her perspective.

I have to find out what you know! I thought, directing my unspoken words towards Karen, a silent plea to uncover the source of her unwavering faith in Luke.

"I better check in with Joel," Jamie finally broke the heavy silence that had settled like a shroud over the camp. His words carried a weight of concern as he seemed to hesitate, unsure of what to make of our new companions. "Nice to meet you both," he added, offering a brief half-wave before disappearing inside the tent.

"Joel?" Karen's voice held a note of curiosity, her raised brow indicating her desire for more information.

"Jamie's son," I replied, offering a hint of context to ease her confusion.

"He's not been well," Paul chimed in, his eyes briefly darting toward me, as if seeking my approval before revealing more. "I'm sure he'll be fine after a few days' rest."

"Yes," I agreed, interpreting Paul's discretion as a cue to refrain from delving deeper into Joel's enigmatic condition. I returned his sidelong glance with one of my own, a silent acknowledgment of our shared understanding. "Perhaps you and Kain would be best moving back in there for a short time," I suggested, nodding in the direction of Jamie and Joel's tent. It was the practical thing to do, given the limited shelter.

Shadows cast over Paul's face for a moment, but then a glimmer of hope brightened his eyes. "We have another tent," he exclaimed enthusiastically, pointing towards the ute.

"Brilliant!" I couldn't help but exclaim with genuine relief. *The discovery of Luke's supplies couldn't be timelier,* I thought to myself, silently thanking the absent Luke for his foresight.

"Looks like they got a little dusty," Kain remarked, his words carrying a hint of amusement as he hoisted the first box from the back of the ute. With a rough shake, he attempted to dislodge some of the clinging red dust that coated the top, causing a small puff of the fine particles to scatter into the dry air, creating a fleeting crimson cloud.

I watched with a mixture of fascination and trepidation as the cloud dissipated, the dust settling slowly back to the ground like a veil of forgotten memories.

"Here, let me take that," Chris offered, his voice calm as he stepped forward to take the box from Kain's hands.

"Thanks," Kain responded.

"May as well put it next to ours, I guess," Paul suggested, his eyes scanning the expanding campsite, and he pointed to the location of the third tent on the far right. It was clear that our makeshift settlement was growing, slowly but surely.

Chris nodded in agreement and began making his way toward the indicated spot, the box cradled carefully in his arms.

"Tent pegs," Paul declared, holding up a small box he had retrieved from the ute. He extended it toward Karen, offering her the essential items.

"Thanks," Karen said, her voice reflecting a hint of relief as she accepted the small box, her eyes drifting towards her husband's retreating figure as he set down the box he was carrying.

"I'm going back to the Drop Zone for the concrete," Kain announced as he swung open the front door, causing the hinges to creak in protest. Meanwhile, Paul redirected his attention towards the ute, preparing to collect the final box.

"Hold up," Paul interjected abruptly, his hurried steps nearly causing him to fumble with the box in his grasp as he rushed over to grab hold of Kain's arm.

"What?" Kain retorted, yanking his arm free with an easy, fluid motion. "If you want these sheds up, we gotta get this concrete poured asap."

Paul's brows furrowed in contemplation. "Five to seven days?" he inquired, seeking confirmation.

"Five to seven days," Kain affirmed, nodding as he spoke. "Although if we're going to keep getting these cloudless skies, we might get away with four."

I leaned against the opposite side of the ute's roof, observing their exchange with a sense of curiosity. Their conversation had captured my interest, but now I found myself somewhat perplexed. "What takes five to seven days?" I interjected, seeking clarity.

"We have to let the concrete rest," Paul explained.

"Ahh, that makes sense," I acknowledged, nodding in agreement. "How many sheds are we talking about?"

"Not sure," Kain replied. "I'll check how many Luke's left us."

"We may as well do as many slabs as we can for the concrete we have available," Paul suggested, his gaze sweeping across the barren landscape surrounding us. "I don't think we can have too much storage and protection here."

"And Luke can always bring us more sheds," I added optimistically, hoping to inject a note of encouragement into the conversation.

"I'll bring all the concrete supplies we have then," Kain declared, a sense of purpose in his voice as he swiftly climbed into the driver's seat, preparing to head back to the Drop Zone.

"I'll come with you," Paul offered, taking a step toward the passenger side of the vehicle.

"No offence," Kain began, his tone cautious, "but maybe you'd be better off helping Glenda with the new tent."

"Chris and I can help," Karen chimed in, rejoining the group with her husband in tow. "We're accustomed to camping on our short research trips. It shouldn't take too long."

I welcomed the offer with a sense of gratitude. The prospect of additional assistance brought a measure of relief.

Paul's enthusiasm was undeniable, but I couldn't help but acknowledge Kain's preference to work without him. *His practical skills are somewhat... lacking*, I thought to myself, casting a glance toward Paul.

"Okay," Paul replied, his shoulders slumping slightly as he shrugged. "So, what am I doing now?"

As the group fell into a heavy silence, all eyes turned toward Paul. I couldn't help but feel a twinge of pity, watching his initial excitement begin to wane. "You're helping us put the tent up," I said, my voice as cheerful as I could muster, hoping to buoy his spirits and make him feel included in our efforts.

CORIANDER EXPRESS

1338.208.5

"Where the hell did that come from?" I blurted out in my thick Swiss accent, my words a sharp contrast to the quiet focus that had enveloped our small group. The suddenness of my exclamation seemed to startle the Owens, who were crouched beside the tent, their attention riveted on several tiny seedlings that had miraculously sprouted from the barren ground.

"There's a thick crust beneath all the layers of dust, and there appears to be living soil beneath that crust," Chris explained patiently, his words deliberate and clear.

I couldn't help but be captivated by the revelation, my curiosity driving me to crouch beside them. My long fingers gently brushed against the delicate, green leaves that reached for the sun. "Fascinating," I murmured softly, awe colouring my tone as I marvelled at the resilience of life in this harsh environment. "And the plants?"

"Coriander seeds," Karen answered, her voice filled with a mix of wonder and intrigue, as she waved a small zip-lock bag in the air for emphasis.

I regarded the couple with an inquisitive expression, my curiosity piqued by their revelation. Chris and Karen had stumbled upon something unexpected, and I couldn't help but wonder about the story behind their find.

"She's always carrying some sort of seeds... or bugs," Chris remarked, his words tinged with a hint of amusement, as if he had grown accustomed to Karen's peculiar habits.

"They're not bugs," Karen interjected flatly.

The tiny seed Karen held in her hand beckoned my attention. "May I?" I inquired, extending my palm toward her. My interest in the reasons for Karen's seed collection was minimal, but I was acutely curious about the rapid transformation of a seed into a seedling. I wondered if that was indeed what had happened.

"Glenda, grab the pole!" Jamie's urgent shout interrupted my thoughts. Impatience welled up within me, and I couldn't resist joining in Jamie's exhortation. "Yeah!" I yelled impatiently, not turning my attention from the small coriander seed that Karen had placed in my hand.

With a sense of anticipation so palpable it felt like an electric charge in the air, I pressed the small seed into the soil in Chris's cupped hands and stared at it, my eyes unblinking, as if willing it to reveal its secrets.

It didn't take long for the magic to unfold before my eyes. A gasp escaped my lips as I watched the seed crack open, small roots sprouting and eagerly anchoring themselves to the soil particles. A tiny stalk emerged, adorned with the first delicate leaves, as the coriander seed rapidly transformed into a seedling.

"What the fuck are you doing?" Jamie's angry voice cut through the air as he approached us, his frustration palpable.

"Come take a look at this," I responded, unfazed by his harsh outburst, my excitement overriding any concern for his anger. I waved him over with exaggerated enthusiasm, eager to share our discovery.

"What is that?" Jamie demanded, his gaze fixed on the coriander seedlings in Chris's hands. Frustration still etched deep lines on his forehead, refusing to dissipate.

"They're coriander plants," Karen answered, her tone lacking the same level of enthusiasm that had infected me.

"Did you bring those plants here?" Jamie pressed, his voice tinged with suspicion.

"In a manner of speaking, yes, I did," Karen admitted.

"In a manner of speaking?" Jamie echoed, clearly puzzled.

"We found the soil beneath the hard crust hidden beneath all the dust and sand," Karen elaborated, her words delivered with a sense of justification. "A few seeds accidentally fell out of my pocket and landed in the soil."

"And look what happens," I interjected, eager to demonstrate the wonder of our discovery. I reached into the bag and retrieved another coriander seed, placing it in Chris's trembling hands.

"My hands are getting a little tired," Chris complained, his palms slightly shaky as he held the seedling.

"Last time," I assured him, and Karen reached under her husband's hands to provide additional support.

"Just because you've planted something doesn't mean it's going to grow," Jamie retorted impatiently, skepticism etched in his tone.

"Just watch. It's incredible," I whispered, my gaze unwavering as I fixated on the small ecosystem taking shape within Chris's hands.

A wide, exhilarated smile stretched across my face as the coriander seed cracked open, just like the previous one, and rapidly began to form tiny roots, a delicate stem, and its very first leaves. The miracle unfolding before me filled me with a sense of wonder, and for a moment, the harsh reality of our situation seemed to fade into the background.

"This is great news," Chris remarked, his gaze lifted towards the vast expanse of empty land that stretched out around us.

My eyes widened with a sudden influx of thoughts and possibilities. "Perhaps this might help explain Joel's condition," I ventured, looking up at Jamie, my voice tinged with a newfound hope. *Maybe my father's stories still held some truth, and there was indeed a place teeming with life somewhere out there.*

"I'm not sure that Joel was buried in the dirt," Jamie responded bluntly, his skepticism unwavering.

"Maybe not," I conceded, my optimism tempered but not extinguished. "First, it was the lagoon water, and now the soil. There is definitely something different about this place," I mused, my thoughts racing as I contemplated the mysteries hidden beneath the desolation of our surroundings.

"Chris and I will make the study of the soil our priority. It may be possible to get a controlled ecosystem up and running," Karen declared, her energy surging as she spoke, her eyes bright with newfound determination.

"Hold up. Don't get too ahead of yourselves," Chris interjected, his cautionary tone slicing through the buoyant atmosphere. "We should still exercise a great deal of caution. Sure, these plants are a great sign, but we don't know what the conditions here are really like. You and I have been here for less than a day, and the others not much longer. We have no idea what dangers we might yet face. Cracking the surface could release more than we realise."

"With miracle soil like this, it can only get better from here," I chimed in eagerly. Somewhere in the recesses of my mind, I acknowledged the wisdom in Chris's warning, but the thrill of bringing life to our dreary settlement quickly overshadowed my caution. I looked up at Karen, my eyes ablaze with enthusiasm. "I'm ready to paint that masterpiece with you, Karen," I declared, fully embracing the possibility of transformation and renewal in our challenging new world.

All four heads snapped in unison towards the roaring sound of an approaching vehicle, the sudden intrusion shattering the moment of hope and excitement that had enveloped us.

"I'll go," Jamie declared with a disgruntled huff, turning on his heel and striding away towards the source of the disturbance.

"What do we do with these plants now?" I inquired, my gaze shifting from the approaching vehicle back to Chris and Karen.

"We keep them safe," Chris replied, lowering his cupped hands and carefully planting the fragile seedlings. "The tent should provide a little shade and protection from the sun."

"We had better finish putting it up," I suggested, pushing myself to my feet and extending my hand to Karen, assisting her in standing.

Karen cast an expectant look toward her husband, awaiting his decision.

"I want to see how far this soil spreads," Chris declared after a moment, his voice carrying a mix of curiosity and determination. He rose to his full height, placing his hands on his hips as if to physically brace himself for the vastness of the task ahead. His gaze swept across the landscape, taking in the expanse that surrounded us—a sea of dust and dirt that seemed both oppressive and oddly liberating in its boundlessness.

HOPE

1338.208.6

"What do you make of them?" Kain inquired as I squatted beside him, watching as he and Jamie meticulously ran the screed over the freshly poured concrete slabs for the sheds.

"It looks mostly even. Maybe a bit more over there," I replied, extending a finger to indicate the spot that required a touch-up.

"I meant the new people," Kain clarified with a chuckle, his eyes briefly leaving the concrete to meet mine.

I glanced in the direction that Karen and Chris had wandered off to. Chris's determination to follow the trail of fertile soil had been unwavering, and after assisting with the tent, Karen had eagerly joined him in his quest. "They are well educated, especially Karen. I can see why Luke chose to bring them here," I mused, my thoughts drifting towards our new arrivals.

"You really think..." Kain began to ask, but our conversation was abruptly interrupted by the enthusiastic barking of a dog.

Looking up, a wide, joyful smile instantly spread across my face. I recognised that bark, and my heart leaped with excitement. Rising to my feet, I scanned the surrounding landscape, searching for the source of the familiar sound.

"Lois!" My voice carried across the camp, filled with excitement and anticipation. I began jogging towards her, my heart lifting with each step. The sight of my beloved golden retriever cresting the nearest hill and bounding towards me with unbridled joy, was a balm to my soul. Her silky fur seemed to catch the sunlight, rippling with each movement, embodying the essence of freedom and loyalty.

As I crouched down to welcome her, Lois wasted no time in lavishing me with a sloppy greeting across my cheeks, her tail wagging furiously. I laughed, a sound of pure joy, as I clapped her shiny fur enthusiastically. The feel of her warm, soft coat under my hands, the genuine affection in her eager licks, momentarily grounded me in a sense of normalcy and home.

As Joel emerged from the tent, Duke and Henri flanking him like a pair of mismatched guardians, Lois's exuberance was palpable. She bounded over, her energy infectious, her golden fur a blur of motion and light.

"Lois, down!" My voice, firm yet affectionate, aimed to temper her enthusiasm, not quell it. Approaching the trio, I watched as Joel, despite his recent ordeal, crouched down to welcome Lois's affection. He wrapped his arms around her, his actions gentle, a soft smile playing on his lips as he stroked her fur. The sight was heartwarming, a small but significant testament to the healing power of companionship.

"Seems she likes you," I observed, my smile broadening at the sight.

Duke began his approach, his movements deliberate as he circled around, sniffing curiously. The suddenness of his sniffing caught Lois off guard, prompting a playful jump backward. Her tail, however, continued to wag excitedly, a clear sign of her enjoyment of the moment.

Meanwhile, Henri, displaying his usual reticence, made a swift retreat into the tent, likely seeking the safety and comfort of his bed.

Lois, undeterred by Duke's cautious assessment, continued to jump around playfully, her joy uncontained. Watching Duke proceed with his careful investigation of Lois, I was reminded of the delicate dance of animal interactions, each movement and response a language of its own.

"We need a road," Paul's declaration cut through the air as he made his way down the final slope into camp, his voice carrying the weight of a decision that seemed overdue. The dust kicked up by his steps settled slowly, marking his path.

Lois immediately left Duke and Joel's side to greet Paul, her tail a blur of excited wagging. It was a simple joy, the kind that Lois always brought with her.

Caught off guard by Paul's sudden toss, my reflexes kicked in, and I managed to catch the keys thrown in my direction. The unexpected action brought a brief moment of surprise, quickly replaced by curiosity.

"Ooh, you're a gorgeous girl," Paul cooed at Lois, his attention fully on her as he crouched down to lavish her with affection.

"My car's here?" The question slipped out, laced with disbelief as I held up the keys for Paul to see. His casual confirmation, "Yeah," as he continued to focus on Lois, sparked a mix of relief and concern. "It got bogged just over the hill," he added, almost as an afterthought.

"We definitely need a road," Kain chimed in, finding humour in the situation.

"I wouldn't be laughing if I were you," Paul retorted, his tone playful yet pointed. "You wanna be the one to collect the stuff in it or dig it out of the dust?" His question, a gentle jab at Kain's amusement, underscored the reality of the task ahead.

"Honestly," I huffed, my patience thinning. "This camp is like living with a bunch of children sometimes." My words, though spoken in a moment of frustration, carried a hint of affection for our makeshift family. Turning, I began to walk towards where Paul had indicated, Lois and Duke trailing behind me, their presence a comforting constant.

"I don't think she's got any children," Jamie's voice followed me, his joke a light-hearted attempt to ease the tension.

"I heard that!" My response, shouted over my shoulder, was a mix of mock indignation and amusement. Despite the challenges, the jests and jibes, there was a sense of camaraderie that bound us together, a reminder that we were not just survivors but a community, navigating the complexities of this new world side by side.

❖

As the BMW finally came into view, my heart sank a little. There it was, my once shiny charcoal vehicle, now cloaked in a layer of ochre dust that seemed to mock the efforts of keeping anything clean in this environment. With a hefty sigh, I approached, my palm automatically reaching out to brush against the bonnet in a futile attempt to restore some of its former glory. The realisation of my mistake hit immediately, but with no better option available, I resignedly wiped my now dust-covered hands down the front of my slacks, grimacing as I did so. The fabric, already bearing the marks of camp life, accepted another layer of the land's signature.

"Fuck! You've done a good job, Paul," Jamie's voice, laced with a mix of sarcasm and disbelief, cut through my resignation as he crouched beside the car's buried back wheel. His tone was light, but the underlying critique was clear.

"It all happened so quickly," Paul defended, his voice carrying a note of frustration mixed with resignation

"I bet it did," Jamie retorted, his skepticism barely masked by the casualness of his reply.

Kain's soft chuckle offered a momentary reprieve from the tension. Turning my attention to the passenger door, I opened it to find a collection of blankets and pillows stuffed into the seat—a makeshift storage solution that now seemed almost comical.

The movement of Paul walking away caught my attention, prompting a reflexive call from me. "You're not staying, Paul?" My voice carried a mix of surprise and concern. His departure felt premature, especially given the task at hand.

Paul paused, his response hanging in the air between us. "I don't think Luke's done yet," he said, the ambiguity of his statement leaving more questions than answers. Then, without further explanation, he turned and continued walking.

"Think we can dig it out?" Kain's voice broke through the quiet as he crouched beside Jamie, assessing the situation with an eye for action rather than resignation.

"We're gonna need more than just our bare hands," Jamie countered, his tone realistic yet not defeated.

"Lois!" My voice cut through the air, a reflexive attempt to call back the golden retriever now trailing after Paul, her loyalty split between her human friends. But the call was ignored, or perhaps unheard, lost to the vastness of the landscape. I watched, a twinge of sadness mingling with resignation, as Lois and Paul's figures blended into the horizon beyond the next rise.

"Do you want to carry anything back now? Or wait to see if we can dig this car out?" Jamie's question, pulling me back from my thoughts, was pragmatic.

"Hmm," was my initial, non-committal response as I poked my head back through the passenger door, my hand reaching for something familiar amidst the uncertainty. My fingers found my memory-foam pillow, a small piece of comfort in a world that had been turned on its head. "I'll take this one for now," I decided, pulling the pillow out with a decisive tug.

"Joel?" Jamie's voice held a mix of surprise and concern as he called out. His tone immediately put me on alert, the casual conversation forgotten.

"I'll check on him when I get back to camp," I had replied initially, assuming Joel was safely resting. But Jamie's next words sent a jolt through me.

"Joel! What the hell are you doing here?" Jamie's voice, now filled with urgency, propelled me into action. I spun around so quickly that the pillow I was holding smacked against the car door, nearly slipping from my grasp.

"Help," came a weak, croaking voice from Joel. It was barely more than a whisper, but it was laden with determination.

"You need help?" Jamie rushed to Joel's side, his voice laced with concern, while gesturing for me to come over.

Joel, however, shook his head quickly, his eyes bright with a different kind of plea. "Help," he repeated, his finger pointing not at himself, but at the car ensnared by the dust.

Jamie's protective instincts kicked in. "I don't think that's a good idea. You should be resting," he argued, trying to coax Joel back towards the safety and comfort of the camp with a gentle, guiding pressure on his shoulders.

"Here, take this," I interjected, stepping forward. My movement was swift, brushing aside Jamie's hand as I reached out to offer the pillow to Joel. "As long as you are careful, I think some movement will be beneficial," I said, my voice firm yet encouraging. It was a delicate balance, acknowledging Joel's desire to contribute while mindful of his ongoing recovery.

Jamie's pout was almost palpable as he turned back to face Joel, his concern evident. "Are you sure you can manage?" he asked, his voice a mixture of resignation and hope.

Joel's response was a silent nod, a gesture of quiet confidence that spoke volumes.

Hands now free, I turned my attention back to the car, delving into the chaotic assortment of items that had been hastily thrown into the backseat. As I sifted through the pile, my heart leaped, a surge of joy washing over me as my fingers brushed against the familiar, hard case. *My violin!* Extracting it with care, I cradled the case in my arms, a sense of relief and unexpected happiness enveloping me.

"This must mean that Luke spoke with Pierre!" The realisation burst from me in a mix of excitement and wonder, my voice echoing slightly in the open air as I rested the case on the car's bonnet. Carefully, I opened it, half expecting to see Pierre smiling back at me from within. The violin lay there, untouched and serene, a bridge to a life that felt both distant and achingly close.

"Your husband?" Jamie's voice, laced with curiosity, cut through my reverie.

"Yes," I answered, the mere mention of Pierre's name stirring a whirlpool of emotions within me. "I miss him terribly already." The words were a mere whisper, an admission of the loneliness that had taken root in my heart since I arrived here.

"How does your violin imply that Luke spoke with Pierre?" Jamie's skepticism was not unexpected, yet it stung a little.

"I highly doubt that Luke would have known to bring me my violin," I countered, my voice carrying a mix of conviction and hope. The violin wasn't just an instrument; it was a piece of my soul, a connection to Pierre and the life we shared. It was inconceivable to me that Luke would have known its significance without Pierre telling him.

"You'd be surprised," Jamie retorted, a hint of amusement in his tone that implied he knew more about Luke's capabilities and thoughtfulness than I did. His words hinted at a depth to Luke that I had yet to fully appreciate, a reminder that we all had layers and secrets yet to be uncovered.

Returning the violin to its case, my emotions swirled, teetering between relief and a sudden spike of anxiety. "Where is Kain?" The question slipped out, laced with concern. His absence, unnoticed until now, sent a brief wave of panic through me, quickening my heartbeat.

"He went to the Drop Zone to see if there are any more shovels so we can dig this fucking wheel out," Jamie's response was matter-of-fact, though his choice of words betrayed his frustration with our current predicament.

A thought occurred to me, prompting me to tilt my head inquisitively. "Aren't there shovels near the shed site?" It seemed a logical place to find such tools.

Jamie's expression twisted, his nose scrunching up as if the answer left a bad taste. "They're covered in cement." The simplicity of his statement did little to mask the underlying implications of a day that had clearly not gone as planned.

My eyes narrowed, a mix of disbelief and resignation colouring my tone. "How the hell did they get... never mind." The question died on my lips, the details of their misadventure suddenly irrelevant. In this new reality, the absurd had already become commonplace, and I found I didn't really want to know the answer.

Turning my attention back to the violin, I pulled the case closer, wrapping my arms around it in a tight embrace. A wave of warmth cascaded down my spine, a sensation that seemed to echo the faint stirrings of hope within me. Lois's joyful return and now my violin—these were not mere coincidences but symbols of a thread connecting me to a past that still held sway over my heart. A silent thank you formed in my mind, directed at Luke, wherever he might be. His actions, whether directly intended or not, had brought me a measure of comfort and a reminder that amidst the uncertainty and challenges, there were still reasons to hold onto hope.

OLD & NEW

4338.208.7

The distinct woodiness of the smoke emanating from the blazing campfire filled the air, wrapping me in a blanket of unexpected comfort as I settled my log-seat into the dust. Just forty-eight hours earlier, the thought of calling this arid, seemingly desolate landscape home would have been unfathomable. Yet here I was, finding a sense of belonging in a place where, beneath its harsh exterior, lay a force so compelling and mysterious it defied easy explanation.

"Lois!" My voice was a sharp whisper, a mix of admonishment and affection, as I tugged firmly on her collar, urging the golden retriever to sit beside me. Lois, with her boundless energy and loyalty, had taken to following Paul around all day as if he were the sun itself. While Paul's patience with her was something I was deeply grateful for, I knew Lois well enough to recognise the signs of her potential for overexuberance. Years of companionship had taught me the fine line between her joyful enthusiasm and the moment it could tip into intolerance.

"Butter chicken for you?" Luke's voice broke through the evening air, a welcome sound amidst the crackle of the campfire. He extended a plastic container towards Paul, filled to the brim with the rich, aromatic Indian dish. My mouth watered at the sight, a visceral reminder of meals shared in far-flung places, of a time in Borneo where the exotic had been commonplace. Here, amidst the dust and challenge of making this place home, food had taken on a new significance—a luxury rather than a given.

"Yeah, thanks," Paul's voice carried a note of genuine gratitude as he took the container from Luke.

Luke then turned to Karen, who sat somewhat awkwardly on her log-seat next to Paul. "Chicken tikka?" he offered, the casualness of his tone belying the careful consideration behind the choice.

"How did you know?" Karen's face lit up with a smile as she accepted the container, her delight unmistakable. She quickly ran a finger down the side, catching a dribble of sauce before it could escape.

"Lucky guess," Luke replied, his grin wide and infectious.

"Oh my God, Lois," I muttered in hushed exasperation as Lois, ever the bundle of boundless energy, slipped from my grasp. Her bum wiggled with excitement, her tail a frantic pendulum, as she lovingly nudged her head against Paul's thigh, her affection for him obvious.

"Anything is fine," Chris chimed in, his attention momentarily diverted as he accepted a container from Luke, a grateful nod accompanying the gesture.

"Lois, sit!" My voice, firm yet filled with affection, aimed to corral her enthusiasm as I reached over to regain control, my hand clasping her collar and pulling her back towards me with a gentle firmness.

"Look, Lois, even Duke has settled," Jamie joined in, attempting to coax Lois into emulating Duke's calm demeanour. Duke himself lay serenely between him and Joel, a picture of tranquility with his head resting on his paws, a stark contrast to Lois's vibrant energy.

"And butter chicken for you," Luke directed towards Jamie, his attention on distributing the meals rather than the canine commotion, handing over a container with a practiced ease.

"Thanks," Jamie responded.

I leaned over to Lois, pressing a kiss atop her furry head and letting my hand glide along her side in a gesture of praise for her fleeting attempts at calmness.

"Hey, what about Joel?" Jamie's voice cut through the evening calm, an edge of concern sharpening his words as Luke, carrying an array of fragrant Indian dishes, moved past Joel to offer me a choice. In that moment, Lois, perked back up, her attention captured by the tantalising scent wafting through the air. Her nose twitched with interest, a testament to the allure of the spices mingling in the containers Luke held.

"I'm sorry," Luke's voice carried a mix of apology and surprise as he retreated a few steps, the revelation catching him off guard. "I didn't realise he could eat." His admission was sincere yet tinged with uncertainty.

My brow arched, a silent observer to the unfolding drama, my interest piqued not just by the situation but by the palpable tension that seemed to thicken with every exchange.

"Of course, he can fucking eat!" Jamie's response was sharp, a flash of anger punctuating his words, a protective fervour for Joel evident in his tone.

"What do you want?" Luke shifted his attention to Joel, offering an assortment of food with an open, questioning gesture. The variety in his arms suggested a willingness to accommodate, yet the simple action felt weighted with deeper significance under the current circumstances.

Joel's response was a silent shrug, his quietness not born of indifference but perhaps uncertainty or even discomfort.

To be honest, I found myself caught between skepticism and hope. Joel's condition had rendered him nearly voiceless, casting doubt on his ability to partake in something as normal as eating. Yet, here we were, contemplating it. Keeping Lois by my side, I watched closely, a part of me analysing the situation with a clinician's eye. The learning opportunity was undeniable, the situation unfolding before me a vivid reminder of the resilience of the human spirit and the adaptability we were all forced to embrace in this new and uncharted existence. The necessity of medical observation in these moments wasn't just academic—it was a lifeline to understanding, to adapting, and perhaps, to healing.

"Beef madras okay?" Luke inquired, his gaze intently fixed on the container in his hands, as if the meal selection required his full attention. The simplicity of the question belied the care behind it, a reminder of the small choices that now felt significant in our stripped-back existence.

"Sure," Joel's voice was a raspy whisper, a stark contrast to the lively discussions around us. His acceptance, though quiet, was a sign of his gradual reintegration into our makeshift community, each meal shared a step towards whatever semblance of normalcy we could muster here.

"I don't really like anything too spicy," I found myself saying as Luke approached, the warmth from the container he held seemed to radiate a comforting promise of a hearty meal.

"Looks like butter chicken it is for you, too," Luke's response came with a light-hearted ease as he handed me a container, the heat greeting my palms through the plastic. "Good thing that's what I got the most of."

"You really can't go wrong with a good butter chicken," Kain chimed in, his voice carrying a mix of anticipation and contentment. It was a sentiment that resonated with us all, a shared appreciation for the familiar comfort found in food.

"You can have the last one then," Luke declared, passing the final container of butter chicken to Kain before settling down with his own meal.

The aroma that escaped as I cracked open my container was immediately intoxicating, a rush of spices and warmth that felt like a hug in the cool evening air. *Smells delicious!* The thought was a silent celebration, my anticipation heightened as I allowed the scent to envelop me.

"Sorry, not for you," I whispered down to Lois, who had been drawn by the smell, her eyes wide with the hope of sharing, as I leaned down to place another kiss on her head.

❖

"Ahem," Paul's throat clearing cut sharply through the ambiance of clinking utensils and satisfied murmurs. The camp fell into a momentary hush, all eyes turning to him as he stood, imposing a pause on the evening's casual camaraderie. "I need everyone to check in at the Drop Zone regularly to see whether Luke has brought any of your belongings. Or perhaps there might be something there that you find you need."

"That sounds reasonable enough," Chris responded, nodding in agreement, the simplicity of the request seeming to resonate with him.

"Reasonable?" Karen's voice was laced with disbelief as she turned to her husband, her incredulity mirrored in her eyes. "It's a long way to walk just to check. I'm too busy to wander over to simply... check."

I was about to voice my thoughts when Jamie quickly chimed in, aligning himself with Karen's stance. "I'm with Karen on this one," he asserted, his tone edged with a hint of irritation. "Too busy."

"Busy!" Paul's retort was sharp, a flash of frustration breaking through his typically measured tone. "All you've done is sit in the tent for the past two days!"

"Fuck off, Paul!" Jamie's outburst was sudden, his frustration spilling over as a piece of chicken tumbled from his fork to his lap, a visual accent to the tension that snapped in the air.

Amidst the escalating disagreement, Chris's voice emerged once again, calm and practical. "I'm happy to wander over. It'll be a nice break and good to see what's there," he said, his demeanour unbothered by the brewing storm, as he continued to eat with an unshaken focus.

The exchange, a snapshot of our collective struggle to adapt and prioritise, left me pondering the balance between necessity and convenience, individual tasks, and communal responsibilities. The friction, though unsettling, was a reminder of the varied perspectives and coping mechanisms within our small group, each of us navigating this new existence with our own set of expectations and limitations.

Seizing the moment to affirm Paul's contribution, I voiced my support. "You make a good Drop Zone Manager, Paul," I commended him, a statement meant both to acknowledge his efforts and to foster a sense of unity and purpose among us.

Kain, ever the joker yet not always at the most opportune times, couldn't resist adding his quip, "Well, he is shit at building things," barely audible yet clear enough for those of us nearby to catch. The tension it briefly introduced hung in the air.

In the pause that followed, I addressed the group. "I think our settlement has more chance of thriving if we each focus on our strengths," I stated, a gentle reprimand in my glance towards Kain, who avoided my gaze, his attention suddenly captured by his meal.

Lois stirred at my feet and after her sniffing nose got pushed away from the food in my lap, with wagging tail, she decided to bother Duke. *She's done well*, I told myself, conceding to allow the two dogs more play time. *Probably best they tire themselves out now before bedtime, anyway.* The thought made me reflect on the circumstances of Lois's arrival. *So unexpected.*

Turning back to the matter at hand, I reinforced the suggestion to Paul. "With Luke bringing supplies through so quickly now, perhaps it would be best if the Drop Zone had a dedicated manager." It was a role that, despite the levity and occasional jibes, was crucial for our nascent community's organisation and efficiency.

Paul's acceptance, though resigned, was a commitment to take on a role that utilised his strengths and contributed to the greater good. "Fine," he acquiesced, the weight of responsibility settling on his shoulders. "I'll be responsible for notifying people when things arrive for them and for keeping the Drop Zone in some sort of order."

Karen's enthusiasm was palpable, her exclamation serving as a bright, affirmative beacon in the growing dusk. "Marvellous!" she declared, her voice carrying a spark of excitement, perhaps a bit too eagerly.

"But–" Paul's interjection carried a weight of practicality, drawing the word out as if to brace us for the inevitable complexities his suggestion might unfurl. "If I am going to be going back and forth so often, we need to do something about this bloody dust! We need to build a road." His point, albeit laced with a hint of frustration, resonated with undeniable logic.

"That sounds fair enough," I concurred, the memory of my recent struggle with the dust clouding my agreement with a personal understanding of the task's urgency. The thought of regularly facing that ordeal was less than appealing.

"I can help with that," Chris offered, his enthusiasm almost tangible as he raised his hand, embodying the spirit of a committed volunteer.

"Yeah, I guess we could all pitch in," Kain added, his voice carrying a mix of reluctance and resolve. His gaze wandered, seeking, and perhaps needing, the reassurance of consensus from the group.

"I'll help too," came Joel's contribution, his voice raspy but determined.

This consensus, quickly reached, was a telling moment, a reflection of our evolving dynamic. It was interesting to observe how readiness to assist became more pronounced when the issue directly impacted them. *Guilt, responsibility, or simply a growing sense of community?* The motivations might vary, but the outcome was a collective commitment to improvement.

Draining the last of my sauce, I indulged in a moment of personal satisfaction, a small, silent celebration of not wasting anything, especially in such sparse conditions. *Never let a good sauce go to waste*, as my mother would say, her words echoing in my actions. The slurps, loud in the quiet that followed our decision, were more than just the consumption of sauce; they were a nod to preserving and appreciating the small comforts, even here, even now.

❖

The fire's glow was a beacon in the night, casting long, flickering shadows that seemed to play upon the faces of those gathered around, creating a tapestry of light and darkness that danced across their features. It was a vivid contrast to the all-consuming blackness that enveloped everything beyond our small circle, turning the surrounding desert into a void of unseen mysteries. The air was tinged with a crispness that heralded the night's chill, sending shivers down my spine and causing goosebumps to erupt along my arms where my sleeves fell short.

Wrapped in a blanket of silence, save for the occasional crackle of the fire, my senses seemed heightened, attuned to the slightest whisper of sound. It was then, amidst the tranquil stillness, that a soft, raspy voice cut through the quietude, pulling at the edges of my awareness. My heart skipped a beat as the realisation dawned on me. "Joel!?" I whispered, my voice a mix of surprise and incredulity. The humming, barely discernible at first, gradually took shape into words, weaving a melody that seemed to resonate with the very air around us. Since he had offered his help earlier, Joel had remained a silent, almost spectral presence among us; hearing his voice now felt like uncovering a hidden layer to the young man I had yet to truly understand.

*"Let us celebrate our story
The words we've yet to write."*

Joel's song, simple yet profound, stirred something within me, a feeling of connection to the moment, to the people around me, and to the vast, untold future stretching out ahead. It was as if his words were a call to arms, a reminder of the stories we were living and those yet to be written. The resonance of his voice seemed to vibrate through me, touching a chord deep within my soul and awakening an almost magnetic pull toward my violin. It was a feeling beyond explanation—a deep-seated need to join in, to meld my own musicality with his in the creation of something beautiful.

I couldn't help myself; I moved, almost without thinking, my actions propelled by the force of the emotion his song had evoked. My sudden movement, a disruption in the stillness, caused him to halt, his voice trailing off into the night. "Please, don't stop. You have a beautiful voice," I found myself saying, the words tumbling out in a rush of earnestness. I wanted more than anything for him to continue, to fill the night with the beauty of his song and allow me to become a part of it with my violin.

Joel's response was a faint nod, a subtle acknowledgment that carried with it an air of humility and a depth of emotion that words could not convey. As he resumed his humming, the melody weaving its way back into the night, I felt a profound sense of gratitude and connection.

Cursing under my breath, the darkness felt almost tangible as I navigated my way into the tent, the fabric flap closing behind me with a swish, severing the last tendrils of light from the campfire outside. The world within was swallowed by an inky blackness, leaving me momentarily disoriented. Groping forward, I sank to my hands and knees, the cool, rough texture of the tent floor pressing against my palms as I crawled. The space felt both familiar and alien in the darkness, my hands guiding me towards the far corner where, nestled amongst my belongings, lay the treasure I sought: my violin case.

Grasping the case with a sense of urgency, I turned to make my way back, moving with a blend of haste and caution. My hip collided with an unseen obstacle—a heavy, unmoving presence in the darkness that I swore wasn't there before. The impact sent a jolt of pain radiating through my side, prompting a frustrated groan. "We really need more light," I muttered, nursing the tender spot with a rub. The lack of visibility was not just inconvenient; it was a tangible reminder of our precarious situation, where even the simple act of retrieving an instrument could become an ordeal.

With the violin case in hand, I emerged back into the night, the warmth of the campfire a welcoming contrast to the cool, dark confines of the tent. My return was marked by a small, triumphant smile.

Taking my seat once more on the log, I cradled the violin with a reverence reserved for the most intimate of companions. The bow, an extension of my own arm, hovered in anticipation as I tuned into Joel's melody, a repetitive tune that had woven itself into the fabric of the evening. The first few notes from my violin were hesitant, a squeaky overture that seemed almost apologetic for the intrusion. Yet, with each stroke, my confidence grew, guided by muscle memory and a deep-seated love for music.

The violin soon found its voice, blending seamlessly with Joel's melody. The notes I played danced around the fire, intertwining with his song in a harmonious partnership that spoke of resilience, of shared experiences, and of the unspoken bonds forming between us. This was more than just accompaniment; it was a conversation carried out in the universal language of music, a dialogue between two souls momentarily lifted above the harshness of our reality.

As the music flowed, I found myself swept up in the moment, my earlier frustrations and the pain from my collision with the unseen furniture fading into the background. Here, in the glow of the campfire, with my fellow settlers gathered around, I felt a profound sense of belonging.

Karen's inquiry floated to me through the night air, her voice tinged with curiosity and a touch of wonder as her head swayed softly with the rhythm, embodying the music's gentle sway. "You know this song?" she asked, her eyes reflecting the flicker of the campfire.

"Not until now," I responded, my fingers moving deftly over the strings of my violin, not missing a beat. The music had become an extension of my thoughts, a spontaneous creation that bound us together in this slice of time. My attention briefly wandered to Luke, who moved among us with a tray of drinks, his steps lively, a visible bounce that matched the energy of our impromptu performance.

Joel's voice, carrying the melody of the same four lines, became a beacon of hope in the enveloping darkness. Each repetition of the verse seemed to weave a stronger spell, binding us closer with the promise of a future crafted by our own hands.

"Let us celebrate our story
The words we've yet to write.
How we all wound up with glory
In the world we fought to right."

The simplicity and depth of the lyrics spoke volumes, echoing our shared dreams and the silent vows we made to each other and the night. It was a hymn for the hopeful, a ballad for the brave, sung by a voice that had known weariness yet refused to bow to it.

As Joel's voice dwindled into silence, a profound stillness enveloped us. I played through the stanza once more, my bow drawing out the last notes, a final salute to the resilience and spirit of our small community. With the conclusion of the melody, I lowered my violin, the silence marking the end of our musical interlude.

I turned to Joel, compelled to acknowledge the gift he had unwittingly bestowed upon us. "Your music... it's more than just words or notes. It's a spark," I said, my voice laden with a mixture of admiration and gratitude. In that moment, it was crucial to honour the talent and hope he shared, recognising how his weary yet determined voice had ignited a light within us all, a reminder of the strength found in unity and the power of shared dreams.

"To Joel!" Luke's voice, buoyant with admiration and gratitude, cut through the night air, his glass held high as if it were a beacon in the darkness. The camp responded in kind, a chorus of voices merging to form a powerful echo that seemed to carry our collective spirit into the night, resonating far beyond the confines of our immediate surroundings. The energy within the camp surged, a palpable wave of renewed hope and camaraderie washing over us all. Amidst the revelry, my thoughts turned introspective, drawn to the enigmatic figure whose song had inspired this outpouring of unity.

From my vantage point across the campfire, its flames casting a kaleidoscope of light and shadow across his face, I pondered the origin of Joel's profound lyrics. *Was his musical talent a natural gift, a beacon of hope in these troubled times? Or,* as my thoughts dared to wander into darker territories, *was there a more mystical explanation?* The notion that Clivilius, a name whispered in hushed tones, laden with fear and reverence, might be communicating through Joel sent an involuntary shiver through me. The visible scar of a slit throat served as a stark reminder of the brutal realities we faced, the unspoken battles yet to be fought, and the sacrifices already made.

My gaze then shifted to Karen, whose earlier mentions of a breeding facility among other revelations had stirred a whirlpool of questions within me. These were topics shrouded in mystery, subjects my father had never broached, suggesting layers of complexity to our situation that I had yet to uncover. The reality that there was so much beyond my understanding weighed heavily on my mind, tethering my soaring spirits with a gravity I couldn't easily shake off.

Joel's song, with its poignant call to celebrate our unwritten stories, now resonated with a deeper significance. It was a clarion call not just to remember the past or to revel in the present, but to bravely face the unknowns of our future. His words, imbued with hope and defiance, had unwittingly sown a seed of determination within me. A determination to delve deeper, to understand the full breadth of our circumstances, and to arm myself with knowledge.

The realisation that our stories were indeed unwritten, that our paths were ours to chart in the face of adversity, steeled my resolve. The mysteries surrounding my father, the truths Karen hinted at, and the enigmatic presence of Joel—all these were threads in a larger tapestry I was now compelled to unravel. As the cheers for Joel faded into the background, replaced by the comforting crackle of the fire and the soft murmur of conversation, my resolve hardened. I was more determined than ever to learn, to explore the depths of what had been kept from me, and to prepare for the challenges that lay ahead. In this moment, surrounded by the warmth of the fire and the strength of my newfound family, I felt a quiet determination take root, fuelling my desire to face the unknown with courage and an unquenchable thirst for the truth.

CHEWBATHIAN TENSION

1338.208.8

The sudden shift in Karen's demeanour broke through the intensity of our discussion like a cold wave, redirecting our focus from the heated debate to the palpable tension between her and Chris. Her voice, sharp with irritation, sliced through the night air, targeting Chris with a question that seemed to echo my own observations. I had been so engrossed in our conversation that Chris's restless movements had been nothing more than a peripheral blur until now. Yet, with Karen's pointed inquiry, his unease became the centre of our collective attention.

I found myself momentarily stepping back from the fervour of our debate, using Karen's interruption as an opportunity to breathe and recalibrate. My fingers pressed against my forehead, a subconscious gesture aimed at smoothing away the creases of frustration and fatigue that had settled there. Around us, the camp life continued in its own rhythm, with small clusters of our group seeking respite from the main fire, their silhouettes fragmented by shadows and light.

Chris's response was almost lost in the shuffle of our movement, his voice low and tinged with a discomfort that seemed out of place with his usual composure. The sheen of sweat on his forehead was a testament to the fire's intensity, or perhaps it was a reflection of his inner turmoil. His words, "It's nothing," felt hollow, a placeholder response that did little to quell the curiosity his behaviour had sparked.

Karen's patience, already worn thin, snapped with a sharpness that startled me. Her demand for honesty, "Just spit it out, would you!" carried an edge of desperation, a plea for clarity amidst the growing confusion. It was a side of Karen that revealed the depth of her concern and her intolerance for evasion.

In that moment, witnessing the strain between Karen and Chris, something within me shifted. The earlier tension from our debate, the sense of being on the back foot, began to dissipate, replaced by a newfound sense of composure. Karen's distraction with Chris's behaviour had inadvertently handed me an advantage, a psychological upper hand that I hadn't anticipated but was now keen to embrace.

This renewed confidence was not born from a desire to exploit Karen's moment of vulnerability but from recognising an opportunity to reassess my approach to our discussion. Karen's weary state, her focus divided between her husband's mysterious discomfort and our conversation, offered me a chance to collect my thoughts and prepare for the next phase of our debate with a clearer mind and a strategic advantage.

The tension in the air was almost tangible as we huddled closer, the campfire casting long shadows that danced around us. Chris's actions had drawn our collective attention, a silent question hanging between us as he reached into his pocket. His movements were deliberate, each one marked by a visible tension, as if he were about to reveal a secret long kept. With his top teeth firmly biting into his lower lip, a gesture of nervous anticipation or perhaps apprehension, he slowly withdrew his hand. It was not empty but instead held several small objects, which he cautiously extended toward us in the flickering firelight.

I couldn't help the gasp that escaped me, my usual composure momentarily forgotten in the face of the unexpected. "Fascinating," I whispered, the word barely more than a breath as I carefully picked up one of the small, metallic objects. Holding it barely an inch from my face, I examined it closely, the intricate details barely discernible in the dim light yet enough to pique my curiosity further.

Karen's voice, impatient and tinged with curiosity, broke the momentary silence. "What are they?" she demanded, snatching another of the objects from Chris's open palm, her gaze intense as she sought to uncover their secrets alongside me.

Chris, wiping away the sweat that had formed on his brow replied with a hint of uncertainty, "I think they might be coins of some sort, but I'm not really sure."

The metal felt cool and heavy in my hand, its surface etched with symbols and letters that spoke of places and stories yet to be understood. "Chewbathia," I read aloud, the name unfamiliar yet filled with an inexplicable significance. My eyes, squinting in the attempt to make out the letters, suddenly lifted to meet Chris's gaze. "Yes, it's a coin," I stated, my voice now filled with a confidence that surprised even me.

Karen's skepticism was immediate, her eyes narrowing as she challenged my assertion. "How do you know for certain?" she asked, her tone reflecting her doubt and pushing me to defend my newfound conviction.

I barely heard Karen's question as I continued to study the coin, my mind racing to connect this moment with the fragmented pieces of stories my father had once shared. The skepticism in Karen's voice faded into the background as I delved deeper into my thoughts, trying to recall any mention of Chewbathia in my father's tales. This was more than just a coin; it was a piece of a puzzle that I hadn't even known was missing, a clue to histories and worlds that suddenly seemed within reach.

"I think the markings of the twenty cliv make it rather obvious," Chris said, his voice steady, imbuing the air with a gravity that demanded consideration. The coin, small yet significant, lay between us as evidence to his claim.

"It means we're not alone," I found myself responding, the words tumbling out in a rush of excitement that I couldn't contain. The possibility, the mere hint of another civilisation, sparked a torrent of thoughts and emotions within me. Yet, as quickly as the words left my mouth, a silent command took hold. *Say no more. Not yet.* There was a caution in the back of my mind, a whisper urging restraint amidst the thrill of discovery.

Karen's skepticism served as a counterbalance to our growing enthusiasm. "We don't know that," she cautioned, her eyes narrowed in the dim light as she examined the coin with a critical eye. "This looks quite dated." Her words were a reminder of the chasm between discovery and understanding, between the thrill of speculation and the weight of proof.

Her observation echoed within me, resonating with a truth I had long sensed but never fully acknowledged. *It is,* my mind whispered back, a silent acknowledgment of the coin's age and the vast history it represented. Chewbathia, as my father had described, was a world apart, a civilisation that had flourished in secrecy, its culture and people evolving along paths divergent from our own Earthly experiences. The realisation that the fragments of information my father had shared were but a glimpse of a much larger, much older story caused a tightness in my chest, a mix of wonder and frustration.

As Karen scrutinised the coin, my thoughts drifted to my father, to the fleeting mentions of Chewbathia and the palpable tension that had always accompanied those discussions. My shoulders tensed reflexively, a physical manifestation of the unease that memory evoked. There had been something in his demeanour, a hesitancy, perhaps even fear, that had led him to steer away from the topic, leaving me with more questions than answers.

What had he been so afraid to tell me? The question hung heavily in the air, its weight suffocating in the silence that followed Karen's words. A dark foreboding clouded my excitement, tainting it with the bitter taste of unanswered questions and unexplored truths. The acidic taste of uncertainty lingered, a stark reminder of the complexities and potential dangers that lay hidden within our newfound discovery. The coin, for all its physical insignificance, had become a symbol of a vast, uncharted territory that we were only beginning to understand, a key to a door that had long been closed.

Chris's assertion sliced through the silence that had momentarily enveloped us, his excitement barely contained, giving his words an urgency that resonated with my own swirling thoughts. "But it must mean that people have been here before us," he declared, a revelation that seemed as profound as it was unsettling. "We're not the first." The weight of his conclusion hung in the air, thick with implications and unspoken questions.

Indeed we're not, echoed silently within me, my mind racing to piece together the puzzle laid bare by the discovery of the coins. The presence of such artefacts here, in the wilderness, far from any known civilisation, hinted at a history and a connection to Chewbathia that was both thrilling and terrifying. My brow creased with concern, the thrill of discovery now shadowed by the practical implications of our find. *What are the coins doing out here?* The question churned in my mind, giving rise to a more pressing concern: *Are we near the city?* The possibility that we might inadvertently be treading on the doorstep of an unknown civilisation, potentially under the watchful gaze of its inhabitants, sent a shiver of fear down my spine. *Are we being watched?*

Karen's voice, pragmatic and grounded, broke through my spiralling thoughts. "We should tell Paul," she suggested, her hand outstretched, expecting the return of the second coin. Her suggestion, though well-intentioned, struck me as premature, a potential misstep given the myriad of unknowns we were facing.

"I don't think that is wise," I found myself responding, my grip on the coin tightening reflexively. The instinct to protect our discovery, to shield it from scrutiny until we had a clearer understanding, was overpowering. There are too many unknowns. The realisation that sharing this information prematurely could trigger a defensive, possibly obstructive response from Paul was clear in my mind. His protective instincts, while invaluable, could inadvertently quash any hope of further exploration or understanding. *I need to find Chewbathia!* The thought was a beacon, guiding my resolve to tread carefully, to keep the secret just a little longer.

Karen's reaction was immediate, her mouth tightening, lips pressed into a thin line of disapproval. "Why not?" she pressed, her voice tinged with frustration and disbelief. Her demand for justification hung between us, a challenge to my decision to withhold information.

"He is too busy," I offered, a simplified excuse that veiled my true concerns. The decision to keep my thoughts and the coin to myself was not made lightly, but out of a necessity to navigate the delicate balance between caution and curiosity. *If Karen's doing the same, then it's only fair*, I rationalised, seeking to justify my reluctance to share, even as I recognised the complexities of the situation.

Karen's response was a huff of frustration, her impatience manifesting in the sharp gesture of her fingers, a silent demand for me to relinquish the artefact. The tension between us was palpable, a reflection of the broader uncertainties and fears that the discovery of the coins had unearthed.

Chris's words, though hesitant, offered a sliver of validation that my stance might hold merit. "Perhaps Glenda is right," he mused, his gesture to take back the coin from Karen a physical endorsement of his newfound agreement with my perspective. His shrug, seemingly nonchalant, belied the gravity of our discussion. "Until we know more about them, there's probably no point saying anything to Paul."

"Yes," I chimed in, eager to bolster this line of reasoning before Karen could mount another counterargument. "Paul has enough on his mind with trying to get the settlement up and running." The mention of Paul's myriad responsibilities was not just a diversion; it was a stark reality. The weight of establishing a new community from the ground up was immense, and every additional concern could tip the scales towards chaos.

"And dealing with Luke," Chris added, reminding us of the interpersonal dynamics that further complicated our leadership's already Herculean task.

Yet, Karen's resolve was unyielding, her belief in transparency with Paul unshaken. "As our delegated leader, I still think Paul should know." Her insistence, while admirable in its loyalty, felt dangerously naïve given the stakes.

Driven by a mix of frustration and urgency, I found myself snapping, a rare loss of composure on my part. "No," I declared, seizing the momentary shock on Karen's face to reclaim the second coin from her grasp. The act was impulsive, driven by a conviction that the risk of wider knowledge was too great.

Karen's reaction was immediate and fiery. "Give that back!" she demanded, her anger palpable, almost as vivid and threatening as the campfire that crackled in the background.

Yet, in that moment, my resolve hardened. "We say nothing to anyone," I stated, the finality in my voice reflecting my determination as I secured the coins in my bra, a makeshift safeguarding that felt both desperate and necessary.

Karen's retort, a visceral "That's not your decision to make," accompanied by a bold, unwelcome reach toward my bosom, was met with a fierce rebuke. "Fuck off, Karen!" I snapped, recoiling from her advance with a protective twist of my body. My words, sharp and unyielding, echoed my physical rejection. "I said no."

Her response, a silent, seething retreat into crossed arms and laboured breathing, marked the end of our confrontation. The tension between us, now a tangible divide, left me no choice but to withdraw from her presence. Walking away, the fire's crackle felt like a cautionary backdrop to my retreat, its sparks a warning of the dangers of letting emotions fan the flames of conflict.

"I don't care," I muttered under my breath, a whispered defiance against the turmoil. Catching a glimpse of Karen heading toward her tent, a part of me lamented the rift that had formed. *That woman needs to learn her place*, I thought, not with malice, but with a weary realisation that our paths to leadership and decision-making were fundamentally at odds. The night's events, a microcosm of our larger struggles, left me questioning not just our immediate dilemma, but the sustainability of our cohesion as a fledgling community.

❖

The tent flap announced my entrance with a loud, unsettling rustle, a prelude to the chaos that ensued. "For fuck's sake!" escaped my lips in a harsh whisper as my foot ensnared itself on the tent's treacherous floor. The world seemed to tilt alarmingly, and in a desperate bid to save myself, I pitched forward. My hands, previously clenched in determination to safeguard the coins hidden within my bra, flew open in an instinctive effort to break my fall. The sensation of the cool metal slipping from my grasp added a pang of panic to the rush of adrenaline. There, in the pitch black of the tent, I found myself sprawled awkwardly on the ground, the indignity of the fall compounded by the urgency to recover the coins. My fingers, now unbidden explorers, scuttled across the tent's rough fabric, seeking out the escaped treasures in the darkness.

As I searched, Joel's song echoed hauntingly in the recesses of my mind, its melody a stark contrast to my current predicament.

"Let us celebrate our story
The words we've yet to write."

The irony of the situation wasn't lost on me. Here I was, fumbling in the dark, literally and metaphorically, as I grappled with the tangible symbols of an unknown narrative. The cool, rounded edges of the coins finally met my fingertips, their familiar texture a small comfort in the disarray. Clutching them close, I nestled the coins back into their makeshift sanctuary, their presence a reassuring weight against my skin.

"How we all wound up with glory
In the world we fought to right."

The words resonated deeper as I sat in the darkness, cross-legged and disoriented, not just by my fall but by the weight of our situation. The act of reciting the lyrics aloud brought a moment of clarity amidst the turmoil, a brief respite that allowed my racing heart to steady. Each breath I drew was a conscious effort to anchor myself, not just within the confines of the tent but to the reality of our collective endeavour.

"In the world we fought to right," I murmured to myself, a soft echo of Joel's optimism tinged with my own burgeoning doubts. "But which world?" The question hung in the air, palpable and heavy with implications. *Were we fighting for the world we had left behind, or for the one we were attempting to forge here?* The duality of the struggle, of our past against our potential future, crystallised in that moment of solitude.

4338.209

(28 July 2018)

GROWL

1338.209.1

Adjusting the log on the campfire, its embers sending a cascade of sparks into the night like a miniature galaxy being born, I couldn't help but cast a contemplative glance over our makeshift encampment. Each of the settlers, my unexpected family in this vast wilderness, was settled into their chosen spots for the night, their bodies relaxed in the trusting embrace of sleep. The air, though cool, was a gentle reminder of the wild's indifferent embrace, suggesting that even without the fire's warmth, survival wouldn't have been in question tonight. Yet, the fire wasn't just a source of warmth; it was a beacon of hope, a circle of light against the darkness of the unknown.

Passing Lois, I couldn't resist giving her a gentle pat. She responded with a soft nuzzle against my hand. Convincing myself that dragging out blankets or sleeping bags for the human members of our group wasn't necessary felt like a small lie I told myself to ease the burden of leadership. After all, it was just Luke, Paul, and Kain remaining outside, the men seemingly content with their spots near the fire.

My mind wandered to the whereabouts of the others. Karen's earlier departure, fuelled by frustration and anger, replayed in my mind, her silhouette storming off to her tent a vivid image against the night's canvas. Chris, too, was absent from the circle, likely seeking to mend fences with Karen in the privacy of their tent.

Jamie, on the other hand, would be in his tent, but not alone—Joel, his son, would be there with him. The dynamic between father and son, especially in these trying times, was something I often pondered. It was a relationship tested and forged anew in the crucible of our circumstances.

Lois, ever the curious soul, had initially been fascinated by the mysterious coins that had sparked so much debate and conflict. Her snout had been irresistibly drawn to them, her golden retriever instincts piqued by the scent of adventure they carried. However, after a few gentle reprimands aimed at preserving the coins' secrecy, she had found solace and companionship beside Paul, who had unwittingly become her new favourite human. Her choice was both amusing and telling; in this new world, alliances were formed not just by necessity but by the innate bonds of friendship and trust.

Satisfied the fire was well-fed for the remainder of the night, I withdrew into the sanctuary of my tent, seeking solace in its familiar confines. As I lay there, the darkness of the tent's canopy a vast expanse above me, I found myself absentmindedly playing with the coins. Their cool metal surface slid between my thumb and forefinger, a tactile reminder of the day's discoveries and the mysteries they heralded. My thoughts inevitably drifted to my father, the man who had first spoken the name Chewbathia in hushed tones, imbuing it with a sense of wonder and secrecy.

I tried to summon more details from the depths of my memory, wishing I could recall more of his tales about that distant place. With my eyes shut tightly, an effort to block out all distractions, my father's image materialised in my mind's eye with startling clarity. I could see him, his gentle expression as he brushed my hair from my face, his voice a soft whisper in the quiet of my memory. "Glenda," he seemed to say, his presence so vivid it was as if he was there with me in the tent.

"Father," I whispered back, uncertain whether the words had truly left my lips or merely echoed in the chambers of my mind. "Where is Chewbathia?" The question felt as heavy as it was heartfelt, a plea for guidance across the boundaries of time and space.

His answer was cryptic, yet imbued with a confidence that felt both reassuring and daunting. "You know how to find it. You know how to find all of them." The assertion left me bewildered, my brow furrowing in concentration as I grappled with his meaning. *Could it be true? Did I possess knowledge, however buried, of how to uncover these secrets?*

"The secret key that you kept hidden in your study?" I ventured, the memory of a forbidden space filled with the promise of untold mysteries surfacing in my thoughts. His laughter, light and filled with affection, seemed to dance around the confines of my tent. "Well, it was hardly secret nor hidden then, was it?" he teased, and I could almost see the twinkle in his eye, the shared joke illuminating a connection that time had not diminished.

His next words struck a chord, a revelation of my childhood antics known yet unspoken between us. "I always knew that you used to spy on me through the crack in the door, late at night when you should have been tucked away in bed and fast asleep," he said, and I could feel a warmth spreading across my cheeks, a flush of embarrassment mingled with a deep, abiding love.

But then, the moment was shattered by a sound from outside the tent—a deep, ominous growl that snapped me back to the present, to the reality of our encampment nestled within the unforgiving desert. My father's comforting presence dissipated like mist at dawn, leaving me alone with the night and its untold threats. The sudden intrusion of danger, real or imagined, cast a shadow over the warmth of my reverie

The tent's entrance stirred, a soft, insistent rustling that cut through the silence of the night. "Father?" My voice broke the stillness, an irrational hope flickering briefly as I called out. The heat of the moment, sweat beading on my forehead, betrayed my rising panic. "Father, is that you?" I knew it couldn't be, yet the part of me clinging to the remnants of my dream couldn't help but reach out.

Lois's response was immediate, her barks sharp and alert, slicing through the tension like a warning bell. The sensation of fear prickled at the back of my neck, a physical manifestation of my growing unease. In the almost oppressive darkness of the tent, my vision was useless, my eyes squinting as they tried in vain to penetrate the night that had swallowed the interior of my shelter whole.

Driven by a mixture of concern and a determination to prevent Lois from waking the entire camp, I moved. My hands and knees felt the familiar fabric of the tent floor as I made my way toward the entrance.

From her place at the campfire, Lois's growl, a short, warning snarl, heightened my alarm. Something was amiss, and the protective instinct for my companions, both human and canine, surged within me.

"What's going on? Why is Lois barking?" My questions were a half shout as I emerged, finding Paul, Luke, and Kain, their figures etched in the dim light, suddenly as vigilant as sentinels. The cold shiver that cascaded down my spine was as much from the sight of their alertness as from the unknown threat that had disturbed our peace.

"We don't know," Paul's reply came, his voice steady but his gaze locked on the unseen, his attention fixed on the darkness beyond our camp. The intensity of his focus was unnerving, a silent acknowledgment that the night held more secrets than we were privy to.

"Probably just the wind picking up dust," Luke ventured, his attempt at reassurance sounding hollow against the backdrop of our collective apprehension. Yet, as if to affirm his words, a sudden gust swept through the camp, a tangible force that whipped a spray of fine dust over us. The wind, capricious and unyielding, tangled my hair, sending strands flying across my face in a wild dance.

Luke must be right, I conceded silently, even as I fought to free my vision from the unruly locks. The wind, a natural explanation for the disturbance, offered a sliver of rationality amidst the fear. Yet, the mention of Clivilius, even in thought, imbued the moment with an eerie significance. The suddenness of the wind, its timing almost too perfect, left me wrestling with a mix of relief and residual unease. Was it merely the wind, or had we inadvertently drawn the attention of something—or someone—far more formidable?

The urgency in Luke's voice sliced through the tension like a knife. "We'd better get inside the tents!" he bellowed, his command echoing the rising panic among us. My immediate concern turned to Lois, whose instincts seemed far sharper than our own in this moment of crisis. "Come, Lois," I called out, my hand reaching for her collar in a desperate attempt to guide her to safety.

But Lois, ever the protector, ignored me completely, her growls deepening—a clear sign of her perceived threat. Her defiance was unnerving, amplifying the fear that had already taken root within me.

From the darkness, Jamie's voice added to the unease, his own panic for Duke mirroring my struggle with Lois. "Duke! Get back here!" he yelled, his concern palpable in the night air.

"Lois!" I hissed, a last-ditch effort to gain control, but my voice seemed to dissolve into the tension that enveloped us.

Kain's exclamation, "Shit! We're surrounded!" sent a wave of dread crashing over me. His retreat to the campfire, a beacon of false safety, underscored the desperation of our situation.

Frustration and fear battled within me as I attempted once more to coax Lois. "I mean it, Lois. Get inside," I growled, more to convince myself than her. My efforts, however, were futile against her steadfast determination to stand her ground.

Karen's voice, tinged with alarm, cut through the night. "What's going on?" she demanded, emerging from her tent into the brewing storm of fear and confusion.

It was then, amid the escalating panic, that an inexplicable phenomenon caught my eye. The Portal, a spectacle of bright rainbow colours, shimmered across the dunes in the distance—an otherworldly light show that seemed both beautiful and terrifying. *What the hell?* The sight was disorienting, challenging everything I thought I knew about our Portal.

Karen's confusion only heightened the surreal nature of the moment. "Is that Luke?" she queried, mistaking the cause for the Portal's eerie illumination.

"I'm right here," Luke responded, confirming my fears that he wasn't our Guardian that had activated the Portal.

With my patience depleted and Lois unyielding in her vigilance, my attempts to move her resulted in my own ungraceful fall to the ground. The thump of my backside hitting the earth was a jarring punctuation to the night's madness.

"Duke, stop barking!" Jamie's shout was a desperate plea for order amid the disarray.

Lying there, momentarily defeated, I was overwhelmed by a sense of helplessness. The reality of our predicament—a clash between the known and the unknown, between invisible dangers and the unfathomable mysteries of the Portal's activation—loomed large.

The night air, already tense with unease, was shattered by a scream—a sound so raw and terrifying it seemed to freeze the very blood in my veins. The dust, whipped into frenzied spirals by the wind, became an eerie backdrop to the nightmare unfolding before us.

In that moment of disruption, Lois reacted with a decisiveness that I couldn't match. As I fumbled to rise from the ground, dirt clinging to my palms, she bolted. "Lois!" The name tore from my throat, a desperate plea as I watched her sprint into the void beyond. My heart raced, not just with fear but with the overwhelming need to protect her from whatever horror had pierced the night with its cry.

Driven by a mix of dread and determination, I found my legs propelling me forward, chasing after Lois's rapidly disappearing form. The relief at sensing Paul's presence close behind me was a fleeting comfort, a thin thread of solidarity in the face of the unknown.

The desert beneath my bare feet shifted treacherously, the fine dust a hindrance that seemed determined to drag me back. Each step was a battle, the dunes rising and falling like the swell of a stormy sea. As I crested the second dune, my footing failed me. The ground crumbled, and I was sent tumbling downward, the world a blur of motion and disorienting flips. Dust clouds erupted around me, my descent a chaotic dance with gravity.

Paul's voice, a beacon in the tumult, reached out, "Are you..." His words were a lifeline cut devastatingly short by another scream. This one was closer, a visceral sound that clawed at the fragile veil of courage I had drawn around myself. The immediacy of the threat, now so near, hammered home the reality of our perilous situation.

As the night sky momentarily erupted into an otherworldly spectacle of colours, my attention was drawn to a small, incongruous shape in the dust, mere feet from the enigmatic Portal. The world plunged back into darkness, but the image of the object was seared into my mind, guiding me through the shadows.

Nearing the object, a faint glow beckoned from beneath it —a beacon in the overwhelming dark. *A phone!* The realisation hit me with a mix of shock and intrigue as I scooped it up from the cool dust. The device must have belonged to the source of those harrowing screams, a silent witness to the terror that had unfolded. Locked, its screen offered a sliver of illumination, a lifeline in the pitch-black desert.

With the phone's dim light carving a path through the darkness, I made my way to Paul, who sat disoriented in the dirt, the blackness of the night having eroded his sense of direction.

As I reached for him, his instinctive recoil spoke volumes of the heightened tension we all felt. "It's me," I reassured, securing a firmer grip on his arm to anchor him.

"Where the hell did you get that?" His voice was a mix of surprise and skepticism as he eyed the phone in my grasp.

"I found it face down in the dust, over there, near the Portal," I explained, my grip on his arm unyielding.

Together, we stood, just as the Portal erupted once more into a vibrant display, its colours casting our shadows into stark relief against the night.

Luke's voice cut through the tension, his concern palpable. "Everyone okay?" His glance back at us offered a momentary connection, a shared acknowledgment of the ordeal we'd just endured.

"I think so," Paul's voice carried a hint of relief, his gaze meeting mine in search of reassurance.

I nodded, signalling my unspoken agreement, even as I questioned how much Paul could actually see in the fluctuating light.

"Good. I'm going in," Luke declared with a resolve that bordered on defiance. His statement, laden with determination and the unspoken risks it entailed, left us in a momentary pause. And then, as abruptly as it had flared to life, Clivilius went dark.

The sudden cessation of the Portal's light, the disappearance of Luke, sent a ripple of anxiety through me. The phone in my hand, a silent testament to the night's events, felt heavier—a symbol of the unknown dangers and the fragile hope.

A sudden brush of fur against my leg startled me, disrupting the tense silence that had enveloped us. "That darn dog," I muttered under my breath, a mix of affection and irritation colouring my tone. Lois had once again positioned herself at the heart of the chaos.

"Lois! Stay!" My command was firm, a desperate attempt to exert some control over the situation as I let go of Paul's arm to secure Lois. Illuminating her with the phone's screen, I hastily examined her for any signs of injury, my heart racing with concern for her well-being.

From the darkness, Kain's exclamation, "Whoa!" pierced the night, adding to the already heightened sense of urgency.

Lois, sensing something we couldn't, pulled fiercely, her strength surprising. As she bared her teeth, a growl vibrating through her throat, my worry deepened. "She's baring her teeth," I informed Paul, the worry in my voice unmistakable. "She's never done that before." The behaviour was uncharacteristic, a clear indication that the danger, whatever its source, was real and immediate.

Paul's reaction, a sharp intake of breath as he shielded himself from a gust of wind laden with dust, was instinctive. The night had turned against us, the environment itself seeming to conspire to heighten our fear.

Then, cutting through the turmoil, Kain's scream—a sound so raw and filled with agony—it froze me to my core. It was a scream of pain, unmistakably different from any cry of frustration or fear. It was the kind of scream that told you its emitter was experiencing a level of pain that was visceral and immediate.

In that moment, my fear for Lois, for Paul, for all of us, crystallised into a sharp, painful point in my chest. The realisation that we were not merely spectators, but active participants in a drama far beyond our understanding, was overwhelming. The darkness, once merely an absence of light, now felt alive with threats, both seen and unseen, and Kain's scream was a harrowing reminder of the stakes involved. The night had turned hostile, and every shadow seemed to hide a new danger, every gust of wind a harbinger of further terror.

"Go and find him, girl," I urged Lois, my voice laced with desperation as I gave her a gentle push on the backside, signalling her release. As she darted off into the night, I hurried after her, the phone's dim light my only guide through the oppressive darkness. Calling out for Kain became a mantra, each shout a blend of hope and dread, the silence that followed each call twisting my heart tighter with worry.

"Where are you, Kain?" Paul's voice, heavy with concern, boomed through the darkness, mirroring my own anxiety.

Then, a small victory against the night; "I see tracks," I announced, spotting the distinct imprints of Lois's paws in the dust, a fleeting sign before the wind threatened to erase them. My pace quickened to a jog, the phone's light bobbing ahead as I followed the trail. "Lois found him!" Relief flooded through me as the figures of Lois and Kain materialised from the shadows.

I rushed to Kain's side, dropping to the ground with a sense of urgency that eclipsed the threats around us. "Kain," I said, gently pushing Lois away as she attempted to lavish him with concerned licks. "Kain, are you okay?" My voice was a mix of fear and hope, seeking any sign that he was not beyond help.

"Is he alive?" Paul's question cut through the tense air, loaded with the weight of unspoken fears.

Kain's response was a grimace of pain, his face twisted in a silent scream that spoke volumes of his suffering. The garbled sounds that escaped him were barely human, yet his nod towards his leg was a clear communication of the source of his agony.

As the phone's light swept over Kain, revealing the extent of his injury, a cold, sharp intake of breath escaped me. The sight of the deep, jagged gash across his thigh was a stark reminder of the dangers lurking in the shadows. The fabric of his trousers, now a mere relic of the attack, was soaked through with blood, clinging desperately to the wound as if trying to shield it from further harm.

Years of medical training surged to the forefront of my mind, pushing aside the initial shock with a wave of focused determination. "Yes, but his leg is wounded. Come help me move him," I called out to Paul, my voice a mixture of urgency and command. Despite the fear clawing at my thoughts, a semblance of calm settled over me, a testament to the countless times I'd faced medical emergencies back on Earth.

Kain's scream, a harrowing sound filled with pain and fear, pierced the night. "My leg!" he cried out, a mist of bloody saliva painting the air with his agony. "I think it's bleeding," he managed between sobs, the realisation of his own vulnerability breaking through his shock.

"It is," I confirmed, my voice steady despite the turmoil within. The light flickered across his injury, casting eerie shadows that seemed to dance with the pain radiating from his wound.

Paul's arrival was a relief, his presence a tangible support in the madness. "We need to move him out of this dust storm," I stated, turning to face him, my mind racing with the logistics of safely transporting Kain without exacerbating his injuries.

"You hold the light, I'll help him," Paul responded.

With the phone's light our only guide, the full gravity of Kain's condition was shrouded in shadow and uncertainty. The desolation surrounding us, once merely an inhospitable backdrop, now felt ominously alive with hidden threats. The realisation that something—or someone—had inflicted such harm on Kain sent waves of fear through me. The thought of not being alone on this planet had once held a tinge of hope for companionship, for allies in this unknown world. But this violent encounter shattered that hope, leaving behind a gnawing dread of what else might be out there, watching, waiting.

"Try not to put too much pressure on the leg," I instructed Kain gently, aware of every grimace and twitch of pain that crossed his face. My voice carried a blend of concern and command, hoping to ease his journey to standing despite the gnawing fear that we were far from being out of danger.

Paul crouched beside Kain, positioning himself as a human crutch. "Okay. We can take shelter at the Drop Zone for now," he suggested, though his voice betrayed a hint of doubt, as if questioning the safety of any haven in this unpredictable world.

As they prepared to stand, Paul's assurance to Kain, "We're going to stand," was more than just a statement of action; it was a declaration of solidarity, of shared burden. Watching them struggle to their feet, a surge of admiration for their resilience mingled with my anxiety.

Illuminating the path ahead with the phone's light, I took the lead towards the Drop Zone, each step a balance between haste and the need to ensure Kain's stability. The sight that greeted us—a makeshift shelter comprised of large boxes and unused shed materials—was ironically comforting. My initial chagrin at our slow progress in building the settlement now transformed into gratitude; our "incompetence" had inadvertently provided us with a means to protect Kain from the harsh elements and potential predators.

The Portal, igniting once more, painted the night with surreal hues, its beauty a stark contrast to our grim reality on the ground. It was a reminder of the thin veil between the extraordinary and the perilous that we navigated.

"Paul!" Luke's voice, unmistakable and imbued with urgency, cut through the tension, momentarily drawing our attention.

"We're almost at the Drop Zone," Paul responded, his voice carrying through the darkness, a beacon of our location and a signal of our continued struggle for safety.

Luke's declaration, "I need to check the house. I'll be back soon!" and his subsequent departure back into the darkness left us in a renewed state of isolation.

Passing between the two stone piles that marked the entrance to the Drop Zone, following my directions, our small group weaved in and out in search of a suitable place to stop.

"Do you think we're safe here?" Kain's question, voiced as we huddled amongst the protective embrace of the larger shed boxes, was laden with vulnerability. The uncertainty in his voice mirrored the anxiety that clung to my own thoughts, a persistent shadow that no amount of reasoning could fully dispel.

As I carefully arranged Kain's leg, keeping it extended to minimise further injury, I reached for Paul's shirt. Transforming it into an impromptu bandage, I wrapped it around Kain's thigh with as much precision as the dim light allowed. The action was both a distraction and a necessity, a way to focus on the tangible problem in front of us.

"Lois hasn't growled once since we found you," Paul observed, his voice carrying a note of hopeful relief. His hand found Lois's head, offering comfort to both the dog and himself. Lois seemed to have relaxed, her heavy panting a sign of her own exhaustion from the night's events.

"As soon as the wind calms, we need to get back to camp. Kain's leg needs prompt medical care," I stated, the weight of leadership pressing down on me. The urgency of the situation allowed no room for delay; every moment we remained at the Drop Zone was a moment lost in the battle against time and injury.

"Of course," Paul agreed, his exhaustion palpable as he sought rest against a makeshift support.

Alone with my thoughts as I buried the phone to hide its betraying light, my back against the cold, unyielding surface of a box, I allowed myself a moment of vulnerability. The adrenaline that had fuelled my actions began to wane, leaving behind a tide of emotions that I had fought to keep at bay. In the darkness, with only the silhouettes of our temporary shelter for company, a silent tear escaped, a quiet testament to the fear and loneliness that threatened to overwhelm me.

I can't do this on my own, my mind sobbed as I wiped a silent tear from my eye. *I need you, Pierre.*

THE HUNTER AND THE HUNTED

4338.209.2

The unexpected sound of a woman's voice slicing through the darkness snapped me out of the creeping edges of exhaustion. "I mean you no harm," she called, her words a stark contrast to the silence that had preceded them. My head jerked up, a rush of adrenaline dispelling the drowsiness that had begun to claim me. Despite my efforts to stay vigilant, the night's mild but persistent wind, coupled with Kain's soft, pain-filled whimpers, had lulled me into a state of near-sleep, a dangerous lapse in this unknown territory.

With a sense of urgency, I retrieved the phone, its screen a beacon in the enveloping darkness. As I swept the light across our makeshift encampment, searching for the source of the voice, my heart pounded with a mix of fear and anticipation. The light finally settled on a figure emerging from the shadows, and I gasped aloud at the sight, the sudden appearance of a stranger sending shockwaves through my already tense body.

"Shit," Kain's whispered exclamation broke the momentary silence, his voice a raspy testament to the ordeal he had endured. His reaction, a mix of surprise and pain, mirrored my own shock at the sudden intrusion into our precarious haven.

The sharp pang of guilt for not having provided better care for Kain's injury was swiftly supplanted by the immediate and pressing reality before us. The young woman who emerged from the darkness, armed with a bow in one hand and a bloodied arrow in the other, commanded our full attention. The sight of blood, still oozing down the arrow's shaft and disappearing into the dust at her feet, sent a wave of cold dread through me. Memories of my time in Borneo, where violence had lurked in unexpected corners, flooded back with startling clarity. Despite the warnings about the challenges of my assignment there, nothing had truly prepared me for the visceral reality of human cruelty and the capacity for bloodshed.

As I stood there, facing this armed stranger in the midst of an alien landscape, the horrors I had witnessed in Borneo seemed to converge with the present moment. My body reacted with a primal shudder, a physical rejection of the violence that seemed to permeate every facet of existence. The harsh truth that life, in its most basic form, was an unending cycle of violence and survival, was a lesson I had learned all too well. Yet, it was a conclusion I fought against internally, refusing to accept that Darwin's brutal axiom of survival of the fittest was the sole governing principle of our nature.

In the face of this young woman, her weapon poised and bloodied, I found myself grappling once again with the dichotomy of human existence. The stark contrast between the capacity for brutal violence and the equally powerful potential for compassion and empathy lay before me, embodied in her silhouette against the dark backdrop of the night. Despite the evidence of violence in her hands, I couldn't help but cling to the hope that compassion remained a vital component of our survival as a species. It was this belief, perhaps naïve but fiercely held, that had guided me through the darkest moments of my past experiences and what I hoped would see us through this current ordeal.

As the woman's command to follow cut through the tension-laden air, I found my grip on Paul tightening, an instinctive reaction to the uncertainty that cloaked her intentions. Her step forward, each movement measured yet fraught with an unspoken threat, compelled me to act. "Step back!" My voice, louder than intended, echoed my rising panic, my fingers pressing into Paul's arm with an urgency that mirrored my fear.

The woman's sudden change in demeanour, dropping the arrow and raising her hands in a gesture of peace, did little to assuage my apprehension. "Keep your voices down," she hissed, a warning that hinted at dangers lurking in the shadows beyond our sight. "It's not safe. We have to go. Now." Her words, meant to hurry us, only tangled further with my doubts, weaving a complex web of fear and necessity.

Paul's questioning gaze, illuminated in the sparse light cast by the phone, sought answers I wasn't sure I possessed. "Where are we going?" he asked, his voice threading through the darkness with a vulnerability that echoed my own uncertainties.

"To your camp," the woman stated, her answer simple yet laden with implications that sent my mind racing. *Could we afford to lead this stranger, this potential threat, back to our sanctuary?*

Paul's whispered caution, "I don't think we should trust her," vibrated with a skepticism that mirrored my inner turmoil. As Kain's pained sounds punctuated the night, a stark reminder of our vulnerability, I was torn between the instinct to protect our group and the possibility that this woman could offer us a way out of our current torture.

Lois's soft growl, a sound so subtle yet laden with instinctual warning, sent a shiver down my spine. My instincts screamed caution, a lifetime of learned wariness against the unknown battling against the pressing need to find safety for Kain, for all of us.

The growl that broke through the silence was unlike any sound of the night thus far—a deeper, more menacing rumble that seemed to originate from the very heart of the darkness surrounding us. My mind raced, trying to reconcile the immediate danger with the woman standing before us, arrow now back in her hand, blood still tracing its path down the shaft. If she had intended to harm us, surely the opportunity had already presented itself. This realisation, however dimly it flickered in the sea of my fears, held a semblance of reassurance. My gaze, locked on the weapon that seemed both a threat and a promise of protection, couldn't ignore the fact that Kain's injuries were not her doing.

"There's something else out there," I whispered urgently, directing the phone's beam towards the abyss that Lois seemed fixated on. The darkness remained impenetrable, a void that refused to reveal its secrets, leaving us with more questions than answers. The woman remained the only certainty in a landscape shrouded in mystery and danger.

"Shit!" The exclamation slipped from both Paul and me as we realised the immediacy of the threat, our collective alarm peaking as the woman positioned herself within arm's reach. Her proximity, under different circumstances, might have been a comfort, but now it only heightened the tension.

"My name is Charity. Don't be afraid; you can trust me," she insisted, her voice cutting through the fear with a clarity that demanded attention. Her hand found Paul's arm, her grip firm, a physical manifestation of her urgency. "We must go."

Lois's growls deepened, a raw display of primal instinct that I had never witnessed in her before. Each bared tooth, each ripple of tension through her body, sent an echo of unease down my spine. This side of Lois, protective and fierce, was unfamiliar, unsettling even.

"Come on," Paul's voice broke through my spiralling thoughts, his hand firm on my arm, urging me back to the present. His words mirrored my earlier attempt at reasoning, but instead of offering solace, they propelled my mind into darker territories. "If this woman wanted to kill us, she would have done it already."

"Or feed us to some creature," I retorted, the words slipping out in a whisper tinged with fear and regret. My own dramatic suggestion immediately felt like a betrayal of the composure I was supposed to embody. *Glenda!* The internal reprimand was swift. After the harrowing experiences in Borneo, where I had faced and overcome unimaginable challenges, I chided myself for succumbing to panic now. I was supposed to be the anchor, the calm in the storm.

"Quickly now," Charity's voice, steady and urgent, prompted action rather than further reflection. Her command, coupled with Paul's support, galvanised me into motion. With a collective effort, we lifted Kain. It was a moment that demanded all the resilience and strength I could muster.

"Give me your light," Charity's request snapped me back to the task at hand. Her outstretched hand, waiting for the phone, was a pivotal moment of trust—a decision point that could define our fate. In handing over the light, I was placing our lives in the hands of someone who, until moments ago, had been a potential threat. Yet, her calm demeanour and the urgency of our escape lent her an aura of credibility that was hard to deny.

Finally trusting the intruder, I passed the phone into her waiting hand. It was an act of faith, a leap into the unknown that underscored the desperation of our circumstances.

"Stay close," Charity instructed, her tone imbued with a confidence that belied the chaos of our escape. "And keep up." Her words were a lifeline, a directive that promised a chance at survival if only we could muster the strength to follow.

My head nodding in agreement, the familiar words stirred a deep-seated memory within me, transporting me back to a time fraught with danger of a different kind. I had issued the same command to young children, their lives precariously hanging in the balance as we navigated fields marred by the remnants of war—unexploded mines, hidden threats that demanded the utmost caution with every step. The gravity of instructing those children to place their trust in me, to step where I stepped to avoid unseen dangers, resonated strongly now as we followed Charity through this perilous landscape.

The sudden explosion of a mine in my memory jolted me back to the present, a stark reminder of the ever-present dangers that lurked just beyond our awareness. Though the explosion was a spectre of the past, the visceral reaction it evoked was a testament to the scars such experiences had left upon me. I clenched up involuntarily, the shockwaves of remembered blasts brushing against my skin as if to underscore the danger of our current journey.

Forcing my gaze away from the horrors of my past, I focused intently on Charity's back, placing one foot in front of the other with deliberate care. Paul and I, burdened yet determined, supported Kain between us, each step a testament to our collective resolve to return to the safety of our camp.

As we trudged on, the relentless winds that had tormented us earlier began to abate, granting us a reprieve from the biting sand and dust that had threatened to overwhelm our senses. This small mercy was a balm to my frayed nerves, a sliver of solace in the midst of our arduous trek.

Approaching our destination, the glow of our camp began to pierce the darkness, the flickering lights beckoning us home from across the dunes. The sight of the firesticks, strategically placed around the perimeter of the camp to ward off the darkness, filled me with a sense of relief and security. Their warm, protective glow cast a barrier against the night.

❖

Stepping into the protective circle cast by the firesticks, the question from Charity pierced the relative calm that had settled over us. "Who is the camp leader?" Her inquiry, straightforward yet loaded with implications, awaited an answer.

"I am," Paul's response was immediate, firm, and devoid of hesitation. His declaration of leadership, under the circumstances we found ourselves in, was reassuring. It was a mantle he assumed without falter, and his acceptance of this role resonated with a sense of rightness within me. Observing Paul step into this responsibility filled me with a mix of pride and relief. In the severity of our situation, having a clear leader was a beacon of stability.

"We need to talk. You and I," Charity's words, directed at Paul with a firmness that brooked no argument, hinted at discussions that held the weight of our current predicament. Her insistence on a private conversation suggested matters of urgency or information crucial for our safety.

Paul prioritised our immediate concerns. "We need to see to Kain's wounded leg first," he countered, his commitment to our well-being evident. Yet, Charity's examination of Kain's injury seemed cursory, almost dismissive. "It's barely a scratch. He'll live," she declared after a brief look, standing up from her squat. Her assessment, in stark contrast to the blood-soaked bandage and the fresh trail of blood marking Kain's leg, did little to ease my growing apprehension. The quick dismissal of what was clearly a serious injury felt rash, and Paul's attempt to voice his own concern was abruptly silenced by Charity's shushing motion, her nervous glance around adding layers of unspoken tension.

Chris's arrival, taking over the support of Kain from Paul, underscored the need for immediate medical attention. "We need to get him to the medical tent," I stated, my voice carrying the urgency I felt. The sight of Kain's leg, the reality of his condition, demanded more than what Charity's brief assessment offered. My insistence on proper care stemmed from a place of deep concern, a reflection of my protective instincts.

❖

In an instant, the urgency of the moment had Chris leaping into action, aiding me in steering Kain toward the sanctuary of the tent. The air was thick with concern as we navigated the compact space, the tent flap offering a whisper of resistance before giving way to our determined push. We lowered Kain carefully onto the mattress that seemed too meagre for the gravity of his condition.

"What happened to him?" Chris's voice cut through the tension, a mix of worry and confusion as we settled Kain down.

"We don't know," I replied, my voice steady yet tinged with an undercurrent of frustration. I was certain Charity wasn't behind this, yet the true cause eluded me, shrouded in a mist of uncertainty that seemed to thicken with every passing second.

"I think..." Kain's voice was a fragile thread, barely audible over the rustle of our movements.

As Chris stayed by Kain's side, a silent sentinel of support, I moved with purpose across the tent. The darkness seemed to close in around me as I sifted through the medical supplies, each item a potential lifeline in my hands. The air was heavy, charged with a palpable tension that made my every movement feel monumental.

"I think it was an animal," Kain managed through gritted teeth, his voice a testament to the pain he was enduring. I knelt beside him, my hands working deftly to remove the makeshift shirt-bandage. The seriousness of his condition was laid bare before me, a stark reminder of our vulnerability in this wild expanse.

"A shadow panther," Chris gasped.

"A what?" The question slipped from Kain's lips, mirroring the confusion within my own mind.

"Enough talk," I snapped, more sharply than intended. The urgency of the moment demanded focus, not fascination. The spectre of intrigue had to be banished, for Kain's well-being hung in the balance. "I need to concentrate, or Kain might lose his leg."

Chris's response was immediate, his hand finding Kain's in a gesture of unspoken solidarity. His eyes met Kain's, a beacon of reassurance in the shadowy confines of the tent. "You're going to be fine," he said, his voice a soothing balm. "Just fine."

"I'm going to give you a dose of morphine," I announced to Kain, my voice steady, betraying none of the inner turmoil I felt. The vial of morphine glinted in the dim light, a small beacon of relief. As I expelled the excess air from the syringe, watching the liquid form a small droplet at the needle's tip, a part of me marvelled at the power contained within that tiny cylinder—to ease pain, to bring a semblance of peace.

Without waiting for an acknowledgment from Kain, whose face was etched with lines of suffering, I gently but firmly inserted the needle into his upper arm. His grimace softened slightly at the contact, a silent testament to his trust in my actions.

"Try to relax," I whispered to him, my voice a soft caress against the backdrop of his pain. "You're safe now." It was as much a reassurance for him as it was a mantra for myself, a reminder of the sanctuary we had created here within the tent's canvas walls.

Chris watched our interaction with a mix of concern and awe. His gaze shifted to me as Kain, under the morphine's burgeoning effect, squeezed his hand—a gesture laden with gratitude and a plea for comfort.

"Brianne," Kain murmured deliriously, his hand reaching out to gently caress Chris's face, mistaking him in his morphine-induced haze. It was a moment of vulnerability, a breaking down of walls that hardship often constructs.

A brief smile flickered across my face, a momentary lapse into satisfaction as I noted the drug's effect. "I think the morphine's got a hold of him now," I shared with Chris, catching his gaze. The relief in his eyes mirrored my own, a shared moment of respite in our relentless reality.

"What do you need me to do?" Chris asked, his voice tinged with readiness, his eyes darting to the gruesome wound that marred Kain's leg.

The sight of the wound was a visceral blow, the severity of the gash enough to make my stomach churn with unease. *You've seen worse and had less, Glenda,* I reminded myself sternly, drawing upon reserves of strength I sometimes forgot I possessed. It was a mental pep talk, one I had given myself countless times before in moments of doubt and despair.

"Just hold his hand," I directed Chris, my voice firm yet gentle. I knew the limitations of our situation—Chris's medical expertise might not extend to suturing wounds or administering care, but his presence, his unwavering support, offered a different kind of healing. The simple act of holding Kain's hand was a lifeline, a physical manifestation of our collective will to survive, to fight, to persevere.

The flickering light from the campfire outside cast long, wavering shadows across the interior of the tent, its illumination meagre and insufficient for the task at hand. My eyes strained in the dimness, the contours of Kain's wound blurring and sharpening as I tried to focus. The thought of bringing a firestick inside was fraught with danger, the risk of disaster looming large in my mind. Yet, the stark reality of our situation left us teetering on the edge of a precipice—one where Kain's life hung in the balance.

"I need more light," I confessed to Chris, the words tumbling from my lips in a mix of desperation and resignation. It felt like a defeat, acknowledging the lengths to which we might have to go to save Kain.

"A firestick?" The alarm in Chris's voice was palpable, his eyes reflecting the severity of what I was suggesting. The air between us charged with a silent understanding of the risks involved.

I nodded, the weight of the decision pressing down on me. "We have no choice. I can't stitch Kain's leg without it," I admitted, my voice firm despite the turmoil churning inside me. The necessity of the situation left no room for doubt, even as the danger of our actions loomed ominously.

"It can't wait until morning?" Chris's plea was laced with hope, a desperate clutch at any alternative to the perilous course we were contemplating. His face twisted in distress, the grip on Kain's hand a testament to his fear and concern.

"He's already lost too much blood," I responded, my tone laced with the urgency of our predicament. As I dragged another clean t-shirt through the blood that pooled around Kain's leg, the stark reality of his condition was laid bare. Time was not a luxury we could afford.

Chris's response was a mix of fear and determination. "There has to be another way," he insisted, his voice breaking with the weight of the moment. The thought of endangering all of us with a single misstep was a burden he was loath to bear. "One false step and I'll set this whole tent ablaze!"

"I know," I found myself responding, my voice laced with a tension that seemed to echo the tightness in my chest. "I just need light long enough to close the wound to stop the bleeding. We'll take him to the lagoon as soon as the sun begins to rise, and hopefully, the water will speed up the healing process." The words felt heavy on my tongue, a mixture of hope and desperation clinging to the idea of the lagoon's healing waters—a beacon in our dark night.

"I don't understand how the water will make any difference," Chris's voice broke through the tension, his confusion palpable even in the dimly lit confines of our makeshift infirmary. The shadows played across his face, deepening his expression of concern into one of outright skepticism.

For a moment, I hesitated, caught in the internal debate of how much to reveal about the lagoon's enigmatic healing powers. The water's secrets were not widely known, and in the current context, explaining its mystic properties felt almost frivolous against the backdrop of Kain's critical condition. "Just get me some light," I finally said, settling on a practical request over delving into explanations that would do little to alter our immediate situation.

As Chris hurried out, a silence descended upon the tent, thick and almost tangible. It was a quiet that amplified every other sound—the steady rhythm of Kain's laboured breathing, the unsettling thud of my own heart—as if in the absence of light, our senses sought to compensate by heightening our awareness of everything else.

Left alone in the tent, my eyes attempted to navigate through the oppressive darkness, a futile effort to prepare for the task ahead. The darkness seemed to swallow up every hopeful thought, leaving a residue of anxiety that was hard to shake off. The faint glow from the campfire's embers at the tent's entrance barely penetrated the interior, casting ghostly shadows that danced across the canvas walls in an eerie display of light and dark.

Feeling the weight of the situation, I allowed myself a brief moment of surrender, closing my eyes tightly in an attempt to block out the uncertainty and fear that threatened to overwhelm me. My fingers found my temples, massaging in small, circular motions in a feeble attempt to ease the pounding headache that mirrored the turmoil within. In that moment of forced calm, I found myself grappling with the harsh reality of our predicament, the delicate balance between life and death resting heavily on our next actions. The responsibility was a tangible weight, a burden I bore with a determination fuelled by necessity and the faint, flickering hope that dawn—and with it, salvation—was not too far off.

❖

The abrupt rustling at the tent's entrance sent a sharp spike of adrenaline surging through my veins, a primal response to the potential threat lurking just beyond my field of vision. In a reflexive, albeit clumsy, attempt to face the unknown, I pivoted too swiftly on the tent's uneven floor, losing my precarious balance and tumbling backward. The impact with the ground sent a jolt through me, and for a moment, I lay there, disoriented, my heart pounding a frenetic rhythm against my ribcage.

Scrambling to a somewhat dignified position on all fours, I could sense—more than see—the presence of whatever creature had decided to visit us in these vulnerable hours. The darkness of the night seemed to solidify around me, and in that moment, the weight of isolation pressed down, a tangible reminder of our remoteness. The creature advanced, and its eyes, unseen yet palpably fixed on me, pierced through the shadows, sending a wave of fear coursing through my already tense body.

As it lunged forward, my hands shot up instinctively, a feeble barrier against the impending threat. My mind raced with images of ferocious beasts, each more terrifying than the last, conjured from the depths of my anxiety. The realisation that my efforts would be utterly useless in the face of such raw power did little to quell the panic that had taken hold, my breaths coming in short, sharp gasps as my chest tightened in fear.

Then, unexpectedly, the harshness of the situation melted away with the rough, wet sensation of a tongue sliding across my cheek. The creature, far from the monstrous entity my mind had envisioned, paused and retreated slightly, its heavy breathing punctuating the silence that had fallen over us.

Tentatively, I parted the fingers that shielded my eyes, braving a glimpse of my would-be assailant. Relief washed over me in an overwhelming wave as the familiar sight of Lois came into focus. Her tail wagged in a blur of motion, her panting breaths a sign of her excitement—or perhaps relief at finding me.

"Lois!" The tension drained from my body, replaced by an immense relief that left me breathless. I gathered her into my arms, pulling her close, her warmth a stark contrast to the cold dread that had moments ago gripped me. Her rough kisses, interspersed with my attempts to calm both our racing hearts, coaxed a faint smile onto my lips—a rare moment of lightness amidst the shadows.

"Will this do?" Chris's voice cut through, a beacon of hope in the form of a simple question. He stepped into the tent, the smartphone in his hand glowing like a modern-day torch against the canvas backdrop. It was a stark contrast to the primitive solution we had dreaded to employ, and in that moment, the sight of it seemed almost revolutionary.

As a wave of renewed optimism surged through me, invigorating my weary spirit with a much-needed dose of adrenaline, I couldn't help but feel a glimmer of hope. "It's better than a fire," I responded, my voice laced with a relief that was as palpable as the cool night air. The soft smile that my words coaxed onto Chris's round, bearded face was like a visual sigh of relief, a shared moment of lightness.

With a renewed sense of urgency, I quickly gathered my medical instruments, laying them out with meticulous care. The smartphone's light, though not as broad or as warm as the campfire's, cast a focused beam that cut through the darkness, illuminating the task at hand. It was a critical lifeline, one that transformed Chris from a bystander into an indispensable part of the life-saving process we were about to undertake.

Lois, too, seemed to sense the gravity of the moment. She sat close by, her presence a silent source of comfort and watchfulness. Her eyes followed my movements with an intensity that mirrored the protective instinct I felt swelling within my own chest. Together, we formed a makeshift triage team, united by a common purpose—to save Kain's leg, and with it, perhaps a part of ourselves.

❖

Having expressed my gratitude to Chris for his indispensable help and wishing him a restful night, the silence of the tent enveloped me, allowing a moment of solitude as I went about tidying the makeshift medical area. Lois had settled herself beside Kain, her body a comforting presence in the dimly lit space. "Stay," I gently instructed her as she made a slight movement, her head lifting as if to follow me. With a soft sigh, she obeyed, returning her head to rest atop her front paws, her eyes watching me with a mixture of loyalty and concern.

As I stepped out of the tent, the night air greeted me with its cool embrace, a stark contrast to the stifled atmosphere I had grown accustomed to inside. The open sky overhead seemed to stretch infinitely, a vast canvas of inky blackness. I took a moment to wipe the sweat from my brow, the residue of the night's endeavours still clinging to my skin, before allowing myself the luxury of stretching my tired muscles.

The stillness of the night was broken by Paul's voice, his figure emerging from the darkness like a ghost materialising from the ether. "How is Kain?" he asked, his tone laced with the undercurrent of concern that had been our constant companion since the ordeal began.

I paused my stretching, turning to face him, the vast, vacant heavens above serving as a backdrop to our solemn exchange. "He should be okay for the next few hours," I responded, trying to infuse my voice with a confidence that felt somewhat forced given the circumstances. As I rolled my neck, releasing the tension with a satisfying crack, I pondered the fragility of the situation we found ourselves in.

As Paul's weary figure came into focus, his exhaustion mirrored my own, a silent testament to the night's trials. My gaze drifted past him, landing on the hulking silhouette of a large, black creature lying ominously still beside the campfire. The sight sent a jolt of alarm coursing through me, my heart pounding against my ribcage as if trying to escape the confines of my chest. With cautious steps, I moved closer, the creature's formidable presence casting a shadow that seemed to chill the night air further. Its large tongue lolled from an open mouth, nestled among teeth that promised death with their razor-sharp menace. The sight of the gaping wound in its belly, from which blood seeped into the dust, stirred a visceral unease within me, my stomach churning in revolt.

"You've done enough tonight, Glenda. You should get some rest," Paul's voice broke through my focused observation, causing me to startle slightly under the unexpected touch of his hand on my shoulder. His words, meant to comfort, instead wrapped around me like a shroud, heavy with the reminder of the night's grim realities.

"Are you sure we are safe?" I couldn't help the tremor in my voice, the lingering images of Kain's injury intertwining with the present danger before us.

"Charity's doing another perimeter sweep. There's nothing more you can do, Glenda." Paul's assurance was a balm, yet it did little to quell the storm of thoughts raging within me. Despite the reassurance, the seed of doubt planted by the night's events refused to be easily dislodged.

The weight of exhaustion began to assert itself more forcefully, the adrenaline that had sustained me through the night ebbing away, leaving a fog of weariness in its wake. Acknowledging the futility of resistance, I acquiesced to Paul's suggestion. My hands, stained with the evidence of the night's endeavours, were mechanically wiped down my pants, a futile attempt to cleanse away the physical reminders of the hell we had experienced.

Retreating to the sanctuary of my tent, I was confronted with the task of shedding the soiled clothes that clung to my skin, a fabric barrier saturated with the night's toils. The moment the cool air hit my skin, a shiver of vulnerability coursed through me, the reality of our situation pressing in. The thought of being caught unprepared in the event of another emergency halted my actions, prompting me to hurriedly redress. The decision, born of a blend of practicality and a lingering sense of foreboding, was a concession to the unpredictable nature of our existence at the edge of civilisation.

Collapsing into my makeshift bed, the exhaustion that enveloped me was a physical entity, dragging me down into the depths of a much-needed, albeit uneasy, sleep. My eyes, heavy with the weight of the night's vigil, closed with the hope of rest yet haunted by the spectre of what the morrow might bring. In the quiet solitude of my tent, the line between wakefulness and sleep blurred, as I drifted off into a restless slumber, the events of the night weaving through my dreams like dark threads in a tapestry of survival.

SAVE A LEG

1338.209.3

As dawn's early light began to paint the sky with strokes of pink and orange, the world around me stirred gently to life. The fabric of the tent swayed with a softness that belied the tumultuous night we had just endured. My approach was tentative, the absurdity of my actions dawning on me as I reached out to knock on the canvas. The realisation washed over me in a wave of embarrassment, my cheeks burning with a flush that felt absurdly out of place in the wilderness. "Psst, Chris. Are you awake?" I whispered, my voice unintentionally escalating into a louder hiss, betraying my attempt at stealth.

The sudden interjection of Karen's shrill voice from within the tent, "Chris! Get up!" momentarily shattered the morning's calm and redirected my thoughts away from the recent disaster. The mental image of Karen, exasperated and prodding her husband into wakefulness, sparked a rare flicker of amusement amidst the gloom. A small, involuntary smile tugged at the corner of my mouth, a brief oasis of levity in the desert of our current predicament.

Standing there, in the quiet of dawn, the realisation that Chris was now undeniably roused from sleep halted my next call to him mid-breath. The small victory of having achieved my immediate goal—waking him—was overshadowed by the pressing need for his assistance. "Chris, I need your urgent help," I found myself whispering again, this time with a sharp urgency that pierced the tranquil air.

Karen's voice, laden with irritation, cut through once more, "Get up, would you?" Her tone, scolding yet laced with underlying concern, resonated with me.

As the sleeping bags inside the tent rustled with the promise of activity, I waited with a patience born of necessity, my body tensed and ready to spring into action. Within moments, the flap was cautiously unzipped, and Chris's head emerged, a visual embodiment of grogginess. His eyes, clouded with the remnants of sleep, briefly met mine, a silent acknowledgment passing between us. The sleepiness etched into his features spoke volumes of the night's toll, yet the urgency of our situation brooked no delay.

"I need you to help me get Kain to the lagoon. We need to hurry," I implored, the weight of responsibility pressing down on me. The morning's golden light did little to dispel the shadows of concern that lingered from the night before.

"Of course," Chris mumbled, his voice rough with sleep as he rubbed a hand across his face in a vain attempt to stifle a yawn.

"Put some blinkin' pants on!" Karen ordered, her command echoing slightly in the crisp dawn. Chris's expression, caught between confusion and the slow realisation of his state of undress, was almost comical. His mouth opened, then closed, words failing him in his half-awake state.

"I'll meet you at the medical tent," I said, turning away to give Chris a moment of privacy. Despite the gravity of our mission, I couldn't suppress a twinge of sympathy for him. It was hard to judge a man's morning disposition under such circumstances, especially when the night had been anything but restful. The thought that Chris might not be a morning person lingered in my mind, yet the events of the previous night rendered any such judgments moot. Our focus was singular now: to ensure Kain's safety and recovery.

As Chris disappeared back into the tent, urgency propelled me forward. The campfire, now a smouldering reminder of the night's vigil, lay on my path, its faint glow casting eerie shadows on the ground. My heart urged me to look away, to ignore the remains of the creature that had brought such turmoil to our camp, but my eyes betrayed me with a compulsive flicker in its direction. The sight of it, lifeless and eerie in the cold light of dawn, with the dried blood marking its final struggle, sent an involuntary shudder coursing through me.

The cool shudder that danced across my shoulders and threaded its icy fingers down my spine was more than fear; it was a tangible reminder of the unknown dangers that lurked in the darkness beyond our camp. The question of how many creatures had besieged us during the long night lingered heavily in my mind. The uncertainty of facing one or many adversaries added a thick layer of tension to the already strained atmosphere of the camp.

In the chaos of the night, there had been no time for thorough assessments or headcounts of our attackers. The need to tend to Kain's injuries, coupled with the immediate threat to our safety, had pushed all else to the periphery of my concerns. Paul and Charity, each having played their roles in the night's events, would have insights, perhaps even answers, but the luxury of debriefing with them seemed distant in that moment.

As I made my way, the promise of a later time for reflection and strategy offered a sliver of solace. Yet, the pressing need to secure Kain's well-being and ensure the safety of our camp weighed heavily on me. The uncertainty of what lay ahead, of whether the night's horrors were a singular event or a harbinger of further dangers, clouded my thoughts. The hope that we could come together, to share knowledge and fortify our defences, was a beacon in the swirling fog of my apprehensions.

As I quietly navigated my way into the medical tent, the early morning light cast a gentle, ethereal glow through the fabric, illuminating the space with a soft radiance. My steps were guided by a singular purpose as I moved towards Kain's makeshift bed in the right wing of the tent. The events of the night had left a heavy imprint on my mind, and despite the quiet that now enveloped us, the echo of urgency from our nocturnal ordeal lingered palpably in the air.

The thought of Kain waking to the reality of his injuries, coupled with my own uncertainties about the adequacy of my surgical efforts under such less-than-ideal conditions, propelled me forward. My hands, steady despite the exhaustion that clung to me like a second skin, were swift in preparing a fresh syringe of antibiotics. This was a routine I had performed countless times, yet each instance carried the weight of responsibility anew.

Kneeling beside Kain, the fabric of the tent floor pressing cold against my knees, I leaned in close, "Kain," I whispered, my voice soft but firm, a tentative probe for any sign of consciousness. His response, a smile that seemed both surprising and heartbreakingly innocent given the circumstances, brushed a wave of relief through me, even as his eyes remained closed in peaceful oblivion.

"Kain," I called again, this time with a gentle but decisive poke in the ribs, a more insistent summons back to the world of the waking. The heavy veil of sleep that had claimed him began to lift, his eyelids fluttering open in a slow, hesitant dance with consciousness.

"Good, you're awake," I greeted, the relief and a touch of mischief mingling in my voice, giving rise to a broad smile that stretched across my weary face. The sight of him awakening, despite the pain and confusion that was sure to follow, was a small victory in the grand scheme of our situation.

As I tore open an alcohol swab and began the methodical process of disinfecting an area on his arm, the clinical familiarity of the task provided a momentary anchor. "Try and hold still," I instructed, my voice imbued with a gentle firmness. The needle, a slender beacon of healing, pierced his skin with ease.

Kain's breathing, shallow and quick, broke the stillness of the medical tent with its urgency. "I can't feel my leg," he gasped, the words tangled in laboured breaths, a palpable fear lacing each syllable.

"Are you certain?" My response was automatic, clinical, even as my heart raced in tandem with his fear. My eyes, trained on his face, searched for signs of panic or confusion that might skew his perception of pain—or its absence.

"Am I going to lose it?" His question, loaded with the weight of unspoken fears, hit me harder than expected. The sight of his eyes, glistening with the onset of tears, tightened my chest in empathy.

Remain calm, Glenda. The mantra echoed in my mind, a source of strength in the face of my own rising tide of emotion. With a steadiness I didn't feel, I took the empty syringe, aiming for a response that would reassure us both. The sharp plunge into the arch of his foot elicited a cry, raw and filled with surprise.

"What the fuck was that for!?" The sense of betrayal in his voice was unmistakable, a clear reflection of the shock and pain I had just inflicted.

I forced a soft smile, an attempt to ease the tension, "Your leg still has feeling." The words were meant to comfort, to provide a silver lining to the cloud of fear that hung over us.

"No!" His retort came as he frantically wiped away tears, the vulnerability of his youth laid bare in this moment of crisis. "I meant the other leg."

My professional façade wavered at the revelation, a cold stab of worry knotting my stomach. "That doesn't make any sense," I murmured, more to myself than to him. The logical part of my brain scrambled for an explanation, even as I instructed him, "Close your eyes."

He complied, a sniffle punctuating the heavy silence that followed. My examination became more deliberate, my fingers pressing into the flesh of his calf, moving towards his foot, each touch a silent prayer for a reaction. "Do you not feel anything?" The question was a whisper against the storm of fear brewing within me.

When his eyes met mine, void of the reaction I had desperately hoped for, my heart sank. "No," he responded, his voice a mix of confusion and fear. "Should I?"

The reassurance I offered next was hollow, the words tasting like ash in my mouth. "You're going to be just fine," I lied, the lie of confidence crumbling as I faced the grim reality of his condition. The professional in me knew the gravity of his symptoms, yet the human in me clung to a sliver of hope, desperate to believe in the possibility of a positive outcome.

The tent's fabric whispered a soft protest as Chris made his entrance, the urgency of the situation reflected in his brisk movements.

"We need to get Kain to the lagoon, now!" The words tumbled out of my mouth, fuelled by a mixture of determination and desperation. The lagoon, with its whispered promises of healing, seemed our only hope.

Turning my attention back to Kain, I caught the flicker of fear in his eyes, wide and imploring. His vehement shake of the head, "Not the lagoon," he whispered, struck a chord of confusion within me. His resistance was unexpected, a puzzle piece that didn't fit the image I had been constructing of our next steps.

"Why not?" My question was laced with curiosity and concern, my brow furrowing as I tried to decipher the root of his fear. Kain's continued silence, punctuated by the persistent shaking of his head, only deepened the mystery.

Chris chimed in with reassurance, "It's okay. The beast has been killed." His words were meant to soothe, to dispel the shadows of fear that seemed to cling to Kain.

"Help me lift him," I instructed Chris, my focus shifting back to the task at hand. The urgency to act, to do something that might tip the scales back in our favour, was overwhelming. Chris positioned himself beside me, his posture one of readiness.

Together, we attempted to navigate the delicate balance of supporting Kain, of offering physical assistance. Chris's arm slipped beneath Kain's shoulders with ease. Yet, the reality of Kain's condition—a wounded leg and the terrifying, inexplicable paralysis of the other—transformed what should have been straightforward, into a moment fraught with difficulty.

The inevitable stumble, a dance of desperation and determination, ended with them both on the ground. The thud of their fall was a stark reminder of our vulnerability, of the precariousness of our situation. In that instant, the weight of responsibility bore down on me with renewed intensity, a silent demand for action, for solutions, in a world that seemed determined to offer neither.

As I acknowledged the gravity of Kain's situation, my gaze shifted to Chris, the silent communication between us speaking volumes. "I'll get Karen," I declared, feeling the weight of our predicament pressing down on us with an urgency that demanded immediate action.

"No need," Karen's voice, both unexpected and welcome, cut through the tense atmosphere as she appeared at the tent's entrance. Her timely arrival, propelled by a keen sense of intuition or perhaps the unspoken bond that often forms in times of crisis, was a small beacon of hope. "I figured you might need some more help," she stated, her presence bringing a new surge of energy as she approached us with determined strides. "What do you need?"

"We need to carry Kain to the lagoon," I explained, locking eyes with her to convey the seriousness. My voice softened as I addressed her directly, sharing the grim reality: "He currently has no use of his legs." The words felt heavy in my mouth, each syllable a reminder of the dire situation we were navigating.

Karen's reaction—a brief widening of her eyes followed by a quick nod—was all the confirmation I needed of her understanding and unwavering support. Without hesitation, she moved to Chris's side.

"I'll take the bulk of his weight," Chris announced, outlining a plan that relied on teamwork and mutual trust. "Can you support his waist and legs?"

"Of course," Karen responded, her voice imbued with resolve as she offered a reassuring squeeze to her husband's shoulder.

As they prepared to lift Kain, the air filled with grunts and moans. Seizing the moment, I leaned in to inspect the hastily applied bandage around Kain's leg. The sight that greeted me —a rag tightly bound around the limb, fresh blood seeping through the rough stitches I had placed in the desperate darkness—sent a wave of self-reproach through me. *That really doesn't look good,* I silently admonished myself, my grimace a reflection of my dissatisfaction with the work I had been forced to perform under less than ideal conditions.

♦

Standing atop the dune, the lagoon unfolded before me in a spectacle of serene beauty, its tranquility belying the turmoil that had led us here. The clear, pristine waters carved a vivid contrast against the canvas of earthy hues that framed it—browns, reds, and oranges blending into a backdrop that seemed almost otherworldly in its quiet splendour. The absence of life around such an inviting oasis added a layer of mystery, its untouched surface mirroring the sky with an almost eerie perfection. *Then again, this place is anything but usual,* I mused, a reminder to myself that the rules of the ordinary world seemed to bend and shift in this secluded haven.

As Karen and Chris gently lowered Kain onto the bank, the solemnity of our mission settled around us like a cloak. The lagoon's edge, where water met land, became a threshold between hope and uncertainty. The moment my fingers breached the surface of the cool water, a familiar zing—a whisper of energy—danced across my skin, rekindling memories of past miracles witnessed at these very shores. The sensation, both invigorating and unnerving, served as a silent affirmation of the lagoon's mysterious healing properties. It was a feeling I had encountered before, with Joel and when treating Paul's wounded arm, a tangible connection to the unseen forces that lingered in these waters.

Compelled by a mixture of desperation and hope, I eschewed the idea of a cautious approach. The urgency of Kain's condition, the visible marks of my nocturnal efforts to stitch his wounds, underscored the need for decisive action. With a resolve fortified by the memory of past successes, I opted for a full leg submersion. This decision, born from a blend of intuition and experience, was a leap of faith in the lagoon's ability to mend what lay beyond the reach of my medical expertise.

As I prepared to lower Kain's leg into the healing embrace of the lagoon, the air seemed to hold its breath, the world around us pausing in anticipation. The act, while simple in its execution, was laden with the weight of all our hopes, a silent plea for restoration and relief. In that moment, the boundaries between science and the inexplicable blurred, leaving us suspended in a space where only faith and the healing powers of nature held sway.

The moment Kain's foot touched the water, a sharp, pained groan broke from his lips, slicing through the quietude of the lagoon's edge. Reacting instinctively, Karen and Chris pulled him away, their movements quick, fuelled by concern and fear. Yet, I held firm, my grasp on Kain's leg unyielding. "He's fine," I told them, as the memory of Paul's similar reaction flashed through my mind, a beacon of hope amidst the panic. *This is no different,* I reassured myself, even as I felt the collective resistance of our small group. The conviction that the lagoon's waters held healing powers was a belief I clung to, even in the face of their understandable apprehension.

Kain's voice, strained yet resolute, cut through the tension. "I want to be alone for a while," he declared, his rapid blinking and bitten lip betraying the effort it took to remain composed. His request, born from a place of pain and vulnerability, was met with immediate dissent.

"Don't be such an idiot. You can't be alone in your state," Karen's response was swift, her tone laced with a mix of frustration and concern. It was a harsh rebuttal, yet underscored by the undeniable truth.

Kain's gaze then shifted to me, his eyes a mirror to the turmoil within, seeking an ally in his plea for solitude. It was a moment that demanded a delicate balance between compassion and the harsh realities of our circumstances.

"Karen's right," I found myself echoing, the weight of my professional judgment and personal concern melding into a single, unwavering stance. "It's not safe for you to be alone out here."

As Kain began to voice another plea, Chris stepped in with a solution that seemed to bridge the gap between Kain's desire for independence and our collective concern for his safety. "I'll stay here with him," he offered, his tone firm. "I can clean his wound."

The resolution, swift and unexpected, was met with a silent consensus. Kain's nod of agreement was quick, a visible sign of his trust in Chris's capability to care for him. "I'll be safe with Chris," he added, his plea imbued with a mix of hope and resignation.

Kain's insistence on solitude, despite the precariousness of his situation, left me momentarily taken aback. His resolve, a blend of stubbornness and bravery, was as admirable as it was concerning. I found myself capitulating, my professional judgment mingling with respect for his wishes. "As long as you make sure his leg stays submerged for a reasonable amount of time," I advised Chris, emphasising the importance of the treatment despite Kain's anticipated protests.

The sudden twitch of Kain's leg under my grip was a stark reminder of the pain he was enduring. I tightened my hold, a silent vow to myself to ensure his well-being as much as possible. "Regardless of how much he groans and tells you to stop, okay?" My words were firm, a directive that brooked no compromise. Chris's nod, though quiet, carried the weight of his commitment.

As I released Kain's leg and rose to my feet, the gravity of our decision seemed to hang in the air between us. Karen's voiced concern, "Are you sure this is a good idea?" echoed the doubts that shadowed my mind. Her uncertainty was palpable, her worry for Kain's well-being manifesting in the tight press of her lips.

"We're sure," Kain's response was quick, a flash of determination cutting through the haze of anxiety. His words were a plea for trust, a declaration of his readiness to face the consequences of his choice.

Our collective gaze shifted to Chris, seeking some semblance of reassurance, but his response was noncommittal—a shrug that left us floating in a sea of uncertainty. *I guess we just have to trust him,* I thought, a silent concession to the faith we had placed in one another.

"You could lose your leg if you don't let the water help you," I cautioned Kain, my voice tinged with a mix of sternness and concern. My hand squeezed his shoulder, a physical manifestation of my support and a silent promise that we were there for him, no matter the outcome.

As I extended my hand to Karen, pulling her to her feet, the action was more than just a gesture of solidarity. It was an acknowledgment of the journey we had undertaken together, a path fraught with challenges but also marked by moments of profound connection and mutual reliance. Our decision to trust in the healing properties of the lagoon, in the strength of our bond, and in the resilience of the human spirit was a leap of faith—one that we hoped would carry Kain through this trial and bring him back to us, whole and healed.

HOPE OF CHEWBATHIA

4338.209.4

The warmth of the early morning sun promised a day devoid of clouds, a stark contrast to the internal storm of questions and uncertainties that swirled within me. Karen's voice broke through my contemplation of Clivilius's unforgiving weather, bringing me back to the immediate concerns at hand.

"Did those two seem a little odd to you?" Her question, seemingly casual, hinted at underlying worries.

"I'm sure they're just being men," was my attempt at light-hearted dismissal, though it felt hollow even to my own ears. The simplicity of the explanation did little to address the complex web of concerns that had entangled us since our arrival at the mysterious lagoon.

Karen's persistence, however, unearthed the deeper apprehensions I had been trying to tamp down. "You don't think that maybe there's something weird going on with the water?" she probed further. "I mean, look what we discovered with the soil."

As we walked, my foot disturbed the dust beneath us, creating small clouds that the breeze whimsically erased from existence. It was a momentary distraction from the weight of our conversation. "I believe the water has some interesting healing properties. I suspect the healing process hurts a little," I mused aloud, trying to piece together the puzzle of the lagoon's powers with the scraps of evidence I had gathered.

Karen's scoff at my explanation, labelling our companions' stoicism as a "manly façade," elicited a brief, shared moment of levity between us. "Exactly!" I agreed, clinging to the camaraderie that helped to lighten the burden of our situation.

However, her next words, left hanging as I abruptly stopped and grasped her arm, were a stark reminder of the fine line we walked between discovery and danger. "I'm sure they'll be fine. Chris will come and get us if they have any problems," I reassured her, and perhaps myself, with more confidence than I felt. The reality was, we were navigating uncharted waters, both literally and metaphorically.

Karen's sigh was heavy with resignation, a sound that seemed to carry the weight of our shared concerns and the unspoken fears that lingered between us. As she attempted to withdraw, I tightened my grip on her arm, not out of restraint but in a silent plea for connection, for reassurance in the face of the unknown. It was then that my eyes caught sight of the scratch marring her forearm, a stark contrast against her skin.

"How did you get that scratch?" My inquiry was more than casual curiosity; it was tinged with the undercurrent of anxiety that was becoming my constant companion.

Karen's demeanour shifted at my question, her previous resolve dissolving into a visible unease. The shadow that suddenly loomed over us seemed to echo the dark turn our conversation had taken, amplifying the sense of foreboding that had been simmering just beneath the surface.

Brow furrowing deeply, my heart skipped a beat with the fear that Karen was another victim of the shadow panther.

"Duke accidentally scratched me when Chris and I attempted to help Jamie and Duke." Her explanation, intended to allay my fears, only served to deepen the mystery, prompting more questions than it answered.

My suspicion, impossible to mask, pushed me to probe further. "Why did Jamie and Duke need help?"

Karen's hesitation, the visible struggle to articulate her next words, did little to quell the growing apprehension within me. "You haven't heard?" Her question, hinted at a tale of loss and despair that I had yet to uncover.

"Heard what?" I asked, tentatively.

"Duke," she began, the difficulty with which she spoke betraying the gravity of what she was about to disclose. My heart clenched in anticipation, a dreadful premonition taking root as I waited for her to continue.

The pause that followed, filled with Karen's attempt to compose herself, seemed to stretch on indefinitely, the silence punctuated only by her cleared throat. "Duke was attacked last night too. He didn't make it."

The revelation of Duke's fate sent a shockwave through me, my reaction instinctive as my hand flew to my mouth, a barrier against the audible gasp of disbelief. The notion that a shadow panther, a creature of such lethal grace and power, had claimed Duke was almost too surreal to digest. Karen's nod only solidified the grim reality, anchoring the tragedy firmly in the harshness of our current existence.

A sharp sting pricked behind my eyes, the onset of tears for a small dog that, despite our lack of a warm relationship, had become a part of my extended family in this wild place. "I know Duke and I weren't exactly on the friendliest of terms, but..." My voice faltered, a mixture of sadness and disbelief muddling my words. The silence that followed was heavy with the unspoken acknowledgment of our loss. *I can't believe this is happening,* I thought, struggling to wrap my mind around the cruel twist of fate.

"Are Duke and Kain our only losses?" The question, while necessary, felt cold, clinical even, as if trying to quantify our grief could somehow make it more bearable.

Karen cast me a sideways glance, "We haven't lost Kain yet," she rebuked.

"Of course not," I retorted, the correction doing little to ease the tension that had woven itself tightly around my heart.

"But yes, I'm pretty sure that Duke and Kain were the only ones injured."

The news was unfortunate, but I was grateful that there were not more serious injuries sustained. Processing the gravity of our situation, Karen and I continued toward camp, the silence allowing us both to consider our own thoughts and emotions.

❖

The silence that greeted us upon our return to camp was disconcerting, a stark contrast to the usual morning bustle that signified the start of another day's struggle for survival. My unease grew with each step, the absence of familiar faces only adding to the growing apprehension within me. Besides Kain, Chris and Karen this morning, I hadn't seen Joel, or anybody else for that matter.

Entering Joel's tent with a sense of foreboding, the emptiness that met me was a silent scream in the quiet of the morning. No Joel, no Jamie, no Henri, and, of course, no Duke. The realisation that so many were unaccounted for sent a shiver down my spine, the implications of their absence weaving a tapestry of fear in my mind.

"Where are Jamie and Duke?" The question was directed at Karen, who had quietly followed me into the tent. Her response, "I'm not sure," accompanied with a simple shake of the head, did nothing to quell the unease that had settled over me like a heavy cloak.

As we stepped back outside, the sound of voices drew my attention. Moving towards the source, the sight that unfolded before me was one of solemnity and grief. Jamie, standing by the river's edge with a small, lifeless form cradled in his arms, was a poignant reminder of the loss we had suffered. My heart sank at the confirmation of Duke's fate, a sight that, despite the preparation, was no less harrowing to witness.

Paul, Charity, and a woman I didn't recognise were engaged in what appeared to be a tense conversation with Jamie. The strain in their voices, even from a distance, was palpable, a clear indication of the stress and sorrow that had enveloped our camp.

As I approached, the need to account for everyone became paramount. A quick scan of the faces confirmed that all were present, save for Joel. The realisation tightened its grip around my heart, the worry for our missing companion casting a long shadow over the already sombre mood. My brow furrowed, a physical manifestation of the turmoil within, as I braced myself for the challenge of piecing together the events that had led to this moment.

"Has anyone seen Joel this morning?" The urgency in my question was palpable, my voice betraying the panic that had steadily been building within me. The absence of Joel, especially under these circumstances, was a concern that I couldn't shake off, each passing moment adding to the fear that something else had gone terribly wrong.

The response from the shorter woman, a newcomer to our group whose presence was as striking as it was mysterious, did little to ease my worries. "I've been with Jamie since I arrived," she stated, her voice calm, betraying none of the chaos that seemed to envelop her appearance. My gaze lingered on her, taking in the contrasting details - the long silver hair that seemed almost ethereal, the cuts that marred her arms, and the tattered state of her dress. It was a visage that spoke volumes of the night's events, a silent testimony to the ordeal she had endured. The screams that had haunted the night, now had a face, and the realisation sent a chill down my spine.

Paul's input, though well-intentioned, offered no comfort. "I've not seen him at all this morning. I just assumed he was still resting in his tent. Is he not there?"

"No," was all I could manage, the word sharp, a clear indicator of my escalating worry. The conversation was abruptly cut short by Jamie's sudden collapse, the distress in his movements drawing our collective attention. The sight of him, struggling to maintain his grip on Duke even as he fell, was a poignant reminder of the grief that we were all grappling with.

"Jamie!" Our voices merged into a singular cry of alarm, our individual concerns momentarily set aside as we rushed to his aid.

Crouching beside Jamie, the urgency of the moment sharpened my focus as I quickly scanned his chest, searching for any indication that the blood might be his own and not solely Duke's. The sight of Jamie's face, marked by the unmistakable signs of a night spent in turmoil—swollen, red eyes devoid of rest—painted a vivid picture of his suffering. It was a silent testimony to the depth of his grief.

I directed Paul with a sense of purpose. "Gather everyone to the campfire," I instructed, my voice carrying the weight of both command and necessity. As I turned my attention back to Jamie, a second, more thorough assessment confirmed my initial observation: his physical condition, while marred by the evident signs of a night spent in grief and the minor injuries sustained in his fall, bore no trace of more serious harm.

"You must be Glenda," the silver-haired woman's voice broke through my focused assessment, her cautious gaze meeting mine as I stood. Her presence, both intriguing and enigmatic, added another layer to the already complex tapestry of our situation.

"I am," I confirmed, the act of brushing dust from my clothes serving as a brief interlude to the morning's grim proceedings. "I'm going to find something suitable to wrap Duke in. Please help Jamie get himself cleaned. I'll meet you back here before we take the dog to the campfire." My instructions were clear, each task a step towards not just preserving Duke's dignity but also allowing us a moment to come together in our shared grief.

"Yes, doctor," the woman's response, formal yet tinged with an undercurrent of shared understanding, acknowledged the role I had assumed within our group.

As I turned away to fulfil my grim duty, the weight of leadership pressed heavily upon me, a mantle borne of circumstance rather than choice. The task ahead, while simple in its execution, was laden with significance. It was not just about finding a suitable shroud for Duke; it was about providing a semblance of order, a moment of collective mourning that might offer a measure of solace to our fractured spirits.

❖

Finding a suitable sheet for Duke was a small mercy in the midst of our turmoil, allowing me to act with a semblance of purpose. However, as I exited the tent, my resolve was momentarily sidetracked by the sight of Charity examining the carcass of the shadow panther that had caused so much grief. My steps, initially brisk with intention, slowed as curiosity and concern drew me towards her.

"Was there only one shadow panther?" The question emerged almost reflexively, my scientific mind grappling with the need to understand the extent of the threat we faced.

Charity's response sent a chill down my spine. "They are pack hunters. There would have been at least four or five of them in the area last night." The implication of her words, the realisation that we had been surrounded by such lethal predators, was staggering.

"That many?" My response was a whisper, disbelief and fear mingling in equal measure. The notion that we had been so close to a larger catastrophe was unnerving.

Charity's confirmation, though expected, did little to quell the growing unease within me. Her next revelation, however, was utterly unexpected and shifted the ground beneath my feet. "Now that they have lost two of their pack, it's unlikely that they..." Her words trailed off as my interruption, sparked by surprise and confusion, cut through the air.

"They lost two?" The question was out before I could temper my reaction, my eyes darting around in search of evidence of another fallen predator.

Charity's explanation, far from clarifying the situation, only deepened the mystery and widened the chasm of my understanding. "There's this one and the second one followed Beatrix through the Portal to Earth."

"What!?" The exclamation was a reflex, a verbal manifestation of the whirlwind of questions that assaulted me. "We can get back to Earth now? And who's Beatrix?" The possibility of a return, of escape from this relentless survival, was a beacon of hope in the dense fog of our predicament.

Charity's response, however, quashed that flicker of hope as swiftly as it had ignited. "We can't, but there are some creatures, like Guardians and these shadow panthers, that can." The distinction she made was a bitter pill to swallow, a reminder of the barriers that still stood firmly between us and home.

"And Beatrix?" The question hung between us, a thread seeking to weave through the tapestry of confusion that enveloped me.

"The silver-haired girl," Charity clarified, indicating the direction of Joel and Jamie's tent. The pieces began to fall into place, albeit slowly, the mention of Beatrix now linked to the mysterious newcomer with striking silver hair. "I believe she is your newest Guardian."

My eyes widened in disbelief, a sensation akin to a cold shiver cascading down my spine. "There's more than one Guardian?" The words tumbled out of me, tinged with a mix of awe and incredulity. The very concept seemed to unravel everything I thought I knew, expanding the boundaries of my understanding in an instant.

Charity, with her ever-present calm demeanour, chuckled softly, a sound that somehow managed to be both comforting and unsettling in this strange new context. "It would seem you've got a lot more to learn," she remarked, her voice a gentle nudge towards the vast unknown that lay ahead of me. As she spoke, her actions belied the softness of her tone. She deftly pulled a knife from the sheath strapped to her waist, the metal gleaming ominously under the morning light, and with a precision that spoke of countless such instances, thrust the blade into the black panther's neck.

The immediate stench that burst forth from the incision was like a physical entity, assaulting my senses with such ferocity that my stomach executed violent somersaults. My mouth gagged reflexively, a bitter taste clawing at the back of my throat. The smell was a vile mixture of death and decay, so potent it seemed almost tangible, a miasma that clung to the air and threatened to overwhelm me.

Undeterred, Charity began to work the blade across the beast's throat with a grim determination, her movements efficient yet brutal. "It's unpleasant," she acknowledged, her voice strained as she hacked and ripped at the bloody flesh. The understatement of her words did little to mask the gruesomeness of the task. "But the scent will warn the pack members to keep their distance." Her explanation did little to comfort me.

"I'm not surprised," I mumbled, the words barely audible even to my own ears. Pressing the back of my hand against my mouth in a vain attempt to shield myself from the assault on my senses, I quickly backed away, eager to put as much distance between myself and the source of my discomfort as possible.

It was then, in my haste to escape, that I nearly collided with Beatrix as she exited the tent, her arms laden with fresh clothes for Jamie. The suddenness of our near encounter elicited a soft, startled gasp from her, a sound that, under different circumstances, might have sparked a moment of shared amusement between us.

"Please take this with you and give it to Jamie," I told her, my voice steadier now, the urgency of the situation lending me a semblance of composure. I offered her the folded sheet, a makeshift solution for a problem that seemed both immediate and trivial in the grand scheme of things. "He can wrap Duke in it until we can organise more suitable arrangements."

With a silent nod, Beatrix took the sheet from me. Her actions, though simple, were imbued with an understanding and a sense of solidarity that transcended the need for words.

"Charity is right, Beatrix," Paul's voice cut through the tension, clearly continuing a conversation that had been happening before I arrived. His words hung in the air as he emerged from the tent, his presence commanding yet weary.

As my eyes darted suspiciously between the two, trying to piece together the context I had missed, Paul approached with a weight in his steps that seemed to press down on the very atmosphere around us. Beatrix's response was immediate, her frustration palpable. "You take charge of it then," she huffed, her tone laced with resignation and a hint of challenge before she turned on her heels, her departure swift and final.

Taking a deep breath to steady my nerves, I turned to Paul, my gaze questioning, seeking clarity in the midst of confusion. Before Paul could reply, Charity chimed in, her actions as decisive as her words. "The dog needs to be cremated," she declared, getting to her feet. Her movements were precise, almost ritualistic, as she wiped the bloodied blade across the bottom of one of the tassels that hung from her short leather skirt before sheathing it with a finality that left no room for argument.

I frowned, my discomfort growing. This new woman, Charity, with her blunt statements and stark pragmatism, was an enigma. *She has even less tact than I do*, I noted mentally, a wry observation that did little to lighten the gravity of her words. *And that's saying something!* My internal dialogue stumbled over itself as I struggled to articulate a response, my mouth opening and closing in silent protest. *But it's not okay*, I admitted to myself, the worry lines etched deeply into my forehead a testament to the turmoil within. *Hardly anything about this place is okay.*

Just as the weight of the situation threatened to engulf me, Paul's voice offered a momentary reprieve. "Look! Karen and Chris are returning with Kain," he announced, his finger pointing towards the dunes behind me, pulling me back from the edge of despair.

"And Lois too," I managed to add, a flicker of warmth igniting at the mention of familiar faces. A brief smile found its way to my lips, a rare beacon of hope in a landscape marred by uncertainty. I crouched down, my arms open in anticipation, ready to embrace the energetic girl who bounded towards me with an innocence that stood in stark contrast to the grim realities we faced. In that moment, as Lois reached my embrace, the harshness of our situation was momentarily softened by the purity of her unbridled joy.

The approach of the three settlers towards our makeshift camp was measured, their movements punctuated by the rugged terrain that seemed to challenge every step. The older couple, with a resilience born of necessity, took turns supporting Kain, whose determination to walk was evident despite his stagger.

"The feeling has returned in my good leg," Kain announced, a broad smile lighting up his face, casting a brief shadow of normalcy over the grave situation. His optimism was contagious, yet it carried with it an unspoken acknowledgment of the challenges yet to come.

"Well, that's a relief," I found myself saying as I pushed myself to my feet, drawn to the hint of hope in his words. "And the injured one?" I inquired, my professional curiosity mingling with a genuine concern for his wellbeing.

"Seems to be quite the miracle," Karen interjected, her voice tinged with a mixture of surprise and gratitude as the group came to a halt near the warmth of the campfire. The morning air, cool and crisp, seemed to pause in anticipation of my assessment.

Crouching in front of Kain, I took a closer look at the wound. *A miracle indeed*, I mused silently, my fingers gently probing the fresh skin that had begun to knit together with astonishing speed. The healing properties of the water here had exceeded my wildest expectations, compensating for my less than perfect sutures. A moment of professional pride flickered within me, quickly tempered by the realisation that nature here held powers beyond my understanding. *I won't have to redo them after all*, I thought, a small victory in the grand scheme of things.

Rising to my feet, I addressed Kain with a mix of sternness and care. "You'll still need to give the leg plenty of rest," I cautioned, aware of the fine line between recovery and relapse in such unpredictable conditions.

"We can make you some crutches," Chris offered. He shifted his weight, subtly adjusting to Kain's movements as he leaned heavily on Chris's shoulders for support.

"Forget making crutches," Karen huffed, her voice cutting through with a mixture of impatience and pragmatism. "Just get Luke to bring us some real ones, okay?"

"That's a much better idea..." I began, my voice trailing off as I caught myself.

The atmosphere around the campfire shifted palpably as Beatrix and Jamie emerged from behind the tents. My gaze, drawn irresistibly to the small bundle cradled in Jamie's arms, became heavy with the weight of unspoken grief. Beneath the sheet lay a silent testament to our sorrows, a reminder of loss in a place where every life held the weight of a community.

Feeling Lois tug at the frayed edges of my emotions, I instinctively pulled her closer, my hand finding solace in the softness of her head. The air around us seemed to thicken with her soft whimper, a sound that pierced the veil of gathered silence. "I know," I whispered back, crouching to meet her gaze with a tenderness I scarcely felt in my own heart. "He was your new friend." The words felt hollow, a feeble attempt to bridge the chasm of her understanding with my own. I pressed a soft kiss atop her head, a gesture of comfort that felt achingly inadequate, and stood once more.

Paul's voice broke through the gathering, his usual composure frayed at the edges by the strain of the moment.

His voice cracked, a rare display of vulnerability that mirrored the collective unease. His eyes, searching the faces around the campfire for any semblance of readiness, found only a shared hesitance.

"Jamie," he began, the weight of his duty as a leader evident in his faltering start. "I know things are a bit painful right now, but we need to know when you last saw Joel."

Jamie stopped abruptly, taking a moment to think. "It was just before the attack last night. He was in his bed in the tent when I took off after Duke," the reply was measured and heavy with unspoken guilt.

Paul's next question was delicate, a careful navigation through the minefield of our collective dread. "And when you returned?" he asked.

Jamie's response, a simple shrug, carried the weight of finality, his face a mask of resignation that mirrored the sinking feeling in my own heart.

"Then it's settled," I found myself saying, the words forming a barrier against the tide of despair threatening to overwhelm me. My arms crossed over my chest in a feeble attempt to ward off the chill of realisation that crept through the gathering. "Joel is missing."

As Charity brushed past me, her presence commanding and determined, she addressed the group with a certainty that both alarmed and galvanised us. "I am certain Joel has been taken by the Portal pirate. I will hunt him down and bring Joel back." Her words, decisive and bold, sliced through the heavy air of despair that had settled around us.

Portal pirate? The term ricocheted around the confines of my mind, a myriad of questions springing to life, each vying for precedence. My mouth, however, failed spectacularly to articulate any of them, opening and closing in a futile attempt to give voice to the whirlwind of thoughts and concerns.

Jamie's declaration cut through my internal chaos. "I'm coming with you," he stated, the resolve in his voice leaving no room for doubt or debate. It was a testament to his courage, or perhaps the depth of his desperation.

Charity's nod in response was swift, her agreement sealing their pact with an urgency that underscored the criticality of the situation. "Prepare your things. We leave immediately." Her command, though directed at Jamie, seemed to ripple through the rest of us, a call to action that was both thrilling and terrifying.

As Jamie's gaze fell upon Duke, the magnitude of what lay ahead seemed to crash down upon him. His eyes, wide with a mix of terror and determination.

Charity moved towards Jamie with long, confident strides. The moment she placed her hand beneath his chin, compelling him to meet her gaze, was charged with an intensity that drew a collective breath from those of us watching. "If you want any chance of finding Joel alive, we must leave immediately." Her words, though meant to steel Jamie for the journey ahead, reverberated through the group, a stark reminder of the peril Joel faced and the slim window for his rescue.

My heart plummeted into my empty stomach at the realisation of the direness of Joel's situation. The audible gasps from our small assembly echoed my own feelings of dread and helplessness. In that moment, as we faced the reality of embarking on a rescue mission into the unknown, the bonds that tied us together as a community were both tested and reinforced.

"I need to say farewell to Duke first," Jamie's voice cracked as he spoke to Charity, the tremble of his bottom lip a silent echo of the heartache in his words. It was a moment of raw vulnerability, a painful reminder of the cost of survival in this harsh new world.

Charity, with her gaze unwavering, held onto Jamie's eyes with a determination that seemed to anchor him amidst the storm of his emotions. "Life is full of decisions and consequences, Jamie. You need to make a choice: Joel or Duke." Her words, though spoken with a certain hardness, carried the weight of our grim reality. The necessity of her stance was clear, yet it did nothing to soften the blow of the ultimatum she presented.

The harshness of the choice laid before Jamie struck me deeply, sending a sharp pang through my chest. Despite the emotional turmoil unfolding before my eyes, I couldn't look away. My hand moved instinctively, seeking comfort in the familiar warmth of Lois' fur, the softness a stark contrast to the harshness of our situation. *I could never make such an impossible choice!* The thought circled in my mind, a whirlwind of empathy and despair for Jamie's predicament.

Finally, Jamie's slight nod towards Beatrix was a silent surrender, a relinquishment of one heartache in the hope of preventing another. Beatrix, her own sorrow mirrored in her slow approach, accepted the unspoken transfer of duty with a grace that belied the heaviness of the moment. The tear that traced its way down her cheek caught the sunlight, a single, glistening testament to the collective grief that hung over us.

Carefully, with a tenderness that spoke volumes, Beatrix took Duke from Jamie's arms, her voice soft and soothing as she tried to offer comfort. "Duke knows you love him, Jamie. He won't ever forget that." Her words, meant to heal, were a balm to the open wounds of our hearts, yet the ache they carried seemed to only deepen the sorrow.

Tears broke freely from Jamie's eyes, each one a silent bearer of the love and regret that filled him. Leaning in, he placed a gentle kiss on Duke's wrapped form, his whisper barely audible above the crackle of the campfire. "I'm so sorry, Duke." The simple, heart-wrenching apology was a final goodbye, a moment of closure amidst the horrors that threatened to engulf us.

An unexpected surge of anger swelled within me, its intensity taking me by surprise. It coursed through my veins like a tempest, directed not only at the situation at hand but at Clivilius itself, the mysterious and cruel force behind our predicament. In that moment, I made a silent vow, promising to harbour a grudge against it as unforgiving and relentless as the arid wasteland that stretched endlessly around us.

As I wrestled with my inner turmoil, Jamie's resolve seemed to solidify. Taking a deep, steadying breath, he stood with a newfound determination. "I'll grab my things," he announced to Charity, his voice carrying a mix of resolve and underlying sorrow. I couldn't help but admire his courage, even as my heart ached for him.

My gaze followed Jamie's retreating back with a mix of anger and concern. It was a silent protest against the unfairness of it all, the dangerous mission he was about to embark on, and the sacrifices being demanded of us. Then, unexpectedly, Jamie paused and threw a glance over his shoulder. "Take good care of Henri for me." His voice, tinged with a vulnerability he rarely showed, cut through the tension like a knife.

Henri, ever the oblivious companion, perked up at the sound of his name. He snorted several times, a sound that momentarily lightened the heavy atmosphere, before his attention was diverted by a scent near one of the logs by the campfire. It was a small, almost comical moment that provided a brief respite.

Paul scooped the chubby dog into his arms with a gentle ease. "We'll keep him safe, Jamie. You have my word." His assurance was firm, a solemn promise in the midst of uncertainty.

As Jamie continued towards his tent, with Charity following close behind, a wave of sadness washed over me. *If only you knew you could keep that promise*, I thought despairingly. My mind was plagued with doubts, the fear that the growing list of dangers we faced might one day be insurmountable. The thought that we might not all make it through this ordeal lingered in the back of my mind, a shadow that even the promise of safety couldn't dispel.

Watching them prepare for what could very well be a mission from which they might not return, I felt a profound sense of vulnerability. The reality of our situation was stark and unyielding; the safety of our small group was a fragile thing, easily shattered.

Glenda! The voice of my father boomed within the confines of my mind, echoing with a sternness that transcended time and space. *Ich habe dich eines besseren belehrt!* His words, laden with disappointment, sent a jolt through me, igniting a tumultuous wave of guilt that threatened to overwhelm my senses. *Ich weiss. Es tut mir leid, Vater.* I replied silently, the acknowledgment of my shortcomings mingling with a deep-seated yearning for his guidance.

In the midst of this emotional tempest, my thoughts drifted unexpectedly to the Chewbathian coins, now secured to the chain around my neck, their cold presence a stark contrast to the warmth of my skin. The coins, a tangible link to my father's past and now, seemingly, to the presence of a Chewbathian Hunter, felt heavier against my chest. *Was this alignment of events merely a coincidence?*

There are no coincidences, Glenda, the soft, insidious whisper of Clivilius infiltrated my thoughts, bringing with it a chilling sense of inevitability. *Your father...*

The implication hung in the air, tantalisingly out of reach. My heart skipped a beat. *My father is alive?* The hope that sprang forth was immediate and overwhelming, a beacon in the darkness of uncertainty.

There are no coincidences, Glenda, the voice echoed, its repetition doing nothing to quell the storm of emotions within me.

Clivilius, answer the god damn question!

But there was only silence, a void that seemed to mock my desperation.

Clivilius!?

Silence.

Hot saline tears scorched my cheeks as I called out to the void, "Clivilius!" My plea was both a scream into the abyss and a silent beg for answers, for a sign that I was not alone in this fight. Sinking to my knees, the barren ground beneath my fists became the physical manifestation of my anguish.

As I lifted my head, the sudden awareness of the settlers' eyes on me was a jolt back to reality. A strange warmth began to stir within me, growing hotter, spreading through my veins like fiery tentacles seeking out the cold fear that had taken root in my heart. My hand reached for the Chewbathian coins, their heat intensifying, becoming an extension of my burgeoning resolve.

"Glenda, are you alright?" Paul's voice, laced with concern, barely registered as I clutched the coins tighter, their heat a beacon of hope in the growing darkness.

The fire behind my eyes, fuelled by determination and a newfound hope, met Paul's gaze with an intensity that felt foreign yet empowering. A grin began to form, unbidden, spreading across my face as the realisation took hold.

The words, once a whispered hope, now rang out with conviction, a declaration that cut through the despair and uncertainty that had shrouded us.

"My father is alive!"

TO BE CONTINUED...